The Glowering Woman

A Victorian Murder Mystery

Diana Lee

Libri et Scientia

2025

For wonderful, talented Amy,
thank you

Chapter One

London, England
October 1894

I didn't need the bells of St. Anne's tolling to know I was more than an hour late. I raced down the street, weaving with precision through the crowd, only to be brought up short by a stout matron pushing a pram.

I usually skirted this main thoroughfare with its crush of humanity and gauntlet of interchangeable abusive arseholes. But today, having spent the better part of the morning in heated debate with my tutor over the merits of Lamarckian evolution (me clinging stubbornly to Darwinism), I didn't have time to plot an alternate route.

Like clockwork, a grubby urchin yelled from across the street, "*Oi, ching chong.*" He added to the insult by pulling the corners of his eyes up to imitate this Chinese feature.

"Oi, ignoramus," I retorted, relaxing my face into a slack-jawed parody of his stupid mug.

"Who ya callin' igno . . . igno-armous?" He balled his hands into fists and made like he was going to cross the street towards me. His ragged compatriots hooted and snarled like a pack of hyenas from the shadowy protection of the rancid alleyway behind him.

I smirked. This hostile display was all for show.

Here in Limehouse, a tiny island of Chinese lived in uneasy proximity to the rest of this vast metropolis. Within its boundaries, the threat of retribution by "Oriental thugs" kept the wretched miscreants at bay.

"Mongrel," he spat with impotent rage.

I shrugged and dashed through a narrow opening between the woman and a shopkeeper with a broom. I'd heard plenty worse.

There were lots of mixed-raced kids like me in Limehouse, though most had English mothers and Chinese fathers. I was one of few with an English father.

"You inhabit a dangerous middle ground, an inauspicious no-man's-land," my grandfather often warned me. "Never be caught unawares."

Good advice for the teeming avenues and narrow alleyways I navigated on a daily basis. But truth be told, I typically eluded that "dangerous middle ground" with ease.

People actually *see* very little. They go on their merry way, minds occupied, rarely even glancing from side to side. More than anything else, the cloak of human self-absorption shielded me. It was a rare occasion when I did not go completely unnoticed.

I dodged past a couple of young clerks and finally rounded the corner to our apothecary. As I made the final dash to our door, a cab skidded to a stop beside me. Its wheels threw up a cloud of dust to mix with the perpetually sooty air of London. I coughed and squinted through the haze, surprised to see my grandfather's head emerge from the window.

"Hop in, Kuo, we have a patient to see."

His lips twitched at my obvious surprise. The expense of traveling by cab was not a luxury in which we typically indulged.

I jumped in and settled beside him, making sure not to sit on the folds of his simple black *chanshang*, a traditional Chinese robe he wore every day, as well as the embroidered silk skullcap atop his head. I, on the other hand, dressed in trousers and jacket, and except for my wide-brimmed slouch hat, looked much like any other boy my age.

"I'm sorry, Grandfather. I forgot the hour in my preoccupation with—"

He waved away my apology. "Mrs. Hudson has referred us to yet another patient. One who was kind enough to provide transportation."

"Mrs. Hudson," I murmured, picturing the thin, frayed woman who had hobbled into our store several months ago last spring.

She used a cane, and her knees creaked so loudly I thought a floorboard or two loose. One look at her face convinced me that only tremendous pain had forced so respectable a lady into the far reaches of Limehouse where, in the minds of upstanding Englishmen and women, opium dens abounded, and white slavers lurked around every corner, waiting for their next victim.

Like most Londoners, I'd read the lurid stories of Limehouse in newspapers and periodicals. But sinister opium dens and "dastardly Orientals" lying in wait to kidnap beautiful white maidens existed mostly in the overheated imagination of the English reading public. Opium dens, although there were those to be sure, were no more sinister than a tavern, and much quieter. I had stepped over the inert forms of drunks passed out in the gutters of Whitechapel more often than those of opium eaters on the Limehouse Causeway. As for white slavers, I had encountered none to my knowledge.

Mrs. Hudson's expression of distaste mimicked that of many of our English customers, and I experienced a twinge of irritation at her entrance. My mother, being deeply empathetic, hurried over to assist the woman, who was in obvious distress. Mother's kindness put people at ease, and Mrs. Hudson relaxed into a comfortable armchair for a consultation. Since that time, she had referred many new customers our way.

"Who's the patient?" I asked.

Grandfather grinned and winked. "Why, none other than her 'particular' boarder."

I laughed, Mrs. Hudson having regaled us many times with complaints about her tenant and his penchant for attracting trouble. "Such a particular, particular man," she would bemoan, wringing her hands.

"What's wrong with him?" I probed further.

Grandfather shrugged. "I don't know. The message only requested our immediate presence."

He adjusted a brown leather medical bag on his lap. The bag and a stethoscope within were his only concessions to Western medicine.

We adhered to a Taoist philosophy, though my grandfather spouted the odd Confucian saying when the mood struck him. Our path embraced the oneness of all things and a faith in the universal life force of *chi*.

"Everything comes from the same place," my grandfather had instructed me over the course of my apprenticeship. "Evil flourishes and diseases run rampant when people abandon their connection to the universe and each other."

Unfortunately, this and other imparted Chinese wisdom found little fertile ground in my heart. I struggled to grasp with certainty the Universal Connection—a certainty my grandfather wore like a second skin.

He often shook his head with sad conviction. "You are too English."

No truer words were ever spoken. I was too English, although, to the English, never English enough.

I stared out at the swarm of carriages, enjoying the novelty of jostling through traffic without having to worry about the pickpockets that stalked the omnibuses. After a while, I asked, "What's the patient's name?"

Grandfather handed me the missive. "The note doesn't say. It is signed by a Dr. John Watson. I assume him to be the patient's regular physician."

My hand froze in the process of unfolding the heavy piece of stationary. "Dr. Watson?" I exclaimed. "As in Sherlock Holmes and Dr. Watson?"

"Sherlock who?" Grandfather returned as we pulled up to that well-known address, 221B Baker Street.

Unlike my grandfather, I knew exactly who Sherlock Holmes was and had read many of his case studies. I admired his abilities but did not view him as some unique intellect.

In Chinese literature, we have extolled for hundreds of years the wise detective, usually in the form of a judge or magistrate. Fanciful stories, to be sure, for ghosts often assisted in the investigations, but the importance of astute observation and reasoned deduction played a central role in solving any mystery.

While I did not hold Sherlock Holmes in the same high esteem as did many of my countrymen, I confess to a feeling of anticipation at meeting him. Anticipation that faded in the face of the shivering, emaciated man lying on a settee in the littered room. He clutched at the lapels of his smoking jacket with fevered hands, and a stale, sickly sweet odor clung to his skin.

His recent return from the dead shocked the world, though there had been little word of his exploits since then. Now, I knew why. The great detective's cocaine habit was no secret, but what we beheld was a man in the throes of opiate addiction.

Dr. Watson confirmed the obvious. "Holmes wandered the Far East during his absence and there developed a taste for opium. I believed him abstinent upon his return, but he went missing for two days before the constables found him stumbling around, lost and confused.

"I fear he has fallen into a deep dependence. Though I have tried, I'm at the limit of my abilities as a physician to help him."

My grandfather spoke and understood English well, but I "translated" Dr. Watson's words to feign his ignorance. Grandfather stroked his beard and muttered under his breath in Cantonese, "How often have we seen this, my child?" In my fifteen years, the last five as an apprentice, I had witnessed the ravages of opium consumption countless times.

We gathered around the settee as Grandfather, with a cultivated expression of supreme wisdom, examined the suffering man. He relayed his observations to me in his native tongue, all the while keeping a keen, unobtrusive eye on Dr. Watson. I repeated these to our host in my unaccented English, diminishing somewhat the foreignness of our presence.

When he finished, Grandfather clasped his large, boney hands in front of him and prompted me with a knowing smile. "What do you think? Will this English doctor recognize the chasm that has opened between his friend and the very cosmos? Because the rift is wide and deep."

Dr. Watson looked from my grandfather to me. "What has he concluded, my boy?"

His tone carried a hint of skepticism, but he maintained a respectful manner and appeared a better sort than most Englishmen. All the same, I could not tell him Grandfather had determined Mr. Holmes to be so disassociated from the larger universe as to render his friend unknown even to himself.

"He has rarely seen such a sad case and will, no doubt, recommend a strict course. You must follow it to the day, hour, and measure if it is to help Mr. Holmes in his recovery."

"Yes, yes, but what *is* the course of action?" Dr. Watson asked with an impatient nod. "We're talking opium here, and at a quantity proving resistant to treatment."

Only I saw the flicker of irritation cross my grandfather's face. "Ah, the poor English, consumed by the same drug they forced upon us," he grumbled in a quiet aside to me, referring, of course, to the concerted efforts of the British East India Company to smuggle opium into China against the emperor's edicts.

"I can hardly tell him that," I complained.

Our little exchange had gone unnoticed by Dr. Watson. His mind preoccupied with the sufferings of his friend, he stared down at Mr. Holmes with a worried frown and pulled at his overgrown mustache. I translated his question before my grandfather could say anything more.

Grandfather considered the pitiful form on the sofa with an intent gaze. I stood with my head bowed in deferential silence as he pondered the next step. This show of contemplation was entirely for the benefit of Dr. Watson. My grandfather had known within moments how to proceed.

As with other such cases of opium dependence, he prescribed an extended period of weaning Mr. Holmes off the drug with lower doses and supplements to reduce the pain of withdrawal and increase appetite. The process would be slow and require constant vigilance on the part of those caring for him.

I explained this to Dr. Watson, telling him that we would supply the necessary medications each week with written instructions on how to administer them. He nodded, seeming satisfied with the prescribed treatment.

A knock on the door and Mrs. Hudson entered, carrying a tea tray. "Hello, Mr. Cheng, young Kuo," she greeted Grandfather and me in her usual harried manner, to which I had become familiar on her many visits to our shop.

With an absentminded smile, she put the tray down on the parlour table and turned to survey the room. Sheets of music lay scattered about the apartment, and piles of newspapers leaned against the walls.

Mrs. Hudson wrinkled her nose. "Goodness, it's musty in here."

She opened a window and made a vain attempt to tidy up. Her stride, while aimless, was nonetheless free and easy, much changed from when she first entered our store. Witnessing the cluttered disarray—or disharmony, as my grandfather would say—of their lodgings, I gained a greater sympathy for the broken condition in which she had first come to us.

"Tea," Mrs. Hudson urged.

We sat and I translated more of my grandfather's instructions. Dr. Watson wrote everything down, and soon afterwards, we left.

On our way home, my tutor came to mind, the famous (or rather, infamous) polymath, Lord Clive Brudeford. He, too, had succumbed to the lure of opium, but to such an extent as to exile him in disgrace from his family and society. In his more lucid periods, which could last for many months, he exchanged his services as a tutor for medicines from my grandfather. Sadly, the need for oblivion always drove him back into the arms of opium, a situation made even more tragic by the many contributions he could have made had he but resisted the drug.

Believing I had experienced an epiphany, I proclaimed, "Grandfather, perhaps great intelligence is as much a curse as a gift."

"Hmm."

I persisted. "In his case accounts, Dr. Watson notes that Mr. Holmes is most susceptible to his addictive habit when he has no clear purpose or complicated crime on which to concentrate. Like Lord Brudeford, he cannot turn his mind off without the help of drugs."

"It is more," my grandfather explained, "that they cannot tolerate the everyday or commonplace. They have not integrated their intellect with the universe. They believe the capacity of the mind finite and create a false dichotomy between what is worthy of their attention and what is not." He gestured to the bustling city around us. "If they cannot pause to appreciate what is easily understood, then they cannot fully comprehend the complexity of existence and, therefore, themselves."

"Appreciate what is easily understood? Lord Brudeford would call that stupidity."

Grandfather laughed. I loved his laughter, a man's laugh, a rumbling in his chest, low and tolerant. "Then I prescribe for you, Kuo, a pinch of 'stupidity' every day. For it will keep you sane."

Chapter Two

On the appointed day to deliver medicines to Mr. Holmes, the morning dawned at its usual time for early autumn, though the air still hung heavy with summer-like humidity. The distance from our shop to Baker Street being considerable, I left just after sunup.

Even amidst the grinding poverty of Limehouse, the thought of familiarizing myself with another part of the city buoyed me. I set out on my long journey across London with a spring in my step that did not abate until reaching my destination.

At his door, Dr. Watson greeted me with a frown and twitchy mustache. "You? I'd expected Mr. Cheng."

My eyes narrowed with irritation at his assumption that Grandfather had the time to cater to one patient. I bit back a sharp retort, replying instead, "The examination is a simple one. If I find anything amiss, my grandfather will come."

He grumbled his displeasure, but as I proceeded with the checkup, he warmed to my presence. This being the end of the first week of treatment, Mr. Holmes, while now sleeping peacefully, still lay insensible to the world around him.

Dr. Watson gazed down at the great detective. "He awoke last night and spoke to Mrs. Hudson regarding the need to restock his chemical cabinet. In my opinion, the conversation was more a reflex than a conscious effort. His chemical experiments occupy a good deal of his thoughts, you see."

I glanced up at the overstuffed bookshelves and found them lined with tomes on chemistry, botany, geology, anatomy, and obscure fields of study, such as graphology. "Does Mr. Holmes not read for pleasure?" I asked, having noted the absence of any literature.

Dr. Watson laughed with a good-natured shake of his head. "Unless you count newspaper articles and police reports, then no, he does not. Holmes believes the mind has just so much room for facts and information and will only fill his with those which helps in solving our cases."

"My grandfather believes, through its connection to the universe, that the mind is infinite," I replied, not sure what had prompted me to share this piece of Chinese wisdom with an English doctor.

His dismissive wave, with the words "mere nonsense," pricked my pride, and I snapped, "Yet you have turned to my grandfather to cure your friend where you have failed."

If his mustache twitched when he was irritated, it positively bristled when he was angry. "Young man," he began in a stern tone.

I have discovered the best way to avoid a lecture from an adult is to turn them from your wrongdoing to one of their own. I sniffed the air as if just becoming aware of something.

"Excuse me, Dr. Watson. Has someone been smoking in here?"

My lucky guess proved correct. He drew back with a guilty expression.

"A few puffs on my pipe, no more. I put it out immediately upon remembering Mr. Cheng's instructions."

"It cannot happen again," I admonished him. "Tobacco smoke can trigger the addictive response and must be avoided. Although, I'm sure no harm will come from your unintended mistake."

He glared at me from beneath bushy brows. I pivoted quickly into an entertaining story of an old woman I'd passed on my way over with four Yorkshire terriers all dressed as famous queens, including, scandalously, Queen Victoria herself. This did the trick, for he laughed, clapped me on the back, and told me I was too clever by half.

A gust of wind rustled the pages of a nearby stack of newspapers and brought with it the smell of rain. Dr. Watson hurried over to shut the window.

"Did you bring an umbrella?"

I shook my head.

He grabbed a neat, black number from an ornate umbrella stand. "Here. Take this. We're in for a downpour. You'll be soaked to the skin. Bring it back the next time you come." He chuckled. "I may know nothing of the infinite mind, but I do know autumn colds are the very devil."

Ah, a humorous attempt to acknowledge his own shortcomings while still belittling my grandfather's beliefs. As I said, better than most Englishmen, though a low bar, to be sure.

I took the offered umbrella and thanked him. A final nod and I was out the door.

The landing, darkened from the overcast sky, lay empty before me, and I made my way to the staircase. Halfway down, a creaky floorboard in the hall below caught my attention, and I hastened in an attempt to catch Mrs. Hudson.

Grandfather would want to know exactly what Mr. Holmes had said to her during their nighttime chat. In the treatment of drug dependency, nothing should be dismissed as too insignificant.

I reached the foyer expecting to see the neat bun and starched skirts of the landlady. Instead, a broad-shouldered man wearing a heavy wool jacket and with a battered bowler hat atop lank, dark-red hair sped down the hallway.

Curious as to his business, I caught up with him at the back door and tapped him on the shoulder. "Excuse me, sir."

Instead of greeting me with the courtesy due a polite stranger, the man whirled and threw me a facer. Instinctively, my arm shot up, and I batted his fist away with the umbrella just in time so that his ring only grazed my right cheek. I lost my balance and fell hard onto the polished wood floor.

He burst through the door and out into the alley, making good his escape. I scrambled to my feet and brushed my trousers off with shaking hands.

"Heavens." Mrs. Hudson's head popped into view over the railing. "What's all the commotion? Did you fall, dear boy?"

I couldn't speak for trying to catch my breath. I had until now successfully avoided any form of fisticuffs. The sudden jolt to my body proved unsettling and oddly exhilarating.

"Yes," I answered once able. "A man attacked me and fled out the back door."

"Man? What man?" Mrs. Hudson fluttered down the staircase, twittering in alarm, and met me in the hallway. "Are you hurt?"

"No," I told her, adding, "A tall man with red hair. Do you know him?"

"Nobody by that description lives here, but disruptions are quite common in the vicinity of Mr. Holmes." She wrung her hands. "Red hair is a bad omen. Is it not?"

Though kindly, Mrs. Hudson believed some of the stupider superstitions and prejudices common among her set. I sought to calm her fears. "It means nothing more ominous than hair color. I assure you. He's probably a petty thief looking for easy money. You should lock your doors more securely in the future."

She nodded in her vague, distracted way and left once she was satisfied I had come to no harm. I touched my cheek where a small scratch had formed and tried to picture the man's face, but the only image that came to mind was that of a large, beefy fist and a carved silver ring.

How strange that a man dressed as a deckhand could lurk unseen by the landlady in a respectable abode. My interest was such that I followed his path out the back door.

I stood on the wooden porch and gazed at the overflowing trash bins and rain-soaked cobbles. My skin prickled with the sensation of danger.

"He fled down the alley and turned onto Baker Street. He didn't notice me here, just ran off."

I suppressed a startled yelp and swung around. A girl sat on an overturned barrel surrounded by grubby exposed brick walls with eaves dripping dirty rainwater.

Within this dreary frame, she stood out like a bird-of-paradise. Not that I had ever seen a real bird-of-paradise before. But Chinese paintings depicted a creature of delicate bones and colorful plumage, both of which she displayed in abundance.

Perched on the barrel, her toes barely touched the ground. She stared down at her hands resting in her lap and clutched in one tiny fist a crumpled linen handkerchief.

She wore what women's magazines refer to as a walking suit. I cannot imagine why, since the narrow, fitted skirt hampered that particular activity. The brilliant red and green tartan pattern of her dress struck me as garish and too mature for one so young.

I took her little hiccups to be suppressed sobs until realizing she was, in actuality, gasping for air. "Are you quite well?" I asked.

She looked up. Her face was the standard in English beauty and of the type often seen in advertisements for cosmetics. Tears drenched heavily lashed, large, and intensely blue eyes. Her hair gleamed a deep gold and was swept up in the back with a curly fringe over her forehead.

"No, ninny, I'm not. As anyone can plainly see," she snapped. Her little rosebud mouth trembled with emotion.

Used to being either ignored or brusquely dismissed by girls of her station, I touched the brim of my hat with a polite nod and turned to go. I cared little for the opinions of such pampered creatures.

"No, wait. I'm sorry." The girl pushed off the barrel and stood bent at the waist. She took shallow breaths, straightening a little with each one, like a balloon inflating. At last, she stood upright, one hand resting on the barrel for support and the other pressed against her stomach.

"My evil Aunt Sadie insisted on tightening my . . . well, let's just say you're lucky to be a boy and not have to endure such torture," she finished, tossing her head with a dramatic flourish.

A blush threatened to spread across my cheeks. Speaking with a girl about female undergarments, even obliquely, was not a common occurrence for me. Although, I had overheard my mother counsel many a suffering woman on how to lessen the pressure from a corset.

"If you soak the laces in cold water and vinegar over several days," I advised her with admirable control, "the mixture will break down the material and the laces will give even when tightened."

She blinked, taken aback. "What an odd thing for a boy to know."

I shrugged. "My grandfather and mother are knowledgeable in all areas of health, including breathing. And the first thing they will tell you"—I glared down my nose at her—"is not to wear anything that impedes it."

"Easy for you to say." An angry flush enhanced her pale complexion. "You weren't sent up from the lovely countryside when your dear, sweet guardian died and accused daily by a vindictive old maid aunt of not understanding proper etiquette, and 'running wild,' and having an 'ugly, clumsy figure.' Were you?"

"No," I admitted.

"Well, there, you see," she spat. "And now, I've been turned away *again* from seeing Mr. Holmes, this time by his horrid housekeeper."

"Mrs. Hudson is his landlady and a gracious hostess," I countered in her defense, but also just to annoy the girl.

She blinked again in surprise. How silly and vapid it made her look.

"You're acquainted with Mrs. Hudson? Have you seen Mr. Holmes? Are you coming from him now?" With each question, she inched closer to me until we stood toe to toe.

Her golden head bobbed just below my line of sight. Tiny though she was, her intense gaze pushed me back a step or two.

I cleared my throat and assumed a professional manner. "I am not at liberty to speak of Mr. Holmes, only to tell you he is of no use to you or anyone else in his present state."

Her shoulders drooped, and she sagged against the barrel, declaring in tragic accents, "Then I am lost."

Chapter Three

Of the girls who live in my part of London, few can indulge in flights of fancy. Many work as domestics, in factories and taverns, or worse. They trudge home past our store in the evenings, bent with exhaustion and weary of spirit. Therefore, it was with little patience and less tact that I rolled my eyes at the girl's dramatic pronouncement.

Her head snapped up, eyes flashing. "You doubt me? What do you know? My name is Charlotte Gaines, and I have been cursed since birth. And you are an extremely ill-mannered boy."

I stopped myself from blinking in surprise, knowing how stupid it made one look, but could not keep a note of disbelief from my voice. "Great Scott, you can't possibly be 'My Lovely Little Lottie Love.'"

She drew herself up. "I can . . . and am."

Unlike Mr. Holmes, I read for pleasure whenever I could, and the books of John Harold Gaines were some of my favorites. He was the most famous author in Britain and, in his time, perhaps the world. I knew of no other writer of such renown and acclaim.

"You're the granddaughter of John Harold Gaines?"

"Yes, of course. Didn't I just say that?"

"Well, sort of," I hedged, not wanting to set her off again. My caution was for naught.

Charlotte Gaines stomped her delicate boot-encased foot. "I know what you're thinking, *Spoiled little rich girl, poor, poor 'My Lovely Little Lottie Love.'"*

I gave her points for perception, for I was thinking exactly that. She struggled to draw in a deep breath.

"Well, I *am* pitiable," she gasped out. "For almost everyone in my family is dead. Everyone dead long before their time. And I am sure to be among them soon."

On this histrionic note, the girl pulled a folded envelope from her handbag and waved it under my nose. "I received this just last week on my sixteenth birthday. Read it and tell me I have no reason to be distraught." She thrust the missive into my hands.

I pulled from an ordinary stationary envelope a piece of heavy, textured paper. Lines ran across the creamy surface, and a delicate gold paint tipped its edges. An elegant hand had scribbled the following words:

The lowering sky benights the day,
and the cowardly man has his way.
The sister lost betrays the nave,
and the glowering woman defies the grave.

I raised my eyebrows. "Bit of a riddle, no?"

Charlotte snatched the paper from my hands. "It is clearly a poem foretelling calamity, thus the words 'benights,' 'betrays,' and 'grave.'"

It did sound rather grim, but I wasn't convinced the poem foretold anything more sinister than a birthday prank. "Who's it from?"

"If I knew that, I wouldn't be seeking the help of Mr. Holmes."

"Perhaps a cousin or uncle?" I suggested, thinking the culprit likely a male relative making game of an impressionable girl.

"Do you know nothing of my family?" she asked with a heavy sigh.

I crossed my arms. "I've read all your grandfather's books and novellas, even his collection of nursery rhymes. I can recite *My Lovely Little Lottie Love* by heart."

Charlotte bared her even, pearly white teeth in a stiff smile. "No need for that."

She stood up on her toes and pushed herself back to sit on the barrel again. With a majestic wave, she indicated I should sit as well. Curious, I controlled my natural inclination to balk at her imperious attitude and sat on the top step of the stoop.

"My grandparents were married for almost twenty-five years," Charlotte began. "They had five living children: Thomas, Cecil, Sadie, Eliza, and Archie." She blushed but added in a flat, matter-of-fact tone, "Although my grandmother had countless, well, babies that didn't live to be born."

"And your Aunt Sadie, she is with whom you live now?" I asked.

She nodded. "Thomas was my father. He and my mother, Frances, died in a carriage accident when I was a baby. Not long after that, my grandmother was committed to an asylum and later died there. Because my mother's parents were dead, I was raised by her sister, dear Aunt Beatrix, until just last year when she died."

Charlotte sniffed and dabbed the corner of one eye with a damp handkerchief. I had to acknowledge the unusual amount of tragedy in those few short sentences and waited out of sympathy for her to continue.

The uncomfortable silence stretched on, and I grew impatient, finally asking, "Why didn't you live with your grandfather after your parents died?"

Her color heightened further, and she answered without looking up, "He had taken a mistress, Nora Davies, an actress young enough to be his daughter. After my grandmother died, he married Miss Davies."

She raised her chin in a gesture of defiance and met my eyes. "It was just as well I went to live with Aunt Beatrix, for my grandfather and his wife drowned in a boating accident off the coast of Cornwall, having been married less than a year."

I studied her set, disapproving expression and wondered fleetingly what this privileged girl would make of my family so far removed from hers in wealth and status. I pushed the thought aside, realizing that she was unlikely to think of me at all, having not once even asked my name.

Her lack of manners, though, suited me just fine. I was fascinated with her story and eager to know if anyone else had survived this particularly ill-fated family.

"What of the others?" I asked.

"What others?"

"Cecil, Eliza, and Archie."

"Oh, well, Uncle Cecil is still alive. I suppose. I haven't heard otherwise. He was the only one who stood up to Grandfather, from what Aunt Beatrix told me. He fought hard to keep my grandmother out of the asylum, saying she was only sad to have lost her children. You see, Eliza died in a fire at a boarding school in Scotland when she was twelve. Poor Archie died as a baby of scarlet fever. He was much younger than the others and would have been only a few years older than I am now."

"Your Uncle Cecil doesn't visit?"

"Oh no, that's the best part." She laughed and clapped her little hands together. "He's a monk and resides in some northern monastery. Sent my grandfather into an apoplexy. I'm told he hated most religions and especially the show and pomp of the Catholic Church. When Uncle Cecil took orders, my grandfather disowned him. I don't think anyone has seen or heard from Cecil in years. Certainly I never have."

Charlotte's manner evidenced an undercurrent of hostility towards her grandfather, an interesting contrast to the veneration in which he was held in England and around the world. Yet, here sat his only grandchild openly contemptuous of him. Perhaps her Aunt Beatrix had held him in dislike and foisted her feelings unfairly upon her gullible niece.

"I'm sorry to hear of your family's hardships." I chose my words with care. "But you must feel some sense of pride in your grandfather's works. His books illuminated much of the injustice and hypocrisy that still plagues English society to this day. Many of them have inspired important reforms."

She looked away. "Much good it has done his family."

I pursued the matter no further and, since the rain had stopped, stood to take my leave. I still held the envelope and turned it over in my hand. There was no address for either recipient or sender, nor was there a stamp, only Charlotte's name written in elegant script across the front.

"How did you get this? The letter could not have been delivered by post without a stamp or address."

"I don't know. Nellie, our housemaid, gave it to me with my breakfast four days ago."

I brushed my fingers across a raised area near the bottom of the envelope and squinted at a small oval indentation. "Was there something else inside besides the letter?"

She drew back and blinked. I hoped one day that her "evil" Aunt Sadie would tell her to stop batting her eyelashes like an idiot every time she was surprised.

"Why, yes. How did you know?"

"Whatever it was made an impression on the envelope."

"How clever of you to notice. There was, indeed, a small gold locket within, but no picture or strands of hair or anything inside it. I showed the locket to Aunt Sadie. She had a fit and snatched it from me."

I frowned. Did the girl not understand the significance of what she had just said? "You must know your aunt has some idea what this is all about."

"I'm not a simpleton." Charlotte sniffed with indignation. "Of course I know my aunt recognized the locket. I've asked her a dozen times to explain her actions and to give it back to me. She refuses. I didn't show her the poem for fear she'd take that too."

I returned the envelope to her. "Have you read any of Mr. Holmes's cases?"

"No. Aunt Sadie deplores what she calls 'frivolous diversions.'"

"I think he would start with the paper on which the verse is written," I proposed. "Mr. Holmes is quite methodical in his investigations and knows a great deal about obscure matters. The paper might give you some idea who wrote the letter. Another clue is the poem. Does your aunt allow poetry?"

Charlotte nodded and pushed off the barrel. She clutched at the rim for support. "Yes, though the library is always locked. She chooses what I read, typically the classics and a good deal of female writers. Aunt Sadie is a staunch believer in women's suffrage but has a great fear of the scandalous. I think it has to do with my grandmother's madness." She struggled to look understanding and sympathetic but failed, managing only an angry frown.

"Gain access to the library, if possible," I suggested. "You might find something relating to the poem. Someone obviously believes it is of significance to you. Also, ask your maid who gave her the letter. Maybe it is that simple."

Charlotte drew in a deep breath, stopping just short of filling her lungs. "Drat this hateful thing." She pulled at the bottom of her jacket and straightened her shoulders.

"One last matter," I told her. "You must get the locket from your aunt. A jeweler could have some idea where it came from." With those final words, I tipped my hat and made to leave.

She detained me with a hand on my arm. "You can help me?"

I had given no thought to helping her beyond how I believed Mr. Holmes would proceed with such a case. "I work. My family owns an apothecary in Limehouse, and I'm required to help," I informed her, thinking my lowly origins would surely quash further appeals for assistance.

"I can pay you," she persisted, undeterred. "My aunt is exacting in many things, but I have a generous allowance and, though she natters on about respectability, she rarely troubles herself with my whereabouts."

Grandfather says there is a purpose in all things, but it is not always evident at the time. I considered her upturned face. What purpose was there in meeting Charlotte Gaines?

Lord Brudeford's visage arose in my mind. Though I deplored the use of drugs and alcohol and the oblivion they offered as a sign of moral weakness, I sympathized with my tutor. My mixed heritage and mutinous nature alienated me from the larger English society. How simple to find solace, or at the very least, escape, in opium dreams or drunken revels.

If I hoped to avoid his fate, perhaps I should direct my energies to some need outside myself. Besides, what harm could come from tracking down the source of an ill-conceived birthday jest?

"I'll help you."

She clasped my hands in a fervent grasp. "Thank you."

I disentangled myself. "Give me the poem. I have an idea where to begin. Retrieve the locket if you can and try to get into the library.

Also, speak with your maid about the letter and meet me here next Monday at noon."

I turned to go, but she detained me once more. This time with a question: "What is your name?"

Chapter Four

I've lived in London all my life and can find my way through the streets and alleyways of Limehouse blindfolded, but to know every twist and turn of this immense city is impossible. In unfamiliar parts, I asked directions of shopkeepers, or barmen, or other neighborhood fixtures. As a backup, I always slipped a pocket map into my jacket.

Most Londoners wouldn't admit to being lost and rather hang than use a map to get around. To avoid their ridicule, I studied my map at home before leaving and only pulled it out in a secluded spot if the need arose.

Truth be told, I loved maps, all kinds, even nautical charts. Fortunately, Lord Brudeford shared my fascination and owned a wide variety (although his opium habit forced him to sell the most valuable). One recent addition, a detailed map of London's East End by the cartographer Charles Booth, made a close study of poverty in the area and color-coded each street by earnings, or lack thereof.

Our street and those around it were coded a deep blue, indicating extreme poverty, some even coded black, meaning "vicious, semi-criminal." I bristled at this description. Not because there were no vicious crimes in the East End; certainly there were, the Whitechapel murders being some of the most heinous.

No. My anger arose because the poorest of the poor were the only ones identified by something other than their earnings. Wealth does not rule out crime or viciousness. As my grandfather was wont to observe, great wealth was often the fruits of crime.

Some of the most ruthless criminals in this city hailed from the richest families. But I had to admit, the rich were unlikely to steal your purse or cut your throat on their own pristine streets and broad avenues. For that reason, I studied closely the maps of Charles Booth and committed to memory the blue and blackened streets of the poor.

Though my family prospered compared to many of our neighbors, I rarely used anything other than my feet to get around. Still, crossing London occasionally required the combined use of trams, omnibuses, and trains, and I'd have to part with a few precious coins to arrive at my destination.

Sometimes I got lucky, as I did the morning after meeting Charlotte Gaines, and hitched a ride with Mr. Wei, a most resourceful Chinese businessman. A rich man by our standards, he nevertheless lived in humble lodgings near the West India docks. He was a well-known figure in our neighborhood and contributed generously to local charities.

I joined him shortly before dawn outside the stable where he boarded his sturdy, dapple grey Welsh pony, Chester. Mr. Wei harnessed him to a compact, two-wheeled wagon, somewhat larger than the rickshaws used in the Far East. An oiled canvas covered an ingeniously constructed cabinet fitted exactly into the wagon bed. Like an intricate puzzle, the drawers moved and shifted to hold all types of exotic and rare ingredients used in perfumes and cosmetics.

Chester swished his lovely, flowing tail and pawed the ground, impatient to be gone. I took my cue from him and jumped up onto the bench seat next to Mr. Wei. The first delivery of the morning was at Floris of London, a perfumery on Jermyn Street near St. James Square. This suited me fine since I planned to visit a bookshop only a few streets north of there.

Mr. Wei handled the reins with smooth, quiet efficiency, and we pulled out onto the dark and narrow street. I glanced over at his craggy, weathered face.

He flashed me a warm smile. "What takes you so far afield? An errand for your grandfather . . . or mother?"

The muscles between my shoulder blades tightened. Mr. Wei's casual mention of my mother did not fool me. His interest in her was no secret. The gossips loudly marveled at Mother's coolness towards so eligible a prospect, never failing to mention her less than virtuous past.

You see, my parents met on the ship carrying my mother and grandfather from China to England, and I was the result of that brief encounter. My father was more myth than man to me since they never married and he died at sea when I was but a newborn.

My illegitimacy was a well-known fact in our community. Even so, I believed if my mother had not been so beautiful, the gossips would have been kinder. As it was, she made a rich target for the barbed comments and ugly innuendoes of some of the neighbors.

Mother ignored them, disdainful of their opinions. I envied her composure, for I longed to punch them in their spiteful faces.

She had mentioned Mr. Wei to me only once. "He is a dangerous man, my child. You would do well to remember that whenever you chance to deal with him."

I puzzled over this. Mr. Wei seemed no more dangerous, and much nicer, than any of our other neighbors, so that I asked my grandfather why Mother held him in dislike.

"Dislike?" He had shaken his head. "No. She is wary of him. Ask yourself why a man who trades in rare and valuable commodities never employs a guard. He moves about the city unbothered and untouched by the thieves who lurk on every corner. For this reason alone, it is wise to be cautious in his presence."

I heeded his words and therefore changed the subject from that of my mother. "I've met Mr. Sherlock Holmes."

"Ah, the great detective." He stared straight ahead. "Strange."

"Strange how?"

"His sudden reappearance after everyone believed him dead."

I nodded in agreement. The whole world now knew of the criminal mastermind, Moriarty, and we all mourned Sherlock Holmes when he fell to his death locked in struggle with the evil professor. I assumed Dr. Watson knew what had truly transpired at Reichenbach Falls and hoped one day he would write an account.

"I've read nothing new of his exploits since his resurrection," my companion commented.

"He's between cases," I hedged.

Mr. Wei did not pursue the subject. He knew better than to ask in what capacity I had met Mr. Holmes, since my grandfather kept our patients' needs in the strictest of confidence.

Even at this early hour, the racket of the city forced us to raise our voices to converse. Much of our way took us along the Thames, where the shouts of deckhands and the groans of ships and barges created a ceaseless din. The stench off the sewage-filled river was a bracing reminder of why we always kept incense burning in our shop.

Mr. Wei wove through the maze of boxes, bags, and people with ease, never once held up by the obstacles experienced by larger, less maneuverable carriages. It was not long before we turned off the Thames Byway and headed north past the Nelson Monument.

The smell eased here as boys dodged hooves and wheels to scoop up steaming manure and shove it into burlap sacks. Despite their efforts, keeping the city clean of waste from thousands of horses was like digging out from under an erupting volcano of shite.

The ragged, underfed boys dashed in and out of the pressing traffic. I was grateful not to be among them.

We slowed to a standstill, giving the costermongers a chance to sell their wares. Mr. Wei gestured to a woman with a tray of meat pies and purchased two, giving me one. The hot, flaky bun warmed my hand, and the smell of savory meat and spices made my stomach growl.

I shook my head and tried to give it back to him. "Thank you, but I'm not hungry."

He pushed my hand away with a curt laugh. "I hear your stomach. Don't worry. I won't force your mother into a loveless marriage because you accepted a meat pie from me."

I blushed and turned away to look out on the crowd rushing along the pavement. My gaze chanced to fall on the broad back and lank, shaggy red hair of the very same man who had thrown me a facer just the day before on Baker Street.

My curiosity piqued, and making what was, in hindsight, an exceedingly stupid decision, I shoved the pie into my pocket and leapt from the cart. "Thanks for the ride, Mr. Wei. Only a few more blocks. It'll be quicker for me to walk." I gave him no opportunity to object and darted through traffic towards the square.

Though I had never followed anyone before, I have found that with a little nerve and some good fortune, I could slip unnoticed in and out of most places. I avoided the truly observant by pulling down the wide brim of my hat and fading from sight with the ease of long practice.

This skill at blending in served me well when tracking the unsuspecting man. I trailed behind him from Pall Mall to Waterloo Place, shielded by three shop girls in close conversation.

The man crossed diagonally at the intersection to the southwest corner in front of the Athenaeum Club. The exclusive men's club dominated the corner with its impressive columned portico and the helmeted statue of Athena standing sentry over its entryway.

The redheaded man strode the length of the façade and turned the corner into the gardens behind the club. I sped across the intersection, worried I'd lost him. But peeking round the corner of the building, I spotted my quarry talking to another man obscured from view by a large tree trunk.

To get a better look, I skirted the boundary of the garden unseen and came onto a path that wound between the trees and a sparse hedgerow. I stopped about ten feet away from the two men and peered out from between the twisting branches of the hedge.

The other man emerged into view, but only in profile. His trimmed beard and distinguished bearing gave the impression of wealth and social standing. They were a study in contrasts, the redheaded man, rough and shabby, and the other, neat and polished in his expensive overcoat and shiny top hat.

"So, you've found out nothing," the rich man sneered. "Twice she's been to his lodgings, and still, we don't know why."

"You're welcome to give it a go." The redheaded man's anger flared but quickly flickered out in deference to his social better. "Just give me more time. It ain't easy getting close to her."

"I don't pay you to do the easy tasks," the rich man snapped.

Their voices lowered as the conversation intensified. I leaned in through the branches, intent on catching every word, and came nose-to-beak with an enormous magpie.

The bird reared back and puffed up its feathers in fury at my trespass. If it had been any other kind of bird, it would have hopped away or scolded me with a gentle chitter. But an angry, loudmouthed magpie was not about to let me off that easy.

It emitted a deafening squawk.

I stumbled out of the hedge and onto the pathway. My retreat did not appease the bloody thing. The bird balanced on a swinging branch and flapped its wings, screeching, as if to pronounce: "Here he is, spying on you. Get him."

The men pinned me with their startled gaze. Too late, I pulled my hat down and faded back into the trees.

"Hey, you, boy," shouted the redheaded man. "Stop."

I ran.

The most obvious route was to dash back out onto Waterloo Place and get lost in the crowd. Instead, I shot up the pathway between the buildings and burst onto Pall Mall.

I raced across the wide avenue and into Saint James Square with its many small branching byways. Here the crowd was thinner with fewer hands to grab me should he employ the "stop thief" tactic.

I turned and twisted through the streets and emerged onto Piccadilly almost to Green Park. Only then did I slow my headlong dash and duck around the corner of a building.

My chest heaved as I gasped for breath and pressed my back up against the hard, red brick. I threw a quick glance behind me out onto the street.

Carriages rolled by and people strolled along the pavement. They paid me little heed.

Their disinterest highlighted the menacing aspect of the redheaded man carefully searching each offshoot and alleyway. My heart skipped a beat, and I jerked my head back behind the building.

He would find me in a matter of seconds. I chanced another look. The man had his face turned away from me.

I took off my hat and tucked it out of sight under my arm. In two swift strides, I left my hiding place and fell into casual step beside a nursemaid clutching the hand of a small boy.

The woman glared at me. "Get away with you. I've no money."

"Don't want anything, ma'am," I replied with as sweet a smile as I could muster. "Just to get to the next street up."

My attempt at wide-eyed innocence only made her more suspicious. She drew the boy close in a protective gesture. Before she could make an abrupt move away from me, I darted down a darkened, narrow alleyway.

The recessed entry at the dead end had stood since the Middle Ages. I pounded on the solid oak door, hardly daring to think what would happen if it did not open.

But open it did to a kind, wizened face and raspy greeting, "Young Master Cheng, how nice to see you."

I slipped inside, and my shoulders relaxed as the door closed behind me with a solid thud.

Chapter Five

I inhaled a deep, calming breath and with it, the heady scent of ink and parchment. The backroom at Cohen and Sons Booksellers cloaked me in dust and old leather. Diffuse light filtered in from high windows, and a comforting maze of piled books seemed to grow ever more twisting and intricate with each passing year.

Ebenezer Cohen stared at me over the rims of his half-moon spectacles. His eyes held a perpetual squint, and wispy gray hair created, to my grateful mind, a halo around his balding head. Ebenezer, a third generation Cohen, managed acquisitions and appraisals, leaving the storefront to his eldest daughter, Rachel, and her husband, Jacob.

"To what do I owe the honor of so unexpected a visit?" His good-humored voice crinkled like the turn of a page. "And by the back way, no less. One might assume you have something to hide." A smiled quivered on his thin lips.

I laughed with unconvincing bravado. But before I could answer, Rachel bustled in, hands on hips.

"Huh." She glared at me. "I might've known. A rude, disreputable-looking man was just in asking if we'd seen his nephew, 'thin, wiry boy with dark hair and big, floppy hat.' Said he'd lost track of him on Saint James's Square, and his sister was going to give him what for if he couldn't find the boy. He's checking all the stores up and down the street."

A tingling shock raced up my spine. Only a short while ago, I was the hunter. But I'd misjudged my prey and now had, by all appearances, a persistent and dangerous man on my trail.

Mr. Cohen dropped a gnarled hand on my shoulder and said in Cantonese, "No worries, my boy, he won't find you here."

Rachel harrumphed. "I don't know what Papa just told you, but we've got more exits out of here than Buckingham Palace." With a brusque nod and swish of her skirts, she turned and left.

"What've you gotten yourself into?" He reverted to English and gestured to a stool pulled up next to his workbench.

"I don't know, to be honest." I sat on the stool and rested my arm on the long, polished tabletop scattered with all sorts of tools used in the repair and restoration of old books. "That man broke into a patient's house yesterday. He tried to land me a punch when I confronted him. He appeared to be just a common thief, but when I saw him on the street, my curiosity was roused, and I followed him."

Mr. Cohen chuckled. "Quite the coincidence."

I shrugged. "Grandfather says a coincidence is the universe telling us to pay attention."

He raised his eyebrows, unconvinced. "Heeding a coincidence and following a suspected criminal are two very different things."

Ebenezer Cohen was one of our few English friends my grandfather trusted implicitly, as did I. His trade in rare books and religious texts had led him to the Kaifeng Jews in the Henan Province of China. He spent many years among them and returned to this country fluent in different Chinese dialects and an expert on their community.

I flashed what I hoped was a rueful, disarming smile and confessed, "I think I've stumbled onto something strange." I told him of my meeting with Charlotte Gaines and the mystery with which I was helping her.

"And this redheaded man—you say the landlady didn't know him?"

"Mrs. Hudson had no notion of him. And as I said, I thought him a thief until he spoke with the other man behind the Athenaeum Club. He must have followed Charlotte yesterday to Mr. Holmes's lodgings."

"A logical conclusion," Mr. Cohen agreed, holding out his hand. "The paper, please."

I pulled from my pocket Charlotte's poem. My whole purpose in venturing out that day had been to get his opinion on the origin of the paper.

He turned it over in his hands. "The page has been cut down. It looks to be torn from some sort of ledger or accounts book."

"Isn't the paper too heavy and expensive for a ledger?"

"I've known some owned by important men to be quite elaborate." He pushed his spectacles further up his nose and leaned closer to the lantern. "Look at this, Kuo."

I scooted my stool next to his and stared hard at where he pointed. "The lines aren't printed on, they're drawn. Well done, and a steady hand that one. So, not a ledger, a writing album perhaps?"

Mr. Cohen picked up a small book from a stack resting on the table and opened it to the back. He placed the torn side of the paper against the binding. "The poem is written on the backside of the page."

"Does that matter?" I asked.

"Don't know." He ran a finger along the paper's edge. "The gold trim suggests a scrapbook or picture album, something put on display instead of filled with personal entries. The paper is good quality but of ordinary stock, nothing unusual. It can be bought in any stationary store in England." He handed it back to me. "The verse is strange."

I put the piece of paper into my pocket. "The girl is histrionic and flighty, but I can't blame her for being nervous. And now, this man . . ."

Mr. Cohen nodded absently, his mind on the poem. "Religious in some ways, wouldn't you say? Day becoming night, betraying the nave, defying the grave, and so on."

"I think the emphasis is more on the man and woman. A cowardly man, a glowering woman speaks more to me of contempt and rage."

"Excellent, Kuo. Your time with Lord Brudeford has not been wasted."

I blushed and jumped up from the stool, never one to accept compliments with good grace. "Thank you. I'll be going. I shouldn't take up any more of your time."

Mr. Cohen stood and rubbed his hands together. "Well then, let me show you out. But before that . . ." He snatched up my battered felt slouch hat from the workbench where I'd laid it. "For all your talk of blending in, my boy, this hat doesn't lend itself to that particular end."

I tensed. A few years ago, I found the hat in a trunk shoved under some shelves in the basement of our store. Along with the hat was a dark blue woolen men's suit stripped of any identifying labels. I imagined them having belonged to my father, though neither my mother nor grandfather made any comment when I came up from the basement wearing the hat.

I kept wearing it every day. The soft felt and wide brim made it easy to hide my face; just a quick tilt of the head and only my chin was visible.

Mr. Cohen noted my reaction. "Don't worry. The hat will be here when you want it, but right now you need something less obvious."

From a wall rack thick with coats, he took a worn, tweed flatcap, like the Irish wear and which had become popular with young men, and handed it to me. The thing fit well enough, but without the wide brim of my old slouch hat it was as if a thin coat of armor had been stripped from my body.

I followed Mr. Cohen out of the practical workroom and into the magical realm of books. There weren't many places in this city I loved more than the front showroom of Cohen and Sons Booksellers.

A whimsical cross between the London Library and Ali Baba's Cave, books lined the store's walls from floor to ceiling, cataloged in meticulous order, yet yielding surprising treasures in unexpected places. Stairways and ladders connected the three stories of shelves. Lamps with beaded and colorful shades stood on tables covered with velvet runners and displays of expensive stationary and sealing wax.

We climbed a spiral staircase to the next floor, where Jacob knelt dusting a set of pocket books for children. He glanced up as we passed and smiled in his dreamy way. I'd never understood the unlikely pairing of the methodical Rachel with her vague and wooly husband, but the laws of romantic attraction tended to escape me in general.

We continued all the way to the back of the store and around a corner. Mr. Cohen stopped at the end of a row of books and pushed on a panel between a set of heavy shelves. It swung inward to reveal a narrow hallway.

My heart skipped a beat. "A hidden passage," I whispered.

Chapter Six

Even better than Ali Baba's Cave. I grinned with anticipation at the thought of sneaking through its twisting branches, perhaps carrying a torch and eavesdropping on the secret plans of dangerous criminals.

"It's just an old servants' corridor that once connected the bedroom wing of a residence to the kitchen," Mr. Cohen informed me, throwing cold water on my flight of fancy. "Our shop and Godfrey's Hotel used to be one very large house."

With the neat flare of a match, he lit a lantern hanging just within the passageway. "Here, take this. You'll come out in the cellar of Godfrey's. You needn't worry. The door opens behind the wine racks. Use some care and check for people. A bit early in the day for a wine order, so you should be fine."

He gave me a pat on the back and a gentle push through the opening. "Extinguish the lantern before you leave. There's a hook at the other end to hang it. I trust you'll use your typical good judgment in getting home. No more spying on strangers." He smiled, his squinty eyes alight with laughter at his mild joke.

"I'll do my best," I answered as he shut the panel behind me.

Far from the dark and perilous tunnel of my imagination, the hallway stretched level and straight before descending in a series of steep stairs. Cracks from beneath the eaves lit the close space in a gray haze. After a short minute or two, I arrived at a narrow door.

I flipped up the simple hook latch and peeked through a cracked opening. No one was about. I blew out the lantern and wiggled out from behind the wine racks into the cool, still air of the cellar. A door near the far corner opened out onto steps leading up to the mews.

The rush of horses, carriages, grooms, and stable boys camouflaged my sudden appearance from the bowels of the hotel. I paused amongst the flurry to get my bearings, drawing in a deep breath of the sooty air.

A tabby cat brushed my leg. I bent to scratch it behind one tattered ear.

"You there," a man called out. He stopped directly in front of me.

I straightened, and my gaze traveled up him from his well-worn country boots to a finely tailored wool jacket. A flatcap, much like my own, sat atop dusky curls and overshadowed a classically handsome face with its firm jaw and wide apart blue eyes. His ruddy complexion and close-cropped whiskers typified a man more at home walking a country estate than the grounds of a fashionable hotel in the heart of London.

Dr. Watson, in many of his accounts, has described this type as the ideal physical embodiment of the essence of English manhood, decent and upstanding. I took a more skeptical view of "English manhood," since I had often borne the brunt of their prejudiced opinions.

I touched my cap with a respectful nod. "Yes, sir?"

"There's a good lad." His voice held the faint trace of a Yorkshire accent refined by an elite boarding school. "Who is the most fashionable florist in London?"

I cocked my head to one side, contemplating. Not the question, of course, for I had not the slightest notion who the most fashionable florist in London was. I considered the man.

Despite the whiskers, he appeared to be young, somewhere in his mid-twenties. His country attire fit a slim, broad-shouldered physique, and his mild blue eyes shone with a tolerant, kindly disposition.

"Can't say, sir. Someone with the hotel staff could advise you better," I answered.

He cleared his throat, cast a furtive glance around, and lowered his voice. "I'm down from Yorkshire. Not much of a city man, and these hotel types take me for a bit of a country bumpkin as it is. You look a bright lad, surely you know someone."

"There's a woman in Covent Garden sells flowers," I admitted. "Knows all about what they mean, but it's only a cart, not a fancy shop."

"Just the thing." He clapped me on the shoulder and tossed a coin to a passing stable boy. "Call me a cab."

"Right you are, sir." The boy pocketed the coin and ran to do his bidding.

"Come along, then. Show me where this flower lady resides." The man propelled me out of the stable yard to where a cab waited at the curb.

He gave me no opportunity to object. My skin prickled with a vague sense of unease. I sat poised to jump from the carriage should this turn out to be some sort of trap.

"Covent Garden," he told the driver. The cab jerked away from the curb and into the stream of traffic.

I kept a keen eye on the crowds, intent on spotting the redheaded man. My companion glanced at me with a sheepish smile.

"I hope, my lad, you've no pressing business, because I'm a man in love." He made a wide, encompassing gesture with his arms. "I'm letting no obstacle come between me and the woman of my desires, as my sister urged me to do."

A blush crept up from under his beard and spread across his

cheeks. He flashed me a schoolboy's self-conscious grin. I relaxed at this guileless confession.

"Nothing pressing, sir," I assured him. "But I've an errand needs doing not too far from Covent Garden on Gower Street. So this suits me fine."

This wasn't exactly true. My errand was no more than a half-conceived plan to warn Charlotte of the shadowy men watching her. (Though, considering her fondness for drama, I would not use the word "shadowy" when telling her.)

The problem being I didn't know precisely where Charlotte lived. I assumed she and her Aunt Sadie resided in the house once owned by John Harold Gaines, and everyone knew that it was a modest Georgian townhouse on Gower Street across from University College. I figured a few discreet inquiries in the area would put me on the right track.

"Excellent," the man replied, clapping his hands. "My ladylove lives not far from Gower Street on Russell Square. I mean to surprise her with a posy."

Ladylove? I cast him a sidelong glance. His blush deepened. He did not seem the type for poetic speech.

"Lucy, my sister," he explained, "says I should be more generous with endearments and romantic gestures if I'm to win the woman I've set my heart on."

"My grandfather says the heart must speak with a true voice to be understood."

He leaned forward with an intense expression. "I say, that sounds wise. What exactly does he mean?"

I shrugged. "Tell her how you feel but in your own words."

He sat back in the cushions and stared out the window. "When I first met the woman of my dreams, I thought her a strange sight." He lowered his voice, as if someone might overhear us. "She was wearing one of those riding outfits for a bike. It wasn't a dress, more like bloomers, but on the outside."

I suppressed a laugh. Did he not realize that his "ladylove" was a rational dresser? My interest piqued, I nodded, encouraging him to continue.

"She and two of her friends were on a biking tour of Yorkshire, including our little hamlet, Worseton-on-Tees. I'd just come onto the lane from our estate. Bruno, my horse, shied, unused to encountering bicycles. It took me a bit to bring him to hand. The other girls giggled, but Margaret—that's her name—maintained her composure and said, 'Sorry to startle such a magnificent beast.'

"I told them of a path leading to a wide vista that circled back around behind our manor. Invited them to tea after their ride."

His expression softened with a dreamy, faraway look. "She has large brown eyes, a sweet smile, and a quiet, dignified manner. I consider her quite fine. They came to tea, and"—he rubbed a hand over his face—"well, I've not felt the same ever since."

"I think a lady might prefer hearing that instead of some endearments or poetic verses," I opined.

"No," he returned, with a vehement shake of his head. "You and I might feel that way, but we're *men*." He tapped his chest. "Men want to hear things direct and honest. Women are softer creatures. We can't be too open with our feelings. They're easily upset and frightened."

My mother came to mind. She was soft in the way many women were, kind and yielding, but that wasn't the same as weak or frightened. In fact, I'd never known my mother to be frightened, and there was nobody stronger.

"Here we are," the driver yelled and pulled to a stop at a corner of the busy piazza.

Chapter Seven

I jumped down from the carriage and waited amongst the color and flurry of Covent Garden for my companion to alight. The lively, raucous market jolted my brain to attention and brought a smile to my lips—another one of my favorite places in a city full of them.

Once a year, on the first day of May, Mother, Grandfather, and I rise before dawn to watch the market come to life. The vendors travel through the night, bringing their leaden wagons in on all the major byways from the countryside and outer suburbs. Other wagons come empty, ready to take goods from the market to surrounding stores, hotels, and green grocers. Servants arrive from the great houses to stock up on meats, cheeses, and produce.

My mother brings rice cakes and dried fruit to give the old women sleeping beneath the stoops. She leaves them with jars of herbal rub for their joints and sore feet. Grandfather explains the "harmony of chaos" as we watch each random action weave through and around another to create a vibrant tapestry of both gaiety and commerce.

But more than honest merchants plied their trade here; the market also teemed with the sharp-eyed energy of thieves. As a precaution, my mother had sewn hidden pockets along the inside of the waistband of all my pants in which to stow my few coins.

I wasn't a rich target, but the same could not be said of my new acquaintance. Many men wandered the area dressed as country squires, but only he nervously bit his upper lip as we made our way through the crowd.

"Is this your first visit to the city, Mr. . . .?" I asked, curious as to why someone obviously wealthy and well educated was not more at ease in the nation's capital.

"Hughes, Jack Hughes, and no." He huffed, indignant. "What gave you that impression?"

I didn't answer. He shook his head and laughed at my reluctance.

"Sorry, lad, not meaning to sound full of myself. I've been here many times since a child, but I don't have a liking for the place. I haven't stayed long enough to know it. Back home, I can wander our grounds in the darkest hour of night and never get lost. I like knowing my way around."

I pushed through the throng, making a path to the flower market with Jack Hughes at my heels. "Here," I told him. "Mind your purse, because the most light-fingered thieves in all of England haunt these grounds." He thrust his hands into his pockets and swiveled his head with renewed attention to the people jostling past us.

"You might want to get a map of London, sir. There are lots to be had, some that'll even fit in your pocket. The more you study the map, the more you'll grow familiar with how the city flows."

"I never thought of that." His eyes widened at so novel an idea.

"Just make sure you don't take it out in a busy place. Wouldn't want folks thinking you're a tourist."

He shook his head. "No, indeed."

We arrived at the flower market just in time, a quarter of an hour before the doors closed. Most of the stalls were packing up, and the vendors busy trying to sell off the last of their stock. This was the best time to make a bargain, a fact made obvious by the flower ladies filling their baskets for a day of selling on street corners.

I led Jack Hughes through the maze and stopped at a stall with buckets and crates near empty. Mrs. Tooley's supply of fresh flowers and arrangements sold out quick, but I knew from long experience, she held a good amount back for the street sellers. A gaggle of these ladies hung about her stall trading jokes and gossip as they arranged flowers in their baskets.

I waded into the group and gestured for Jack to follow. He cleared his throat and stiffly sidled in between the women, saying, "Beg pardon" every time he bumped up against one of them.

They giggled. A few coarse comments on the fit of his trousers and the color rose again on his cheeks.

"Mrs. Tooley," I said upon seeing thick, gray hair piled high in a bun and the back of her trademark colorful shawl. She turned, and her lined face lifted in a good-natured smile.

"Kuo." She crossed her arms over a well-worn smock that covered the front of her dress. "Where's that grandson of mine?"

I shrugged. Last time I'd seen Teddy he'd nicked a gold watch off a fat cat right here at the market. The reason I no longer kept company with him.

"Sorry, Mrs. Tooley, I haven't seen him in weeks," I answered truthfully. I didn't approve of Teddy's latest venture, but I wasn't going to rat him out either.

"I'm afeared he's fallen in with some bad sort," she lamented.

Plenty of the "bad sort" roamed a city the size of London, and you couldn't hunt for marks at Covent Garden without owing allegiance to one of them. But Teddy wouldn't tell me who had put him up to it.

"He'll come back in good time, Mrs. Tooley," I told her, feeling guilty at her worried frown.

"Mayhap, you're right." She nodded and squinted up at Jack Hughes. "You've brought me a customer?"

"Yes. Mr. Hughes needs a posy for a lady."

The women edged in closer and whispered among themselves. The musty smell of wool garments mingled with the fragrance of flowers pressed in around us.

"A long attachment?" Mrs. Tooley asked.

Jack cleared his throat, something of a nervous habit I was realizing. "No. We've just met, but um . . . ahem . . . she has made a tremendous impression on me."

The flower ladies tittered. Mrs. Tooley shushed them, her expression serious.

"So, you'll be needing a tussie-mussie to tell this young lady how you feel." She reached past a crateful of flowers to pull towards her a pail of greenery and fresh herbs. "In the case of you just meeting, you won't want to be too forward." The women nodded wisely in unison.

Jack straightened his shoulders and offered, "A small nosegay of roses, white perhaps, being as I'm a Yorkshire man?"

A collective intake of breath from the gathered women and a forceful shake of Mrs. Tooley's head gave him reason to believe he was mistaken. I cast him a sidelong glance and smiled at the intimidation writ large across his face.

"The rose is a serious flower, Mr. Hughes, the white in particular. Any lady of fashion worth her salt will know what a white rose means. It best be avoided this early in the courtship."

"Yes, of course." Humbled, he gestured to the flowers before him. "What do you propose?"

"What is the lady's character?"

"She is a person of deep sensibilities and quite proper . . . ah . . ." His voice trailed off. He frowned down at the ground, struggling to list the qualities of his "ladylove."

I raised my eyebrows. "Proper" wasn't a word most people used for a woman cycling through the countryside in bloomers.

Mrs. Tooley held up a hand to relieve him from further description. "Proper with deep sensibilities it is," she repeated. "I have just the thing." While she spoke, her deft, practiced fingers wove together ivy and lavender. "The ivy can have many meanings, but combined with lavender suggests grace and remembrance."

A vase-like structure emerged from the tangle of ivy tendrils and lavender sprigs. In the middle of this, she placed a bunch of short-stemmed purple irises. "The iris means strong attachment, either love or friendship. We'll leave it to the lady to figure your meaning. A good tussie-mussie can't be too direct in case she don't share your feelings. Best let her take the lead."

Jack returned a solemn nod as if receiving sage advice from an ancient oracle. Mrs. Tooley finished the bouquet with a lacy paper doily and ribbon to tie it all together.

My new friend smiled with satisfaction at the simple, elegant confection. "Thank you. How much will that be?"

"Nothing, Mr. Hughes. This first one's a gift. You just tell your family and friends where to buy their flowers."

"But I . . . ah . . . I should pay you. I'm, um, not often in town."

Mrs. Tooley shook her head and narrowed her eyes with wily insight. Jack Hughes was a man easily put under obligation. Both she and I had little doubt he would strive to fulfill any debt owed.

Jack thanked her again and removed himself from the gaggle pressed in around him, taking great care not to bump into any of the grinning women. On our way back to the waiting cab, his steps slowed and stopped.

He stared down at the vivid purple irises with an expression of terrified indecision. "I've been thinking. Perhaps it would be best if *you* delivered this posy."

"Whatever for?" I objected, shocked at his about-face. "She doesn't know me from Adam."

"Yes, well, you could deliver the flowers with my card, so she'll know they're from me."

"Wasn't the whole purpose of this venture to talk to her yourself?"

He blew out a long breath. "I'm not much of a ladies' man. I get tongue-tied. Lucy says I should work harder at making myself more polished and agreeable or I'll never get married."

I stopped myself from rolling my eyes and wished us back among Mrs. Tooley's gang, knowing they'd have strong opinions about his predicament. Backing out after going to all this trouble seemed self-defeating, and so I told him.

He straightened his shoulders. "Self-defeating? No, lad, this posy represents the, ah, vanguard, so to speak." Jack cleared his throat yet again and smiled. "I'll write her from Yorkshire. Next time I'm in London, she'll be primed to see me."

He puffed out his chest with masculine bravado, but his eyes gleamed with deep insecurity. He had seemed a simple man at first, but after observing him this past hour or so, I deduced him to be a man out of his element.

I nodded. "If you give me her name and address, I'll deliver the flowers."

Jack relaxed, and his broad, straight outline softened. He grinned in relief, pulling from his breast pocket an ornate silver card case. In contrast to the elaborate case, the card he handed me displayed only his name—"John Jeremy Hughes, Esq."—printed in simple black ink across its face.

I deduced the case to be a gift just before he said, tucking it back into his pocket, "From my sister." He shook his head with a fond smile. "Always trying to make me look smart, Lucy is."

I thrust his card into my pocket. "And the direction?"

He told me the address and pressed some coins into my hand. "Here, for your trouble . . . ah, well, I didn't catch your name."

"Kuo Cheng."

Jack drew back with a frown. "That sounds Oriental."

"Yes, sir. My mother and grandfather are from China. We have an apothecary in Limehouse."

"Except for horses and"—he blushed—"a pretty girl, I'm not the most observant of men. Now you mention it, there is a bit of the Orient about your eyes. Still, I've seen some with similar features up my way."

"My father was an Englishman."

"Well now, that would explain it, wouldn't it?"

I didn't answer and pocketed the coins. Jack gestured back towards the cab.

"Take the cab to Russell Square," he insisted. "I've a need to stretch my legs. Send a note round to the inn. Let me know how it went."

My new acquaintance gave the driver the address and some change. I climbed in, and the carriage jolted out into traffic, leaving Jack alone to walk back to his hotel.

Chapter Eight

Outside of Shakespearian plays and popular novels, I knew little of romantic love. Stories fraught with suffering, and even suicide, baffled me. Unlike Romeo and Juliet, I rejected the idea of taking my life in love or despair. I'm too logical and practical for such a gesture.

Besides, grand passions were reserved for the wealthy, or at the very least, poor governesses who caught the eye of rich and powerful men. I imagined a more commonplace romance for someone like myself.

However, I understood enough to know that Jack's last-minute retreat did not bode well for his chances of winning the lady—faint heart and all that. But a good half an hour later, when I finally stood before an intimidating tangle of three laughing girls, each dressed more outrageously than the other, I understood both his infatuation and reluctance to face the object of his affections.

My knock had not brought forth the expected butler or housekeeper, but shrieks of laughter, and with it, the heavy pounding of feet. I stood well back from the door expecting it to burst forth upon a herd of stampeding cattle. Burst open it did, but far from commonplace cows, I beheld three of the loveliest young women I had ever seen.

Their dress, or rather costumes, ranged from a velvet Little Lord

Fauntleroy suit with a cutaway jacket and matching knee breeches to a revealing Grecian robe, and an elaborate riding habit from the last century. They grouped together in the open doorway, arms wrapped around each other's waists and with hair loose and hanging down their backs.

Once she had caught her breath, the Grecian fixed me with a perplexed stare. "I say, Meg, he doesn't look like a painter."

Meg, whom I assumed to be the Margaret of Jack's desires, stood taller than the other two, her shapely figure encased in a riding habit of deep forest green that contrasted magnificently with her chestnut curls and large, dark eyes. She frowned. "Certainly not. Mr. Sawyer is a man of sixty, if not more. Who are you?"

I doffed my hat and made a little bow, holding the bouquet of irises before me. "I am delivering this posy to Miss Margaret Scott on behalf of Mr. Jack Hughes."

My pronouncement was greeted with a collective look of puzzlement and the question "Who?" from all three pairs of lips simultaneously.

I pulled his card from my pocket and presented it with the posy. "Mr. Jack Hughes of Yorkshire."

Still the blank looks.

"You met on a cycling trip and lunched with him and his sister, Lucy, at his estate near Worseton-on-Tees."

Little Lord Fauntleroy threw her head back with a peal of laughter. "Why, Meg, he's referring to your 'magnificent beast.'"

The girls collapsed into a heap of giggles. My hands, still holding the posy and card, dropped to my sides.

The Grecian, gulping for air, declared, "He's certainly handsome, but I can't imagine the set of his shoulders being compensation for his plodding conversation."

"He did seem more at home with the cows in the pasture than with ladies in the parlour," Little Lord Fauntleroy added, choking with laughter.

"Not cows, sheep," sputtered the Grecian. "They're even more stupid."

I straightened with indignation and pursed my lips in distaste.

"Oh look, we've offended his messenger." Margaret's mouth curved into a delicate, mocking smile.

I tossed the posy at their feet and let Jack's card flutter to the ground. "Not at all, ma'am." I doffed my hat again. "You are not the first people of my acquaintance to mistake cruelty for wit."

I turned on my heels and stalked off. Their expressions of shock and anger followed me down the steps and out onto the pavement.

"How *dare* you speak to us . . ." the Grecian called out to my retreating back.

I ignored her. I despised bullies, even pretty ones.

The driver having left, I strode up the street and ducked into an alleyway leading to the mews behind the houses. My mother told me that as a small child, whenever my will was thwarted, I threw terrible fits of rage. I screamed and ripped at my clothes, sometimes even bending over and banging my head against the floor.

I have no recollection of this. My earliest childhood memories are those of long sessions with my grandfather focusing my thoughts inward to a place of quiet. I did that now.

I leaned against the wall. Cool moisture from the bricks seeped into my back. I uncurled my fists, closed my eyes, and slowed my breathing. My mind reached out and focused on the monotonous drip of water from the overhanging eaves. I followed a single drop as it fell from the roof and plopped against the cobblestones, shattering into smaller drops of water. I wound with them through a maze of interwoven stones, regrouping at the gutter and sliding off into oblivion, again as one.

"You alright, lad?"

My eyes flew open. An old groom in worn cotton pants and a woolen jacket stood before me, a tattered knit scarf about his neck. He held the reins of a dainty little thoroughbred that blinked at me with large, soft eyes fringed with impossibly long lashes. I was reminded of Charlotte.

I straightened. "Yes, sir, I'm fine. Thank you. Just a little lost. Would you happen to know the residence of the late author John Harold Gaines?"

"Right, I would. Everyone hereabouts knows where he lived. They have a plaque out front on the house. It's just over on Gower, number fourteen."

I thanked him and exited the alley, making my way to Gower Street. With the hour tending towards noon, my stomach growled.

I took a small detour to Bedford Square, where only months before the city had removed the gates used to enclose this upper-class estate, allowing traffic to flow unchecked through the area. Bedford's oval garden lay at its center, a peaceful, grassy oasis with shrubbery and large London plane trees ringing its perimeter.

A fence prevented us commoners from entering the garden, but this did not discourage me. I could still enjoy the first changing colors of autumn from my spot leaning against the wrought iron barrier.

I pulled from my pocket the meat pie Mr. Wei had bought me that morning, still wrapped in a piece of crumpled wax paper and miraculously intact. Though no longer hot, the savory meat and spices still tasted delicious, and I wiped my mouth with a sleeve to keep from drooling.

Lord Brudeford often led me through the streets of London, praising its "architectural treasures," one of his favorites being Bedford Square. "Note the uniformity of the classical Georgian façade, Kuo. Unlike the drab appearance of similar architecture along Gower Street, here the pigmented stone over the doorways enlivens the presentation while still maintaining an overall air of elegance."

I couldn't disagree more. I found the "enlivened presentation" and "air of elegance" of the square as dull and uniform as the houses on Gower Street. My only real interest in the buildings centered on the decorative ceramic Coade "stone" developed by one Eleanor Coade in the middle part of the last century.

Mrs. Coade (as she was known, though she never married) bought a struggling stone business in 1769 and developed the high-quality ceramic stone that proved resistant to the extreme weather and caustic air of London. Her company designed statues, busts, friezes, moldings, panels, and all types of ornamentation for both inside and out. She even made decorative stone for royal residences.

I liked to imagine her poring over designs and instructing her workers on the proper ceramic mix and exact temperature of the kilns. I marveled at her finding a purpose and a place in a business where someone like her had no right to be.

I licked the last flaky crumbs from my fingers and pushed away from the fence. In a short block or two, I stood in front of number fourteen Gower Street, a Georgian townhouse almost identical to its neighbors. A brass plaque adorned the wall:

John Harold Gaines
London residence
1850-1879
"Through the darkness and strife,
we see a candle on the sill."

A mix of autumn flowers ran across the fence, and stone pots thick with ivy flanked the entrance. I knew better than to knock on the front door with no official business.

I walked down the exterior stairway to the kitchen entrance below. As I came off the last step, I collided with a harried girl holding up the ends of her apron full of potato peels and apple cores.

Chapter Nine

"Goodness, but you gave me a start," the girl chided, her voice a dry, husky growl. "You shouldn't be down here. This entrance is for those who belong to the family. I could've dropped this mess. Then where'd we be?" She tipped her apron and dumped the kitchen debris into a wooden crate by the door.

Her long, skinny arms dangled from a reed-thin torso set atop equally long and skinny legs. A pair of kind, hazel eyes softened her angular face. She looked no older than fifteen or sixteen. I identified her correctly as the housemaid, Nellie.

"I'm here to see Miss Charlotte Gaines. My name is Kuo Cheng."

Nellie gasped and lowered her voice to a hushed, even deeper growl. "I shoulda known, with your face and all." She frowned and peered closer. "Can't say I'd notice in passing."

I kept my expression blank, used to this type of offhanded remark on my appearance. "Is Miss Gaines at home?"

"Sure she is, but so's Miss Sadie, both of them in the sitting room sewing." She laughed. "Miss Charlotte hates embroidery and lacks the skill of it, but her aunt insists on a few hours every week."

"I need to speak with her."

"This about the letter? I told Miss Charlotte I'd no idea who delivered it. Just showed up on the silver dish in the foyer one morning."

I tucked this piece of information away in my mind and shook my head. "No. I have news. I need to speak with her. It's vital."

Nellie puffed out her cheeks and released a long breath. "If you'd come just a fortnight ago, I coulda snuck you into her room easy. Now, we got this new housekeeper, Mrs. Marshton." She grimaced. "A right stickler for rules and 'proper management.' I've never known one for sneaking up on a person all quiet-like out of nowhere, almost like a ghost, and as pale as one too." The girl shivered. "Can't risk it. I'd get the sack for sure."

"Is there anywhere else we can meet?"

Nellie pulled at her cap. "Well, there's the community garden behind this row of houses. It's private for them who lives here. Each house has an entrance into it from the back, but there's a large gate off the path behind. I can get you the key."

Long legs carried her across the landing and into the kitchen in two swift strides. She moved with the undulating grace of an octopus. A hard-earned accomplishment, I deduced. She must have forced herself early in life not to get tangled up in her limbs or trip over her large, floppy feet.

She returned with a whoosh and a large, brass gate key clutched in her hand. "Give it back to Miss Charlotte. There's brickwork right inside with shrubs and a big, black walnut tree along the back. I'll tell her to meet you next to the tree." With those brief instructions and a firm nod, she was gone.

I turned the skeleton key over in my hands. From the looks of it, I could've easily picked the lock. At least with the key, I wouldn't look suspicious to any passersby.

A narrow track stretched behind the houses and bordered the garden. The path was strangely unkempt for this well-to-do neighborhood, with tendrils from overgrown hedges stretching across the rough pavement. The boughs of the common plane trees met overhead, creating a leafy tunnel running along the entire length of the block.

A tall, elaborate wrought iron gate glowed with a new coat of black paint and stood in well-maintained contrast to the path. The key turned smoothly in the lock, and the gate swung inward on its oiled hinges. I stood just inside, enchanted by this hidden gem.

A broad swath of deserted green lawn lay at the garden's center. Large maple trees ringed the grass in a long oval, and broad-leafed bushes hid most of the iron fence from view. I spotted the black walnut with its leaflets turning a vivid yellow in the far corner. Instead of crossing the empty lawn, I ambled along between the hedge and the fence until reaching the cracked and gnarled trunk of the old tree. Sparse tufts of grass grew beneath its heavy branches.

I lay my hands against the rough bark. Few such magnificent trees populated London. I longed to step inside the trunk and follow its roots to the center of the earth.

"The black walnut is poisonous to other plants. That's why nothing grows beneath it."

I jumped at Charlotte's voice and turned, ready to fling an angry retort at the girl forever startling me. But my sharp words died at the sight of a damp lump of curly fur she clasped to her breast.

"What is that?" I demanded, repulsed, as the thing twitched and made a strangled gargling noise.

"Rose-Marie, my little French poodle."

She set the creature down, for I had yet to determine whether the thing was truly a dog (though most certainly not a French poodle). Four boney legs emerged from the mass of fur, and a snout with protruding snaggleteeth sniffed at the ground.

"Rose-Marie just had a bath," Charlotte said as explanation for the "dog's" bedraggled appearance.

The ragged animal tottered over to the tree trunk and hitched up a hind leg. "Rose-Marie is a boy," I observed.

"I *know* that."

"So why not Pierre or Claude?"

Charlotte snatched the little dog up and cradled it in her arms. "I like the name Rose-Marie, and he doesn't mind. So why should anyone else?"

"He's not the sort of dog I'd have imagined your aunt owning."

Her eyes grew wide, and she pressed the wiggling creature even closer to her chest. "Aunt Sadie doesn't know about Rose-Marie. I found the poor thing trapped in the gutter of our back garden. He stays hidden in my room, and Nellie helps me care for him."

Charlotte rubbed her cheek against the mass of wiry fuzz, her expression soft. A surge of pity coursed through me for the lonely girl who, surrounded as she was by wealth and comfort, had by all appearances only a housemaid and an ugly, abandoned dog for friends.

I resisted the feeling. Empathy, a condition I struggled with, and for which I blamed my mother, overwhelmed me at the most inopportune times. I have nothing against identifying with another's suffering, but too much emotion serves only to cloud the brain. I strive more for compassion, an understanding of another's pain without feeling it myself.

"Miss Gaines—" I began.

"Can we dispense with the formalities? Charlotte will do, at least in private." She sat cross-legged on a thin patch of grass. Rose-Marie nestled on her dress, stretched hammock-like between her knees. "I am heartily sick of Aunt Sadie's lectures on my 'unnatural behavior' and 'insufficient education,' so that I long sometimes just to be comfortable."

I studied her. In contrast to the fashionable dress she had worn to Baker Street, the loose-fitting cotton smock needed no corset and allowed her to breathe and move with ease. She pulled a light woolen shawl tighter around her shoulders and petted the dog.

Society frowned on familiarity between the sexes, especially when they were not of equal rank. But what harm could it do when we were alone? I leaned against the tree trunk. "Charlotte . . ." I began again.

She smiled her approval.

"You are being followed."

She blinked. "Me?"

"You remember the redheaded man who ran out the back?"

She nodded.

"He was following you. I believe he must have seen you enter the building, and when you didn't exit the same way, he went in search of you." I told her about the conversation I overheard between the redheaded man and his accomplice and the rest of my adventures of the morning.

Charlotte again clasped the poor creature in a close embrace and declared in breathless tones, "*Now* you believe me."

"I didn't disbelieve you . . ." I attempted to explain my skepticism and the importance of an analytical process, but thought better of it, saying instead, "You must take precautions."

"Good heavens." Her voice throbbed with emotion. "What precautions do you suggest? Lock myself forever in my room?"

I sighed. Would the drama never cease?

I pushed away from the tree and sat next to her. "Nothing so extreme. In fact, we must become more aggressive in our investigation." I picked up a stick and drew a crude map in the dirt. "Here is Mr. Holmes's residence on Baker Street, and here is the Athenaeum Club, and finally, your house." The triangle that emerged as I drew a line from one point to the other encompassed some of the wealthiest parts of London.

When I told her this, she squinted at the ground. "All I see is dirt."

Remembering my map, I pulled it from my jacket and unfolded it before us. Charlotte sucked in her breath. "How ingenious, a little map."

I pointed to the area within the triangle on the map. "Our

unknown adversaries likely live and work within, or just outside, this triangle. We should concentrate our efforts in this area. People rarely move far from their base of operations, whether it be their homes or businesses."

"You do."

"What?"

Charlotte pointed to the south and east on the map. "Your home and business are in Limehouse, yet you were at all these places in the past two days alone."

I frowned, irritated by her astute observation. "I suppose you're right. Still, the redheaded man was at Baker Street, the Athenaeum Club, and here—"

"Was he here?"

I shot her an exasperated look. "I don't know for sure, but if he was following you . . ." My voice trailed off as the logic of my analytical process fell in the face of her questions. I had let guesses (educated ones, to be sure) override the facts, of which there were, admittedly, few.

Charlotte leaned over the map. "It's as good a place to start as any, I suppose. But I would include"—she drew her finger from the Athenaeum Club, bowing out one side of the triangle to encompass Jermyn Street—"your friend's bookstore."

I nodded. "Agreed."

The girl scrambled to her feet. Rose-Marie wiggled and yipped.

"I should be getting back. Aunt Sadie may spy me through the window. Too bad the paper didn't tell us anything truly useful."

I stood and brushed off my trousers. "I think it told us, at the very least, we are dealing with an exacting person."

"How so?"

"The lines were so expertly drawn, Mr. Cohen thought at first they were printed on."

"I guess that's something," she acknowledged. "Oh, I almost forgot." Charlotte thrust a hand into the pocket of her smock and pulled from its depths a delicate gold locket.

The necklace glinted in a shaft of weak sunlight, and I squinted at the tiny glowing heart with an engraved dragonfly design. "Did your aunt return it to you?"

Her lips curved in a small, grim smile. "No. She had no right to it. When she went out, I took it from her room."

"Was she angry?"

"She raged at me and demanded it back, but she can't really do anything. Once of age, I'm the sole heir to my grandfather's estate. She has a pension and lifetime occupancy of the house, but that is all." Charlotte nudged at a tuft of grass with the toe of her shoe. "If she wasn't so mean, I'd feel sorry for her. Aunt Sadie should have an equal share, but I'm told my grandfather was scornful of spinsters. Him leaving me everything wasn't fair. I have a mind never to marry, just to spite him."

I ignored this bitter declaration, saying, "I'll see what I can find out about the locket." I handed her the map. "Here. You take it. I have another one. Learn the streets around your house and pay attention when you go out. Let's keep our meeting at Baker Street, but only if you're not followed."

Charlotte nodded and pressed several coins into my hand. I didn't count them, not wanting to seem coarse, but put them, along with the locket, into the hidden pocket at my waistband and left.

Chapter Ten

I clung to my seat on the omnibus as we careened down the twisting streets. Sitting up top, I could avoid the choking dust kicked up by hundreds of wheels and horses' hooves, but not the ever-present pickpockets. Packed tight and shoulder to shoulder with the other passengers, I kept one hand gripping the railing and the other resting against my waistband—just in case.

We neared my stop, and I pushed my way through the throng and down the stairs off the back. I reached our store before teatime. The bell jingled as I pushed the door open and stepped into a tiny slice of China.

The delicate scent of sandalwood washed over me, and the Chinese lanterns hanging from the ceiling danced in the chill draft. My grandfather, having never bothered with the pretense of not knowing English in our own neighborhood, leaned over the heavy, scarred wooden counter, deep in conversation with Mr. Johnson, the local tobacconist.

Behind him loomed an enormous cabinet of small square drawers holding every medicinal herb, plant, or dried animal part known to man. Stoppered glass bottles lined the shelves along with heavy tomes on anatomy, acupuncture, massage, and diet, among others.

I wove in between small tables stacked with boxes of tea, china, jade balls, amulets, jars of anise seed, candy, bundled incense, intricate ivory fans, and whatever else our customers might need from the far-flung reaches of the East. Through the beaded curtain at the back, I found my mother in the storeroom.

She sorted medicines into small paper packets and labeled each using an inkwell and a feathered calligraphy pen. Mother looked up and smiled. The tension eased from my neck and shoulders. Her name was Yu Yan: beautiful smile.

"Kuo, just in time . . ." She frowned. "Your hat?"

I pulled off the Irish flatcap and threw it and my jacket onto a stool. "Mr. Cohen felt my hat too, ah, noticeable."

She narrowed her eyes. My mother's eyes were singularly lovely, like twin shiny half-moons. "Noticeable to whom?"

I gathered a stack of the small paper squares we used to wrap our medicines. I tapped them on the table to align the edges and handed them to my mother.

By the color and texture of the powder, I could tell that she prepared our usual weekly delivery to Colonel Rockwell. A decoction of the herb *artemisia annua*, that when seeped for several minutes in cold water relieved the fever of malaria.

"I was, um, out, and, ah, this rogue . . ."

"Stop." Mother walked to the beaded curtain and poked her head out into the store. "*Ba*, when you are done, please come back."

She continued packaging the medicine in silence, and I labeled each neat little folded square. After some time, Grandfather closed the store and joined us.

He pulled from his pocket a small tin of butterscotch candy and placed it in the middle of the table. He, too, lent a hand filling papers and folding them.

Butterscotch being his only English weakness, he ordered the candies from a small confectioner in Doncaster, a market town in

South Yorkshire. We each took a piece. The sweet, salty taste made my mouth water, and I slurped.

After I had labeled the final little packet of medicine, Grandfather crossed his arms and prompted me with a nod. "Yes?"

"You know how you say there is a purpose in all things," I blathered. "And sometimes we should let events—"

"Do you take me for a fool?" His voice rumbled low in his chest.

I bowed my head. "No, Grandfather."

"Then spare me the repetition of my own words. What are you up to?"

I told them of meeting Charlotte and her request for help in solving the mysterious poem. Mother's face creased with concern when I described my narrow escape from the redheaded man.

"—and so, I *must* help her. She has only a bitter old aunt who doesn't really look out for her . . ." My voice trailed off.

Mother closed her eyes and sighed. Grandfather shook his head, and I steeled myself for his objections.

"How old is this girl?" he asked instead.

"Sixteen. She received the poem and locket on her birthday."

"And she was seeking assistance from Mr. Holmes when you met her?"

"Yes, sir."

"Do you believe this redheaded man to be dangerous?"

I looked from him to my mother. I could not lie. "Yes."

"Kuo—" Mother began.

Heavy, frantic pounding on the door halted our conversation. We exchanged startled glances.

Grandfather turned and strode into the store, my mother and I close on his heels. He opened the door.

Mrs. Tooley stumbled in, her hair disheveled and face twisted in pain. I grabbed for her, but Mother was before me and steadied the old woman with an arm around her waist.

"What has happened? Are you injured?" Grandfather asked as Mother led her to the comfortable armchair.

She collapsed into the chair and doubled over, burying her face in her lap. A haunting keen issued from deep in her throat. Mother threw her arms around the distressed woman and held her close.

"Kuo, run to the kitchen and brew up a cup of chrysanthemum tea."

Our small kitchen doubled as a laboratory and was, for that purpose, meticulously clean and organized. A large oven took up half the back wall and warmed the little room. Mother kept a kettle of water on the stove, and I stoked it to a boil.

I pulled from the pantry a small tin and broke the dried petals up into a teacup. The boiling water released the distinct smooth and calming aroma of chrysanthemum.

With teacup in hand, I went back into the store. Mrs. Tooley sat huddled in a miserable heap between my mother and grandfather. Mother's eyes met my questioning gaze. Her expression of profound sadness stopped me in my tracks.

Grandfather took the cup and gave it to Mrs. Tooley, steadying it between his two strong hands before letting go. "The authorities have informed Mrs. Tooley that Teddy's body was pulled from the Thames."

My lungs froze on an indrawn breath. In that instant, I think my heart even stopped. Teddy, with his gap-toothed grin and shock of white-blond hair, had been my friend since we were small children.

Mrs. Tooley first came to us with a painful and unsightly red rash on her hands. She left with a pair of gloves woven from raw silk and an herbal ointment to apply twice daily. A week later, her rash gone, she returned with five-year-old Teddy in tow, suffering from the sins of his mother, who had died from gin and dissipation. Grandfather did what he could for him, but Teddy couldn't quite escape the damage done to him in the womb, and he struggled to read and write.

He wasn't exactly stupid, but he lacked judgment and even a measure of self-preservation. Teddy trusted easily and often turned to me for guidance.

But as we grew older, he tired of my caution. He idolized the criminals who worked the market and longed for the brotherhood of the streets with the excitement of easy money and women.

"Look at the titties on that one," Teddy had exclaimed the last time we met, pointing out the large breasts of a young prostitute. His loud, excitable voice carried across the market. "She could milk a litter of pups with them bubbies." He laughed, a wide, lopsided grin spreading across his face.

Covent Garden swirled with its usual flash and noise. No one gave us a second look; still, I winced at his crude joke, embarrassed.

I usually kept a firm grip on my temper but lost it that day. I don't know why.

Brushing aside his comment, I snapped, "I saw you nick a watch from halfway across the market the other day. You're no good at it. You'll get caught."

He flushed with anger. "Ain't none of your business what I do. I don't need no lump 'o ice from you."

His bluster and ingratitude irked me. I'd pulled him out of tons of scrapes and never once given him up to his grandmother.

"If you're working for one of the kidsman," I warned him, "you'll find yourself in a right pickle soon enough. Then you'll want my help."

He turned on me, bringing his fists up as if to throw a punch. His sudden movement took me by surprise, but I didn't flinch. Teddy's slim physique matched my own, and though he was taller, I was quicker and more muscled.

"You ain't as smart as you think you are," he growled through gritted teeth. "You should be lookin' to make money and find a woman, but maybe you're some dirty poof."

I drew back. He'd never made such an insult, never said that word before. I calmed my breathing and narrowed my eyes with suspicion. "Who're you working for?"

"Wouldn't you like to know? Rat me out to Grandma, like always."

Blood beat against my temples. He knew better, but still threw the lie in my face.

"Go on then, big man," I jeered. "You don't need me, and I won't worry about you."

A glint of uncertainty flashed in his eyes, but still I taunted, "What're you waiting for? Go on."

"Nothin'," he spat with a dismissive wave and strode away.

I didn't wait to see the crowd swallow him up but turned and left in the opposite direction. I hadn't seen him since.

My heart started back up with a heavy thump, and my chest ached with a deep sense of shame. I knew why I'd lost my temper that day.

I was tired of his company, tired of his coarse talk and dumb ideas. So angry at his ugly insult, I didn't even tell his grandmother he was headed for trouble.

Mrs. Tooley clutched at my grandfather's hand. "You'll go see him, won't you? They say he killed hisself. But that can't be true." Tears ran down her ravaged cheeks. "Teddy didn't despair the same as other folk. He was simple like that. He'd never kill hisself."

I acknowledged the truth of her words. I couldn't picture a less likely scenario than Teddy jumping into the Thames voluntarily.

"What can I do?" Grandfather asked.

Her expression shifted from one of anguish to that of fury. "Find out how he died and who done it to him."

"I don't—" Grandfather began.

"Please," she pleaded.

He looked over at my mother. She nodded.

"It is a risk. But what else can we do?" Mother reasoned.

A small, bitter smile peeked from out of his silky gray beard. "Only what is right."

Mrs. Tooley's intense, tear-drenched eyes never left my grandfather's face.

He sighed. "I'll go."

Chapter Eleven

The distraught old woman planted a fervent kiss on my grandfather's hand. "No need for that," he said with an embarrassed shake of his head. "Kuo . . ." He wavered. "Get my bag."

I understood his hesitation. The leather case held acupuncture needles, herbs and medicines for common ailments, stones and cups, and a modern stethoscope with ivory earpieces and flexible rubber tubing.

The medicine bag was for the living. It contained little to help the dead.

I took it from his desk in the storeroom and stopped just short of the beaded curtain to study Mrs. Tooley. Grief had reshaped her. She stood, wrapped in her colorful shawl, a wilted flower, fragile and wounded outside her market stronghold.

She wiped her face with a grimy shirtsleeve. "You'll need me to get in. Old Dengington don't just let anybody by."

Horace Dengington's pockmarked face arose in my mind. If the presence of death wasn't deterrent enough, his scarred features, along with his hunchback and harsh voice, kept most people from even approaching the small coroner's mortuary at St. George's. I knew from overhearing the conversations of medical students that cadavers for dissection required a hefty bribe, as well as braving Horace Dengington's foul temper.

I swallowed, not wanting to go with my grandfather but knowing I owed Teddy at least that. "I'm coming," I announced, walking through the beaded curtain.

Mother did not object. Her perception when it came to me rarely missed its mark. She read my guilt as if it were branded across my forehead.

"Bundle up, Kuo," was my grandfather's only reply.

I pulled on my wool jacket and wound a scarf around my neck. I snatched up the cap and settled it atop my head as we hustled out the door.

The humidity that had lingered from summer gave way to autumn's evening chill. Fortunately, we didn't have far to go in the cold and climbed into a hired cab waiting at the curb.

Mrs. Tooley's humble appearance deceived many. However, her business sense outpaced even her flower skills, and she lived in a comfortable set of rooms in Covent Garden. She didn't often indulge in the luxuries of life but could afford them in emergencies such as this one.

The carriage pulled out into traffic. An occasional streetlamp flashed past, lighting up the old woman's rigid profile. Her shaky breath reverberated in the quiet of the enclosed cab.

My grandfather sat with the medicine bag on his lap; the hem of his *chanshang* peeked out from below his long, heavy coat. He closed his eyes, no doubt steeling his emotions for the ordeal to come.

The churchyard at St. George's lay dark and deserted. Only a single lamp hung over the entrance of the small building sitting at the far side of the yard. Built about twenty years ago, the mortuary served our poor community and once housed a victim of the Whitechapel Murderer who terrorized the city only a few short years before.

The hunched outline of Horace Dengington greeted us at the door. The man grunted, turned on his heels, and led us in a silent single file down a dank and narrow corridor. The heavy, rank air pressed in around me, making it difficult to draw in a deep breath. Grandfather appeared untroubled by our oppressive surroundings.

His silk robe rustled around him like leaves in a gentle wind. I concentrated on the comforting sound as we turned a corner and entered a tiny, bare room with an elevated wooden table in its middle.

"Thirty minutes and no more," Horace growled and left.

A gas lantern sat on the windowsill. Its flickering light cast an eerie glow over the figure lying on the table. A clean cotton sheet covered the body.

Mrs. Tooley stood just inside the threshold. She stared with unseeing eyes at the slim outline beneath the sheet, her arms crossed and fingers digging into her woolen shawl.

"Mrs. Tooley, please step outside into the churchyard," my grandfather bade her.

She answered him with a curt nod and left. He set his bag on the end of the table and bowed his head. I did the same.

A moment passed. The catch on the bag clicked and released. I looked up.

It sat open, and Grandfather drew from its depths a pair of close-fitting leather gloves. He handed me another pair, and I slipped them on.

"Pull back the sheet, Kuo."

I swallowed hard and removed the sheet to reveal . . . tears started in my eyes. Horace Dengington had taken care to lay him out properly, with tenderness even. Teddy's pale skin was washed, and his limbs rested in a natural and respectful position. A loincloth-like garment covered his private parts. His eyes were closed and his expression relaxed and peaceful.

I shook my head in silent self-reproach for my harsh opinion of the old caretaker. I knew that no matter how much coin the medical students pressed into Horace's palm, they would have to wait for another corpse to dissect.

Grandfather examined Teddy as he would any living patient. Beginning at the head, he checked pressure points and followed the major meridians that managed the flow of *chi* throughout the body. He paused right below the rib cage.

"Help me lift him."

Stepping forward, we turned the body. I gasped.

On the backside, just where the liver would be, a large, purple bruise spread halfway across his narrow frame. "Tell me, Kuo, could this be the result of trauma after death?"

I shook my head. "Unlikely. Bruising requires blood flow." I forced back tears. "Teddy was probably injured before dying."

He nodded. "It could be he jumped into the river and was pushed by the current against a solid object before drowning."

We laid the body back down, and Grandfather continued to trace the now barren map of life down Teddy's legs to his feet. He peered in between the toes. His beard drooped with a frown.

"What is it, Grandfather?"

"A needle mark."

I squinted at the tiny red speck between the big and long toes. "What does it mean?"

"Many things, perhaps, but most certainly that it was not meant to be found."

Horace Dengington appeared at the door. "Time's up."

We covered the body and followed him out into the hallway. "When is the inquest?" Grandfather asked.

The caretaker shook his head. "No inquest."

We stepped outside into a hazy drizzle. Mrs. Tooley stood on the corner closest to the churchyard, her outline illuminated by the dim light of a streetlamp. A pipe hung from her lips. The rain and smoke combined to blur her face.

"A suicide and no inquest?" my grandfather probed.

Horace's face registered disapproval. "Even the tanner's boy, him that was trampled by horses, got an inquest. But word is there's no need, suicide being clear and all."

"Who examined him?"

"The magistrate, Lord Marlington, looked in, and a police inspector with him, a Jonas Lloyddyn."

"No doctor?"

Horace grunted again with disapproval and shook his head.

"Mrs. Tooley knows?"

"Aye, she knows. Figured that's why she brung ya."

"I see. Thank you."

We left Horace standing on the stoop, his expression as fierce as a gargoyle protecting a cathedral. I glanced at Grandfather. What would he tell Mrs. Tooley?

She straightened as we neared and tapped her pipe against the iron lamppost. Red cinders fell from the bowl and sizzled on the damp pavement. "Well?"

Grandfather gestured towards the cab, and we climbed in, settling ourselves among the cushions. "You must insist on an inquest."

"He was killed?" she managed to ask through tight lips and barely controlled grief.

"I cannot be sure. But I believe there is reason to question the official conclusion."

She gasped for air and fell forward, grasping the padded side of the coach for support. Grandfather gripped her forearms and pushed her back against the seat.

"Stop." The severity of his tone startled me. "Hysteria may be a rational reaction to this terrible death, but it will not help. Not now."

Mrs. Tooley swallowed her sobs. She drew in a deep breath and nodded.

"Mr. Dengington mentioned a police inspector," he continued. "Did you speak with him?"

"Yes," she croaked and cleared her throat. "Said me boy jumped."

"Speak with him again. Insist on an inquest. If he refuses, tell him you will talk to the newspapers. Just that. Nothing specific, a vague threat."

"I will," Mrs. Tooley agreed.

"Come home with us. You must not be alone."

She shook her head, having gained control of her emotions. "No. I can go to me sister's boy. He's a good lad, and his wife'll look after me."

"Excellent," my grandfather replied, his voice now gentle. He reached into his bag and took out a small packet of medicine. "Dissolve this in boiling water and drink it right before bedtime." He gave her the brown paper packet. "Just tonight to help you sleep."

She clutched at his hand. Large tears rolled down her cheeks. "Will I dream? I couldn't stand to dream about me poor boy."

Grandfather returned the pressure of her clasped hands. "No dreams, just sleep."

Chapter Twelve

I awoke the next morning heavy eyed and with the sensation of a jagged knife sawing through my skull. Pounding headaches had plagued me since childhood. Some so bad they fractured my eyesight, leaving me to see the world through a bewildering prism of colorful glass. A combination of acupuncture and the herb *yan hu suo* helped with the pain, but some days, the headaches left me so wobbly on my feet I couldn't stand.

My mother hovered over me, a cup of steaming herbal tea cradled in her hands. "Drink this."

I sat up and groaned. My head swam, and I closed my eyes against the nausea.

The stark image of my dead friend arose in my mind; a flickering gas lamp threw shadows across his shrouded body. I swallowed and opened my eyes.

"Thanks, Ma." Taking the cup, I sipped the tea, comforted by my familiar surroundings.

We lived above our store. My cramped bedroom barely held the narrow slat bed on which I sat, a small desk pushed up against the dormer window, and a simple wooden washstand. At one end, the ceiling sagged with the weight of years.

A patchwork of old maps adorned my bedroom walls, and stacks of books lay scattered on every clean, available space. Though hardly the English ideal of middle-class respectability, I lived mostly secure and content in my humble surroundings.

Mother sat on the bed and plucked at a loose thread on the colorful quilt. "Your grandfather is disturbed by the course the authorities have taken in Teddy's death."

I frowned at her through a haze of herbal steam. "They haven't taken a course."

"Exactly."

I rested the cup on my lap. "That's why he told Mrs. Tooley to insist on an inquest?"

Mother nodded. "It is usual to have one in such cases."

She stared out the window. I studied her tense profile. "What is worrying you?"

"That the police will discover your grandfather was at the morgue. An unapproved examination, and by a Chinese doctor . . ." She looked down at her feet. "Well, they could make things unpleasant for us."

Mrs. Tooley's distress and Horace Dengington's disgust of the arrogant officials arose in my mind. "They won't learn of it from anyone present. I assure you."

She stood. "Unlikely, I agree, but secrets are hard to keep from the powerful."

I swung my legs over the side of the bed and set the half-empty cup on the floor. "Ma, the magistrate thinks Teddy is poor and insignificant. That's all. They don't want to be bothered with him. Why would someone powerful be interested in his death?"

"Good question." She nodded at the cup, and I handed it to her. "How do you feel?"

"Better."

"You have a lesson with Lord Brudeford today. Best get dressed and eat something."

She left, closing the door behind her. I stared at the brass knob. I had learned long ago not to dismiss my mother's concerns. But a scheme by someone powerful to hide the cause of Teddy's death seemed outlandish.

Could it have something to do with the unknown kidsman for whom he was working? Did this man influence the magistrate's decision to forego an inquest?

I wasn't fool enough to believe the authorities above a criminal alliance. But whoever this man was, if he existed, would have to be powerful indeed to have a magistrate in his pocket.

I reached for my clothes folded over the back of the desk chair. Dressing with haste, I descended to the kitchen for my breakfast and, less than a quarter of an hour later, left the store with a wave to my grandfather.

My head still tender, I walked with some care, wondering if I should take the Underground. But just the thought of the choking smoke from the trains made me nauseous. So, I adjusted Mr. Cohen's flatcap more firmly on my head and prepared for the long trek to Lord Brudeford's lodgings.

In an effort at good cheer, I whistled a jaunty tune and strode out, thrusting my hands into my pockets. My fingers touched a forgotten piece of paper, and I stopped midstride. Groaning, I pulled the envelope from my pocket.

Last night's traumatic events had so occupied my mind I'd forgotten I'd even written this note. A few quick lines telling Jack Hughes that Margaret was out and his flowery tribute left with the staff was all I'd managed. I didn't lie as a rule but deemed it necessary in order to spare his feelings.

Wanting to dispatch with this obligation as quickly as possible, I ducked into Needer's corner store and flashed a wide smile at Dora Needer behind the counter. Her thin lips thinned even further into a scowl of disgust. Dora hated me.

She hated all Chinese, but me being the product of a mixed union, I was an "abomination" and an especially deserving target for her vile insults. Old Mr. Needer, Dora's father, took seriously his responsibilities as proprietor of one of the many post office receiving houses around the city and forbade anything but polite treatment of his diverse clientele.

On the street, all bets were off, but in the store, Dora had to bite her tongue. I was a frequent patron.

I touched my cap with a bright "Good morning, Miss Needer. The store looks fine and natty. Your doing, no doubt." I slid my letter across the counter.

Her angry, squinty eyes never left my grinning face as she reached for the envelope with the stamp already affixed. She looked ready to bust a stay.

Loud, off-key humming preceded Mr. Needer from out of the back room. "Why, young Kuo, how is your grandfather and lovely mother this fine morning?"

Dora turned beet red at mention of my mother. I chuckled, feigning good-natured neighborliness.

"Both well, thank you, sir."

Mr. Needer sniffed, and his large belly heaved up and down. He moved with ponderous grace, his stomach parting all that came before him like the bow of a ship through the waves. Known for his mild, genial disposition, I wondered at the bitterness of his daughter.

"Some spirits break from oppression and others curdle," my mother had said when I mentioned the odd contrast between father and daughter.

"Oppression? How is Dora Needer oppressed?"

"A cage is still a cage, even one built of kindness. Mr. Needer may be pleasant of temperament, but he is also selfish. As a widower, he fears loneliness. He binds Dora to him, though she would like to marry and have a family of her own."

I raised my eyebrows. "Filial piety?"

Mother had smiled. "Not the same, perhaps, as with us Chinese, but Dora is dependent on her father. The community holds him in affection, making it even more difficult for her. Whatever she wants appears to others as peevishness or ingratitude."

Did I mention my mother was empathetic? Often the brunt of Dora's vicious words, Mother still felt for the woman. It boggled the mind.

Catching the expression of hatred on Dora's face as she watched her father putter around the store sent a chill down my spine. It would not surprise me if we were to find him one day with a kitchen knife through his heart and Dora long gone.

"Did you hear about that boy who was fished out of the Thames last night? The towhead?" Mr. Needer asked. "Spotted him a time or two visiting your shop. He a friend of yours?"

I faked a look of shock. "Teddy Tooley? We *were* friends, but I haven't seen him in a while," I hedged, remembering my mother's warning. "How'd he end up in the river?"

"Suicide." Mr. Needer's face shone with the glow of a natural gossip. He puffed up with the importance of passing on tragic news. "Heard it this morning. A beggar outside the church saw the boy brought in, and his grandmother, poor thing, was in a state."

I conjured up an image of the ragged old man who begged on the corner across from the churchyard. My stomach lurched with fear, but I recovered quickly, figuring that if he'd seen us, Mr. Needer would be asking *me* the questions.

"The beggar was sure they'd haul her away in a straight waistcoat," he continued with relish, "yelling at the magistrate as she was. But she up and run off, crying and wringing her hands, before they could stop her." Mr. Needer shook his head in sympathy.

"Why'd she yell at the magistrate?" I probed.

"Not the magistrate exactly, him just standing there and all. But some police inspector, a Welshman what told her it was a suicide."

"Lloyddyn?"

His eyes narrowed. "How'd you know?" The shrewdness rumored to lie beneath the jovial exterior flashed of a sudden in his sharp, suspicious gaze.

"Colonel Rockwell," I hastily lied. "He knows all the police inspectors. He's mentioned the Welshman before."

The colonel's reputation for being knowledgeable and well-connected prompted a quick nod from Mr. Needer. "Ah, the colonel, indeed," he replied and questioned me no further.

I bade him good day, tipped my hat in Dora's direction (who sneered in return), and beat a hasty retreat before my careless tongue could betray me further. Out on the street, a heavy draft of air mixed with black smoke greeted me.

The fragrance of the ever-present Thames, pungent with sewage, wafted past my nostrils. I sucked in a deep lungful of London broth and turned my steps towards Covent Garden.

Chapter Thirteen

Lord Brudeford lived above Ainsworth Publishing on Henrietta Street. The converted four-story Georgian townhouse stood out from its neighbors with a riotous display of rosemary, lavender, and ivy spilling out of the decorative wrought iron flower boxes at every window. Even the most preoccupied passerby paused to admire the profusion of greenery that expressed the naturalist tendencies of the publisher within.

I entered the building and slipped past the clerk, springing up four flights of stairs, starting at the elegant carpeted first floor and ending on the much less impressive top-floor landing. I stood for a moment in the dark, narrow hallway before Lord Brudeford's door to catch my breath.

Old, framed handbills advertising the publisher's books and articles adorned the peeling paint-covered walls. Cornelius Ainsworth published scientific books and pamphlets. Some of the most celebrated minds of the day wrote under his imprint, Lord Brudeford among them.

I knocked on the door.

"You needn't pound so. Come in. I'm not languishing in a drug-induced stupor," came his amused response.

My tutor sat at a cluttered table studying what looked to be an

Eastern text. Long, slender fingers skimmed the pages, graceful as reeds at the edge of a peaceful pond. Though not yet thirty-five, his hollowed cheeks and rail-thin figure gave the impression of frailty: an old, dried-out scarecrow a mild breeze might whisk away.

"Another translation?" I asked, knowing Mr. Ainsworth took advantage of Lord Brudeford's lucid moments with work.

He nodded and, with an expansive gesture, indicated the one-room garret that served as his base of operations. "Among the old man's many kindnesses."

Some might think this statement sarcastic, but I knew his words to be sincere. Cornelius Ainsworth founded the company in 1867 as a means to publish the works of his fellow naturalists. Since then, he and his sons expanded that mandate to include the study of languages, astronomy, and philosophy, among other scientific pursuits. When everyone else, even his own family, had given up on curing Lord Brudeford of his stubborn addiction, Mr. Ainsworth held out hope he could be saved from himself.

I contemplated the ravaged face with its proud, patrician nose and arrogant, hooded eyes and doubted the old publisher's staunch optimism. "Arabic?" I asked, pulling a chair up next to him.

"No, Afghani."

I stiffened, knowing that Lord Brudeford's troubles began as a young officer enduring the brutal carnage of the war in Afghanistan. He threw his head back with a laugh so hearty I feared he would break a rib.

"Don't worry, my friend, I won't fall into an opium stupor at the mere mention of Afghanistan," he reassured me. "Your grandfather may believe my malady a result of the ghosts of that merciless country, but my excesses are rooted in decadence and a poverty of spirit. A deep flaw in my soul drives me to destruction."

I narrowed my eyes, remembering Grandfather's words. "Until

Lord Brudeford acknowledges the wounds to his spirit, the violation that is war, he will never recover. Alas, the English see only weakness in confronting this truth."

I trusted my grandfather's judgment. Even more so, Lord Brudeford's attitude smacked of "he doth protest too much" bravado.

"What's the book?" I leaned over to study the elegant script more closely.

"A treatise on simple village life."

"Who wrote it?"

"I don't know. The entries are anonymous. I do believe Cornelius has been hoodwinked. There's no scientific value to the day-to-day traditions and routines of a small rural village." He shut the book with a dismissive snap and sat back in his chair.

"What's your pleasure, my lad? Philosophy? Physics? Ornithology? I am at your command."

"Poetry," I pronounced.

He sat up straighter. "Ah, what has prompted this?"

I pulled Charlotte's poem from my breast pocket. "This came to a girl of my acquaintance. She has no idea who sent it."

Lord Brudeford scanned the paper and frowned. "What girl?"

He misunderstood my hesitation for embarrassment and chuckled. "Normally, I would not be so tactless as to inquire after an affair of the heart, but the provenance of a poem is important to its interpretation."

I scowled at him, though his words were teasing. "Her name is Charlotte Gaines, and as I said, she received the poem anonymously."

"Indeed? Not 'My Lovely Little Lottie Love'?"

"The very one."

Lord Brudeford whistled through his teeth. "That family has known its fair share of tragedy."

A large, handsome, one-legged starling announced its presence with a piercing whistle and noisy, flapping wings. It landed in the flower box and pecked the dirt, disturbing the faded hydrangeas so that they bobbed up and down like buoys on the water.

"Ah, Felix, slim pickings today, eh?" Lord Brudeford called out.

The bird cocked its shiny speckled head to the side. One steady dark eye watched him approach. Felix answered him with a series of eerie vocalizations much like the laughter of children.

I shivered and asked, "What do you know of the Gaines family?"

Lord Brudeford set a plate of uneaten crusts on the windowsill. The bird pecked at them with discernment, as if mining the dried bread for the tastiest morsels.

"We knew them somewhat." He stared with unseeing eyes out onto the street. I recognized the melancholy that descended upon him with thoughts of his family.

Lord Brudeford kept the title of viscount, being the first-born male, but all the responsibilities and prestige of the position had fallen to his younger brother. By his own choice, he lived in exile, refusing to bring more shame to his respectable and upstanding family.

"Gaines had entrée into all levels of society," he explained in a dull monotone. "My mother was close to his wife, Mary, and we spent a long holiday in the Lakes District with her and Gaines one summer."

Felix trilled what sounded like piano scales. Lord Brudeford blinked, the spell broken. He smiled at the mischievous bird. "I admit I never liked the man."

"John Harold Gaines?"

"Are we speaking of another?" He frowned in my direction. "Yes, of course, John Harold Gaines."

"I imagined him generally admired is all," I explained. "And now, both you and Charlotte hold him in disgust."

He strolled back to the table and sat. "She can't have known him."

"No. She did not. I believe her late guardian was prejudiced against him, and her surviving relatives are somewhat . . . eccentric. Her uncle is in a monastery up north, and her aunt is a bitter spinster."

"Ah, yes, Sadie. We are of an age. I didn't know the others. They weren't with us that summer. Thomas and Cecil were older by a few years and off doing what young men do. Eliza and Archie were younger by as many and still in the schoolroom." He waved a languid hand. "Sadie and I got up to some good fun that summer, you know, rafts on the lake, hide-and-seek in the forest, that sort of thing."

"Why didn't you like him?"

"Gaines?"

"Are we speaking of another?" I shot back.

"Touché, my boy." Lord Brudeford grinned and traced a contemplative finger along the edge of the table. "Gaines gave his children nicknames. He charmed everyone with them, so clever and affectionate they were, but there was an undercurrent of . . ."

He hesitated, searching for the right words. "Meanness and intimidation. He used nicknames designed to bring attention to their shortcomings. Called Sadie bumblebee for her, um, round figure. Harmless enough, I suppose, but she didn't like it. I don't believe Gaines could tolerate anyone outshining him, even his children, and most certainly not his wife. My mother didn't like him either," he concluded as if this fact settled the matter.

Rubbing his hands together, Lord Brudeford cleared his throat. "Back to your poem, my boy. I've a notion the verse was written by a woman."

I picked up the scrap of paper and read aloud:

"The lowering sky benights the day,
and the cowardly man has his way.
The sister lost betrays the nave,
and the glowering woman defies the grave."

"Not a professional poet," he pronounced. "A bit curt and rudimentary. Don't you think?"

"Maybe it's part of a longer poem."

"Hmm, perhaps," he mused. "Though something about it strikes a chord of familiarity."

"Mr. Cohen mentioned the religious overtones, but I am not convinced that's the main theme."

"Ah, the bookseller. Good lad. He would know something about the paper." Lord Brudeford grinned. "So, this Charlotte has roped you into tracking down whoever wielded the poison pen. Eh? What did Mr. Cohen have to say?"

"I wasn't roped into any—" I pursed my lips, determined to ignore his teasing comments. "The paper can be bought at any stationary in England, but the lines are so expertly drawn as to appear printed on. The page was cut down and tipped with gold ink, perhaps to make a writing album."

"Um, not much to go on." He steepled his fingers and stared off into space. "We have a dark day, not a night, a day benighted by a lowering sky. Clouds?"

"A storm?" I offered.

He grunted. "As with a great deal of poetry, we should not seek a literal explanation. A life ruined, perhaps, blighted by a cowardly man?"

"Exactly," I agreed. "But the third line doesn't follow. A lost sister . . . a nun? Betrays the church?" I batted at a tickling sensation over my left ear and startled to find Felix perched on the back of my chair.

The bird glared at me with its beady, black eyes. I'd never known him to come into the room before.

Lord Brudeford chuckled. "The conversation must interest him."

"How does anyone 'defy the grave'?" I asked, trying to ignore the ominous specter looming over my shoulder.

"Depends on what the author meant by defy," was my tutor's unhelpful reply.

Even at his most sober, Lord Brudeford resisted order, and stacks of paper and pieces of clothing lay strewn about the room. I wove my way through the mess to a tall bookcase laden with a random assortment of titles and pulled from the topmost shelf a dictionary.

I flipped through the massive tome and found the entry for defy. "Challenge, elude, escape, foil," I read off.

"Challenge, hmm." He frowned, considering. "An angry woman defies the grave by challenging death?"

"Foil," I countered. "The glowering woman's actions are not in isolation but in contrast to the cowardly man who has gotten his way. In defying the grave, she foils him?"

"A good guess."

"But the sister lost? How does a nun come into it?"

"Assuming it is a nun."

I snapped the dictionary shut. Without more information, discovering the poem's true meaning was near impossible.

A sharp rap on the door frightened Felix. He stretched his neck, flapped his iridescent wings, and made straight for the window.

"I'm not bloody deaf," Lord Brudeford bellowed.

The door cracked open, and the bespectacled face of the clerk peered around it. "Mr. Ainsworth asked if you'd finished with the text."

Lord Brudeford shut his eyes. A pained expression crossed his face. "Enough to know it's worthless."

The clerk drew back in alarm. "I can't tell him that," he protested.

My friend pushed himself up from the table. "I'll do the deed."

The clerk left with a grateful nod, and Lord Brudeford pulled on his jacket. "Sorry, Kuo, duty and my benefactor calls."

"Of course." I slipped the poem into my pocket. My fingers

touched the gold locket, and I asked him if he could recommend a knowledgeable jeweler.

He paused in the process of opening the door. "That serious, huh? She must be lovely, indeed."

I scowled and bit my lip, irritated at his teasing but not wanting to reveal any more of Charlotte's secrets. I trusted Lord Brudeford, but his drug habit made him unreliable. I could not run the risk of divulging to him all the facts of the case.

"A childish reply, I must say," I countered with as much dignity as I could muster.

"Sorry, my boy, couldn't help myself." He grinned and clapped me on the back. "Don't know a jeweler, but I do know a pawnbroker, likely as knowledgeable or more so. Not far from here, over on Drury Lane. Bit seedy, but Old Abe is more honest than most."

Pawn shops were as common as pubs, though I'd never stepped foot in one. I often stopped to admire the window displays but knew the items within to be unredeemed, lost forever to their former owners. I imagined many a tale of woe attached to them and resisted the urge to purchase anything, no matter how cheaply priced— superstitiously fearful of the sadness fused to such objects.

I followed him down the stairs, and we stood in the elegant foyer, much different from the stark fourth-floor landing. Here, creamy paint lay thick and smooth over walls decorated with tasteful illustrations from some of their most famous works.

Lord Brudeford waved his goodbye and turned down a branching hallway to Cornelius Ainsworth's corner office. He hesitated in mid stride and looked back at me with a puzzled frown. "I say, where did you happen to meet Miss Gaines?"

Though I had hoped to avoid revealing any more information about Charlotte, I considered this a harmless detail and so told him of our meeting. At mention of 221B Baker Street and Sherlock

Holmes, all languid indifference dropped away from him like a heavy cloak landing with a muted thud at his feet.

"Holmes, that arrogant bastard," he hissed through clenched teeth. "You would do well to steer clear of him. He is a most dangerous man."

Chapter Fourteen

Lord Brudeford spun on his heels and strode away down the hall, leaving me to stare after him in utter bewilderment. Never before had he mentioned knowing the famous detective.

I had walked several paces down Henrietta Street, my mind occupied with his strange outburst, before remembering my mission and turning back around towards Drury Lane. According to the cartographer, Charles Booth, I made my way through streets coded red to light pink, indicating wealth. Pockets of dark blue and black popped up from time to time, like threadbare patches on an old, expensive brocade waistcoat.

"Hey, hey, wait for me," piped a shrill voice from behind.

Knowing I could not escape, I settled my face into a bland mask before turning around. A grubby urchin in ragged knee breeches and an overlarge jacket dodged around skirts and trousers to come panting up beside me. "Almost didn't peg ya in that hat."

"Thanks, Danny," I replied with some sarcasm. "Been nice if you'd told me earlier the old hat served more as a target than a shield."

A dimple quivered on one dirty cheek. "You're the all-knowing one."

We fell into step, and I tried not to smile. Ever since correctly identifying Danny as a girl, she insisted I wielded supernatural powers. Little did she know I had simply chanced to see her pull a ribbon from her short curls before covering them with a cap and dashing from the shelter of some bushes at the west entrance of St Paul's. So occupied was she with her hurried transformation, Danny had not seen me sitting on a bench in the quiet of the church garden.

As one of the factotums used to run the odd errand for the old publisher, Danny had crossed my path many times in the hallways and on the staircase at Ainsworth Publishing. One morning, just for fun, I tipped my hat to her in passing and dropped the greeting, "Good day, miss."

To which she responded by grabbing my arm in a vice-like grip, shoving her dirty face to within an inch of my own, and growling, "Who ya callin' miss."

That was the beginning of our "friendship" in that she tagged along with me wherever I went, whenever she chanced to see me. Her full name was Daniela Flora de Silva, and she lived not far from the Theatre Royal with her mother, the famous Spanish actress Madame Honoria de Silva. Although Danny had once let slip that her mother was "as Spanish as a Cockney chimney sweep."

"Where ya headed?" She squinted up at me from beneath the brim of her cap. I'd seen her once or twice out with her mother, dressed and beribboned. I had to admit the costume she donned for her street activities suited her better.

"Where did you find that getup?" I nodded at her ill-fitting jacket and breeches. "The rubbish bin at the theater?"

"Ha, ha," she responded with feigned laughter. "This here is a *real* costume. Mrs. Watts, the dresser, give it to me."

I raised an eyebrow in Danny's direction. Her laughter wasn't the only thing she faked. The coarse accent and bad grammar were definite put-ons. "Does your mother know what you're about?" I asked.

She shrugged, ignored my question, and repeated, "Where ya headed?"

I sighed. Not for the first time, I wished I had not given in to the smug urge to reveal my knowledge of her true gender. She would stick with me for as long as I operated on "her patch."

"Old Abe's pawn shop," I told her.

She pursed her lips with a troubled frown. "Got money problems?"

"No," I hedged. "I, um, need to find out the origins of a locket."

"A lady's locket?"

"Is there any other kind?"

"Surely," she scoffed. "Men don't wear them so much nowadays, though."

"Well, this is a lady's locket, and Lord Brudeford tells me Old Abe is as knowledgeable as any jeweler."

"Aye, he is."

I slowed my step and glanced down at her. "Do you know him?"

"When Lord Brudeford don't want nobody knowing he's broke, I take what he wants pawned." She snorted her derision. "Still too much of a stuffed shirt to enter a pawn shop is Lord Brudeford."

We crossed Drury Lane and dived into a deep pocket of poverty down Blackmore and onto Stanhope to Clare Street. Hunched and depressed, the buildings huddled back from the pavement, burdened by decades of dirt and coal dust. The people shuffling down these squalid streets looked no better.

Danny, ever alert to the lurking presence of pickpockets, kept up a steady pace. She made a sharp turn down a half-hidden byway running diagonally to the one we walked.

"Here we are," she pronounced, stopping in front of a narrow storefront squashed between its two neighbors, as if to hide from the casual passerby.

The store window, smoky and tinted with age, displayed a collection of objects that shocked me with their general splendor: a crystal bowl filled with delicate hand-blown glass orbs, fine china, antique miniature portraits set in ornate frames, ivory-handled knives, and the like. Who on these fetid streets could afford such luxuries?

As if reading my mind, Danny explained, "Lots of us theater folk trade here. Even me mum's picked up a bauble or two from Old Abe." She waved me to the side. "Come on."

We squeezed through a stinking alley that was little more than a gutter and entered a side door. "Why not go in the front?" I asked, taking in the jumble of objects crowded together on every inch of shelf space and even hanging from the ceiling. Dust lay thick over some items, and others looked as if they'd just been cleaned and polished that very morning.

Danny emitted a scornful huff. "Don't nobody use the front door. It's just for show."

We wove through the clutter, finally emerging into a tidy showroom. A pretty, dark-haired girl sat on a stool behind the counter. She glanced up at our entrance, and a welcoming smile spread across her face.

"Young Danny, have you brought us a new customer?" Her voice, a melodious alto, warmed the confined space.

Danny grinned back at her. "Not as such, Sybil. This here is Kuo, and he needs to have a jaw with your granddad."

"He's feeling poorly, but I'll ask if he'll see you." Sybil pushed off the stool and grasped the counter for support. I barely stopped myself from tilting my head to one side in order to align my sight with her lopsided stance. She steadied herself and walked with a pronounced limp through a door at the back of the store.

"Twisted foot," Danny whispered. "Pity, her being so good-looking. Almost be better if she was ugly."

I puzzled over this piece of strange reasoning, but before I could come to any sound understanding, Sybil reappeared. "Granddad will see you," she announced, waving us through the door.

Oppressive heat and the familiar smell of sandalwood enveloped us upon crossing the threshold. The incense burned in a small, decorative brazier set on a massive oak desk in the middle of the room. A workbench stood pushed up against the far wall, and an overstuffed sofa sat so close to the blazing fireplace as to practically singe the upholstery.

The huddled mass of blankets on the sofa moved and sat up, revealing a bald head and patchy beard. Swollen, watery blue eyes peered at us, and one gnarled hand pressed a crumpled handkerchief to cracked lips. The old man cleared his throat and dropped his hand from his face.

"What do you want?" His voice surprised me by being as rich and mellow as that of his granddaughter's.

I pulled the locket from my jacket and handed it to him. "My name is Kuo Cheng, and this locket was sent anonymously to a friend of mine. She wants to know where it came from."

The necklace, lit by the red and yellow glow of the flames, glittered in his palm. "Both the chain and locket are fifteen carat gold. I can tell you that right off. Bring me my magnifying glass," he instructed his granddaughter.

Sybil took from the desk a large, silver-handled magnifying glass and handed it to him. "A dragonfly." He harrumphed, his eyes made even more bulbous by the thick, round glass. "These insect designs do persist. Hard to tell when it was made, could have been any time from mid-century."

"Who made it?"

"Hmm, good question. But I have a hunch . . ." He opened the locket and nodded with a satisfied smile. "Here we have someone who could never pass up an opportunity to toot his own horn. And I can tell you it was made after 1860."

We leaned in close over the old man, wanting a good look at what had clued him into the maker. "Back up, back up," he growled. "You're in my light. Give me some room, and I'll show you."

"See here." He turned the glass on the narrow rim near the clasp.

"What is that?" Sybil asked. "A flower?"

"A tiny pine tree. Bosque, Julio Bosque, is the name of your jewelry maker. Before 1860, he used a little willow tree as a mark; afterwards, a pine tree as you see here."

"Bosque, the Spanish word for forest," Danny informed us and winked at me with barely contained amusement.

"Mm-hmm, one of the best designers in London, with insects his specialty. Just like flowers, every damn insect's gotta have a meaning," he groused. "The dragonfly has something to do with change or new beginnings or some such other nonsense."

"Where can I find Mr. Bosque?" I asked, eager to question the jeweler.

"In the churchyard. Julio's long dead."

I straightened and wiped away beads of sweat from my forehead with the sleeve of my jacket. I bit back a frustrated curse.

"But his son, Julio Jr., keeps a shop down where them jewelers all congregate, I believe . . ." The old man's voice trailed off, and his head drooped.

"Hatton Garden?" I prompted.

His head bobbed back up, and he nodded. "But don't ask the direction, cuz I dunno." With that, he fell asleep on the instant and sank beneath the weighty blankets like a drowning man going under the waves.

Sybil padded the mound with a fond smile. "No use troubling him more. If he says he don't know, he don't." She shooed us back out into the showroom.

Another customer waited for her, and we beat a hasty retreat out the side door and into the smelly gutter. We walked in silence until almost back to Drury Lane.

"I must leave you here," I informed Danny. "I've an errand to run for my grandfather. Many thanks for your help."

She tipped her hat. "Happy to be o' service, good sir." She mimicked my formal farewell, stuck out her tongue, and skipped off. Danny must've had somewhere to be. She was usually more difficult to get rid of.

I shook my head with a rueful smile and turned my steps towards Baker Street. I hoped Charlotte would make our meeting, for I had much to tell her.

Chapter Fifteen

Dr. Watson met me at the door with a mustache as full and shiny as a sable stole. I deduced he had slept well.

"Come in, my boy, come in," he greeted me with a hearty clap on the back. "Holmes is asleep. He was up late last evening talking in his usual vein, though still quite weak."

I greeted this good news with an approving nod and pulled from my jacket a small silk pouch containing packets of medicine. "Is he eating?" I asked, handing Dr. Watson the bag.

He frowned. "Only a very little improved, I'm afraid. He is a fussy eater at the best of times. And his memory remains quite faulty, for he can recall nothing of the past two weeks."

"Let me have a look. Still on the sofa is he?"

"Yes." Dr. Watson led the way into the sitting room, notable for being much neater than when I last visited. "We did try to move him to his bedroom, but he wouldn't settle. I believe he is soothed by the presence of his books and equipment."

I studied the man in peaceful slumber on the sofa and noted his deep, even breathing. "We all find comfort in familiar things. When one is quiet in the mind, one will heal faster, as my grandfather says."

I often used the phrase "as my grandfather says" when visiting patients. It helped to remind them that I served as his surrogate, no matter my youth.

"What did you talk about?" I asked.

"Not me, Mrs. Hudson. She checks on him in the evening hours, and I take the early morning. She gave him his medicine at the appointed time, and he drank a little beef broth. He asked her to read him a newspaper article on the theft of some documents from one of the clubs on Pall Mall. After which, he nodded off.

"Poor Mrs. Hudson, our adventures can be quite disruptive, but she is fond of the old boy and was overcome with emotion at this sign of improvement."

I sat on an ottoman next to the sofa and checked his pulse. "Fluttery," I commented.

"Yes, still a bit puny. I've kept a log, as Mr. Cheng requested."

"He is paler than my grandfather would like at this stage. Wake him every three hours during the day to eat, even if it is a little. Encourage him to sit up. Tell Mrs. Hudson she must only read to him if he eats. Maybe some bribery will do the trick."

He chuckled. "That would be a first. Holmes is not known for his compliance."

I studied the hawkish nose and thin-lipped profile, obstinate even at rest. "I was hoping he'd be awake," I admitted. "I could use his advice."

"What?" Dr. Watson's mustache quivered with curiosity.

"A friend of mine received an anonymous poem, and I'm investigating for her. All we have is the verse and the envelope it came in." Now that I had a lead on the locket, I kept that clue to myself.

He perked up at my mention of a mystery. "I say, I'd jolly well like to help if I can. Holmes is quite the eccentric, but I miss dashing about with him on the trail of some nefarious criminal." He rubbed his hands together. "Do you have the thing with you?"

I pulled from my breast pocket the envelope and handed it to Dr. Watson. He drew out the poem and unfolded it, placing the piece of paper on the parlour table next to the envelope.

"Ominous sounding," he mused after reading the poem aloud. "A lady received this?"

"A girl."

"Hmm, well, there's nothing unusual about the paper. Holmes is a master at recognizing watermarks, but even I can see the trace of a scripted *L* and a lion's paw imprint here." He pointed to the upper right-hand corner. "Lyons is good quality stock, but in general use and not hard to come by."

"Yes. I've been told the paper is sold in most stationary stores in England."

"Indeed." He pursed his lips and ran a finger along the paper's edge. "It is common practice to cut paper down to fit a small journal or album, but the gold ink is interesting. And the poem itself, odd, very odd . . ." He straightened in frustration. "Ah, but Holmes would have a theory. And he would be right, too, you know."

He patted my shoulder. "You have your work cut out for you, my boy. However, I do have one thought that might prove useful. Holmes consulted on a case involving a commune of lady poets some years back. They put out a quarterly publication called *The Prophetess* full of verse on the vile nature of men, such as the one you have here." He stroked his mustache. "I've no idea whether the periodical continues in circulation, or honestly, whether the ladies carry on as before. But perhaps, if you can get your hands on an issue or two, it might prove enlightening."

With that, Dr. Watson dismissed the matter and busied himself folding the poem and putting it back into the envelope. I, on the other hand, longed to hear more of the "Case of the Commune of Lady Poets" and said so.

"Oh, no, no." Dr. Watson drew back, and his mustache flattened against his upper lip in alarm. "I wouldn't dream of it. Holmes would be most displeased." He glanced over at the sofa and lowered his voice. "Not one of his shining moments. An old, converted inn filled to the rafters with spinsters in rational dress growing their own food and keeping livestock, as eccentric as he and often a step or two ahead of him, I might add. No, no, that case will likely never see the light of day. A pity, though, quite the adventure."

He pulled a watch from his waistcoat pocket. "I must go. But first, I'll get the log for your grandfather's inspection." He left, and I wandered back to the sofa.

A warm, heavy breeze drifted in through the window, lifting the curtains away from the sill to reveal a large, one-legged starling glaring silently into the room. I frowned.

"Felix?"

Sherlock Holmes mumbled and turned onto his side. The air compressed around me, and sweat trailed down my face. I ran a finger along the inside of my collar and glanced up at the overstuffed shelves. The book titles blurred, and I rubbed my eyes, trying to bring them into focus. I swayed, and my knees buckled.

Two strong hands caught me in mid-swoon and held me upright. "Steady, steady."

My vision cleared, and I met the intense gaze of Sherlock Holmes. "Mr. Holmes," I blurted, regaining my balance. "You are recovered?"

He shook his head as if my question made no sense. His hands dropped away from my shoulders. "Transformation is key, life to death to life. The pretender walks among us. Trust at great peril," he intoned.

"What?"

"Here it is." Dr. Watson bustled in, waving the paper over his head. "I say, are you alright? You're pale as a ghost."

I struggled to regain my composure, but the sight of Sherlock Holmes resting peacefully as if he'd never moved, much less stood, threatened to overcome me. Fortunately, Felix (for it could be none other) trilled from the windowsill.

Dr. Watson turned to the bird. "Get along with you," he demanded, shooing him off with the paper. "Bold as brass, that one." He walked back to me. "I'm off, but Mrs. Hudson will gladly serve you a fortifying cup of tea in my absence."

"No, sir, I am fine." That brief reprieve had given me time enough to gather my wits. "But I will have a word with her before I leave."

"Of course, she's likely ensconced in her own parlour this time of day."

I followed him out into the hallway and down the staircase. He pointed me in her direction and left out the front entrance. I waited until the lock clicked into place and turned my steps towards the back door landing.

Charlotte sat on the same overturned barrel as on our first meeting. She jumped off at my appearance with the energy of someone who could draw a complete breath.

"I've been waiting ages," she complained.

She wore a pale-green silk dress with lace at the neck and wrists. Some sort of gemstones intertwined with silver embroidery weaved its way along the bodice, and a brown ribbon cinched the waist. I bristled at her cross greeting, but was distracted from returning a sharp retort by how much nicer she looked in this elegant outfit than in her "bird of paradise" plumage.

"Dr. Watson had an appointment, and I was obliged to wait until he left," I replied with stiff dignity, still rattled from my encounter with Sherlock Holmes. "I had to make an excuse to see Mrs. Hudson just so he wouldn't expect me to leave with him out the front door."

"Oh, don't poker up so. I had the dickens of a time getting here."

She brushed some stray dirt from her skirt and planted her tiny fists, encased in delicate lace gloves, on her hips. "Aunt Sadie took it into her head, today of all days, to ask me where I was going. All sorts of lies I had to come up with—by the way, remind me to pick up some sprigs of lavender and rosemary and a tin of peppermint candies. And"—Charlotte pulled the pocket map from her velvet handbag with a dramatic flourish—"I followed an indirect route."

She had folded the map back to reveal her path—a faint, penciled zigzag from her house to Baker Street. "I took a cab to Portland Place and walked the rest. I stopped at a number of window displays and glanced behind me once or twice as if I'd recognized an acquaintance. I'm certain no one followed me."

I had recovered my composure enough to wonder at the odd picture her playacting must have presented as she walked down the street. I only hoped she was right and no one had followed her.

"Good work," I replied with a stiff, jerky nod.

Charlotte narrowed her eyes. "What's wrong?"

Much to my irritation, I blinked in surprise. "What do you mean?"

"You know exactly what I mean. Something has happened. Normally, you would contradict me on some obscure matter or point out what I did wrong and how I should improve."

"I say, you act as if I'm some sort of raggedy old curmudgeon."

"Noooo," she countered. "I think you are, um, precise, but that is beside the point. I want to know what has happened."

I plopped down on the top step, and Charlotte sat beside me. "I think I have met one of my ancestors," was my blunt reply.

Her eyes grew large, and the flutter of her dark, thick lashes momentarily distracted me. "Ancestors? What do you mean?"

I cleared my throat and gave her a brief summary on the veneration of Chinese ancestors and our literary tradition of detectives and the ghosts that assist them. To my surprise, she listened without interruption or exclamations of disbelief.

I finished with a description of my recent otherworldly experience. "One moment I was looking down at a sleeping man, the next, Mr. Holmes had grabbed me by the shoulders and warned me of a pretender and to trust no one. Once Dr. Watson returned, he lay still, as if he had not moved a muscle."

"Dr. Watson witnessed none of this?"

"No. He did not," I confirmed and stared out at the grubby alleyway.

Charlotte brightened. "Maybe Mr. Holmes overheard your conversation with Dr. Watson, and like a sleepwalker, just spouted some nonsense."

I took a deep breath and peered directly into her very blue eyes. "In Cantonese?"

Chapter Sixteen

Charlotte drew back in surprise. "He spoke Chinese? Mr. Holmes?"

I nodded.

"Well, that does put the incident in a different light."

"Indeed."

She stood and walked down the remaining steps, her brow furrowed. "But ghosts, ancestors . . . they're just stories, right? Not history."

"Stories and legends often have an element of truth. We have a rich spiritual tradition," I said, intending it as a general explanation. But the words stirred something in my chest, like a long-germinating seed sending out a taproot. "I cannot ignore what happened."

Charlotte nodded. "Yes. People believe all sorts of things. Aunt Sadie invited a spiritualist to one of her women's meetings. Some of my grandfather's old-lady friends and their daughters came. I wasn't allowed to be there, but Nellie told me what happened." Her voice dipped to a hushed whisper. "The woman went into a trance and made all sorts of dire prophecies."

"What did she say?"

"Nellie was too frightened to remember," she replied with disapproval. "She said the woman garbled in a deep, rough voice, like a man's, and wove about the room with wide, sightless eyes. Nellie was worried her presence at the keyhole would be 'sensed' and beat a hasty retreat."

Charlotte planted her little fists on her hips again and lifted her chin. Something she did, I was finding, when she made a pronouncement. "I don't believe such nonsense. I think it was a complete sham."

I stood and joined her at the bottom of the steps. "I can't say about your aunt's spiritualist, but what I experienced definitely bordered on the supernatural."

For the first time in my life, I could not understand events. I knew what happened, even as I also knew that it could not have happened—at least not in a world bound by physical laws. I longed for action and told Charlotte about the pawnbroker and his discovery of the locket's origins.

"Hatton Garden," she expostulated. "Why that's not far from my house. I wish I had known. We could have met there. It's as if I've come all this way for nothing."

"How was I to know—" I began, offended at her petulant remark, but stopped myself from responding in kind. Charlotte obviously considered me the hired help, and so I continued in a stiff, detached tone, "I do apologize for inconveniencing you. We can proceed in whatever manner you like. I am at your service, of course."

She stared down at her feet, and her lips trembled. Remembering her friendless state, empathy—for which I entirely blame my mother—arose in my throat.

"By Jove, that was ill-tempered of me," I replied. "I believe I am still somewhat shaken by what happened with Mr. Holmes."

She flashed a relieved smile. "Yes, well, upon further consideration, my journey here was really quite useful in allowing me to practice my skills of evasion."

"Of course," I agreed. "It is still up to you on how to proceed."

She hailed a cab, as I knew she would, and we jostled through the crowded streets of London. In the past, I'd had few opportunities to view this city from a private carriage, and now was doing so for the third time in as many days. Other than the comfort of not being shoved and squeezed, the vantage point was little different from that of an omnibus or Mr. Wei's horse cart.

The two-seated cab with the driver mounted behind gave us a level of privacy that brought with it, for my part, some unease. I sat as far to one side as possible and tried not to bump into Charlotte. She, on the other hand, appeared unconcerned and fell against me with every jolt and turn of the road.

When we arrived at Hatton Garden, I jumped down from the cab and turned to help Charlotte alight. Since we had no idea where to find Julio Bosque Jr., I suggested we ask his whereabouts in one of the other gem stores.

"Don't you think it rude to enter a shop only to inquire after another jeweler?" Charlotte asked.

"No, I don't," I assured her. "In fact, I think it a sensible course of action."

After several tries with no luck, and a few harsh words and gruff dismissals (Charlotte gracefully declined to crow about it), we found ourselves at the corner of Charles Street. I paused to get my bearings. A public house, The Grizzled Beard, stood about a quarter of the way down the block.

Charlotte spotted it too. "A pub can have any silly old name," she scoffed.

"Yes," I agreed. "But there is no better place to ask about the neighborhood."

She drew back in horror at the suggestion. "I cannot go in there. Ladies do not enter public houses."

I sighed. To which she took further offense.

"Don't you dare roll your eyes at me."

106

"I wasn't going to," I protested, a little shocked she had noticed my previous transgressions.

"You were. When you sigh like that, you always roll your eyes."

"No—"

She waved away my objection. "I know it's a stupid rule. As much as I may like to question the patrons of a public house, I can't go around breaking conventions willy-nilly."

"You break conventions willy-nilly daily," I declared. "Just being here with me is a breach of convention. But if public houses are where you draw the line, I will go in by myself. You can wait here."

"Wait here? You mean on the street? Alone?"

With great effort, I suppressed a sigh and endeavored not to roll my eyes. "There are establishments in which a lady can enter without damage to her reputation, not the least of these being any number of jewelers on this street and the next. You can pretend to shop and meet me outside the pub in twenty minutes," I concluded.

"Yes, but then . . ." Her voice trailed off as her sense of propriety warred with the desire to be in on the hunt, so to speak.

"Kuo. I say, Kuo, is that you, old boy?"

I recognized immediately the friendly deep baritone of Jack Hughes, but was surprised to see him decked out in a natty morning suit of a grey plaid design. A shiny bowler sat atop burnished dark curls, and he carried an ebony walking stick with a folded newspaper tucked up under one arm. He could not have appeared more different from the country "bumpkin" I first met in the hotel stable yard. It was as if some fairy godmother had transformed him into the ideal of a fashionable city gentleman.

Jack laughed. "You're shocked." He spread his arms wide to reveal the perfect fit across his broad chest and shoulders.

"Only to see that you are still in town," I replied with a polite nod and turned to introduce him to Charlotte. "Mr. Jack Hughes, Miss Charlotte Gaines."

He doffed his hat. "Miss Gaines, a pleasure."

I didn't need to look at her to feel the warm glow of the blush that arose upon her cheeks at the sudden appearance of so splendid a specimen of English manhood. Her little hand trembled as he enclosed it in one of his own very large ones.

"The pleasure is mine, Mr. Hughes," she replied in a steady tone.

I chanced to glance at her. Though her color was indeed much heightened, she appeared in complete control of her emotions.

Jack flashed an indulgent grin in my direction. "I was all set to leave town when who should arrive without a 'by your leave' but my sister, Lucy, to set me to rights, as you see. Seems with big brother out of the way, Edward Martin, the son from a neighboring estate, got up the nerve to propose, and so she came to surprise me with the news. Cheeky fellow didn't bother to ask permission. But she's determined to have him, and I'm not one to stand in the way of Lucy's happiness."

"Congratulations on such joyful news," Charlotte replied.

"Yes, um, joyful news," I chimed in, unaccountably irritated at his jovial chatter.

"Thank you. I've just dropped off my grandfather's old watch to have it cleaned and inscribed for Edward."

Jack looked from Charlotte to me as if just taking stock of our situation. He frowned. "What brings you to this part of town?"

Chapter Seventeen

Bristling at his clear disapproval, I replied with stiff dignity, "We are in search of a jeweler."

"Well, you've come to the right place . . ." he began, brightly, then almost immediately narrowed his eyes with suspicion. "What do two young people, such as yourselves, need with a jeweler?"

Jack mistook our furtive glances as masking some romantic intent. "Now look, I'm not one to butt into others' affairs, but do your families know—"

"Heavens," Charlotte interrupted with a trill of laughter meant to convey the absolute absurdity of Jack's insinuation. "There is nothing of courtship between us. Kuo is investigating for me. We are attempting to track down the origins of a family locket."

"That's a relief." He smiled and shook his head. "It wouldn't do, you know. It wouldn't do."

I sneered inwardly at the immediate understanding between them. I was well aware of my race and inferior social status, but their casual talk in my presence of a misalliance left a bitter taste in my mouth.

"Perhaps you would be so kind," I asked Jack through a tight smile, finding some advantage to his unexpected appearance, "to accompany Miss Gaines while I inquire about our jeweler in the pub? A half an hour of your time, no more."

"Why the pub?" he asked.

Charlotte's tight smile matched my own, and I relaxed somewhat. She was just as aggravated by this interruption as I.

"We've already asked in many of the stores for the jeweler who made the locket, but with no luck," she replied. "Perhaps a public house would be more fruitful."

"I say, good idea. Pubs are full of neighbors gossiping." He tapped his chest. "Let me do it. A man of my age and station is more likely to get good information."

In my experience, the exact opposite was true. But I could not convince him otherwise and so told him the name of the man we were looking for. "Julio Bosque, Jr."

"A Spaniard? Unusual. Most of the jewelers here are Jews."

I didn't tell him there were Spanish Jews but only returned his cheerful wave as he crossed the street and disappeared into the Grizzled Beard. Charlotte and I meandered down the street, stopping to admire a display of hats in a milliner's store window.

"My, he does prattle so," she commented, with a lingering hint of irritation. "I'll say this in his favor, he is quite good-natured."

Her comment was gentler than those of Margaret Scott and her companions, but the indifference, even disdain, in which they held Jack Hughes puzzled me. "He is a handsome man of wealth and kind disposition. What more do women want?"

A shop girl with her nose in a book walked past, and a tinker with a pushcart of wares bumped and clattered along the uneven street. But for them, we were alone.

Charlotte's lips curved into a secret, superior smile. "Men do not understand the modern woman."

I admitted to my limited knowledge of women but pointed out that popular stories were full of heroes who looked and acted just like Jack Hughes. "You cannot deny that men like him are held up as an ideal."

She shrugged and continued to stroll down the street. "There are plenty of stories with complicated and tortured heroes as well."

"Who die tragically or are reformed by the book's end," I argued. "The heroine either lives happily ever after with her true love or finds solace in the arms of some suitable, usually wealthy, man who has been by her side the whole time."

"Well, if so, I don't waste my time reading them. Aunt Sadie calls such stories drivel."

My color heightened at the insult, but I countered forcefully, "I read everything. They may be drivel, but these stories reflect a common attitude and are best not scoffed at if one is to understand the larger society."

Charlotte glanced back at me, her mouth opened in retort. She snapped it shut and stared at a spot on the brick wall above my head. A tarnished brass placard gave the name of the narrow alleyway cutting through the middle of Charles Street as that of Bleeding Hart Yard. I knew immediately what had drawn her interest.

"Is . . . is this the place?" Her expression of sadness surprised me, aware as I was that she referred to a fictional character, one of her grandfather's most famous, Letty Drumham.

I nodded. "Yes, Letty died here."

Bleeding Hart Yard had a history of tragedy, likely the reason John Harold Gaines chose it for the demise of poor Letty. As the heroine of one of Gaines's later works, *A Candle on the Sill*, she endured the indignities of poverty with grit and optimism, only to die at the hands of her lover's sister just when things were looking up for the star-crossed pair.

Charlotte walked into the cobbled courtyard. Once, long ago, the location of a prosperous inn, the yard now housed mostly poor families squeezed into cramped, squalid lodgings in the partitioned buildings.

Signs of their shaky existence lay everywhere. Broken furniture piled in a corner only waited for pieces of wood and wire to construct a makeshift repair. Laundry hung from lines strung across the yard on rusty nails, and pails of dirty water waited for the next round of the backbreaking work. Two little girls in stained smocks and worn shoes took turns with a tattered jump rope, while some boys kicked a wadded piece of cloth around like a ball.

"My grandfather modeled Letty after my grandmother's youngest sister, Emma. She came to live with them as a child and was only eighteen when she died of some infectious illness. My grandfather held her and read to her as she slipped away. Her death affected him deeply." For the first time, I heard approval of her grandfather in Charlotte's voice.

I followed her over to the dingy, red-bricked building that had been, in better times, a busy inn. "A murder was committed here over two hundred years ago," I told her. "Though no ordinary murder." Charlotte turned to me, eyes wide and questioning. "Lady Elizabeth Hatton, the wife of Sir Christopher Hatton, who owned all the land around here, was ripped to pieces. Her heart lay on the cobblestones, still pumping blood."

"How dreadful," Charlotte whispered and shivered.

"Legend has it the lady made a pact with the Devil for wealth and position, and when she had gained it, he tore her heart from her chest and left it bleeding here in the yard."

"Oh pooh," my friend expostulated. "I don't believe it, a pact with the Devil. What nonsense. Poor woman was brutally killed, and they turn it into a story to entertain the ghoulish."

I smiled, having successfully diverted her mind from the Gaines family's sad history. "Well, in this case, 'they' would be Thomas Ingoldsby of *Ingoldsby Legends* fame. Very likely, the murder never happened. I am not surprised you are unfamiliar with it, being a story you might consider 'drivel'."

She lifted her little pointed chin and narrowed her eyes at me. "I will not rise to the bait, Kuo Cheng. Besides, we should be getting back. Mr. Hughes is likely searching for us."

As it turned out, Jack emerged from the Grizzled Beard just as we stepped onto Charles Street. "What luck, my friends. I have found your jeweler," he pronounced. "It wasn't easy. A more closed-mouthed lot I've never met; but once they realized I wasn't dunning the man, they gave up his direction right enough. Seems the business fell on hard times, and he has relocated to a less elevated location on Saffron Hill near Clerkenwell Road." He rattled off the address.

I knew the area to be a concentration of Italian immigrants and was not surprised by Jack's next comment. "I'll come with you. The patrons of the Grizzled Beard told me the neighborhood is quite rough. Not a place a young girl of delicate upbringing should venture without an escort."

I *was* surprised by Charlotte's response. "Thank you, Mr. Hughes, but I am ably accompanied by Kuo, and we would not dream of delaying you further."

He drew back with an awkward nod. "Right you are. Nobody better than Kuo to get you where you want to go." He padded his breast pocket. "I even bought one of your fold-up maps, my boy, and it has greatly enhanced my knowledge of London."

Jack gripped his cane tighter and doffed his hat. "I'll be on my way then." He cleared his throat. "Thank you, Kuo, for the, ah, service of the other day. Not sure I'll be able to pursue the matter before we leave at the end of the week."

Not wanting to encourage him but feeling that Miss Scott was unlikely to be as uncivil to the actual man as she was to his messenger, I replied, "At your convenience, I'm sure."

Lifting his cane in a quick salute, he turned and strode off in the direction of Hatton Garden.

Chapter Eighteen

We turned our steps towards Saffron Hill. Only seconds passed before Charlotte asked what I knew she would. "What service did you render Mr. Hughes?"

"I'm not at liberty to disclose the business of another client."

"Really?" she scoffed. "He also hired you to assist in an investigation?"

"No," I hedged. "But I have learned through apprenticeship with my grandfather not to speak of another's affairs. Indiscretion is bad for trade."

"I certainly wouldn't want you telling anyone else of my business," she conceded.

"Exactly."

The Saffron Hill-Clerkenwell area differed from other slums in London only by the Italian words and spices that floated in the air. In every other way, from the desperate activity to stave off hunger to the staunch camaraderie of poverty, it was like any other, including my own neighborhood of Limehouse.

The narrow, cobbled street ran north, parallel to Hatton Garden. Its derelict buildings housed patched and ragged people who spilled out onto the street. Women sat on stoops, babies in their laps, and watched their older children play alongside on the pavement. Carts laden with goods rolled by, squeezing past each other as they navigated the teeming street.

We made our way through the crowd. Charlotte's elegant outfit drew curious looks, but no one bothered us. Except an organ grinder's monkey who followed on our heels, chittering and begging for a handout. My companion drew a coin from her bag and tossed it to the vexing creature, which, amazingly, caught it in its teeth.

"Here we are," I announced as we neared the intersection with Clerkenwell.

A darkened, covered entryway cut between two buildings and stared unblinkingly back at us. Charlotte wrinkled her nose at the fetid smell seeping out from its depths.

"Are you sure?" she asked with a skeptical look, her eyes darting around. "This is the address?"

"There's the number." I pointed to a scarred plaque above the arched entryway. "I can go alone—"

"No. No." Charlotte pressed both hands to her chest and drew in a deep breath, as if preparing to dive beneath the ocean waves. "I am ready."

Most days, the sun had to fight its way through the London haze and usually lost the battle. Still, the dingy, smoke-tinged light of the sun was better than the cloaked darkness of the entryway. We inched our way down the path, each of us trying to breathe as little as possible of the dead air.

Faint, wavering light shone through a dirty window and marked our destination. On the door, a rectangular sign of colorful cut glass shimmered like a jewel in a coalmine. The sparkling words spelled out Bosque and Son. I rapped on the ancient wooden door.

Nothing stirred from within. I rapped again, and a third time. After what seemed an age, we heard the sound of shuffling feet.

The door creaked open a bare inch, and a large, distorted eye glared out at us. We startled and shrank back.

"Yes? What do you want?" an impatient voice asked.

"Um," I stammered. "Ah, we are looking for a jeweler by the name of Julio Bosque, Jr. Are you him?"

The door opened wider to reveal another such eye. I realized the man was wearing magnifying spectacles.

"Who's asking?" he growled.

"Miss Charlotte Gains and Mr. Kuo Cheng. We have a locket made by your father and want to know its origins."

"Oh." His voice expressed curiosity, and he stepped back to usher us inside. "Do come in."

We walked through into a foyer lit by a low gas lamp. Dark wood paneling ran the length of the hallway, and I could just see a courtyard beyond.

Julio Jr. removed the spectacles and rubbed his eyes. "Sorry to give you a fright. I need these for my work and often forget I have them on. Good thing I was passing through the courtyard. I wouldn't have heard your knock from my workshop otherwise."

He stood in startling contrast to the cramped foyer, like a bull in a pen. His head almost touched the ceiling, but stooped, broad shoulders shaved a couple of inches off his height.

"What's this you say about a locket? Made by my father, is it?" As he spoke, we followed him down the hallway and out into the courtyard where raised beds of vegetables and pots of flowers somehow flourished in the dingy atmosphere.

"Yes," Charlotte answered. "There is a little tree engraved near the clasp we were told was his signature."

A chuckle rumbled in his chest. "My father was not a humble man. And why should he have been?" He lifted his palms up in question. "He was an inspired artist."

We dove down another dark hallway, twisting and turning until entering a room so remarkable, Charlotte and I were struck speechless by its splendor. Julio Jr. gestured wide with his arms.

"My domain."

His "domain" reached up to the second floor of the building and was twice as large as the courtyard. Blazing chandeliers hung from the ceiling, illuminating every nook and cranny of the workshop.

Five large tables stood positioned in separate areas of the room. Four were covered in different types of metal in all shapes and sizes, from rings and chains to sheets and nuggets. One table held only gold, the other silver, another brass, and another copper. Upon the fifth table sat an intricate cabinet, something like the one my grandfather used for his medicines; but this one was made entirely of thick glass.

Through its tiny windows, gems and stones of all colors glittered in the intense light from above. A sprinkling of loose rubies lay scattered across the tabletop like drops of blood on aged parchment.

Thick logs stacked in one corner were stripped bare of bark and painted bright primary colors. A long sheet of corrugated copper leaned against the far wall set with glowing crystals.

"Oh," Charlotte breathed. "It's like an enchanted waterfall."

Julio Jr. nodded with an approving smile. "Just so. It goes on exhibition in Paris next month, but connected to a fountain, allowing water to move over it in a continuous flow."

He waved us across the expanse of floor and through another doorway. "I keep our records in here, even my father's, going back to when he established the business in '41."

We stood, once again, in a tiny space with a low ceiling. Cabinets ran along the walls, and a long table stood at the center of the room.

Julio Jr. turned up a lamp on the table. "Let me see it."

I took the necklace from my pocket and dropped it into the palm of his large, calloused hand. He slipped the spectacles back on his face and leaned in closer to the light.

"Hmm, yes, my father's work, to be sure. A nice piece, but not his best. I'd say this went to a person of good means but not of great wealth or nobility."

117

"The pawnbroker said it was made after 1860."

"Yes. My father changed his signature around then. This little tree is an evergreen. In earlier years, he used a willow." Julio Jr. stroked his chin and ran his eyes over the rows of cabinets. "I've done a terrible job keeping them in order. It'll take me a minute or two to find the paperwork," he said, peering closely at the labeled drawers.

I contemplated his bent back. Why had a talented and obviously prosperous craftsman chosen to ply his trade in such squalid surroundings, isolated from his fellow jewelers?

Just as I decided that asking the question would be impolite, Charlotte piped up, "Why do you practice your trade in this place?"

He turned to look at us, his eyes contemptuous. "Those ostentatious fools in Hatton Garden never accepted my father. Most of them were jealous, him getting the richest customers. After his death, I invested my inheritance and built this place. I take commissions and make far more than the petty impostors who churn out the dull, unimaginative trinkets for sale in their little shops." He sneered and turned back to rifle through the cabinets. "Besides, no thief would dream to look here for anything of value."

"Mum's the word," Charlotte chirped in an ill-conceived effort to lighten the mood.

His back stiffened, and I cast her an angry, sidelong glance. She blinked rapidly in response. I held my breath, not sure what to expect, but he merely shook his head and laughed.

"I'm not worried about you talking. Anyone with half a wit would know I'm here. You could tell all of them up and down Hatton Garden, though, and they wouldn't believe it. People see what they want to see, and they want to see me fail.

"Ah." Julio Jr. straightened, waving two small pieces of paper clipped together. "This could be it: 'dragonfly, onyx eye, fifteen carat gold.'" He turned the locket over in his hand and frowned. "No, this isn't the one. There are no initials."

"What?" I drew close and squinted at the paper in his hand.

"M and J," he explained. "There should be the initials M and J, entwined and in script on the back, and a little willow for signature. The one we have here was made later."

"May I?" I reached for the receipts and flipped through them. "Your father made two of the same type it appears, one in 1851, and the other . . ." I turned to the backside of the second receipt. "There's no date, but it would appear the only difference in design between the two was the lack of initials."

Julio nodded. "This would be it then?" He held out his hand with the gold locket resting in his palm. "A later one, with no initials."

"Does it say who ordered them?" Charlotte asked.

"My father would have known, but he kept information like that in his head. He was the soul of discretion." Julio winked. "Always said jewelry was the language of love, and well, sometimes we love where we shouldn't."

A clock sounded with a mournful bellow somewhere in the depths of his lodgings. "I've to get on with my work." He handed the locket to Charlotte and gestured towards the door.

As we preceded him across the workshop, Charlotte leaned close, saying in a fierce whisper, "M and J, Mary and John, my grandparents, and I can guess who this one was for."

I glanced back at Julio Jr. trailing behind us. "Wait until we are away from here to speak."

At the door, we thanked the jeweler and beat a hasty retreat through the oppressive entryway. Back out on the crowded street, we gulped down the noxious, yellow air of London as if we stood on the pristine slopes of the Alps.

Charlotte shook her little fist in which she clutched the locket. "One for my grandmother, and this one, years later for his mistress,

Nora Davies, no doubt. Vile man," she hissed and thrust the locket into my hand as if it burned through the lace of her glove.

"We don't know—"

"Who else?" she demanded and turned, striding off down the street.

I fell into step beside her. "Two different customers could have ordered the same locket for entirely unrelated people."

"And send me the one that is expressly *not* my grandmother's?" She pursed her lips with an impatient shake of her head.

I could not argue with her logic. I also had little doubt that John Harold Gaines had purchased both pieces of jewelry. The locket we held meant something to the Gaines family.

"You're right. Gaines must have ordered the lockets, but we cannot be sure for whom he intended this one. He could very well have given it to one of his daughters."

Charlotte stopped in her tracks and grabbed my arm, causing a near collision with the man walking behind. He brushed past us with a snarled curse.

"Aunt Sadie fell into a fit when she saw the locket." Charlotte planted her fists on her hips and declared, "She must know, and I intend to make her tell me."

Chapter Nineteen

We hailed a cab on Hatton Garden and traveled in silence. Charlotte sat consumed, no doubt, with strategies on how to confront her aunt, while I struggled to suppress a resurgence of last night's headache.

I shut my eyes and deepened my breathing. A prism of light pulsated in the darkness. In my early childhood, the prism was an uncontrollable monster that consumed my sight and foretold debilitating pain. Years of practice centering my mind helped reduce the monster (most times) to a mere squalling baby.

"Are you alright?" Charlotte's concerned voice drew me back to the present.

I opened my eyes. Her hand rested on my own, and I was surprised to find she had removed her glove. Noticing where I looked, she sat back and pulled her hand away.

"Yes. I'm fine." I nodded with a reassuring smile and changed the subject. "I agree the locket could have belonged to Miss Davies." I searched for the most delicate words in which to present my doubts. "But don't you think it too humble a gift for a mistress?"

She frowned. "What do you mean?"

"I don't know much about such affairs, but I believe men strive to impress their mistresses where they do not their wives. Men want to show off with these women, but a locket is domestic, cherished, a private thing."

"He did marry her," she countered.

"In which case why not add initials?" I stared out between the horse's ears. My skin prickled. "No, this feels . . . wrong."

"More wrong than a mistress?"

I laughed and shook off my apprehension. "You have a point."

My mind now clear and the prism vanquished, I alit on an idea. "I have a friend whose mother is a prominent actress. Maybe we can get an introduction to some of Miss Davies's friends in the theater. One of them may recognize the locket."

"Nora's mother is still alive," Charlotte informed me. "Aunt Sadie grumbles about her yearly stipend from the estate. She might know."

"Even better. We should speak with her."

"Blast," Charlotte exclaimed and blushed at the mild profanity. She called out to the driver, "Stop here."

"What're you doing?" We were still blocks from her house, and the light waned as evening approached. I had hoped to get home before dark.

"You forgot to remind me," she scolded. "I must get some sprigs of lavender and rosemary and a tin of peppermints." Charlotte climbed out of the cab, and I followed.

"Do you think she will notice if you return without them?"

"Aunt Sadie notices the things that are important to her." She flicked her hand in the air with a theatrical flourish. "If my shoulders slump a fraction, she notices. If I drop a stitch, she notices. If my complexion freckles, she notices."

"Your aunt cannot possibly believe you've been gone all this time on such a simple errand."

"No?" She ducked into a confectioner's shop. "She concerns herself with me only when I am in her presence. When she sees me, she will remember that I promised to bring home scented herbs and candy, not how long I've been gone."

To my relief, we were able to purchase the items in a scant quarter of an hour and walked the last few blocks to her house in companionable silence. I glanced up at the darkening sky.

On rare occasions, a westerly breeze cleared the early evening air to reveal a dim smattering of stars. I gazed at them, and fragments of an old, recurring dream wavered on the edge of my memory: a waft of damp air, strong, encircling arms, gentle rocking.

"Here we are," Charlotte announced, breaking into my reverie. We stopped before her door.

"You should speak with Nellie about a contingency plan," I suggested, wanting to make sure Charlotte had a way out should her aunt turn vindictive.

"What do you mean?"

"Well . . ." I hesitated, feeling that my reliance on literature for insight into the female mind might prove faulty. "We can't know for sure that your aunt won't prevent you from continuing with the investigation when confronted. She is your guardian, after all. Nellie should know how to contact me."

For once, I was relieved by her dramatic intake of breath. "Oh, yes. Aunt Sadie is quite capable of locking me away, but we needn't bother Nellie. Just tell me. I can always get a note out through her."

I told her the address of our apothecary, noting that we lived above the store. She gave no outward sign of repugnance at so obvious an indication of low class.

"Very well," she replied, adding, "So, you'll speak with your friend, and we will—" A strangled growl cut her off.

"Rose-Marie," Charlotte exclaimed, bending over to scoop the "dog" up from the top stair of the servants' entrance. She cast a furtive glance around to make sure no one had seen the creature. "How on earth—"

I grasped her arm and brought a finger to my lips. The kitchen door stood ajar, not surprising in itself, but no noises drifted out from within. Strange, since dinner preparations should have been in full swing.

"Something's wrong," I whispered in her ear.

Charlotte fluttered her eyelashes. With greater familiarity, I had realized this reaction indicated rapid thought as well as surprise. "We have three servants, Mrs. Marshton, Cook, and Nellie. They should be here," she informed me.

"You stay out—"

"Don't be ridiculous." Rose-Marie yipped, and Charlotte loosened her grip on the animal. "I'm coming. I know the house better than you." She had a point, as usual.

We tiptoed down the staircase together. I peered around the doorframe into the kitchen. "No one here."

We went in, and Charlotte sat Rose-Marie on a cushioned stool. She wagged her finger at the bedraggled dog and whispered, "Stay here. Don't move." To me, she said, "At this time of day, Aunt Sadie is usually in the parlour."

I grabbed an iron poker from the fireplace. Charlotte took a large wooden spoon hanging from the wall.

I frowned at her choice of weapon. "What are you going to do with that? Slap some knuckles?"

"I'm nervous," she hissed and exchanged the spoon for a heavy rolling pin.

We crept down the hallway and up the stairs to the ground floor. The house lay silent around us. I had the uneasy suspicion our decision to search for her aunt was perhaps unwise.

"Just up here." Charlotte indicated a room off the main hallway.

Though spooked, I did not believe, in that moment, danger truly threatened. The shock of my almost fatal mistake would stay with me in the days to come.

I entered the parlour first and froze just within the doorway. Terror loosened my grip on the poker, and I choked out a guttural sound of revulsion.

Beside me, Charlotte's hand flew to her mouth, stifling a scream. The rolling pin fell from her limp fingers to the floor with a thud.

Aunt Sadie, for she could be none other, lay on her side on the sofa. She appeared to have no arms or legs. A thin rope encircled her throat, and a wad of crumpled paper protruded from her mouth. She stared back at us with the glassy eyes of death.

Charlotte ran to a corner of the room and threw up into a potted plant. I swallowed my own rising bile and crept closer to the sofa.

The woman was not dismembered. But the agony of her final moments must have been extreme. Her arms and legs were pulled almost from their sockets and tied together behind her. A series of slide-like knots connected this binding to the one about her neck. Even the slightest movement had closed the noose relentlessly around her throat.

"My God," I whispered under my breath in Cantonese and tightened my grip on the poker.

"What is it? What has happened to her?"

I spun around. Charlotte stood with her back to the garden window, her cheeks pale and wet with tears. My reply turned into a bark of alarm.

A hulking, faceless man threw back the curtains and lunged into the room. He clutched a butcher's knife in his raised hand.

Charlotte screamed and stumbled back, knocking me from gaping paralysis into action. I ran between her and the attacker. With a two-handed swing of the poker, I struck the knife from his grasp.

A blurred streak of wiry fur blazed across the floor and sank its snaggle-teeth into the man's leg. He grunted and sent the dog spinning with a vicious kick.

"Rose-Marie," Charlotte cried and ran to the injured animal.

The faceless monster grabbed her by the hair. I charged again, but he jerked the poker from my weakened grip and struck me across the head with it. I dropped to the floor.

He pulled Charlotte up by her hair. She scratched at his arm and kicked out.

Blood dripped into my eyes. I pushed up onto my feet, only to fall back down.

Our labored breathing and calls for help were in startling contrast to the man's hushed and faceless menace. At that moment, I knew only helplessness.

Salvation came in the feathered form of a starling streaking through the open window. With the high-pitched scream of a woman, Felix raked the man's head with one large claw.

The attacker released Charlotte and staggered around, flailing his hands about his head in an effort to dislodge the determined bird. Charlotte snatched up the poker and raised it to strike. The faceless man ran for the window and leapt into the garden, Felix still clinging to his head.

Frantic battering at the front door indicated that our screams had alerted the neighborhood. Charlotte dropped the poker and gathered Rose-Marie in her arms.

She knelt beside me. I put my hand on the small, motionless animal. A faint stirring of breath warmed my palm.

"Brave creature," I uttered before I lost consciousness and knew no more.

Chapter Twenty

A face swam before my eyes and coalesced into the lovely features of Margaret Scott. The frown on her fair brow cleared, and she drew back with a smile at my perplexed gaze.

"He's awake," she announced to what appeared to be nobody in particular.

"Jack's a good sort," I slurred with the effort to find a logical explanation for her presence.

Her mouth twisted into a cynical smile. "Still on mission, I see, young messenger."

"Oh, thank goodness." Charlotte leaned over me.

Margaret moved aside, and the room, which was now full of people, came into view. I lay on the floor.

"Can you help me sit?" I formed each word with care, trying to connect my brain to my mouth.

They each grabbed an elbow and pulled me up until my back rested against an armchair. My head swam, and I touched the wound with a tentative hand.

"What?" I stared down at my fingers, sticky with a thick, brown substance that could only be honey.

"Nellie says honey is good for wounds. Once I'd stopped the bleeding with a pillow, I ran to the kitchen to get some." Charlotte nodded over to a honey jar set against the table leg, a butter knife comically sticking out the top.

My bark of laughter sent needles of pain through my head. "Bloody—pardon me, I, ah, mean, what happened?"

In a breathless tumble of words, Charlotte recounted the moments after our attacker had knocked me unconscious. "I opened the door to our neighbors, who, as good fortune would have it, were out in their garden and heard our cries for help through the open window.

"Miss Scott here"—She nodded at Margaret—"is a member of the same women's society as Aunt—" Her voice faltered. Tears started in her eyes, and she covered them with a shaky hand.

"Sadie," I finished for her in an even, calm voice, hoping that quiet encouragement would lessen her shock.

Charlotte dropped her hand and nodded. "Yes, indeed."

Margaret placed a fortifying arm about her shoulders. "As chance would have it, I was delivering pamphlets to Miss Gaines from our leader, Mrs. Millicent Fawcett, who lives just a few doors down."

"Cook and Nellie?" I asked with some trepidation.

"They returned only moments ago," Charlotte replied, now in command of her emotions. "I can tell you, they are quite shaken."

"And the housekeeper, Mrs. Marshton?"

"Not here. She told the others they had leave for the day."

I blew out a long breath, grateful no one else was found dead. I glanced over at the sofa.

Someone had thankfully thrown a blanket over the grotesque shape, like a pig trussed up for slaughter. My blood boiled at so cruel a death.

Margaret followed my gaze. "We cannot lay her out properly until the constabulary arrives."

A wet, slimy sensation slid across my hand. "Rose-Marie." The dog had rarely acknowledged my presence, much less bestowed upon me a sloppy kiss. "Good to see you survived, apparently none the worse for wear.

"Are you sure this thing isn't a cat?" I teased Charlotte. "First the gutter and now a crazed attacker. He must be running low on lives."

In an effort at devil-may-care gallantry, I attempted a wink. But even that sent a bolt of pain through my head, and it turned into a wince.

Charlotte snatched the dog up and cradled him in her arms. "Rose-Marie is a hero."

I nodded. "He is. We owe a lot to our animal friends. If it wasn't for Fe—ah, the bird."

"Bird?" Margaret questioned.

"Yes. A bird . . . a starling, as a matter of fact, flew in through the window and clawed the man. It is the only reason we are alive."

"The dog, and now a bird? Why on earth would a bird attack someone inside a house?"

I could hardly tell her I knew the bird. Felix was in some way tied to my encounter with Sherlock Holmes earlier in the day. I was not going to share my thoughts on Chinese supernatural intercession with this woman I barely knew and did not like.

"Starlings are very intelligent," I explained. "They recognize people and can take a strong dislike to individuals. This attacker with his violence and faceless—"

"Faceless?" a quiet, steady voice put in. We looked up at the man who, flanked by two bobbies, stood staring down at our small group.

"Inspector Jonas Lloyddyn, at your service. Allow me." He reached down and with a hand to each, helped both Charlotte and Margaret to their feet. "Now you, lad, let's get you into this chair."

"I am quite able—"

He ignored my objections and grasped my arm. I stood with his assistance and sat in the chair. I looked about me. From the second I had set foot in the parlour, my attention was riveted on the gruesome figure of Charlotte's aunt. In the subsequent fight for our lives, I'd had no opportunity to observe my surroundings.

Now I noted two large windows overlooking the garden, one still opened, through which Felix had entered and our attacker fled. Red, embossed wallpaper gave the room a dramatic glow, and a plush, expensive oriental rug covered the floor. Ornate framed paintings adorned the walls, and photographs sat on the many small side tables scattered about the room. A maroon velvet drape covered the mantel, upon which sat a clock and a bust of John Harold Gaines. The rest—vases, knickknacks, china figurines—lay broken and smashed on the carpet.

I frowned. Was the room like this when we entered, or was the mess a result of our struggle?

I must have spoken the question aloud, because Charlotte squeezed into the chair beside me, Rose-Marie on her lap, and replied, "I don't know. It's as if my mind blanked from the moment we saw Aunt Sadie to when the faceless man jumped out the window."

I straightened in the chair. Grandfather's words echoed in my mind: "Violence tears at the fabric of the universe, leaving us lost and unmoored."

Of course, paralyzing shock was the point. We did not catch our attacker in the act; he had lain in wait for us . . . for Charlotte. My mind churned with this new realization.

Like the director of a play, the killer had staged the scene for maximum impact. When he stepped out from behind the curtains, he had already rendered us senseless with shock.

That I was with Charlotte was an unforeseen obstacle to his plan. He must have wavered only seconds before deciding I would be easily overcome. As indeed, proved all too true.

I studied the inspector, the very one who had ruled Teddy's death a suicide. From the contempt in Mrs. Tooley's voice, I had imagined a self-important oaf. Nothing could have been further from reality.

Inspector Lloyddyn directed his men with competence, instructing the constables to question the neighbors and household staff. He cocked an eyebrow at Margaret.

"Who might you be?"

"Miss Margaret Scott, a friend of the family," she explained, nodding towards the sofa without looking in that direction. "Miss Gaines was a member of our women's group. And as such, I will be offering her niece sanctuary in my home."

"I see." The inspector drew out a pipe from his pocket but did not light it. He tapped the barrel against his palm. "I will allow you to stay, but you mustn't interrupt."

"Of course."

Inspector Lloyddyn wore a simple, yet well-tailored, navy tweed suit of inexpensive wool. A man in middle years, he stood trim and straight, though only an inch or two taller than Margaret. Brown, attentive eyes observed us beneath his hat pulled low over his brow.

If not for his clean-shaven face and pale complexion, I would have figured him for a military man. He exuded a calm, meditative quality that must have served him well during interrogations. His first question surprised me.

"How did you two meet?"

"At the booksellers, Cohen and Son," Charlotte lied with a coolness that greatly impressed me. "Being woefully ignorant of my grandfather's work, I had gone to purchase a critical essay. Mr. Cheng was there and, being a friend of the proprietor and a scholar of my grandfather's writings, my aunt hired him to tutor me. We were returning from touring some of the places my grandfather made famous in his books when . . ." She cleared her throat. "When we found my aunt."

Chapter Twenty-One

"Balderdash," the inspector scoffed.

I maintained a neutral expression. Charlotte had let me know in those few short sentences that she wanted to keep our investigation a secret. Considering the threat to her life, I sat in conflicted silence, unsure whether to honor my earlier (and rather pompous) declaration of client confidentiality or let the inspector know the whole of it.

"Inspector, really," Margaret objected. "Do remember where you are."

"Miss Scott, no interrupting, if you please." He stuck the stem of his pipe in his mouth and declared through clenched teeth, "You expect me to believe this boy . . . a scholar . . . on Gaines?"

I smiled inwardly and proceeded to name the books of John Harold Gaines, his main themes, and both the contemporary and present-day critiques of his work. I threw in for good measure some of his more obscure, earlier novellas and short stories.

"I'd be happy to explain the changing symbolism of the vulnerable urchin throughout his work. As you may know, she has become a classic literary tool, often referred to as the 'Gaines waif.'"

"Good grief, you can't be serious?" The inspector laughed and puffed on his empty pipe. "Seems, my boy, you are quite the knowing one." He folded his arms, his face now solemn. "Go on then, tell me what happened."

I sat back and listened as Charlotte gave the main narrative. Inspector Lloyddyn grumbled what sounded like "foolish children" at the point where we left the kitchen in search of Aunt Sadie.

Charlotte's voice faltered when describing our grisly discovery, but she continued on with determination, "And this faceless man—"

"Faceless?" He repeated the very first word he had uttered in our presence.

"No, not faceless," I replied.

Though my head pounded, I'd had plenty of time to overcome the shock and organize my thoughts. "A mask, one of those masks women wear at night. I believe this one was made of India rubber."

Charlotte bounced on the chair, sending a lightning bolt of pain through my head. "Yes, yes. My dear, old guardian wore them at night to purify her skin. They can look quite unnerving, even on someone as sweet and harmless as Aunt Beatrix."

"A lady's mask, you say. Odd choice for a murderer."

"They are called toilette masks," Margaret put in. "And no, indeed, Inspector, the choice of such a mask is inspired. They are affordable and available everywhere, they obscure the features effectively, and as Charlotte points out, can be unsettling even on someone you know and trust."

"Hmm, well, go on then. What happened next?"

Charlotte continued. The inspector was appropriately admiring of the "hero dog," but stopped her when she got to the "bird rescuer."

"A bird?"

"Yes, a starling," I explained just as I had with Margaret. "We must have disturbed its nest in the garden with our cries for help."

"You expect me—"

A commotion at the parlour door cut him off. Cook pushed her way through the constables, an indignant look on her face.

"That's enough, now. Leave these children to get out of this unholy place," she demanded. "What they've been through, and you standing there questioning them while poor Miss Gaines lies here like she was found. For shame."

Cook took hold of my elbow, and I stood steady enough. "This boy needs that wound looked after."

We made to leave, but the inspector held up his hand. "Wait, Miss Gaines. Do you know of any enemies that would want to hurt your aunt?"

Charlotte shook her head. "No one. Aunt Sadie was not an easy person, but I don't believe she ever harmed a soul."

"And you?"

"Heavens, Inspector, she is but a child," Margaret interjected.

"And yet . . ." He let the grim implication hang in the air.

Charlotte squared her shoulders. "I have been in town for less than a year, and I do not believe I have encountered one person who would see me dead."

He dismissed us and turned his attention to his men. "Eaton, Farley, where's the wagon? We need to get this body to the mortuary. Did you check for footprints in the garden? Statements from the neighbors?"

His orders grew faint as we made our way down to the kitchen. I sat on a stool next to the heavy wooden table while Cook cleaned my head wound. With a hot cup of tea in hand, I began to feel more myself.

"Where's Mrs. Marshton?" I mumbled into the rising steam off the cup.

"Now, there's the question," Cook replied, her deft fingers parting the hair around the cut on my head. "You're lucky, my lad. The blow didn't crack your skull."

At the stove, Nellie stirred a pot of aromatic beef broth. Margaret sat at the table. Her ramrod-straight back and primly clasped hands telegraphed her discomfort at joining the servants in the kitchen.

Charlotte, quite the opposite, could not have been more at home. She made directly for the biscuit tin and nibbled on a wafer with a contemplative look. "Maybe my aunt sent Mrs. Marshton away too."

"No, miss, she didn't," Cook replied. "I asked her . . . Mrs. Marshton, that is . . . just who was going to light the fires and serve the tea with Nellie gone, being that Miss Gaines was right particular about teatime. She said her instructions were clear; we go out and not return until half past six. I'm certain Mrs. Marshton was to stay on."

I flinched as she laid a warm rag against the cut. "Steady, lad. Head wounds tend to bleed and look worse than they are. You won't be needing stitches."

Cook wrapped a clean bandage around my head. Nellie set bowls of broth in front of us, though I was little inclined to eat.

"I think Mrs. Marshton is somehow involved in this business," I reasoned. "Or else she would have returned by now."

Cook tut-tutted. "You shouldn't be making claims like that without knowing. I don't like the woman, but saying she's party to murder—"

"Well, I believe it," Nellie declared. "Pale as a ghost and as sneaky as one too."

"It is late for such speculation." Margaret pushed back her chair and stood. "We must go, Charlotte. I sent a message around to Mrs. Fawcett. She will let your aunt's solicitor know of this tragic event."

Charlotte shot her a rebellious look but reluctantly agreed. "Very well, but Kuo must have a cab home. He cannot travel on public transportation injured."

"Of course, one will be hailed for him."

Charlotte stood and I with her. "Rose-Marie is coming as well," she added.

Margaret smiled. "I wouldn't have it any other way."

The girl turned to Cook and Nellie. She squared her shoulders.

"You mustn't worry about what will happen to you or try to find a new situation. You must stay here until all is settled, and . . . well, I will find something to suit."

Nellie bobbed a curtsey, and Cook dabbed her eyes with the corner of her apron. "Certainly, miss," she said through her tears.

Charlotte grasped my one hand in two of her own. "Thank you."

I cleared my throat, embarrassed by such unwarranted gratitude. "Much good I—"

"You saved my life." She squeezed my hand tighter and released it.

Charlotte gathered Rose-Marie in her arms. "I'm ready."

She and Margaret went out, and I was left to stare down at the note the girl had pressed into my palm.

Chapter Twenty-Two

Grandfather sat across from me at a table much different from the sturdy wooden one in the Gaines's kitchen. A delicate thing of carved maple and inlaid ivory, the table accommodated the three of us comfortably, although my mother was not present. She had left earlier in the evening to attend a birth and likely would not return until the wee hours of the morning.

Grandfather had examined my head wound and declared Cook's efforts "adequate." "Hmm, honey," he had mused at the remnants of the sticky stuff still in my hair. "It can prevent inflammation but should be boiled and cooled before use."

I drank a decoction of *xuefu zhuyu*, an ancient blend of Chinese herbs that stimulated the blood and promoted healing. My grandfather sat impassive as I poured out the story of my long, eventful day.

"What were Mr. Holmes's exact words?" he asked when I finished.

Though my mysterious encounter with Sherlock Holmes happened only hours in the past, I strained to remember the correct wording. "'Transformation is . . . um, key, life to death to life. The false . . . no. The *pretender* walks among us. Trust at great peril.'"

He repeated the warning back to me. "Are you sure this is correct?"

I nodded. "Yes. I'm sure."

He closed his eyes and released a weary sigh. "As intelligent as our patient is, I doubt he adds Cantonese to his list of accomplishments."

Grandfather stared down at his hands clasped on the tabletop. "The one-legged bird is most certainly a sign from the ancestors, although the *Bi Fang* is usually described as crane-like. Your friend Felix has shown up at important times, indeed, to save your life. This is not random. The *Bi Fang* is auspicious . . . an omen of fire. Interpreting such signs is complicated, but we must assume the bird a messenger of sorts."

He looked over at me. "Your mother will not agree, but I can see no alternative but to allow you to continue with your investigation."

"Why?"

"Because the ancestors will it."

The scent of seeping herbs and steamed rice mingled to produce a homey smell, one from which I drew comfort. My thoughts turned to Charlotte, alone but for Rose-Marie in a strange house and with a family she knew only in passing.

No wonder the girl clung to the unsightly bundle of fur she called a dog. In the same way, I clung to this humble abode and the people sheltered within its walls.

How quickly violence upends our lives, changing our perspective and altering our fate. I would have set aside my pride and abandoned, at that very moment, the investigation to protect those I loved. If not for Charlotte, I would have done so without a single misgiving.

"I do not want to bring evil to our doorstep."

Grandfather shook his head with a sad smile. "Evil comes whether we want it or not. More important is what we do when it does."

**

Unable to sleep, I pushed back the bedcovers and sat up. My tender head and the stress of our narrow escape kept me awake. I struck a match and lit the candle on the table beside my bed.

The crumpled note Charlotte had pressed into my hand lay smoothed out on the tabletop. I suppressed a shiver of revulsion, knowing what it must have taken her to pull it from Aunt Sadie's dead mouth before even letting the neighbors in.

The elegant script and gold-tipped edges identified the author as the very same who had penned the anonymous poem. I read the note for the hundredth time:

Treason bites deep and leaves a wound, gangrenous and foul.
Slow, cruel death comes for the betrayer. —The Grey Man

The Grey Man? Like the choking fog of London, a fitting description for a silent, faceless, killer.

I shook off my unease and walked to the window, staring out onto the street below. Dingier streets existed in this immense city, but not by much. The unrelenting grime of London air clung to every nook and cranny.

A lonely streetlamp cast an isolated circle of light on the pavement outside my room. Two shadows wavered just beyond its reach and drew my gaze. I pressed my face to the glass and tried to bring the figures into focus: a man and a woman.

Their heads almost touched in close and intimate conversation. The two drew apart, and the woman turned and walked through the circle of light.

I gasped at the lithe, graceful figure of my mother spotlighted for a fraction of a second before darkness swallowed her up again. I stared after the retreating back of the man and needed no light to identify the smooth stride and strong shoulders of Mr. Wei.

Confused, I went back to bed but could only toss and turn, finally falling into a fitful slumber in the early hours of the morning. I awoke late and entered the kitchen to find Grandfather seated at the table and Mother boiling rice on the stove.

Her straight, rigid back told me more effectively than words that she and Grandfather had argued. She turned and kissed my cheek.

"Sit. You need to eat a proper breakfast."

I sat, and she tilted my head up to examine the wound. Cool, gentle fingers pressed along the edges of the cut. "Does this hurt?"

"No," I replied truthfully.

Mother leaned over and pressed her cheek against the top of my head. She pulled away before I could return her embrace and placed an envelope next to my bowl.

"This came in the morning mail."

I tore open the envelope and found inside a note from Charlotte. "She asks if I can join her at Mrs. Millicent Fawcett's residence on Gower Street this afternoon. The ladies of their group are gathering in remembrance of her aunt."

My mother turned back to the stove and did not answer.

"There is a lurid description of the murder in here." Grandfather looked up from the newspaper. "I think it is wise to learn what you can from those who knew the victim."

He took a final sip of tea and stood. "But first, we have work in the storeroom, and you must remember that the inquest for Teddy is tomorrow. We will all attend in support of Mrs. Tooley."

**

The late afternoon sun hovered over the rooftops of the townhouses lining Gower Street. The façade of number two Gower was almost identical to that of John Harold Gaines's just a few doors down.

I knocked and waited but a moment before a grey-haired woman in late middle age opened the door. "You must be young Mr. Cheng. Do come in."

I stepped into the well-appointed, yet stark (compared to the fashionable clutter of the day) foyer. I recognized the name of the woman who lived in this house, famed as she was for her campaigns in support of women suffrage and education.

"Mrs. Millicent Fawcett?" I prompted, removing my hat.

"Oh, do excuse me. I should have introduced myself. I'm her sister, Miss Agnes Garrett."

I followed her down the hallway, and we entered a combination library and study. As I crossed the threshold into the stylish and airy room, a hush descended upon its occupants. All eyes turned on me, and I knew a moment of complete and utter isolation.

I was the only male at this gathering of older matrons with a sprinkling of younger women. Their gazes ranged from mild hostility to tolerance, even one or two of acceptance. I longed to find comfort in those few accepting individuals, but knew from hard experience their approval was tenuous at best.

"K—Mr. Cheng."

My bubble of loneliness burst at the sight of Charlotte striding towards me. She clutched Rose-Marie, seemingly now a permanent fixture, to her breast.

"I've been waiting ages. Why weren't you here an hour ago?"

"Your letter gave no specific time, so I had to guess when such gatherings usually take place."

"Oh, well." She dismissed her mistake with a shake of her head. "You didn't miss much. Just a lot of talk about county elections and school openings and such things, and how much Aunt Sadie will be missed."

Charlotte led me to a sofa set in front of a bookcase tucked into a corner. Putting Rose-Marie down between us, she cast a furtive glance around the room. The women had resumed their individual conversations, and only one or two still glanced my way with a hint of suspicion.

"You read that dreadful message?" she whispered.

"Yes."

"Do you have any idea what it means? Treason, gangrenous wound, betrayer . . ."

"I think we can reasonably assume the note refers to your aunt. That she, in some manner, was treasonous."

I had rehearsed my response on the way over, determined that we should inform the inspector of the note and its contents. And so, I told her.

She frowned. "What can he do? If we cannot decipher its meaning, how can the inspector?"

"Maybe there is a pattern," I suggested. "Maybe the Grey Man has struck before, and the police have withheld the information."

Charlotte stared down at her clasped hands, indecisive. "I don't know. The note, so personal . . . as if he knew Aunt Sadie and hated her."

The color drained from her face. "And don't you know, he must've had one ready for me, a note to shove in my—" Her voice faltered.

I resisted the urge to grasp her hand. Rose-Marie whined and pressed close to her side.

"Goodness, what intensity of conversation." Margaret had walked over to the sofa, but her playful tone changed upon seeing Charlotte's pale face. "My dear, this is all too much. We should leave."

"No. I am perfectly fine," she protested. "It is good to hear people speak so fondly of my aunt."

Margaret smiled her sympathy. "Especially, when your understanding of each other was not what one would have hoped."

Charlotte returned her smile. "Yes. Aunt Sadie could be conventional and, ah, repressive at times."

"Not a ringing endorsement of one who worked for women's rights," Margaret replied.

They laughed in complete agreement, but I did not share their amusement. I studied the gathered women. There were many contrasts among them: rich and poor, old and young, plain and pretty, married and spinster. Yet, they all met together as an organized group with a common purpose.

Women faced many obstacles in society, a situation made even more difficult by lack of status or good looks. How much more admirable was it that the poorer, unmarried, and plainer women overcame significant barriers to work on improving the lot of all women. The youthful beauties, such as Margaret, with their wealth and position, risked far less in their rebellion.

"My grandfather says when the ground beneath our feet is unsteady, we seek security in what is known. That someone like your Aunt Sadie sought comfort in convention is not surprising, but her commitment to women's rights and willingness to be counted as such took courage."

Margaret raised an eyebrow. "Your friend, my dear Charlotte, is forever giving me lessons in compassion."

Charlotte looked from me to Margaret. "How so, when you've only just met?"

"Ah, but we haven't. Mr. Cheng came to my house bearing flowers and a note from an admirer. Come with me, and I will tell you the whole." Margaret threw me a teasing look and crooked her finger at Charlotte.

I could not tell if the gleam in her eye was kind or cruel, nor what form the story would take. But she had diverted Charlotte's mind from her own hypothetical murder, and for that, I was grateful.

We rose, and our legs pushed the sofa back against the shelf. A book, dislodged by the impact, fell from its place and lay open on the cushions.

Charlotte and Margaret walked away, heads close together. I looked up to see from where the book had fallen.

Identical dark red bound volumes stood in a row. Golden letters spelled out *The Prophetess* along their spines, the very periodical published by Mr. Holmes's commune of lady poets.

Heavy air pressed in around me, and beads of sweat gathered on my brow. With the certainty of foreknowledge, I picked up the volume lying on the settee and read the words at the top of the page: *The Glowering Woman by Mary Stafford Gaines, 1879.*

In hushed undertones, I spoke aloud the first line. "The lowering sky benights the day . . ."

Chapter Twenty-Three

I steadied my breathing and checked the date again. Mary Gaines had written the poem the very same year she died.

"What have you there?"

Glancing up, I met the gaze of a small woman with clear, curious eyes. Her dark hair, shot through with grey, coiled in a thick braid at the back of her head.

I turned the open book towards her. "A bound volume of a periodical."

She took the book and examined the page before tucking it up under one arm. "Ah, yes, *The Prophetess*. I know many of the women who contributed to this publication. It is no longer in circulation, though the group who once produced it is still active. Their farm in Warwickshire grows some of the finest produce in the county, and their honey is second to none." From her similarity in features to her sister, I guessed this was my famous hostess.

"I did not have an opportunity to introduce myself when you first arrived. I am Mrs. Millicent Fawcett." She held out her hand.

We exchanged a brief, firm handshake. "An honor to meet you. I'm Kuo Cheng."

"Yes, I know. Charlotte could speak of little else. 'Where is he? Why is he so late? I do hope he shows.'"

Her accurate imitation of Charlotte's tone and mannerisms

surprised a laugh out of me. "She is, at times, anxious and flighty, but I have learned never to underestimate her," I replied.

"Wise boy." She took the book from under her arm and flipped back to the page with the poem. "Interesting you should find this on the very day we gather to remember the life of her daughter," she said with a sad shake of her head. "I knew Mary well. She was as talented a writer as her husband."

"Oh?" I questioned, a disbelieving note to my voice.

She cocked her head to one side, regarding me. "Hmm, perhaps not so wise."

I blushed. "I did not mean—"

She held up her hand. "No need to explain. Society conditions us to believe men are superior in all things. Even I fall victim to the insidious voice in my head insisting on my own insignificance.

"Nevertheless, what I say is true. Mary was a gifted writer, but as expected, she set aside her abilities to help her husband realize his goals. And for all that, she was still discarded."

Mrs. Fawcett considered the poem. "This is particularly sad, don't you think? Written in the year of her death and from the asylum."

"Where was she institutionalized?"

"Broxburn Inn at Wembley. Certainly a kinder and more genteel place than Bedlam, but many an unwilling woman has been held captive there." Her eyes narrowed, angry and stern. "And captivity, Mr. Cheng, whether physical, intellectual, or spiritual, can kill your very soul."

"Millicent," Agnes called from across the room. "Our guests are leaving."

"Ah, yes, a moment," she replied, and to my surprise asked, "Will you join us for tea in the parlour? Just a small group, Margaret and Charlotte, of course."

"Thank you. I would be happy to."

"Well then, down the hall to your left," Mrs. Fawcett instructed and walked away, adding over her shoulder, "You should find Charlotte there with her little, uh, creature."

She joined Agnes at the threshold, and they shepherded their friends into the foyer. I turned the other way and followed the sound of women's laughter to the parlour.

As with earlier, my entrance produced a hush, and I recognized the two newly arrived young women as the Grecian and Little Lord Fauntleroy. In a graceful surge, Margaret rose from the sofa.

"Miss Florence Bagby," she announced, pointing to Little Lord Fauntleroy, "and Miss Elizabeth Hobson," indicating the Grecian. "May I present, Mr. Kuo Cheng." Their lips lifted in slight, polite smiles. "Flo and Beth, as their friends call them, and so must you," Margaret added.

I looked doubtful, but the two women nodded in agreement.

"Yes, indeed," Flo replied. "Even though you were quite rude upon our first encounter, we don't hold grudges."

"No, we don't," Beth added with a forceful shake of her head.

I sat on the sofa next to Charlotte and decided it best to meet boldness with boldness. They may not hold grudges, but any sign of weakness and these women would eat me alive.

"I only responded in kind," I countered, not giving an inch.

"Certainly." Margaret was quick to insert herself into the conversation. "We were hardly at our best when you knocked. But I do resent the implication that I should look favorably upon a suitor that does not suit me."

"The situation required merely common courtesy," I shot back, "not a lifetime commitment."

She laughed. "Touché, Mr. Cheng."

The atmosphere lightened, and Flo and Beth regaled us with the minutes of the Women's Local Government Society meeting from which they had just come. What I knew of the organization was limited to newspaper articles often critical of its efforts to see women elected to public office.

"You would have exploded, Meg," Beth fumed. "The way they keep changing the law to disqualify women candidates. It's infuriating."

"Even this new legislation that allows for some involvement in minor offices is not enough," Flo interjected. "And always dependent on the support of men."

"My friends." Mrs. Fawcett swept into the room with her sister. "Until women can vote, our very rights are dependent on men."

She sat and Agnes poured the tea. "It is the fight of our lifetime, and we shouldn't expect them to yield the battlefield any time soon."

To my surprise, Rose-Marie crawled onto my lap and curled into a warm ball. Perhaps he felt, as the only other male in the room, there was safety in numbers.

My mind wandered, and I itched to speak with Charlotte in private. She would be eager to learn of the origins of her threatening poem and the possibility of a new clue in the form of Broxburn Inn.

"What do you think, Mr. Cheng?"

I blinked and brought my mind back into focus. "Excuse me?"

"Do you support women's suffrage?" Beth scowled at my inattention.

The women regarded me with varying degrees of intensity. Flo and Beth glared, daring me to disavow a woman's right to chart her own course. Margaret's eyes held amusement, as if she enjoyed seeing me put on the spot. Millicent and Agnes looked on with mild curiosity, and Charlotte simply awaited my response.

I cleared my throat. "My mother is a skilled healer. She's knowledgeable in human anatomy and physiology and medicines used to treat almost any ailment. She's called in on childbirth, and you would be surprised by the grand houses and great ladies who have welcomed her services. Yet, society denies her the title of doctor, even by those of our race who adhere to Eastern medical practices. And certainly, by the English." The women listened with rapt attention, believing they knew where I was going with my response.

"The English system of voting disenfranchises many, including the poor and women and me, though I was born in London." They shifted uncomfortably, now less sure of my intent.

"I am, from my mother's example, well aware of the intelligence and capabilities of women. So, yes, I support women's suffrage. But I ask you, will you extend the same right to me and mine?"

"Yes, of course," Charlotte exclaimed. "Whyever would we not?"

Her confident declaration both warmed and pierced my heart. For while Charlotte had yet to be fully indoctrinated into the British dogma of racial superiority, there was reflected in the eyes of those older, educated women a familiar glimmer of distrust. These were the same people, after all, who believed not even the Irish capable of governing themselves.

"I must take my leave." I put Rose-Marie on the sofa and stood, relieving them of the need to answer. "Thank you for the hospitality."

Charlotte grabbed the dog and jumped to her feet. "I'll walk you to the door."

No one objected. I thanked them once more, and we quit the room.

"How odd," Charlotte whispered. "They're always saying we should be equal."

Once out of earshot in the foyer, I replied, "It is because I'm Chinese. They believe I can never be English, because I am not entirely of European descent."

Charlotte released a long, exasperated sigh. "I *know*. I thought . . . perhaps, well, that they believed so because they were not acquainted with any Chinese people."

I frowned, perplexed.

"Don't you understand?" she explained. "If they know you, they will see we are the same."

My heart contracted, and in that moment, it physically hurt. I stopped myself from clutching at my chest, for once understanding Charlotte's disposition for drama.

"I fear there are few as open-minded as you," I replied and, in a rush to cover my emotion, added, "Your poem is in a bound volume of *The Prophetess* in the library."

She gasped. "What?"

"The volume fell from the bookshelf onto the sofa and lay open at the exact page on which the poem was printed."

"Honestly, I do believe this investigation cannot get any stranger," was her tart reply. Rose-Marie yelped, and Charlotte put him down to scamper about. "Well, tell me."

"Your grandmother was the author, and she wrote it in the year of her death, 1879, from Broxburn Inn at Wembley, where she was institutionalized."

Charlotte placed a hand over her mouth and murmured, "So obscure. How does the Grey Man know of the poem?" She stared up at me, pale and shaken. "That monster is stalking my family. And for all we know, Uncle Cecil is dead too, and I am the only one left."

Chapter Twenty-Four

I walked to the Underground in the gathering dusk. Easing Charlotte's fears had taken some effort, not least because the danger was real. I left, but only after extracting a promise that she would not venture out alone. We agreed on a time two days hence to regroup.

I got off the train at the Mansion Street Station and made my way home. Evening had descended, and only a smattering of people scurried by on the narrow avenues. I pushed up my collar and pulled my jacket closer to ward off the chill.

A musical trill floated out over the rooftops, and I searched the overhanging eaves for a one-legged starling. A cloaked shadow slithered down the wall on the building opposite.

The hairs on my forearms stood on end. I pressed back into a recessed doorway, but the thing did not reappear.

A bird fluttered from its chimney perch, silhouetted against a waning moon. I stepped out onto the pavement and ran the rest of the way home.

The next morning dawned dark and stormy, a fitting complement to my gloomy mood and the sad business of the day. Grandfather, Mother, and I were set to attend the inquest into Teddy's death. The pressure brought to bear by Mrs. Tooley had reversed the decision to skip a formal review.

Twice before (once for the tanner's boy and another for a suspected poisoning), I had attended an inquest. I dreaded the prospect of sitting for hours listening to the minute details of Teddy's sad end. The specter of guilt at abandoning my friend still haunted me.

I entered the kitchen to the smell of steamed rice and fish cakes. Grandfather, already seated at the table reading the newspaper, looked up.

"Fortunately, we do not have far to go in this weather. The inquest is at The Sweet Pea since Teddy was pulled from the river not far from there."

He referred to a local public house that catered mostly to dock workers. A narrow building sandwiched in the middle of a row of narrow buildings, The Sweet Pea backed up to the river and, like its neighbors, appeared ready to tumble in at any moment.

I swallowed a lump in my throat. The pub was one of our familiar haunts when Teddy was in the neighborhood. He and I stopped in on the days they served shepherd's pie.

"We leave in half an hour," Grandfather continued. "By then the jury will be selected."

I was glad not to be among the early observers. The coroner would take his time picking the twelve jurors from the group of twenty-four men summoned for this purpose. Only after they were seated would witnesses be called.

Unlike a trial, an inquest allowed the jurors to question witnesses. Sometimes the proceedings would stretch into the evening hours as each juror tried to outdo the other with clever and probing queries. I hoped, for Mrs. Tooley's sake, the sad nature of this crime would discourage such displays.

I sat and poured myself a cup of tea. "Where's Mother?"

"She left early to meet Mrs. Tooley—to comfort the poor woman in her time of trial and grief."

I spooned up a helping of rice and topped it off with a fried egg and fish cake. I looked up, sensing my grandfather's gaze.

"For what do you blame yourself, my son?"

The question didn't surprise me. Grandfather could read my distress in the language of my movements and the quality of my silence.

"For growing impatient and turning away from Teddy," I replied through the tightness in my throat.

He nodded. "It's good to examine one's actions, but in this case, conceit leads you astray."

"Conceit?" I stiffened, offended. "Isn't it through self-reflection that one achieves humility?"

"Yes, but you place too much importance on your influence. You argued with an old friend with whom you had little in common. Your paths had already diverged. This happens." He leaned towards me, his elbows on the table and his chin resting on his clasped hands. "To keep Teddy from harm, you would have needed to be with him every hour of every day."

I bowed my head, and a choking sob escaped from between my gritted teeth. Grandfather placed a gentle hand on my shoulder.

"Waste no more time indulging in senseless guilt. We must show strength and comfort the afflicted. And let us use what skills we have to find justice for Teddy."

I wiped my eyes and nodded. We ate what remained of our breakfast in silence and left the store under the shelter of a large umbrella. The wind had died down since the early morning, and we reached The Sweet Pea managing to stay dry.

The inquest, like all official business, was held on the second floor. The pub itself was doing brisk trade for this time of day. (Unnatural deaths brought out the crowds like nothing else.) We pushed our way through the horde.

Steam rose off the wet jackets of men with their backs to the fireplace. The smell of damp wool pressed in around me and stifled my breathing. The atmosphere lightened as we went up the stairs to the meeting room. I breathed in a deep lungful of the chill, fresh air that washed in from the open windows.

Grandfather surveyed the room and pointed to a bench near the front. Mother stood out like a priceless painting in a crumbling old mansion.

Her long, black hair pulled back in a low bun revealed her smooth complexion and perfect profile. She had changed from her usual work clothes of a loose-fitting cotton tunic over trousers into a simple dress of Western design. She sat next to Mrs. Tooley, who, wrapped in her colorful knit shawl, huddled in a miserable heap at her side.

Mrs. Tooley shooed two women aside to make room for us. Grandfather sat beside her and patted her hand. "What news so far?"

The old woman appeared shrunken and fragile. Her mouth drooped, and grief etched deep wrinkles around her eyes. "Mr. Blankenship, the coroner over there, he just chose the jury," she rasped. "I figure they'll start now."

On cue, the clerk called the inquest to order, "We'll proceed now with the inquest into the death of one Theodore Edward Tooley, a boy, age fifteen."

I didn't recognize the coroner, but then I wouldn't necessarily. Coroners traveled where they were needed. One might show up for an inquest on one day and an entirely different one the next. Although the same coroner typically stayed should the inquest last longer than a day.

Mr. Blankenship appeared too young for someone in his position. A small man, his thin, wiry frame and quick jerky movements gave the impression of pent-up, nervous energy.

"Do the jurors understand their role in these proceedings?" he asked.

The twelve-man jury seated along the length of the inside wall consisted of local professionals and shopkeepers, including Mr. Needer from the corner store. They nodded their heads in unison.

"Good. Let us begin by calling"—he glanced down at a paper in front of him—"Constable Eaton."

I recognized the young, freckled-face constable as one of those who'd assisted Inspector Lloyddyn at the scene of Aunt Sadie's murder. He sat in a chair next to the table and removed his helmet, placing it on his lap.

Mr. Blankenship cleared his throat. "Now, Constable, can you tell us what happened the night of October second, the year of our Lord 1894."

The Constable wiped his lips with a handkerchief before saying, "Yes, sir. Sometime around five in the ev—"

"Can you be precise with the hour, Constable?"

"Um . . . I, ah, a quarter after the hour of five in the evening, I believe. I'd just made a round by Wapping Basin past St. Johns and heard a commotion down by the waterman stairs.

"A taxi man coming up with a passenger had seen a body floating up next to the dock. A crowd had gathered. They'd already pulled the boy out and laid him on the ground."

Mrs. Tooley stifled a sob. Mother laid a comforting arm across her shoulders.

"There weren't much to be done for him. So I had his body taken to the mortuary at St. George's."

"And did you identify the boy, Constable?"

"No, sir, it weren't me. The caretaker at the mortuary, Mr. Horace Dengington, recognized the boy as being the grandson of Mrs. Tooley over there"—he nodded in our direction—"who has a flower stall in Covent Garden Market."

One of the jurors shifted in his chair, a large man in a high, stiff collar and waxed moustache. "Begging your pardon," he interjected, "but what was a boy from Covent Garden doing in Wapping, and so late?"

It was a good question. My work often took me to different parts of the city, but most people stayed close to their homes and businesses. In the past, Teddy only ventured far from his stomping grounds to visit me. I had no idea how his habits had changed since last seeing him and made a mental note to check out the pier near the waterman stairs.

"We never determined where exactly he went into the water. Could be someplace nearer the market, and the tide brought him to rest where he was found."

The man nodded. Silence fell. Constable Eaton fidgeted as he waited for more questions. The clerk's pen scribbled across the paper.

"Are there any other questions of the constable?" Mr. Blankenship asked.

The members of the jury looked at each other. No one spoke. They shook their heads.

"You can go, Constable Eaton, but stay nearby in case you're needed."

"Yes, sir." He stood and placed his helmet back on his head.

People murmured as he made his way past the spectators and down the stairs. I turned to watch him go and frowned at a familiar face grinning at me from a few rows back.

Chapter Twenty-Five

Danny sat, decked out in her urchin costume, next to the pawnbroker's granddaughter, Sybil. Others from the Covent Garden community were in the audience. Mrs. Tooley had a wide network of friends. I wasn't surprised by their show of support.

Danny waved a "come here" gesture. I shook my head and held out my hands to say "not now." She mouthed "when" and opened her eyes wide to indicate urgency. I jerked my head in the direction of the coroner and mouthed "afterwards." To which she stuck out her tongue at me.

"We next call Horace Dengington, caretaker of St. George's mortuary," Mr. Blankenship intoned.

The crowd shifted in uncomfortable unison at the mention of St. George's dour custodian. He stood from a chair on the back wall and made his ponderous way to the front.

The morning light stripped his pale, pockmarked face and misshapen back of shadows and menace. A few quick, furtive signs of the cross followed him down the aisle, but to me, he appeared dignified in a modest wool suit.

"Mr. Dengington, would you recount for us the events of the night of October second when young Mr. Tooley's body was brought to the mortuary."

"Yes," he replied in a low growl that carried all the way to the back of the crowded room.

I glanced up at my grandfather, worried Mr. Dengington might mention us. He gave me a quick, reassuring smile.

"About three quarters past the hour of five in the night," Horace began, "Constable Eaton arrived at the mortuary bringing in tow the body of a boy. I recognized the child as being young Teddy—"

"How did you know him?" questioned Mr. Needer.

Mrs. Tooley stiffened. A faint blush spread across Horace's cheeks. He cut his eyes away from the jury and stared down at his feet.

"He buys flowers from me, don't ya know," Mrs. Tooley declared.

"No comments from the gallery," Mr. Blankenship admonished. "I'll overlook this breach, Mrs. Tooley, given your grieved state, but this is your first and last warning. And that goes for everybody here." He swept his gaze over the crowd. "Now, Mr. Dengington, answer the question."

Horace, having regained his composure, confirmed, "It's like she says. I buy flowers from her. Just like half the city, if they know what's what."

Mr. Blankenship nodded. "Continue."

"Well, like I said, I knew the boy right off and sent word to his grandma. In the meantime, I laid him out, figuring the constable would report the death and there'd be an examination.

"Almost an hour later, the magistrate, Lord Marlington, arrived with an Inspector Jonas Lloyddyn. They viewed the body, and the inspector determined it a suicide. He told me to bury the boy. Mrs. Tooley showed up round that time, saying her boy wouldn't never take his own life."

The crowd grumbled. Mrs. Tooley glared with hostility at the memory.

"Is it typical for the magistrate to show up for such things?" asked the juror with the waxed mustache.

Horace frowned and stroked his chin. "Well, I won't say it's typical, but it's not unheard of for Lord Marlington to interest himself in such cases. If there's a trial, he's sure to be involved."

"Did he agree with the inspector? About the suicide, that is," asked another juror.

"I weren't privy to their conversation, but they appeared in agreement."

"Can you tell us what more happened that night?" Mr. Blankenship put in.

He cut his eyes over at us. I tensed.

"Nothing more happened that night. Next day, I heard Mrs. Tooley had taken her complaint straight to the magistrate, and he'd given in and ordered an inquest."

I relaxed. It looked like between Mrs. Tooley and Horace Dengington, we were not going to figure into this story.

Next up was old Dr. Winslow. I glanced at Grandfather again.

He winked at me. Dr. Winslow and he were friends. I suspected there had been some consultation between them.

Sure enough, the old man reported on Teddy's injuries, pointing out the bruising. "Finally," he concluded in his high-pitched, nasal voice, "I noted an injection site between the left big toe and the second toe. There were no other needle marks on the body."

"What did you make of his wounds?" asked Mr. Needer.

"It's hard to tell. He could have jumped and been bruised by a hard object in the water before drowning. On the other hand, someone could have hit him and pushed him into the river. Or, he could have sustained those injuries by some other means within a day or two of his drowning."

"What of the needle mark?" another juror asked, leaning forward in his chair.

Dr. Winslow shook his head. "Now that's even harder to figure out. He wasn't, by the looks of him, a habitual user of any injectable drug. And the needle mark being between the toes appears to me that it wasn't to be found."

"What is your summation?" the coroner asked.

"I wouldn't call it an open and shut case of suicide. That's for sure," the doctor concluded with a firm nod.

"A homicide?" the coroner prompted.

"Very possibly."

"Thank you, Dr. Winslow. You may leave."

The old man stood and shuffled towards us, giving Grandfather an almost imperceptible nod. Mrs. Tooley reached out, and he grasped her hand with a warm squeeze and moved on.

Mr. Blankenship cleared his throat and scrutinized the paper before him. "Inspector Lloyddyn," he read out, glancing around the room.

"Yes, I'm here," a breathless voice called from the back. The inspector strode up the aisle, the cape of his ulster coat flapping. His pale complexion shone with a ruddy glow from having just run up the stairs.

"Good," the coroner remarked with an air of self-importance. "I was told you might be late, so we put you last."

"Very much obliged," he returned and sat, removing his hat. He poised on the edge of the chair, a trim and energetic contrast to the other witnesses.

"Can you tell us what transpired on the night of October second, year of our Lord 1894, in regards to the death of one Theodore Edward Tooley, age fifteen years?"

"I can." He nodded. "I was informed by Constable Eaton of the untimely death of Mr. Tooley and left immediately for the mortuary, where I was met by Mr. Dengington. Who is the, ah, caretaker, I believe."

"And Lord Marlington? How come he was there?" a stout, prosperous-looking juror asked.

The inspector drew back as if just remembering the magistrate had also been present. "Ah, yes. Lord Marlington was at the station when Constable Eaton arrived, and the death being that of a child, he came with me."

"Inspector." Mr. Blankenship frowned in his direction. "We have just heard testimony from Dr. Winslow that puts the ruling of suicide in question. Can you tell us how you arrived at that conclusion?"

"Yeah, tell us," Mrs. Tooley demanded with a jerky nod. Others in the gallery growled in agreement, prompting the clerk to call them to order.

The spectators quieted, and Inspector Lloyddyn explained, "Well, the decision was made based on a combination of factors. The absence of injury—"

"But there were injury to my poor boy," Mrs. Tooley shouted.

"Mrs. Tooley, I warned you . . ." Mr. Blankenship began.

The inspector held up his hand in a conciliatory gesture. "No, no, I understand her anger. No need to remove her." He turned his kind gaze on Mrs. Tooley. "You must realize we take many people out of the river. We don't have the resources to investigate every death. It has been my experience that most cases of deliberate murder exhibit serious injury, like a blow to the head or strangulation. In the absence of such clear evidence of violence, it is almost impossible to make a case."

"What about the needle mark?" someone yelled from the crowd.

"I didn't examine the body that closely and saw no needle mark."

More grumbles and protests.

"Listen to me." He raised his voice over the rumblings. "Even the needle mark proves nothing. How can we know whether he or someone else put it there, or even what substance was injected?"

Mrs. Tooley bowed her head. Tears streamed down her cheeks, her face drained of anger, leaving only grief.

The crowd took its cue from her, and their complaints receded just as a familiar voice piped up, clear and strong, "Here, now. How do we know he weren't killed by the Grey Man? Him who's been stealin' and murderin' kids all 'round the city."

Chapter Twenty-Six

Shocked, I turned in time to see Danny's ragged back disappear down the stairs. Mumbled questions bubbled up from the crowd.

"Grey Man?"

"What were he sayin' about killin' kids?"

"Quiet, quiet," the clerk shouted.

Inspector Lloyddyn stood and swept the room with intense, focused eyes. "Who said that? Where'd he go?"

Mrs. Tooley grasped my arm. "That were Danny," she rasped in my ear.

I nodded. "Yes, but he ran out."

"Do you know what he meant 'bout this Grey Man killin' our Teddy?"

I shook my head and cut my eyes away only to encounter the inquisitive gaze of Inspector Lloyddyn.

"Order," the clerk shouted again. The audience quieted and was silent.

The coroner cleared his throat. "I am ready to render a decision."

Mrs. Tooley straightened and clasped her hands in front of her. The crowd drew in a collective breath and held it.

"While I understand and sympathize with the restrictions under which our police operate, I cannot ignore evidence of evildoing. I find enough to question the conclusion of suicide and rule Theodore Edward Tooley's death suspicious."

Mrs. Tooley bowed her head, and the crowd released its pent-up breath. In an unusual move, Mr. Blankenship addressed her directly. "Mrs. Tooley, I agree with the inspector that the likelihood of discovering what happened to your grandson, and by whose hand, is low. I can't imagine that my ruling gives you much solace, but I hope you will find some in the coming days."

She choked out a grateful, "Thank you."

The inquest ended. I jumped up to go in search of Danny when a strong hand gripped my shoulder.

"Mr. Cheng, if I recall correctly," Inspector Lloyddyn pronounced. "How is your head?"

"Much better," I replied. We stood grouped together within the milling crowd. "This is my mother and grandfather. Mrs. Tooley, you know."

"Yes." He nodded. "Can any of you tell me who disrupted the inquest?"

Mrs. Tooley pulled her shawl tighter and refused to meet his gaze. "Don't rightly know. Some local boy, I imagine."

He turned to me, eyebrows raised in question.

"Um," I hesitated, wanting to be truthful, but not wanting to give Danny up.

"You'll have to excuse my son," Mother interrupted, flashing her beautiful smile. "We must be going. We have a business to run."

He stood back, all solicitude. "Certainly, I didn't mean to detain you."

I shrugged his hand from my shoulder and stopped myself from smirking. My mother had a stupefying effect on most men, the inspector apparently among them.

Out on the street, she waved me away and told me to run on and find my friend. The sky had lightened, but my mind remained clouded. Danny's puzzling outburst and her unexpected reference to the Grey Man filled me with urgency.

I stood, indecisive, with no idea where to begin looking for her. Fortunately, I didn't have to.

"Hiya." Danny popped out of the doorway of a haberdasher's shop where she had clearly been lying in wait to ambush me.

I cast a quick, worried glance around the street to make sure no one was watching and grasped her arm, steering her into the nearest alleyway. "What do you know of the Grey Man?"

She wiggled out of my grip. "What do you?" she shot back.

"Who says I know anything?"

Danny rolled her eyes. "You must think I'm stupid. It's clear as day you've heard of 'em."

"You're right," I admitted. "I have. How do you know of him, and why do you think he's killing children?"

"I tried to tell you before everything got going in there, but you were *too* important—"

"Alright, I'm sorry. Next time I'll drop everything at the crook of your finger." I crossed my arms. "Now tell me what you know."

Mischievous dimples quivered on her cheeks. "That's just it. I don't know nothin'."

I straightened. "Explain."

"Like I said, I don't know nothin' about this Grey Man. I come here with Sybil and some other folk from the market to comfort Mrs. Tooley in her time of grief and strife . . ." Danny was winding herself up into a John Harold Gaines length novel.

"Just get on with it," I snapped, growing impatient with her antics.

She pulled an indignant face. "Maybe I won't tell you."

I shoved my hands in my pockets and made to leave. "Fine, have it your way."

"No, no, don't go. I'm sorry." Her expression changed in an instant from indignant to contrite. "It ain't every day I know somethin' you don't."

I relented. "Sure. I get it. Just tell me."

She shrugged. "It's what the man paid me to say."

"What man?"

Danny shook her head. "Don't know his name. Never seen him before."

"What did he look like?"

She frowned. "Ordinary, mostly. He was dark with a bushy, black beard and short hair."

"Tall?"

"Not tall, not short, just average. He wore," she rushed on before I could ask, "a heavy black coat, all buttoned up, and an old bowler up top."

My mind went to the man in the mask. The thin India rubber could not hide a bushy beard, but then, maybe the beard was fake.

I conjured up an image of the crowd at the inquest. "I don't remember seeing a man of that description in the room," I remarked almost to myself.

"The man weren't *in* the room," Danny replied. "He talked to me outside the pub before. A group of us waited around to go in until after the jury was picked."

I wiped nervous sweat from my forehead with the sleeve of my jacket. "Here's the thing, Danny. That man . . . you ever see him again, run as fast as you can in the other direction."

"What're you worried about?"

I answered her question with one of my own. "Why do you think he wanted you to say that?"

She scrunched up her face as if I were stupid. "A lark, don't ya know."

"You're lying. You wouldn't yell those things out of respect for Mrs. Tooley unless you believed it would help her cause."

A suspicious wetness appeared around her eyes. She dashed the tears away with an angry hand.

"They think we're worthless, less than rubbish." She glared at me. "Now everyone will be talking about the Grey Man and dead kids, and that inspector will have to find who killed Teddy just to shut everyone up."

"And the man?"

"Don't know why he wanted me to say those things, just suited my purpose. He paid me too."

A drop of rain plopped on my hand. I looked up. Dark clouds threatened another downpour.

"Now that you're rich, you can buy me some bread pudding and we can get out of this rain."

She hooted. "Not likely I'm spending my blunt on you."

A rush of moisture-laden air coursed through the alleyway. I shivered and turned up my collar against the penetrating cold. The world around us glowed in a strange, washed-out orange light. The rain had pulled grime from the air and left it dripping down walls and spotting the pavement. For once, the breeze tasted fresh and clean.

"Come on then, my treat. We need to get inside before the next deluge, and I have a favor to ask."

Chapter Twenty-Seven

"This is a bad idea." Danny's voice floated out from behind a garish yellow silken screen. "My mother thinks I attend Mrs. Stapleton's parlour for lessons on comportment. She'd lock me up and throw away the key if she knew what I really did."

I leaned against the doorframe of the wardrobe room in the basement of the Theatre Royal. The dim lighting and headless dresser mannequin cast a creepy pall over the place.

Danny stepped out from behind the screen and adjusted the blue sash cinched around her waist. She pulled on a matching blue pleated coat. I smiled.

The girl shook her finger at me. "If you laugh . . ."

"Not me," I protested, swallowing a chuckle. "Your mother might be mollified if you try that street urchin talk on her. Impress her with your acting abilities."

Danny snorted. "My mum's set on seeing me 'elevated' into a respectable marriage." She frowned, and sadness flickered in her eyes. "I don't want to be married just to be married, but I don't want her life either."

"You wouldn't want the theater for a career?"

"It's not the theater, it's the"—she cleared her throat—"demands on Mother's time by her admirers."

Stupidly, I puzzled over this for a second before realizing what she was getting at. "I say—" I began.

"You don't have to say anything. It is what it is." She ran a finger between the high lace collar and her neck. "I don't know how much longer I can stay on the streets anyway. Mother insists on fitting me with a corset, and that is next to impossible to get into and out of without help."

I blushed at the mention of women's undergarments and changed the subject. "How come Mrs. Stapleton hasn't reported your absences?"

A sly smile spread across her face. "She would in a heartbeat if she could, but I got something on her."

Danny walked out the door and turned down the hall towards the exit. I followed as we twisted our way through the bowels of the theatre.

Outside, she set a course for home, and I asked, "Are you going to keep me in suspense? What have you got on her?"

The rain had stopped, and fluffy, white clouds floated with lazy majesty through the sky. A rare sparkling sun shone down on us and warmed the crisp autumn air.

She shook her head. "The whole point of extortion is that I'm the only one with the information. If I tell you, I don't have control over it anymore."

"Who would I tell?" I demanded, indignant at her lack of trust.

"Well, that's the thing. I don't know and neither do you. We never know until we do."

She sounded like a crime boss. The word "extortion" dropped with alarming ease from the mouth of this beribboned twelve-year-old girl. I studied her with some misgiving. Her clear-sighted assessment on how to maintain power through the control and manipulation of information gave me pause.

We walked the rest of the way in silence, finally turning down a small street of respectable residences just off the Piazza. Danny stopped at a narrow, nondescript cream brick house.

"Here we are," she announced. "If this is to work, you must let me do the talking." As she reached for the knob, the door burst opened upon a picture of extravagant perfection.

"Darling girl," Madame Honoria de Silva exclaimed at the sight of her daughter. "Excellent timing, my dear. That such acclaim is mine!"

I had seen Madame de Silva's masterful acting on two occasions. But watching such a presence on the stage, and at a distance, does not prepare one for the experience up close.

Every inch of her was an exaggeration of the female form. Thick, impossibly long lashes surrounded huge, melting brown eyes. Her pale skin glowed. Only a red rosebud mouth indicated that blood coursed through her veins. A mass of black curls piled on top of her head and cascaded about her shoulders in charming disarray.

Her figure, encased in a day dress of deep gold with large mutton sleeves, displayed a waist so small as to defy the need for breath. She stood poised on the threshold, her arms outstretched in loving appeal.

"Sweetheart, come, kiss me," she begged in a throaty stage whisper. "Your mother has been summoned by the queen." Her laugh trilled out over the street. "Yes, an audience with the queen. That such honor is mine." She ended with her hands humbly clasped to her breast, eyes modestly downcast.

An aged butler appeared over her shoulder and cleared his throat, his face impassive. "Madame, would it please Miss Daniela and her, um, companion to enter?"

She drew back with a little intake of breath, as if noticing me for the first time. "A friend?" Her faint Castilian lisp, as if worn away by years of living in England, gave no hint of her Cockney origins.

Danny startled me by clasping my forearm in a frenzied grip.

"Mother." Her voice throbbed with pain. "I was set upon by rough boys who pulled my hair and tried to steal the purse from my pocket."

Even as Madame de Silva reared back in melodramatic dismay, her narrowed, calculating gaze fastened upon me. I was not supposed to be part of her little show.

In her haste to let the whole street know of the queen's notice, she had allowed us an opening. Instead of playing our little scene in the parlour as planned, we had the good fortune of an audience, no doubt peering out from behind curtains or through barely cracked doors. Madame de Silva was given little choice but to follow through with the act.

"And this boy saved me," Danny choked the words out on a sob. Tears streamed down her cheeks.

"Oh, my darling, how horrible." Madame de Silva rushed forward and clasped Danny in a tight embrace.

"It was, Mother. It was." The girl cried into her shoulder. She pulled away and drew in a shaky breath. "This boy chased them away and saved me."

I looked on in amazement. Mother and daughter locked in a dramatic competition, each trying to outdo the other in tears and exclamations of shock.

"Ahem." The butler stood unfazed by the overwrought exhibition. "Annette has put the tea tray in the drawing room, madame."

She straightened with indignation. "Oh, the English, tea, tea, tea. Always tea as the answer to everything, even such distressing news." She sniffed. "But if we must, we must. Come, Mr. . . . ?" She tilted her head to one side. Her delicate frozen smile revealed neat, white teeth.

"Cheng, madame. Mr. Kuo Cheng."

She patted her curls. "How interesting, an Oriental. Well, do come in, Mr. Cheng. We must thank you properly for aiding Daniela in her time of need."

I followed the ladies through the door. Danny hung back.

"A lucky break," she whispered in my ear. "She's stuck now. Once Mother starts a performance, she gives it her all."

Down the hallway, framed playbills and posters of Madame de Silva's greatest triumphs hung on the walls. Portraits and photographs of the actress in her many famous roles met us upon entering the parlour.

An old, upright piano stood in jarring contrast to the sophisticated upholstered furniture and elaborate wallpaper. Painted black and carved with rosettes, twisting vines, and bunches of grapes, the instrument was made even more extraordinary by the two small candelabras extending out from the upright casing.

"I see you're admiring my piano."

"Yes," I replied. "It looks like something out of a saloon in the American West."

She smiled. "It is one such piano. Mr. Cody Driscoll, a famous sheriff in the Texas town of Hazard Springs, gave it to me."

"You've been to America?"

She raised her eyebrows, as if surprised by the fact I didn't know every detail of her famous life. "Yes. I made a tour of that country many years ago and even found my way to the great American West." She smiled with modest charm. "I was an oddity, if you will. A respectable woman performer was not common in those parts, but I was a great success. Though at times I felt unsafe in such rough company, I was sorry to part with the friends I made."

"I think many would be interested in hearing that tale," I said sincerely, being myself captivated with the American West. "Your adventures would make fascinating reading."

Madame de Silva gestured me to a seat next to Danny on the sofa. "Do you think so?" She sank with infinite grace into an armchair and poured the tea. "Well, it is something to consider. Milk and sugar?"

"Neither, thank you."

"How austere. *I*, on the other hand, am a creature of comfort and enjoy my milk and sugar."

I glanced at Danny over the rim of my teacup. She rolled her eyes.

"I'm sure you have many interesting stories to tell of your life and the, ah . . ." I nudged Danny for some help. She was supposed to do all the talking.

"Er, yes." She started up. "Mother has many famous friends, not only other actors but *writers* and politicians too."

"Did you know John Harold Gaines?" I asked, adding, "He's one of my favorite authors," as an explanation for my interest.

She sighed. "I knew him in passing, and his tiresome little wife as well."

"You knew Mary Gaines?"

"No, not the first wife, the second one, Nora Davies. We came up together in the theater. Timorous, affected little thing she was, but butter wouldn't melt in her mouth."

"What do you mean, Mother?"

Madame de Silva placed a hand to her breast. "Oh, one shouldn't gossip, and certainly not about the dead."

"It's not gossip if it's true," Danny wheedled. "I want to hear it."

"Very well, there really isn't much to say," Madame de Silva conceded. "Little Nora wasn't serious about her craft, very much on the lookout for a rich husband. And she snagged one. Not as rich as she'd hoped for, but certainly wealthy, and famous to boot."

She frowned. "It is not the most suitable story for young ears, but Mr. Gaines was married at the time when he and Nora, well, when they became acquainted."

I feigned an appropriately shocked expression.

"Scandalized you should be," Madame de Silva insisted. "The whole affair was quite appalling. I felt great pity for his poor wife, bundled away like a useless piece of baggage."

She sipped her tea and stared off into space as if silently debating with herself, finally saying, "You know, little Nora wasn't quite sure of him until the very end when he married her. She always suspected another woman, though there was never a whisper of anyone else."

Chapter Twenty-Eight

Soon after this startling revelation, Madame de Silva ended our conversation. She bade me goodbye and hoped, with perfectly fake sincerity, to see me again.

At the door, I thanked Danny, but she dismissed my gratitude with a shake of her head. "Mother didn't mention anything about a locket or if Nora even wore one."

I had told her a little about the investigation, and she now appeared greatly vested in the outcome. I shrugged.

"Your mother remembering such a minor detail from so long ago was always unlikely. But the possibility of yet another woman is valuable information," I assured her.

"What can you do with old gossip?" she asked.

Her shoulders slumped, and she looked strangely aged and weary for a child. How exhausting it must be to live with such a mother, constantly demanding drama and adoration.

"Maybe nothing," I observed, and added in an attempt to cheer her up, "You should come by our apothecary . . . meet my mother and grandfather. Teddy used to visit. We'd eat butterscotch and help sort the herbs and medicines in the storeroom. Grandfather knows everything about them."

A calculating gleam lit up her eyes. "Aye, I'd sure like to learn about 'em." I left the house with the uneasy feeling that a criminal genius resided in the body of a twelve-year-old girl.

With darkness approaching, I struck out for home and caught the train to Aldgate East. Instead of my usual habit of taking a tram almost to my doorstep, I stretched my legs and headed for the London Docks.

I retraced Constable Eaton's path that fateful night Teddy's body washed ashore. Like him, I skirted Wapping Basin and walked past St. John's church.

Taverns and pubs lined the street, and the raucous sound of drunken men drifted out from their doors. Fog rolled in off the water and curled its way onto land, extinguishing light as it went.

I found the stairway and went down, cautious with my footing on the slippery surface. The low tide exposed a deserted, pebble-strewn beach.

The stench at this level knocked me back a step or two. I pulled out my handkerchief and placed it over my nose and mouth. The image of Teddy meeting his end in such a dark and lonely place opened a deep pit of sadness in my stomach.

Rocks crunched under my feet as I walked to the rickety wooden pier jutting out into the river. A strange compulsion led me along beneath the length of dock that stood out from the low tide. Looking for what, I knew not.

Until I spied it: a grotesque, pinkish substance caught on a nail. I knew before my fingers pulled it from its perch that I beheld a piece of India rubber.

I recoiled at the slimy material in my hand but kept a firm grip. I didn't want to drop the stuff to be swallowed up by the incoming tide.

My brain raced with the implications of this discovery. Had Teddy ripped this from his killer's face? Had he held it in his hand, stiff with rigor, until his muscles released, bringing him and evidence of his murderer to rest here?

I had no answers, but one conclusion grew until it overshadowed all others: The Grey Man had killed Teddy, just as Danny's mysterious, bearded stranger had suggested.

I shoved the piece of rubber into my pocket. This dank and fetid place depressed me, haunted as it was by the ghost of my poor friend. I turned my back on the murky, rushing waters and looked skyward.

My gaze followed a shadow as it swooped from the eaves of a nearby pub. The motion turned my head a fraction, and the blurred fist of the redheaded man dealt my face a glancing blow.

I staggered back and fell to the ground. He landed a vicious kick against my ribs.

Breathless, I scrambled back and pelted him with fistfuls of pebbles. He cursed and lunged for me. Rough hands grabbed the front of my jacket and jerked me up.

"Filthy little spy, I've got you at last." He pressed his face so close to mine the gin on his breath made me gag.

He shook me. "Where's the book?"

I twisted from his grasp and ran for the street. "Help," I yelled to a group of three men who staggered out from a nearby building. "Help me."

The redheaded man yanked me back and threw me onto the rocky beach. I struggled to keep my balance.

"Get away with you, man," shouted a well-known voice. "Get away."

My tutor descended the stairs. He stood, his thin chest laid bare by an open jacket and unbuttoned shirt. His companions had crumpled, rendered useless, against the building behind him.

The redheaded man jeered as he got the measure of my savior. "Are you a man or a scarecrow?"

Lord Brudeford swayed on the uneven ground. I groaned. He was not in the vicinity of Limehouse to admire its architecture.

"Face me, you brigand, and find out," he declared in a slurred, defiant voice. He braced his feet and leveled his fists.

My hopes rose at his confident posture, only to be dashed as my attacker tackled him to the ground with ease. They thrashed around, Lord Brudeford on the receiving end of punch after punch.

I threw myself into the fray, jumping on the villain's back and grabbing handfuls of dirty, lank red hair. He released my tutor and rolled over, crushing me beneath him.

Lord Brudeford leapt to his feet. His ragged breath rattled in his lungs. He landed two kicks to the man's ribs and forced him off me.

My body ached, every inch of me plastered against the rocks. Lord Brudeford's coughing gasps told me he had little fight left in him.

It would all be over once the redheaded man regained his bearings. I pushed up onto my knees and closed my eyes, gathering myself for one last offensive effort.

"You move and I kill you."

My eyes flew open, and I squinted into the darkness. The bare outline of a man held a knife to my attacker's throat.

"Who?" I called out, certain I already knew the answer.

"It is I, Mr. Wei," he confirmed. "Are you hurt?"

"I believe so."

"Kuo? Is that you, my boy?" Lord Brudeford stumbled over and knelt beside me. "Good God! What happenstance is this?"

"A lucky one," I answered. "Without you, I would be dead."

His cynical laughter rang out over the desolate beach. "Ho, lad, I only delayed it, almost adding my own demise to yours. It is this man"—he nodded at Mr. Wei, who still held a knife to the redheaded man's throat—"who is our rescuer. Am I to assume you know each other?"

I grimaced with pain as he helped me to my feet. "Yes. Mr. Wei, our neighbor, Lord Brudeford." I made the introduction through gritted teeth.

"Well, my man," he called over to our champion. "You will have to teach me how to materialize out of thin air. That was quite the trick."

"It is not a trick but a skill," came his quiet reply. He pressed the knife harder against the redheaded man's throat and said in the same even tone, "Who do you work for, and what do they want with this boy?"

"You're crazy if you think they tell me what's what." He laughed. "And you might as well cut my gullet right now, cuz I'm a dead man if they find out I gave 'em up."

The silence stretched to near breaking, and I feared Mr. Wei intended to slit the man's throat right in front of our eyes. He dropped his hand and stepped back.

"This boy is under my protection. If you harm him, I will kill you." Mr. Wei tapped a finger on his forehead. "I have your face in here. You will never see me coming."

The man turned and ran with swift, even strides over the rocks. His back tensed as if expecting to feel the sharp point of a blade sinking into his flesh.

Mr. Wei placed his hand on my shoulder. "Any broken bones?"

I shook my head. "Cuts and bruises are all."

"And you?" He addressed Lord Brudeford.

"The same, although I can add bruised pride to my list of injuries."

Mr. Wei nodded, unmoved by his self-deprecating humor. "It is hard to fight effectively in an opium fog. Your friends?" He gestured to the two men slumped against the building.

Lord Brudeford cast him a chastened look. "I have no idea who they are." He groaned and touched one injured cheek. "Nothing like getting the 'opium fog' punched out of you."

Mr. Wei grasped my elbow. "I must get you both to the apothecary."

"No," I objected. "That would only upset Mother. Put me in a cab to the Gaines house, fourteen Gower Street. Cook can dress my wounds, and my mother won't be the wiser."

"I do not think she would approve of such a plan." He crossed his arms and regarded me with stern eyes.

I returned his steady gaze. At least now I knew why Mother had met him under cover of darkness. I hoped she had not paid too high a price.

"Let me worry about my mother," I declared, hands balled into fists at my sides. "She is of no concern to you."

He did not rise to my angry words. "I make no claim to your mother. I only express my opinion. If you wish to keep this from her, I will not interfere. But Lord Brudeford, at least, must accompany you."

My tutor, for his part, had watched our exchange with curiosity. "By all means," he agreed with his usual lazy good humor. "I could use some patching up myself by . . . um, Cook, is it?"

Mr. Wei nodded, satisfied, and we walked—me leaning heavily on his arm—back to the street. He propped me up while Lord Brudeford stepped off the curb to hail a cab.

I took advantage of our moment of privacy to say, "You haven't asked why I was at the waterman stairs or any questions at all."

"I can guess rightly enough. That's your business. Mine is to make sure you come to no harm." Mr. Wei flashed his oddly warm and comforting smile. "A task you are not making easy."

I contemplated my feet, silently debating whether to pose my question. Need won out over caution.

"In your line of, ah, work, have you ever heard of the Grey Man?" If there really were a masked killer stalking the children of London, Mr. Wei would surely know of it.

He shook his head. "I know of no such person."

Lord Brudeford joined us on the pavement, and the hackney swung to a stop beside us. I was recovered enough to climb into the cab on my own.

I turned back to belatedly thank Mr. Wei for our rescue but found myself addressing only empty air.

"Bloody amazing," Lord Brudeford mumbled under his breath.

Chapter Twenty-Nine

"This is the second time in as many days I've had to put you to rights," Cook groused, placing a compress against my bruised ribs.

I sucked in my breath, waiting for the pain of the hot material against my tender skin to subside. "Thank you, Cook," I replied when able to speak, "but I did not invite this attack."

She wrapped a length of cotton around my middle to hold the compress in place. Nellie stood at the stove, boiling water and filling cheesecloth with a concoction of bran and herbs.

"And with a gentleman in tow, and him injured as well," Cook continued, eyeing Lord Brudeford with reticence.

Even in his bedraggled state (he, too, sported an assortment of bandages and poultices applied to various parts of his body), my tutor was every inch the great man. He put on no airs or affectations, but aristocrats rarely do with their inferiors. They seek only to impress their own kind.

Unlike Margaret, whose wealthy family lacked noble blood, Lord Brudeford lounged back in the wooden chair, completely at home. He did not feel out of place, because every place was his domain.

"I do apologize, madam . . . Lord Brudeford, at your service," he cajoled with a charming smile and stood to make her a slight bow. "Such an imposition on your good nature. I heartily thank you for your assistance."

She blushed and replied without looking at him straight on, "And right you was, my lord, in coming here. I'm not meaning to chide you for doing so."

Nellie put a tea tray on the table, her face drawn. She turned back to the stove.

"What is it, Nellie? You haven't once scolded me," I joked in hopes of setting her at ease.

She looked over her shoulder with a guilty expression. "You know how when you come in and asked us not to tell Miss Char—"

"You didn't," I exclaimed.

She cast her gaze downward. "I sent a message around to Miss Margaret's."

"Now you've done it," I grumbled.

Nellie's head snapped up, and she straightened her shoulders, a spark of defiance in her eyes. "It's just if Miss Charlotte was to find out you'd been here and us not saying a word . . . well, it wouldn't be right, her being our employer and all. We owe her our loyalty more than we do you."

I acknowledged her point with a graceless nod, but the sound of footsteps flying down the staircase prevented me from saying more. The door burst open upon Charlotte, breathless and with golden curls cascading down her back. She wore, to my surprise, the Little Lord Fauntleroy outfit I had last seen on Miss Florence Bagby.

"Goodness," Charlotte exclaimed, coming to a stop just over the threshold. She blushed and averted her eyes.

I fought hard to suppress my own blush, seated, as I was, shirtless at the kitchen table. Lord Brudeford, in the same state of undress, laughed. I scowled at him.

"Now, Charlotte, we mustn't be squeamish. When it comes to nursing, we should be prepared to assist." Margaret swept in behind the girl, magnificent in the dark green riding habit. "How can we help, Cook?"

I cast a sideways glance at my tutor and gloated. He shifted in his chair, discomfited by a beautiful, well-bred lady finding him in such disarray.

All semblance of casual good cheer fell away, and he pokered up. Lord Brudeford stood and reached for his shirt. He pulled it on with some difficulty and said, "Please excuse our rather disreputable appear—"

"You needn't apologize." Margaret assured him. "The note said you were set upon by a ruffian."

"Yes," I answered, grimacing as I shrugged into my own shirt. "I was examining the site where a friend died, and the man attacked me. Lord Brudeford came to my rescue." He and I had agreed not to mention Mr. Wei.

I had kept to myself the puzzling demand by the redheaded man for a book, I knew not what. But now Charlotte was here, I was eager to have a moment alone to tell her all.

"Lord Clive Brudeford?" Margaret regarded my companion. Her eyes widened in recognition. "I know your sister, Anne. I'm Margaret Scott." She stuck out her hand. "You won't remember me, just another schoolgirl scampering around."

He took her hand in a brief clasp, the armor of cynicism now firmly back in place. "I barely remember my own sister, if truth be told, Miss Scott."

"A pity," Margaret retorted, angered by his dismissive reply. "She always speaks of you with fondness."

"Yes. My absence has endeared me greatly to my family."

Margaret lifted her chin and opened her mouth to counter.

"You refer to your friend Teddy?" Charlotte interjected, casting a glance between the two tense adults. "I read a brief report of the inquest in the evening paper."

Grateful for the diversion, I answered, "Yes, indeed, a sad day for all of us."

"Here, now, Miss Margaret." Cook held out a small round tin. "If you'll just hold this for me while I put some ointment on those cuts to Lord Brudeford's face."

"Oh, no, Cook, quite unnecessary—" he began.

"Nonsense," Margaret declared, taking the tin. "What's a little salve, Lord Brudeford? Sit down. It won't hurt."

I didn't hear his retort, having pulled Charlotte unseen out into the hallway. "I must speak with you."

"Yes?"

In a rushed monologue, I told her about the inquest, the bearded man, and Danny's shouted accusations. I added my conversation with Madame de Silva and the gossip regarding her grandfather's involvement with yet another woman.

"Vile man," Charlotte hissed.

I finished with my discovery of the India rubber at the dock, the identity of my attacker, and his puzzling demand to know the whereabouts of a book.

She glared at me. "How *could* you?"

I started back. "What?"

"How could you have all those adventures without me?" She planted her hands on her hips.

"Well, that's gratitude for you," I declared, angry. "I didn't know Danny would disrupt the inquest. And I can tell you, getting almost beaten to death isn't some adventure."

Charlotte paled. I brought myself up short with the realization that my friend was putting on a brave face. If anyone knew the terror of a violent attack, it was she.

"I say, I'd much rather you were there," I told her. "Not to be hurt or anything . . . but, um, everything just happened. And," I added, coaxing her into a better mood, "you and I are the only ones who know about the India rubber and the connection between your aunt's murder and Teddy's."

Charlotte nodded, somewhat mollified. "But who is this bearded man your friend spoke with? How is he involved, and why pay to disrupt the inquest?"

I stared off into space. My pulse leapt with a sudden realization. "Because you took the note, so no one knows about the Grey Man."

A dizzying wave of nausea swept over me. I pressed a hand against the wall to steady myself. Charlotte caught me by the arm. "You need to sit."

"I'm fine, just a reaction from the fight." I straightened and flashed a shaky smile, adding in a rush, "Don't you see. You took the note. It was meant to be found by the police. Until today, no one but us had ever heard of the Grey Man. Can you imagine the newspapers if they got hold of a message from the murderer? He *wants* people to know about him. He wants attention for his crimes."

"That is truly insane," Charlotte whispered, adding, "Your friend's outburst at the inquest didn't even make mention in the paper. So, he still has not gotten the attention he seeks."

Raised voices floated out from the kitchen. Lord Brudeford had no doubt said something outrageous, creating a babble of recriminations from the women trying to minister to his wounds.

Charlotte squared her shoulders. "Let's go over everything we know."

"A methodical examination of the facts," I agreed and held up a finger. "We know you received a poem on your sixteenth birthday that was written by your grandmother."

"We know it was written the year she died while imprisoned at the asylum in Wembley," Charlotte added.

"We know the locket was not your grandmother's but was likely ordered by your grandfather for someone else." I held up three fingers.

"We know . . ." Charlotte hesitated. "Well, we know someone

wants me dead and killed Aunt Sadie and maybe even your friend, Teddy."

"He calls himself the Grey Man and wears a mask of India rubber." I held up five fingers. "We will assume, for now, he is also the one who sent you the poem and locket." Up went a sixth finger.

"The killer knows we are investigating?" Charlotte put in, uncertain.

"Sure, I'll add it." I held up a seventh finger.

She leaned against the wall, deflated. "Is that it?"

I laughed. "Maybe we should list all we *don't* know."

Her eyes lit up. "Exactly, we need to write it all down." Charlotte grabbed my hand and pulled me further down the hallway.

Only one in every two sconces burned low and cast flickering shadows across the walls. Charlotte pushed open the door of the housekeeper's office.

The room, unused in the time since Mrs. Marshton's disappearance, lay still and silent. A chill met us as we stepped inside. Charlotte struck a match and lit the lamp sitting on the desk. She took from the drawer some paper and a pencil.

We sat on the sofa in front of the barren fireplace. Charlotte licked the pencil tip.

"Now, what *don't* we know?"

"We don't know why the Grey Man wants to kill you or why he killed your aunt and Teddy. We don't know why he sent you the poem and locket or why he left threatening messages in the mouth of a dead woman."

She nodded, writing. "In short, why everything?"

"And who? We don't know who he is." I flexed my fingers, grown cold in the airless room.

Charlotte put down the pencil and sat back. "This isn't helping."

I rubbed my hands together and picked up the pencil. "I believe we must focus on *who* the killer is, and from that, we will learn why."

She shrugged. "Sure, but he could be anybody."

"No, not just anybody. This all connects to your family. Firstly, the poem." I wrote "poem" next to the number one. "It's important to the killer. It means something. And now we know your grandmother wrote it."

"Do you think the meaning will tell us who the killer is?"

"Possibly."

She took the pencil from me and wrote the number two and "locket" next to it. "We need to find out whose locket it was."

"Therefore, nothing has changed," I concluded. "We continue to investigate the poem and the locket."

Charlotte frowned at the paper. She drew a line down the middle of the page and wrote on the right-hand side, "Redheaded man," and "Teddy."

"I never met your friend, and as far as I know, he had no connection to my family," she explained. "And the redheaded man, who is he? Does he work for the Grey Man? And if not, then who? Neither the redheaded man nor Teddy fit with our theory about my family."

She threw the pencil down in frustration. "And now a mystery book?"

"Charlotte." Margaret's voice preceded her down the hallway.

Charlotte shoved the list into the pocket of her velvet knee breeches. We stood as Margaret appeared, breathless, at the doorway.

"What are you two doing in here? Oh, never mind. Inspector Lloyddyn has arrived." She pulled in a deep breath. "They've found the housekeeper, Mrs. Marshton, dead in a Limehouse opium den."

Chapter Thirty

Charlotte's hand flew to her mouth. "Oh, no."

I cast a quick look around. If the housekeeper was dead, then the inspector would want to search this room.

"Stall him," I instructed Margaret.

"What? Who?"

"Inspector Lloyddyn . . . stall him." I ran my hands behind the cushions of the sofa, looking for a clue, anything. "Tell him we're getting some . . . something of Charlotte's. This will only take a moment or two."

"Why—?"

"Do it, please," Charlotte pleaded.

"Oh, very well, I'll do what I can." Margaret turned in a swirl of heavy green silk and flounced off.

"We need to search the room," I told Charlotte. "You take the desk. I'll finish the sofa and do the side tables."

"What're we looking for?" she asked, opening drawers and scrabbling through papers.

"I'm not sure."

My hurried search under the sofa cushions and through the side tables yielded nothing but an old thimble. "Any luck?"

"Only this." Charlotte held up a coin, but not of any denomination I could determine.

She dropped the object into my palm. Made of brass, a flower in open bloom was etched on one side.

"Is it a camellia?" I asked.

Charlotte peered down at the coin, bringing our heads close together. "It certainly looks like one, but it could be any such flower, like a gardenia."

I flipped the coin over. The simple outline of a compass encircled two capital letters.

"EX?" I puzzled.

"Charlotte," Margaret called down the hallway.

I pocketed the coin, and we headed out the door. We entered the kitchen upon a tense scene.

Inspector Lloyddyn stood with his back to the door and commanded a sweeping view of the room and its occupants. Constable Farley, with his droopy mustache and wiry dark brows, stood beside him, an opened notebook and a pencil in his hands.

Lord Brudeford feigned nonchalance, but the rhythmic drumming of his fingers on the tabletop signaled his irritation. Both Margaret and Nellie stood stiffly on opposite sides of the kitchen, like prompters in the wings of a stage ready to cue us should we forget our lines.

Cook, with the end of her apron in one hand, wiped at her red, sweaty face and exclaimed, "Oh, dear me, Miss Charlotte, have you ever known such a wretched household. Mrs. Marshton is dead."

Charlotte gave her arm a comforting pat. "Margaret told us. An opium den in Limehouse, I believe. Is that so, Inspector?"

The inspector glanced from Charlotte to me and back again before answering, "Yes. I came to tell you that your housekeeper was discovered dead from an overdose in an opium den run by a woman named Rose Huang. Do you know her, Mr. Cheng?" He turned his penetrating gaze on me.

"I certainly know *of* her," I replied readily enough. "There would be few in Limehouse who did not."

"And you, Lord Brudeford?"

My tutor stood and drew himself up to his full, impressive height. He stared down his nose at the lowly inspector.

Inspector Lloyddyn appeared unfazed. "Lord Brudeford?"

"I know the woman," he snapped.

"Where were you this evening?" The inspector pushed his coat back and thrust his hands into his pockets.

"I don't know that it's any business of yours, but I can assure you I was not at Madame Huang's establishment."

The inspector narrowed his eyes. "You two have been in something of a scuffle."

"I was set upon by a, um, ruffian down at the waterman stairs," I explained.

Inspector Lloyddyn frowned. "The one where Mr. Tooley was pulled from the river?"

"Yes."

"Why were you there?"

The inspector was the last person I wanted to have any knowledge of our investigation. He would surely seek to put an end to our endeavors.

"His grandmother asked me to lay some flowers at the pier. She didn't have the heart to go herself," I lied.

I was impressed with my confederates. No one batted an eyelash, not even Cook or Nellie.

He nodded. "I see. And was Lord Brudeford with you on this mission of kindness?"

"No, *Lloyddyn*." Lord Brudeford notably failed to address him by his title. "I was alerted to his plight by his cries for help and rushed to, ah, assist."

"So," the inspector replied, ignoring the slight, "you just happened to be in the area?"

"Indeed."

I could hardly believe the warm and open man in whose apartment I had lingered many a day over lessons both profound and trivial could say "indeed" with such snobbery. Again, Inspector Lloyddyn showed no annoyance. His pale face remained impassive.

"And the assailant? Did you get a good look at him?"

"It was dark," I explained. "I couldn't see his face. I assumed the same was true for him or he wouldn't have chosen such a poor mark."

He raised his eyebrows at Lord Brudeford. "And you?"

My tutor sat and rested his steepled fingers beneath his chin. "Like Kuo, I saw nothing that would help you identify the fellow. I took him for a common thief."

Inspector Lloyddyn turned to Charlotte. "I will need to see Mrs. Marshton's rooms and any documentation regarding her employment, letters of references, and so forth."

I cursed under my breath that I had not thought of such things. I would sure like to know for whom she had worked before her employment with Sadie Gaines.

"Of course, Inspector, you are welcomed to look through Mrs. Marshton's belongings." Charlotte smiled. "Though I don't know where my aunt kept her business correspondence. I will have to search her bedroom, as well as the sitting room and the parlour. If you return tomorrow, I can give you whatever I find."

Smart girl. I turned my face away to hide a smile.

"Very well. If someone will show me Mrs. Marshton's room, the constable and I will get cracking."

"Certainly, sir." Cook bustled over to the hallway. "This way, if you will."

With Constable Farley preceding him, Inspector Lloyddyn halted just inside the kitchen. "Begging your pardon, Miss Gaines, what did you retrieve from the house? You have nothing in your hands."

Not a twinge of apprehension troubled me so confident had I grown in Charlotte's abilities to manage almost anything. I was not disappointed.

"I was looking for a book." She clasped her hands together in front of her. "Sadly, I couldn't find it. I was sure I had left it in the sitting room, but it wasn't there."

"Hmm," he replied and followed the constable out.

"Insufferable bore," Lord Brudeford spat once the inspector had left.

"Insufferable indeed," Margaret exclaimed. "The way you treated the poor man was disgraceful, and him trying to solve a dreadful crime."

He poured himself a cup of tea and lounged back in his chair, a smug expression on his face. "The police don't deserve your respect. They were organized to protect the ruling classes, and their ranks are riddled with graft and corruption."

She sniffed. "Wait until you need assistance. You'll be singing a different tune."

"Not likely." He leaned forward with an intent expression. "Are you a campaigner for women's rights as is my sister?"

Margaret straightened her shoulders. "I am. What does that have to—?"

"Well, mark my words, Miss Scott, if at any time, your demands grow too strident, that lot"—he jabbed his thumb behind him towards the door—"will throw you and your similarly inclined associates in a jail cell without a second thought."

"I hardly—" she began.

"Margaret, can we please go home?" Charlotte interrupted, her voice weary with strain. "It's just one dreadful piece of news after another."

"Of course, how silly of me to stand here debating the *famous* polymath, as if I could," she retorted with a brittle smile. "And Flo and Beth will be wondering what's kept us."

"Don't you worry about a thing, miss," Nellie put in. "Cook and me'll see the inspector out."

Margaret gathered Charlotte close with an arm about her shoulders, and they left. Lord Brudeford watched their departure with a thoughtful expression.

"I think you have a winner there with your Charlotte," he said in a low voice.

I glanced over at Nellie, who, busy at the stove, appeared not to have heard. "She is not *my* Charlotte," I whispered with as much conviction as possible without raising my voice.

"Oh, come now. I can tell you're as thick as thieves and up to something, and so can the inspector." He stood and pulled on his jacket.

"I thought the police were useless," I shot back.

"Useless, yes, stupid, no," he countered. "Lloyddyn is no fool, and neither am I."

Chapter Thirty-One

Lucky for me, Lord Brudeford and I parted company outside the Gaines house, with him sauntering off down the street. As with Inspector Lloyddyn, the last thing I needed was my tutor poking his nose into my business.

Darkness enveloped his slim, straight back, and I turned to walk in the other direction. Though I puzzled over the many revelations of the day, I could not help worrying about Lord Brudeford.

He appeared to be slipping back into his old ways, and I feared his fragile health could not withstand much more abuse. Grandfather insisted that he must confront the specter of war and reconcile with his experiences in Afghanistan. I believed Lord Brudeford would rather face death than relive those days.

He had denied being at Madame Huang's, and certainly there were plenty of other opium dens to accommodate both the addict and casual user. Still, his presence in Limehouse on the same night as the discovery of Mrs. Marshton's dead body troubled me.

I shook off my suspicions, unwilling to even contemplate the possibility of Lord Brudeford being involved in these heinous crimes. A weakness on my part, I must admit.

I needed to think, so instead of catching the Underground at Gower, I made my way through nighttime London, heading down to Oxford Street with the intention of boarding an omnibus somewhere along the way. The pain in my side and back eased with movement, and I kept walking.

With a map of London laid out in my head, I cut across neighborhood squares and turned down obscure blocks of row houses to take the most direct route home. The earlier fog had dissipated, and a pleasant autumn chill spurred me onward.

Crossing Lincoln's Inn Fields, I did my best to avoid the profusion of beggars who haunted its every stoop. A long string of cabs halted me at the southeast corner.

I glared as they pelted past, impatient to be on my way. When the last had finally cleared the road, I poised to resume my walk but stilled at the sound of piano scales. A hot, prickly sensation tightened my scalp.

I turned, and there perched a sleek, plump, one-legged starling on the rough-hewn crutch of a beggar. The ragged man sat on the hard concrete, his back up against the base of a streetlamp.

No doubt other plump, one-legged starlings that could sing scales like a concert pianist stalked the city, but the odds of meeting another such one seemed slim. "I say, is that your bird?" I asked the man.

The beggar regarded me with rheumy, bulbous eyes and wiped his nose on a filthy sleeve. "Nah, ain't never seen 'em before in me life. Tried to shoo the beast away, but 'e won't go."

I hesitated, indecisive. Felix cocked his head to one side and stared back at me with a beady, black eye.

"What do you want?" I whispered, frustrated by his hovering, mysterious presence.

"Well, since your askin'," the old man growled, mistaking my meaning. "I wouldn't mind a coin or two." He held out his hand.

My mother often stopped at the sight of a beggar, whether it was to give money, or food, or clothing, or just a comforting word. She told me it was important to see the unseen, to acknowledge those whom society would sweep away like dirt under a rug.

Though I stowed most of my "walking around" money in my waistband, I still had a few coins for easy access in the pocket of my trousers. I drew one out and dropped it into his palm.

"'Ere now," he complained as I turned to go. "This won't do me no good."

"What do you mean?"

"I mean, this here ain't money." He held the object up to the light. I realized with some misgiving I had handed him the bronze coin we had found in the housekeeper's sitting room.

"Though in me younger days," the beggar continued, "I'd of redeemed it right enough."

I took the bronze coin and gave him a real one. "Redeem it?"

He winked. "Well, now, ya don't know what you got there, do ya?"

"I wouldn't be asking if I did." I tried to keep the exasperation from my voice.

"That there"—he nodded at the coin—"is a token for a brothel."

"A brothel?" I examined the token and could see nothing to indicate its origins. "How do you know?"

He chuckled. "I weren't always old and sick. Plenty 'o brothels hand 'em out, hoping to draw in customers, them as would keep coming back."

"But it doesn't *say* anything."

He drew in a deep breath. "Aye, boy, you're a right innocent one, ain't ya?"

I bristled and opened my mouth on an angry retort. He shook his head.

"Now, now, don't get worked up. It's best ya don't dip your wick at them type of places anyway," he insisted. "Diseases and such, don't ya know."

I didn't need his admonishments. The seedier side of romantic relations in this city held little interest for me. "Do you know which brothel this token belongs to?"

He cocked his head to one side, very much like Felix. "I might."

I dropped another coin in his hand. He nodded at the token, and I gave it back to him.

The old beggar peered at it in the dim light and grimaced with distaste. "What ya got here is for the Expedition. It's a right fancy place, but the doings there ain't natural, don't ya know." He tossed the token to me as if he couldn't get rid of it fast enough.

"No, I don't," I prompted.

He shook his head. "Well, I ain't explaining it, and no amount of coin'll make me."

I shrugged. "Where can I find the Expedition?"

"Off Soho Square. Looks like a respectable house, but it ain't."

I pocketed the token and thanked the old man. Felix hopped down to the ground and pecked at the dirt like a regular starling.

"Poor old, one-legged sod, like me," the beggar observed, tapping his own withered leg. "Except he's got wings, he has. Makes all the difference, I figure."

**

With the vague directions of "off Soho Square," I searched for the brothel up and down its side streets. After a good quarter of an hour, I spotted a worn rectangle of stonework in which was carved the faded outline of a compass with a flower at its center. The stone image sat above the doorway of an unremarkable red brick building.

I watched the entrance from the shelter of a dark alleyway across the street. Fashionably dressed men came and went at regular intervals. A well-set-up young sentry in an excessively tight footman's uniform stood just inside the door.

My side throbbed, and I had decided to head home for the night when a familiar figure presented himself at the establishment. His trimmed beard and distinguished profile flashed for a brief second in the lantern light from the open door. Though I had seen him for only moments, and from a distance, I recognized the rich man who had argued with my redheaded assailant only days before.

I sagged with weary resignation. There was nothing for me to do but follow him.

Squaring my shoulders, I crossed the street and approached the building with the outward appearance of confidence. The door opened at my knock.

Whatever else I believed would greet me within, it was not the sentry's courteous nod or the general air of respectability of my surroundings. Lit by the yellow glow of gas lamps, the hallway hung with paintings of country estates and peaceful villages.

I held out the token, and the man took it, saying in a rough, low-class accent softened in an imitation of genteel politeness, "Up the stair, sir, to the parlour, first door on the right."

I thanked him and made my way up the staircase. Upon entering the parlour, all pretense at respectability fell away, and my stomach lurched at what I beheld.

Chapter Thirty-Two

The curated scene before me resembled a sumptuous bacchanal. A fountain of champagne flowed in the center of the room, and tables laden with cakes and fruit lined the walls. Heavy brocade curtains covered the windows, leaving the room illuminated by large, branching candelabras. Richly upholstered sofas shone in the flickering light, upon which lounged children, both boys and girls, scantily clad as cherubs, not one older than fifteen, and the youngest perhaps nine.

They appeared as statues, frozen in seductive poses. The wealthy clientele wandered among them, stopping to speak with a child who caught their interest or trail a finger down a smooth cheek.

"You don't belong in 'ere." A woman's voice hissed in my ear. Thin, boney fingers clamped on my arm in a vice-like grip. "What's that idiot at the door doin' letting you in?"

She jerked me out into the hallway and slammed me up against the wall. My bruised body protested the abuse, and I groaned.

She stuck her face close to mine. Fine lines crisscrossed her skin beneath a thick layer of makeup. Her eyes narrowed, and she grinned. "You're a pretty one. You half-breed boys come out real nice. I could use one like you."

I twisted my arm from her grip and pushed her away. "Get off of me. I didn't come here for a job."

She smirked. "Maybe I'm not asking."

My heart raced, but long years of practice kept my expression impassive. "I'm not one of the hopeless and forgotten. There are those in Limehouse, powerful and remorseless people, who would miss me."

In this instance, I was actually grateful for the gullible English who believed every melodramatic story about the Oriental. She took a cautious step back, and I perceived the gaunt figure of a woman younger than she had at first appeared. Her receding gums and the sagging flesh of her jawline told me readily enough she suffered from the ravages of drink, and possibly laudanum.

"Why're you 'ere?" she demanded

To give myself a moment to think, I feigned an expression of annoyance and brushed off the sleeve of my jacket where she had grasped my arm. "I'm here at the request of Madame Huang."

She cocked her head to one side, unimpressed. "And who might she be?"

"She might be someone you don't want to get on the wrong side of." I attempted a threatening sneer and hoped I didn't make a muddle of it. "Madame Huang is not pleased to find one of your English dead in her opium den." I had no idea whether Mrs. Marshton was connected with the brothel or if the token was even hers, but it was my only play.

The woman frowned. "Someone from the Expedition? Dead? In an opium den?"

"So Madame Huang believes."

"Who?"

"A Mrs. Marshton."

The woman staggered back against the wall and slid to the floor, her face pale beneath the makeup. She covered her eyes with a shaking hand. "Dead?"

I squatted next to her. "Yes. Are you a relation?"

She choked out a bitter laugh. "God, no, not to that vile hag."

A creak on the staircase propelled her to her feet. "Follow me," she hissed.

I jumped up, and we hastened to the other end of the hallway. After descending three flights of a narrow staircase, we entered a well-lit corridor snaking through the servants' quarters. She opened the door to one, and we scuttled inside.

I stopped, brought up short by the sight of a small boy lying on a cot next to the narrow bed. The child sat up and pushed black curls back from his sleepy little face.

"Mama?"

"Shh," she admonished the boy and pulled a carpetbag from under the bed. "Don't make no noise, Joey. You're goin' on a trip with this nice boy 'ere."

I drew back with a vehement shake of my head. "What are you talking about? I'm not taking this child anywhere."

She came at me like a raging bull, but stopped short of ramming me up against the wall again. Her face pressed close to mine. "You've seen what goes on 'ere. I ain't much of a mother"—she pointed a shaking finger at her son—"but I'd die before I see Joey used like . . ."

She swallowed threatening tears. "There's men who trade in boys like 'em, even younger. This is me only chance to get Joey out."

The woman glanced up and down the hallway before closing the door. "Mrs. Marshton, that ain't her real name. She only used that name when she wanted to sound respectable. I figured she was off on one of her other 'enterprises,' as she called 'em, cuz I'd only seen her once or twice in these last two months. Her name is, ah, was Dolly Tibbers, and she owned this place until last year when she partnered up with a man."

"What man?"

The woman shook her head and walked to the cupboard. "I don't know. No one ever seen 'em but her. I tell you what, she weren't scared of nothin' and nobody, but Dolly, she were scared of 'em. Before he come, this were a regular brothel. We didn't use children." She took out folded clothes and put them in the bag, kissing a child-sized ivory brush before placing it within.

I thrust my hands before me in a gesture of disbelief. "You cannot *give* me a child. You don't know who I am."

She threw her head back with an unreserved, bubbling laugh that wiped years from her face. "You have a good, calm-like manner; I'll give you that. But you need to work on the ugly sneers and tough guy talk."

I dropped my hands in resignation. I wasn't going to leave a child to be raped or worse. "What about the others?"

She shrugged. "What about 'em? You want to take all of 'em, do ya?"

"Surely you can just let them go."

"Go where? They got no one. At least 'ere they got a roof over their heads and food in their bellies." She settled Joey on her hip and picked up the carpetbag with her other hand. "That man don't know nothin' about me boy. With Joey outta here and Dolly gone, he'll be safe."

I followed her into the hallway. She threw instructions to me over her shoulder as we hurried to the mews entrance. "I got money stowed in this bag, enough to take care of 'em for a few weeks until I come for 'em."

We stepped out into the shrouded, cobblestoned courtyard. The woman handed me the carpetbag and clutched the child close.

She put her cheek against his black curls. "Madame Huang's, you say."

I nodded, not wanting to give her my true address, or even my name. Who knew what abhorrent people comprised her world?

"Give her my description," I told her. "She'll know how to find me."

This was true. I had never met Madame Huang, but there was little chance she didn't know about me, having many times sent couriers to our store for herbs and medicines.

The woman nodded, hesitating now to let go of the boy.

"If you've changed your mind—" I began.

"No." She thrust him into my arms. "There's a cab stand on the square. My name's Penny. If Joey needs anything, you know where to find me." She stepped back into the house and turned to shut the door.

"Wait," I protested. "About this man? Can you tell me nothing?"

Penny scowled with disgust. "All's I know is his name, Mr. Grey." With that, she shut the door in my shocked face and threw the bolt.

Chapter Thirty-Three

"Mr. Grey, you say," Grandfather mused, Joey now sleeping peacefully on his lap after crying a full hour for his mother.

"Yes. It cannot be a coincidence," I insisted. "He must be the Grey Man, the very same."

Mother crossed from the stove with steaming cups of jasmine tea. "It's best to keep an open mind. Grey is not such an uncommon name, and London is a big place."

She sat with her own cup and looked over at the sleeping boy. "What desperation drives a mother to put her child in the arms of a stranger?" she asked with a sad shake of her head.

My arrival home with the loudly protesting Joey had been the perfect diversion from any uncomfortable questions about my stiff gait and tender side. Grandfather examined him with a trained eye and pronounced, "This poor child has been rendered senseless with laudanum on a regular basis. He is now experiencing some withdrawal from the drug."

I searched the carpetbag and, sure enough, found a vial of laudanum along with three pounds and six shillings, some clothes, the ivory hairbrush, and a raggedy stuffed bear. He howled at the sight of the bear but did not quiet one iota once I had given it to him.

Grandfather allowed him to suck on a candied ginger root while he crushed up a *Fu-Yuan* pellet and stirred it into a cup of warm milk. After much struggle, Joey drank the decoction and had settled eventually into sleep. It would take many more days of treatment for him to recover.

"Desperate, indeed." Grandfather shifted the child in his arms. "But we cannot keep him."

Mother stirred in protest. "We will not send him back."

"No, of course not, but an English boy living with us would draw unwanted attention to the store and censure from our neighbors."

"He can stay a few weeks, surely," Mother insisted. "We can tell everybody that he was left by a friend who . . . who went to claim an inheritance in Scotland or something like that."

It was a good lie but poorly told. She would have to practice for anyone to believe the story.

Grandfather nodded. "He can stay, but we must find a permanent place for him if his mother does not claim him soon."

I leaned back in the chair and winced. Mother's sharp eyes caught my reaction. "You are hurt."

I had omitted from my description of the night's events any mention of the attack. I let them believe my presence at the Gaines residence that evening to be a scheduled meeting with Charlotte. If they knew the truth, Grandfather might decide the ancestors had led me far enough and put a stop to the investigation.

"Yes. I slipped on the rocks down near the waterman's stairs, but it is only a bruised rib," I lied.

"Why were you there?" Mother regarded me over the rim of her cup.

I pulled the piece of rubber from my pocket. "I wanted to see for myself where Teddy came ashore. This was caught on a nail under the pier."

Mother reached for the pink glob but drew her hand back with a quick intake of breath. "What is it?" she asked, apprehension shading her voice.

"Perhaps a piece of rubber from one of those ladies' toilette masks," I answered.

Mother and Grandfather exchanged a look of concern mixed with curiosity. I had told them all the details relating to Aunt Sadie's murder.

"The type used to hide the killer's face?" Grandfather shifted Joey and freed a hand. He picked up the rubber and examined it.

"Women put this on their faces at night?" He grunted. "An insalubrious practice, skin needs to breathe."

"Don't you see?" I prompted. "Somehow Teddy and Aunt Sadie's murders are connected."

"Through this piece of rubber?" Grandfather placed the pinkish lump back on the table where it gave the impression of a sickly, shell-less snail. "You cannot know how long it had been there. An interesting find, but the river is a source of every type of debris, and this may only signify the journey's end of a piece of trash."

"I cannot agree, *Baba*." My mother stared at the rubber with a tiny crease in her fair brow. "If we believe the ancestors to have spoken through Mr. Holmes, and perhaps a one-legged bird, we must not ignore such a significant coincidence."

"Hmm." Grandfather stood. Built more like a farmhand than a scholar, he easily draped the sleeping child over one broad shoulder. "Until the universe turns and nudges another clue in Kuo's direction, we will wait and see. For now, we must put this child to bed."

**

I awoke to find Joey gone, his blankets thrown back and rumpled on the makeshift cot pushed up against the wall in my cramped room. Weak morning light filtered in from the window. I pulled on a pair of trousers, gasping at the movement, my side still sore from the redheaded man's repeated kicks.

Fragrant steam drifted out of the pitcher on the washstand, and I deduced that Mother had already made her customary delivery of herb-scented water. I poured it into the porcelain basin and splashed my face, running wet fingers through my disheveled hair.

Straightening, I caught a glimpse of my face in the small mirror above the stand. A patchy shadow of dark whiskers lay across my chin and cheeks. I rubbed the rough skin and contemplated my features.

Pretty, Penny had said.

Like my inconvenient bouts of empathy, I blamed my mother for my face. I could hardly blame my father, having never seen an image of him. But I knew without a doubt Mother had gifted me her heavily lashed dark eyes.

"Girly eyes," Teddy had teased. "Good thing the rest of your mug's more manly, else people'd mistake you for one of them unnatural types."

Poor Teddy, his descent into petty crime had spiraled out of control. That day at the market, he seemed to pivot on the spot, to make a split-second decision to leave me behind.

"No, mate, it was you left me." The words reverberated off the bedroom walls.

I spun around, fists clenched. Blood pulsed in my brain.

No one. I was alone.

Drawing in a deep breath, I relaxed my shoulders and said aloud, "You're right. It was me. I saw and never raised the alarm. I'm sorry."

I didn't really expect an answer. I waited nonetheless. But the only sounds in the room drifted in muffled from the street below.

I pulled on a shirt, leaving it untucked and half buttoned, and slipped my feet into a pair of worn satin house slippers. The sound of a child's laughter floated out into the hallway from the kitchen. I stopped short just inside the door.

Charlotte sat in my accustomed chair, Joey on her lap, his little face suffused in a huge, delighted smile. "No, no, Joey, Patty Cake. Don't you know Patty Cake, silly?"

They each clapped their hands together, but Joey refused to meet hers in the middle, waving his pudgy fingers over his head instead and laughing as if he'd made a fine joke. Mother looked up from the stove and gestured me to Grandfather's chair.

"Sit. Your grandfather is already in the store."

Charlotte glanced over her shoulder and swiftly cast her eyes downward. A modest blush stole over her cheeks.

I buttoned up the rest of my shirt and sat. Charlotte peeked out from under her eyelashes and, finding me decently covered, smiled.

"I must say, this is quite cozy and nice. We had a lovely little breakfast nook overlooking our garden when I lived with Aunt Beatrix."

Mother placed a bowl of beef noodle soup before me and sat with a cup of tea in her hand. "It is pleasant to have a warm and familiar place to gather for meals."

Joey squealed and grabbed a handful of golden ringlets. Resentment at finding Charlotte seated at our kitchen table tightened my chest.

How was I to eat the slippery noodles and slurp up the soup while she sat there watching me, judging? Typical toff behavior with no regard for us common folk.

"The soup smells delicious, and I don't think I've ever had such lovely tea." She disengaged Joey's sticky fingers from her hair and sipped from the delicate, hand-painted teacup.

"You are welcomed to some soup," Mother offered.

"Oh, no, thank you. I've eaten."

Their politesse irked me, and I asked with some heat, "Why are you here?"

Mother rebuked me with a stern look. But Charlotte did not appear in the least chastened by my rudeness.

"I'm sorry to bother you at home and at such an unfashionable hour," she said. "But I am finding Margaret more difficult to escape than Aunt Sadie."

She plucked a biscuit from an open tin on the table and gave it to Joey. "Margaret had to attend an early morning gathering of ladies to protest something or other in front of Parliament, and I took the opportunity to slip away."

"How did you find our shop?" I asked, unbending, somewhat gratified she had tracked me down.

"You gave me the address, if you recall. The driver only had to ask at a local pub near the docks. Your grandfather was kind enough to let me in, even though he had not yet opened. And your mother told me how you came by Joey at that disgusting brothel." She rubbed her nose against the little boy's, sending the child into a fit of giggles. "Oh, and I do hope you've recovered from your *fall* last night."

Having picked up a pair of chopsticks, intending to eat my noodles despite her presence, I set them back down again. Charlotte, of course, knew the truth of what had happened at the waterman's stairs. I darted a sidelong glance at my mother, fearful the girl would give me away.

I glared back at her. She flashed me a sweet smile.

"And while I'm glad you were able to rescue darling Joey," Charlotte continued, "I really wish you would not follow clues without me, as we agreed. You must promise not to do it again."

I said through gritted teeth, "Well, I really didn't have much of a cho—"

"I insist." She tilted her head to one side, her smile frozen in place.

I narrowed my eyes, not believing she would actually betray me. Even with her flighty ways, Charlotte had a sturdy sense of honor.

"You're right," I acknowledged. "I should have waited for you. I promise to speak to you before following a clue from now on."

Her smile broadened. "Thank you."

"No," Joey exclaimed. "No. No."

I sat back in surprise. These were the first words he had uttered in my presence.

"What is it, Joey?" Mother stood and held out her arms. The child reached for her.

She picked him up, and he laid his head on her shoulder. Tears leaked from his eyes. He mumbled a sorrowful "no" several more times before falling asleep.

"Poor child." Mother patted his back. "I've set up a little pallet for him in the storeroom. He can sleep while I work." She nodded at Charlotte. "Miss Gaines has asked if you can accompany her on an errand this morning, and your grandfather has given his permission. We have a shipment arriving today that will need sorting, so you must be back by teatime. Remember, also, to drop medicines off to Mr. Holmes, as today is the appointed day."

"Of course," I answered, sensing her unease.

She left, and I frowned down into my bowl of noodles. Concern for my safety often occupied my mother's thoughts, but something different marred her peace of mind. The tilt of her head and the quick downward droop of her mouth when she looked at Charlotte gave me pause.

"Are you going to finish your soup?" Charlotte asked.

"What errand was my mother referring to?"

"I hoped we could visit Mrs. Davies, Nora's mother. Maybe she knows something about the locket."

"Ah, yes." I pushed back my chair and stood. "Just a short delay to finish dressing and we can leave."

Charlotte stood as well, a hurt, perplexed expression on her face. "Have I done wrong in coming here?"

I pulled myself together at her obvious distress. "No. My mind's elsewhere. That's all. I'll only be a few moments."

She placed her hand on my arm. "Uncle Cecil is not dead, thank goodness. I received an answer to my letter. Not from him, but his boss, the head monk or some such thing, a Father McCleary."

Charlotte reached into her handbag and took out a folded sheet of paper. "Here, read it for yourself."

I scanned the missive. Did all monks have such an elegant hand? I could easily imagine Father McCleary sitting at a high desk scribbling away on an illuminated text with quill and ink. A vague, elusive notion arose in my mind but slipped away before I could grasp it firmly.

"This says your uncle is in seclusion at the hermitage, and they will not disturb him until next spring," I commented and shook my head. "Not even to tell him his only living sister has been murdered?"

Charlotte shrugged. "I cannot fathom the practices of the religious orders. In that way, I am like my grandfather. However, Margaret explained that each monk takes his turn at the hermitage in prayer and with a vow of silence for a year. The rest of the monks can assume other tasks without offending God." She reached for the letter.

I hesitated in giving it back to her, the printed letterhead having caught my attention: Wickersham Abbey, Worseton-on-Tees, Yorkshire, England.

Worseton-on-Tees? Where had I heard that name before?

I drew in a sharp breath—of course, the very village where Jack met Margaret, the location of the Hughes estate in Yorkshire.

Chapter Thirty-Four

"Jack Hughes? The man who insisted on finding the jeweler?"

We jostled along the stifling streets of the East End in a hired hackney, a manner of transportation to which I was becoming alarmingly accustomed. A quick tip of my hat and a cheery "Good Day" to a scowling Dora Needer sweeping the entryway of her father's store lifted my spirits.

"The very same," I answered, settling back into the cushions.

Charlotte stared in thoughtful silence at the space between the horse's ears. "I don't see how he could be involved. He would have to be a confederate of the redheaded man, in addition to knowing about the secret passageway out of Mr. Cohen's bookstore . . ." She threw me an accusatory look, as if I were somehow to blame for making, in her words, "a daring escape" from Cohen's without her. "And that it would end at the hotel where he happened to be staying."

"We only have his word he was, in fact, residing at the hotel," I pointed out.

"But Margaret . . ."

"Yes," I agreed. "Margaret." It strained credulity that he engineered a meeting with Margaret weeks in advance and used that as an excuse to intercept me on a day and at a time and place he could not possibly know I would be.

"Maybe he was in town to forward his suit with Margaret, but also on other, more nefarious business," Charlotte speculated, warming to the subject. "And was informed by his henchman, the redheaded man, that you had disappeared into the bookshop. He then used his *other* purpose for being in London as an excuse to waylay you."

I considered her theory but shook my head. "The redheaded man didn't know I was in the bookshop. He was checking all the stores along the block. No," I concluded with certainty. "It would take an oracle to know about the passageway and to divine when I would use it."

"I agree. Mr. Hughes appears quite guileless, hardly the oracle type. And one doesn't imagine such a handsome villain, more the countenance of a hero."

I bit my tongue on a harsh retort at such a foolish statement. "Where does Mrs. Davies live?" I asked instead.

"Just off Red Lion Square."

I knew the area in passing. A bit of a mixed bag respectability-wise, and one would never find the truly fashionable at that address, but many middle-class families called the neighborhood home.

"The information was in Aunt Sadie's files. The house was purchased by my grandfather for Miss Davies and left to her mother in his will."

The streets broadened as we moved westward onto Holborn. The day had brightened, and a mild autumn breeze stirred the fetid mix of odors into a semblance of freshness.

Charlotte sniffed the air. "How I miss the smell of lilac and honeysuckle."

I nodded out of politeness, but other than Mrs. Tooley's Covent Garden stall, I had no experience with flower-scented surroundings.

"After this investigation is over," she continued. "I am thinking of moving back to the countryside."

"Oh?"

"Yes. I know," she answered my implied question. "There will be objections from *the adults*, but I'm determined to go my own way. I inherited the cottage from Aunt Beatrix, although it is let to the vicarage. The vicar's mother stays there." She leaned towards me in a conspiratorial manner and whispered, "Poor woman, she was so grateful to have a place of her own away from her censorious son. He once had the gall to scold my aunt for wearing an 'overly frivolous hat' to Sunday services. Well, if there was one thing to earn my enmity it was to criticize dear Aunt Beatrix. Detestable man."

She settled back into the seat. "I can hire a companion. Perhaps the vicar's mother would stay on in such a capacity. With Cook and Nellie to keep house, we will suit just fine."

"And if Cook and Nellie don't wish to leave London?" I asked.

"Whyever not?" She blinked in surprise at such a notion.

"Because London is their home, and they may have family here," I replied with some stiffness at her toplofty manner.

Charlotte's face fell. "Do you think so? And I not know it? Because I have no family of my own, not to speak of, anyway, I had hoped they would . . ." Her voice trailed off.

I admonished myself for my ungenerous manner. Any lingering resentment of the morning melted away.

"It's understandable," I said in a softened tone, "that you would want familiar and friendly faces about you. I know both Cook and Nellie hold you in high esteem and would choose to go with you should they be able."

Charlotte turned her face from me and dabbed the corner of her eye with a handkerchief. I changed the subject by asking if she had discovered any documents referring to Mrs. Marshton's employment in her aunt's files.

"Not a one." She shook her head. "I don't believe it possible Aunt Sadie would hire a housekeeper without references."

"Mrs. Marshton likely took evidence of her connections when she fled. Although one would assume her references to be false, since she was clearly the madam of a notorious brothel."

"And now she's dead and can tell us nothing," Charlotte grumbled.

The cab slowed to a halt off Red Lion Square at the corner of Princeton Street. We climbed down and stood in front of a five-story red brick house with a large, bowed window at every floor.

"Mrs. Davies occupies the first two floors, although, according to Aunt Sadie's correspondence, she has taken in a lodger."

"The other floors?" I asked.

"Offices. Lawyers, I believe."

I twisted the doorbell. We waited a short couple of minutes before hearing a brisk step on the other side.

The door opened to a good-natured face of faded beauty. The woman's pale, wrinkled skin marked the advancing years, but fine blue eyes smiled at us, as lively as any girl's.

"What has brought two such handsome young people to my door?" she asked in an open and friendly manner.

Charlotte swallowed, and her hands clasped together in nervous entreaty. "Mrs. Davies?"

The woman frowned, now somewhat wary. "Yes."

"I'm Charlotte Gaines and this is my friend, Kuo Cheng. We're hoping you might speak to us about a certain matter that has arisen."

Her eyes grew wide with astonishment. "Oh, you poor dear, do, please, come in." She ushered us through the door, her hands fluttering with agitation. "I read, of course, of your aunt's terrible death. I cannot tell you how sorry I am."

The woman placed an arm about Charlotte's shoulders and gave her a quick squeeze before leading us down the hallway and into a small, well-lit parlour. My friend dabbed at her eyes once more, overset by this stranger's brief expression of condolence.

"Do sit." Mrs. Davies gestured to a loveseat by the fireplace. "Give me a moment while I get the tea tray."

In her absence, I examined our surroundings. Embers glowed in the hearth, and sunshine, such as it was, streamed in through the bowed window. Sheet music on a small upright piano, a desk strewn with papers, and a half-knitted shawl thrown across one armchair reflected industry and a busy mind. Well-executed amateur paintings hung from the walls, and though neat, the room had a relaxed and comfortable air.

"I did not expect her to be so kind." Charlotte sat straight and stiff on the edge of the sofa. "Aunt Sadie always spoke harshly of her."

"Mrs. Davies does appear to be a goodhearted creature," I agreed.

The woman returned carrying a tray. After she had settled us with cups of tea and biscuits, we sat in uncomfortable silence.

Charlotte cleared her throat. "You must be wondering why we're here."

"Oh, not at all," she replied. "I had expected some such visit, although I would've thought a solicitor more likely."

"A solicitor?"

"Why, yes, this must be about the house and stipend."

Charlotte shook her head. "No. We haven't come about that, but I can reassure you nothing has changed upon my aunt's death. The house is yours in name and the allowance until . . . well, yours for life."

The woman sighed with relief. "I must say, that is good news. I'm capable of making my own way in the world; still, I have grown accustomed to the little comforts of life."

She sipped her tea and regarded us with questioning eyes. Charlotte gazed back at her, uncharacteristically at a loss for words.

"We have come about a matter pertaining to your daughter, Nora," I explained. "Lately, Charlotte, um, Miss Gaines here, has received some mysterious correspondence, and the murder of her aunt has added urgency to our efforts to uncover its origins."

Mrs. Davies gasped in alarm. "Oh, my dear, you're not in any danger?"

"In fact, she is in a great deal of danger," I returned. "That's why we need your help."

Finding her voice, Charlotte added, "I received this locket with an anonymous letter." She drew the necklace from her bag and handed it to Mrs. Davies. "I was hoping you could tell us if this belonged to Nora."

The woman frowned down at the gold locket with its dragonfly design. She turned it over in her hand and opened the clasp. "Nothing inside," she mumbled. "I am sorry. I've never seen this before." A delicate blush stole over her cheeks. "Mr. Gaines gave my daughter many pieces of jewelry. I couldn't be certain this isn't hers, but Nora was wont to show me every gift she received."

She snapped the locket shut and handed it back to Charlotte, adding, "Dragonflies signify transformation."

A shock coursed through me. Mr. Holmes's words sounded again in my brain: *Transformation is key, life to death to life.*

"What?" I asked.

"The dragonfly symbolizes transformation." She smiled. "I learned that, among many other things, working in the theater. I wasn't an actress like Nora but a costume designer. I collaborated with all sorts of artists." An indulgent chuckle escaped her lips. "The dramatists were the most exacting, demanding all sorts of symbolism and such in the sets and costumes. They worked us at all hours to fulfill their whims."

"Transformation to what? From what?" I pressed her.

"I haven't the slightest notion, only transformation." Her expression grew sad. "Nora transformed from my sweet, biddable girl into a grasping, ambitious woman." Mrs. Davies looked at Charlotte.

"Poverty will do that, you know. But that's no excuse for what she did, and we were not so poorly off as many. Still, for a girl as pretty as she, it was hard to see things she wanted but couldn't get by honest means."

Charlotte nodded, pensive, and said, "I won't deny feeling a bit resentful towards her. But I do understand that without money and position, women are at the mercy of society, more so even than men."

I detected a hint of Margaret Scott in those words, but I could hardly deny their truth. Mrs. Davies stood and walked to the desk. She took a letter from a drawer.

"I've never told this to another living soul. I wrote your grandmother, grieved as I was, that Nora should take up with a married man." Her voice trembled, and she clasped the letter to her breast. "Do not mistake me. I loved my daughter, and she always did right by me. Still, when Mrs. Gaines was put away in an asylum . . . well, I can tell you, I couldn't take the guilt and shame of knowing it was my girl to blame, and me by extension."

"I think we can lay fault at my grandfather's feet, as well," Charlotte declared with some severity.

"Good of you to say, my dear, and I won't refute it, but Nora did set her cap at him. There's no denying." Mrs. Davies sat and put the letter on the table between us. "I wrote telling her I was sorry for her circumstances and that my daughter was the cause of it. I don't know what I expected in return, but . . ." She brought a handkerchief to her trembling lips, eyes filling with tears. "Well, Mrs. Gaines returned a letter, that letter"—she nodded at the table—"of such forgiveness and grace that I don't believe a kinder, gentler soul ever lived."

"What does it say?" Charlotte asked.

The woman placed a hand on her breast and drew in a deep breath. "I'll let you see for yourself, for I'm giving it to you. As her granddaughter, I do not believe there is a better person to have possession of it. Suffice it to say she wrote to me, mother to mother, about her grief over losing her children, and this only a few weeks after the terrible carriage accident that killed your parents."

Chapter Thirty-Five

Standing on the stoop, Mrs. Davies waved us on our way. "Do come again, and if you're crossing the square, watch out for Cromwell's ghost," she said with a wink and retreated back into her house, shutting the door behind her.

"What in Heaven's name is she talking about?" Charlotte asked as we made our way to the leafy public garden at the center of the square.

"I believe she is referring to the ghost of Oliver Cromwell," I replied, grateful for my eclectic education. "With the restoration of the monarchy in 1660, Cromwell's body was dug up and posthumously tried, gibbeted, and beheaded."

"How horrible," Charlotte exclaimed. "I don't understand such savagery in the least."

I laughed. Our meeting with Mrs. Davies had shaken my friend. Her spirited response reassured me of her returning sense of self-confidence.

"Afterwards, the body was buried next to the gallows and the head displayed from the roof of Westminster Hall. However, there are those who believe Cromwell's body switched out beforehand and buried in the field behind an inn that once stood on this very square. Another body entirely was hung and dismembered in his stead." I gestured to the pleasant greenery surrounding us. "Thus, the story that Cromwell haunts this place."

Charlotte sighed and sank down onto a park bench perched alongside the pathway. She stared at the letter in her hands. "I wish I were haunted by the ghosts of my parents. Do you think it is so horrible to be haunted by someone who loves you?" She frowned. "At least, I think they loved me. I can't know for certain, although Aunt Beatrix assured me it was so."

I sat beside her. "I never knew my father. He died at sea."

"Oh, I am sorry." She brushed away a stray tear and straightened her shoulders. "Shall we read the letter?"

"Only if you wish me to hear it."

"What a silly thing to say. Of course I wish you to hear it. We are in this together."

"Well, then," I prompted.

She smoothed the paper, made stiff from being folded for so long, and cleared her throat, reading:

My Dear Mrs. Davies,

I received your letter two days ago, though I have only read it this hour past. The envelope sat on the windowsill overlooking the grounds of this place while I wondered whether to open it at all. You see, I have endured such heartache and such desperate loneliness that I could not believe your words would bring me anything but more pain.

Do you know, I finally read your letter out of sheer, crushing boredom. Strange that in my world, it is better to endure pain than the monotony of my daily life.

Therefore, I have read your words and absolve you of any blame associated with my ostracism. Yes, I am magnanimous, but more than that, I am, like you, a mother.

In this capacity, I advise you, Mrs. Davies, to put aside your disappointment. Seek not to chastise your daughter. Listen to me, who has lost so much. Though you may still, it would sadden me if you suffered as I have.

I count but two remaining children of five, my oldest, Thomas, so recently taken from me. Of the two, only Cecil deigns to visit, my little Sadie shows me only her back. This betrayal is one of many. Of Ada, my older sister, I have not heard a word. Information has reached me that she is housekeeper to my husband, the most egregious betrayer of them all.

What more can I do? My daughter and sister have decided their paths. How can I blame them? Their way is certainly made easier by it.

I wave my hand in weary resignation and will bestow what forgiveness I can muster on all, even my husband, who once loved me.

Most days, I contemplate a question. Perhaps, Mrs. Davies, you can help me with it. What is more painful, betrayal by or death of a loved one?

I have experienced both, and yet I cannot tell you. I do not know, if given the power to abolish only one, which I would choose.

I would like to put the question to my husband. He was always good with moral conundrums. Alas, he no longer acknowledges my existence.

I must go. My jailers have opened the door, and the garden beckons.

But if I may, I will offer a piece of advice for your daughter: Do not get old and fat.

Respectfully Yours,
Mary Gaines

A moment passed before I could express the thought foremost in my mind. "Mrs. Davies considered *this* letter a comfort?" While Mary Gaines certainly wrote of her maternal feelings, barely suppressed anger and bitterness bled through every word and turn of phrase.

Charlotte contemplated the letter. She drew in a deep breath. "For all her liveliness, Mrs. Davies is a simple creature. Perhaps her daughter was the same." She gazed off into the distance. "How maddening to be usurped by such a woman as Nora, particularly if one is, as was my grandmother, a person of deep feelings."

"By Mrs. Fawcett's account, Mary Gaines was as good a writer as her husband," I told her.

Charlotte looked up at me wide-eyed and blinked (odd that I no longer found it annoying). "Is that so?"

I stood and presented her with my arm. "Come, let us walk. Grandfather says that physical exertion also works the mind, and we have much to think on."

Charlotte stowed the letter in her handbag and stood. She smiled and tucked her hand into the crook of my arm. "Since I find your grandfather to be a wise man, I will listen to you this once. Lead on."

Did I detect a coquettish note in her voice? An unaccountable flurry roiled my stomach. I ignored it.

"The theme of betrayal in both her letter and those of the killer is striking," I said as we walked down the quiet lane.

"Her poem as well." Charlotte glanced up at me. "And the locket that is so like her own, but not hers. This has always been about my grandmother, hasn't it?"

I nodded. "Yes. I believe so."

"The locket, whose . . .?" Charlotte let the question hang in the air.

Other than Madame de Silva's vague reference to another woman, I hadn't a clue. "Perhaps we should have asked Mrs. Davies if . . .

well, if there was competition, so to speak, for your grandfather's affections."

"Oh, I wouldn't have had the nerve," Charlotte declared with a firm shake of her head. "The poor woman was already so mortified."

We turned onto Hart Street and passed Bloomsbury Square, the roadway now crowded with people and carriages. The activity and noise of our surroundings barely penetrated the deep bubble of contemplation that enveloped us.

"Your Aunt Sadie . . ." I began.

"I know, the betrayer, like my grandfather, and now dead like him." She clasped her other hand around my arm and leaned into me.

I covered her hands with one of my own. "Some fifteen years between their deaths. Can they truly be related?" I mused.

"And Ada?" Charlotte countered. "What became of her?"

Another turn up a short avenue, and we confronted the British Museum. The imposing Greek Revival façade dominated the block, and we stopped, momentarily taken aback at finding ourselves in its presence.

Chapter Thirty-Six

I uttered the first thing that came into my mind. "Lord Brudeford says the British Museum holds the largest cache of stolen riches in the world."

Charlotte laughed. "I think his lordship was quite struck with Margaret."

I frowned, unsure of her meaning. "In a good way?"

She stared off into space, considering. "Good and bad, but mostly good."

"Hmm," was my careful response. I assumed she meant that some piquancy in a romantic relationship was desirable but hesitated to push for clarification, fearing she would attach some unintended meaning to my question.

"Look, Madame de Silva." Charlotte clasped her hands to her breast, calling my attention to the woman who had so recently occupied my thoughts.

"I saw her in *Lady Windermere's Fan*," she enthused. "So wonderful, and so beautiful. Aunt Sadie was scandalized but didn't want to leave for fear of appearing stuffy and old-fashioned."

The famous actress had created a mild stir among the onlookers by descending from a coach in front of the museum. I stiffened at the sight of the man who accompanied her: the very same wealthy gentleman, and employer of the redheaded man, whom I'd witnessed enter the Expedition.

I spotted a beribboned figure slipping out of the coach after them and scuttling around the outskirts of her mother's admirers. "Danny's with her," I declared and tugged at Charlotte's arm. "Come on."

"Who?" She wouldn't budge. "I'll not be manhandled."

"I'm not . . ." I resisted rolling my eyes and explained, "I recognize the man with Madame de Silva. I must speak with Danny, and we need to be quick about it. If I know her, she will get as far away from her mother as swiftly as possible."

Her eyes widened with comprehension. "Of course, the girl who dresses like a boy. How stupid that I should forget. I should write everything down from now on so as not to lose track of information."

Charlotte kept pace beside me as I searched the crowd for Danny. "There she is." I spotted the girl feeding nuts to an organ grinder's monkey.

We came up beside her, and I tapped her on the shoulder. She glanced up at me with an indelicate grunt.

"What'd ya want?"

"How about a polite greeting."

"Since when?"

"Since I'm introducing you to Charlotte Gaines."

"Ho," Danny crowed, giving Charlotte her full attention. "You're the one gettin' them letters and all."

"'And all' meaning the murder of her aunt and the violent attack upon both her and myself, imp," I reminded her. "You can drop the street urchin slang. It does not go well with your present costume."

She scowled and cut her eyes over at Charlotte. "I don't know what you're talking about."

"You needn't worry," Charlotte reassured the girl. "I would never tell a soul about your adventures. Honestly, I wish I had the courage."

Nothing could have better served to mollify Danny than Charlotte's obvious admiration. "Getting the impression right takes skill—hey!"

The monkey, grown impatient waiting for the next handout, had grabbed the bag of nuts and scampered away. It scurried up the iron fence and chittered down at us.

"Greedy beggar," she called after the unrepentant creature.

"Listen, Danny," I said, regaining her attention. "Who's that man with your mother?"

She regarded the excited crowd milling around Madame de Silva. "Ugh, look at her preening." The girl thrust her hands into her coat pockets and said with fake sympathy, "Poor Mother. So, so bored this morning."

Danny placed a dramatic hand to her forehead. "'Oh, the tedium. I must flee these dreary four walls for the city streets. I must experience something real and alive—'"

"The man?" I insisted.

"Him?" She shrugged. "He's not as bad as some of the others. He doesn't press his affections upon her." The girl grimaced with distaste. "Lord Marlington wants to be seen in her presence. Some of Mother's admirers just like the attention."

I drew back, shocked. Lord Marlington, the magistrate? The fact that the magistrate at St. George's and the redheaded man's employer were one and the same was quickly superseded by alarm at where I had last seen him. I grasped Danny by the shoulders.

"Don't ever be alone with that man. Don't ever let him get you by yourself. Promise me."

She narrowed her eyes. "What're you bleating on about? He's harmless."

I shook her. "I can't go into it here, but he's dangerous. Promise me."

Danny shrugged off my hands. "If it'll make you happy. I promise."

She turned from me to hide a delighted smile. There were few people in her life who truly worried for her welfare.

"Daniela." Madame de Silva's soft Spanish lisp reached us as if projected from a stage. "Come here, my darling."

"How does she do that?" Danny complained. "How can she whisper *so* loud?"

Her mother waved with affectionate urgency. "This is your fault," the girl grumbled, piercing me with a resentful stare. "If you hadn't stopped me, I would've been long gone by now."

"Daniela." Only a practiced ear could have detected the slight hardening of the great actress's tone.

Danny left us with a wave and skipped off to join her mother's entourage entering the museum. Lord Marlington hovered at Madame de Silva's elbow, fawning in his attentions.

Charlotte swiveled her head around in search of something. "There it is," she declared, pointing across the street at a stationary shop. "I knew we'd passed one. I'm going to buy a journal this very minute to write everything down before another piece of information slips out of my brain."

With a swish of skirts, she turned to cross the street. I hesitated to follow.

"Well then, we part here," I informed her. "I've medicines to deliver to Dr. Watson."

Charlotte whirled around with such force the compression of air between us pushed me back a step or two. She clamped her hand on my forearm.

"I'm coming with you."

"I don't—"

"I must insist. Dr. Watson knows about me and the investigation, and it's not at all fair that I shouldn't meet him."

"*I* must insist," I responded, prying her hand from my arm, "that you do not. Mr. Holmes is a patient and deserving of his pri—"

"Oh, pooh. I haven't the slightest interest in what's wrong with him. But if he's in any condition to speak with us, I'd like to hear what he knows about this matter."

"What could he possibly know? Besides, it's very unlikely Mr. Holmes will be recovered enough—"

"To speak Cantonese?" she interrupted me yet again. "If anything strange happens, I want to be there."

I struggled with the desire to uphold some professional standards and the knowledge that her request was a fair one. "When we get there, you must wait on the landing while I ask Dr. Watson if he's willing to admit you."

"Agreed."

As it turned out, Dr. Watson had little say in the matter. For upon our arrival, a man I'd never seen before flung open the door.

Tall and heavyset in a strange, lumpy, misshapen way, the man pinned us with a stare both piercing and indolent. "Ah, Mr. Cheng, and with Miss Gaines in tow. Nothing could be better. Do, please, come in."

Chapter Thirty-Seven

I looked past him to Dr. Watson standing silhouetted with his back to the window. "Come in, Kuo, and bring your friend with you. This gentleman is Mr. Mycroft Holmes, Holmes's brother," he informed us, his voice tense.

Charlotte and I entered the room, and Mycroft Holmes closed the door behind us. Dr. Watson stepped away from the window. Though his expression was calm, his mustache bristled with irritation. "Mycroft has come expressly to speak with you."

I glanced around the room and frowned. Sherlock Holmes no longer slept on the sofa. "Where's Mr. Holmes?"

Mycroft collapsed with a heavy sigh into an armchair; as if the mere act of standing and opening the door had sapped him of his strength. He cleared his throat.

"Sherlock has been removed to another lodging where he is now recovering, thanks to the excellent care of your grandfather."

"His treatment is not yet completed," I objected. "The chances of relapse are much greater if it is stopped prematurely."

Mycroft waved a lazy hand in the air. "I understand. Of course, you will continue to deliver medicines to this address, which will be retrieved and administered to him at his present location."

"I'm sorry to interrupt," Charlotte put in, the sharpness in her voice contradicting those words. "But what on earth is going on here?"

Mycroft inhaled a ponderous breath and produced a slight smile. "Hmm, if you will all unbend enough to sit, I will tell you."

"Oh, very well," Dr. Watson declared, taking a seat. "But I object to the high-handed manner in which this was handled."

"Duly noted. However, as I explained earlier, I could no longer protect my brother while he lived here."

"Protect Mr. Holmes? What has happened?" I asked, thoroughly confused.

Dr. Watson opened his mouth, but Mycroft quickly put in, "Admonish me all you will later, Doctor. Now, I must speak with these two."

Dr. Watson snapped his mouth shut and answered him with a curt nod.

"Last night, there was an attempt on my brother's life," Mycroft told us bluntly.

Charlotte gasped, and I admit to being taken aback. At that moment, a breeze fluttered the curtains and revealed Felix perched on the windowsill. I braced for the hot, prickly sensation that often overcame me in the bird's presence. Instead, the chill, moisture-laden air washed over my face and sharpened my mind.

"How?" Charlotte asked. "Who?"

"A poison-laced packet of tea delivered by an unknown assailant. Fortunately, Mrs. Hudson—not that she would agree—has been associated with Sherlock long enough to recognize the garlic smell of arsenic when heated." He stroked his chin. "A clumsy attempt that could have harmed anyone, but that may have been the point."

"A warning?" Dr. Watson mused.

"Who can say? Though, as you can see, when everyone in the world knows where he lives, my brother was vulnerable to another attempt, perhaps not so clumsy next time."

"The question is why?" I interjected. "And what does it have to do with us?"

"Ah, yes," Mycroft agreed. "Why?"

A knock on the door heralded the arrival of Mrs. Hudson with the tea tray, not that I was eager to partake considering what we had just learned. She strode in, her back rigid with disapproval, and put the tray down with such force the cups jumped in their saucers.

She faced the room and clasped her hands before her. "I don't approve of involving these young people in whatever havey-cavey business you're about, Mr. Mycroft."

He lifted heavy lids, widening his eyes. His every movement seemed weighted with great effort, as if he lived surrounded by a thick, gooey substance.

"*I*, Mrs. Hudson, have not involved these young people in anything. *I* am here with the expressed purpose of extracting them from this very dangerous situation."

She sniffed. "Well, I shouldn't like it if they were hurt, and I know Mr. Holmes wouldn't either." With that pronouncement, she left.

"As much as she protests," Dr. Watson put in. "She's very fond of the old boy, and with Holmes ill, the attempt on his life, and now him being taken away, well, the poor thing is out of sorts."

"Be that as it may," Mycroft retorted. "I am not to blame for this muddle."

"Which is?" I prompted.

"Sherlock was hired to find and retrieve a stolen journal that contains some sensitive information about certain members of the nobility, written by one John Harold Gaines."

Charlotte started and glanced over at Dr. Watson. He shrugged and said, "Don't look at me, my dear. I knew nothing about it." He shot a resentful look at Mycroft. "Apparently, Holmes was sworn to secrecy, even as it related to me."

"This journal," Mycroft continued, ignoring his displeasure, "was used by Gaines as a sort of literary resource for his many novels. Members of his club tell me he used pseudonyms and code to mask the identities of those he noted within its pages. Still, to a person knowledgeable of society, it would not be hard to discern to whom he was referring."

The location where I had first spied Lord Marlington and the redheaded man flashed in my brain. A puzzle piece clicked into place.

"The Athenaeum Club . . . Gaines was a member, no?" I looked at Mycroft for confirmation.

He regarded me through steepled fingers. "Yes, famously so. The Athenaeum boasts a membership of the supposed intelligentsia of London society, Gaines among them. It is from the club that the journal—along with a box of documents, land deeds, and such belonging to Gaines—was stolen."

"Is Lord Marlington also a member?" I asked.

Mycroft scowled with distaste and nodded. "As well."

"Then it all makes sense," I mumbled to myself.

"What does?" Charlotte and Dr. Watson asked as one.

I held up a finger. "First, we encountered the redheaded man—"

"Quidley," Mycroft put in. "His name is Ramsey Quidley, a factotum of Lord Marlington and the rest of the Athenaeum bunch. A common ruffian, well-known to law enforcement."

I nodded. "I ran into Quidley here the same day I met you." I turned to Charlotte. "But he wasn't following you as I first thought. He was watching Sherlock Holmes." I looked again at Mycroft.

"Go on."

I stood and paced to the window. Felix cocked one beady, black eye up at me. "Are we to assume that many at the Athenaeum, including Lord Marlington, are featured in this journal?"

"We are," Mycroft replied, his mouth pulled down into an imposing frown. "And more august even than they."

"Likely, Quidley followed Mr. Holmes at Lord Marlington's request to gauge his success at finding the journal. When Holmes fell, uh, ill and Charlotte showed up here two days running, Quidley became suspicious they were being double-crossed, and that Mr. Holmes would give the journal to Charlotte—her being the Gaines heir, after all."

My friend bounced on the sofa. "Oh, and when we joined forces, Quidley thought you were in on it, and that is why—"

"He asked repeatedly for 'the book' when he attacked me at the waterman's stairs," I added with, I must admit, a bit of a dramatic flourish. "I had no idea at the time what he was talking about, but he must have meant the journal."

"What rot," Dr. Watson exclaimed, his mustache plumbed up with indignation. "As if Holmes would conduct himself so dishonorably. He would never steal a client's property and give it to another. If he objects to their position in the matter, he tells them outright."

"Hmm." Mycroft straightened his large frame and settled deeper into the cushions. "Truth be told, my good doctor, Sherlock wasn't working for Marlington or the Athenaeum set."

"You mean—?" Dr. Watson stopped himself from blurting what I had begun to suspect—that Mycroft Holmes, and by extension, his brother, worked for the Crown.

"I mean, my dear Watson, there are others more important even than the luminaries of the Athenaeum Club who want this journal."

"Oh, good grief, do stop with the obscure references," Charlotte exclaimed. "We all know you must be an agent of the Crown."

Mycroft stiffened as much as his languid mannerisms would allow. "My dear, I have no idea what you are talking about."

"So, the journal was stolen from the Athenaeum Club by persons unknown." I turned the conversation back to the matter at hand. "And these *more* important people want it and hired Mr. Holmes to find the journal. However, Marlington and his confederates are after the journal as well and set Quidley on Mr. Holmes's trail."

"Honestly," Charlotte argued, "I don't understand why anyone should have it but me. I am my grandfather's heir, as Kuo pointed out."

A look of alarm crossed Mycroft's face. "Out of the question. The journal, once recovered, must be destroyed."

Charlotte looked mulish but did not reply. I strolled over to the fireplace and stared into the flames. My mind furiously turned over what we had just learned. A forgotten piece of information burst the surface of my brain.

I spun on my heels and faced the room. "We must speak with Mrs. Hudson at once."

Chapter Thirty-Eight

After a grumbled "whatever for?" from Mycroft, Mrs. Hudson was summoned from her other duties and arrived breathless from climbing the stairs. I ushered her to the sofa.

"Mrs. Hudson," I began. "Do you remember a night—I am not sure of the date, but it was no more than five days past—when Mr. Holmes awoke and asked you to do something for him?"

"Yes. He asked me to read an article, but not that day's paper." She frowned in concentration. "An old edition . . . August eleventh, I believe."

"Is it still here?"

"Oh, goodness, no." She gestured to the room. "I finally removed the stacks and threw them away."

"And the article, what was it about?" I pressed her.

"Some stolen documents from the Athenaeum Club."

Charlotte and Dr. Watson sat up straighter at the mention. I turned to Mycroft.

"Why was Mr. Holmes dispatched to retrieve an item that had already been missing for weeks?"

Mycroft pursed his lips and cut his eyes over to Mrs. Hudson. She made to rise and quit the room, but I detained her.

"No, please stay," I insisted. "You may be needed."

I walked back to the window. A renewed sense of clarity coursed through me. Felix trilled.

"Can you answer my question?"

"Very well," he snapped. "Sherlock was asked to investigate, because several individuals received letters demanding large sums of money to withhold from the public damaging information."

"Good heavens," Dr. Watson expostulated. "Extortion in the highest ranks of society, and Holmes does not tell me."

"As you very well know, he was sworn to the strictest of secrecy."

Dr. Watson stiffened. "Little good it did him, or your illustrious client, when I wasn't there to render assistance. I assumed he had fallen into his former ways, when in all likelihood the opium was forced upon him during the days he went missing. Perhaps they even intended to kill him."

Mycroft grunted. "Such speculation is not help—"

"Mrs. Hudson," I interrupted, turning us once again back to the matter at hand. "Do you remember what the article said?"

"Hmm, just a paragraph or two." She contemplated my question for a moment. "Some documents were stolen and that the police were investigating. That was all."

"Did Mr. Holmes seem interested in any particular part of the article?"

She sighed. "Poor Mr. Holmes, he was so weak. He could hardly speak at all. However, he did ask me to repeat the items reported missing."

"And?" I prompted.

"Business letters, I believe, and a deed to a property in Yorkshire."

I stilled my face at the mention of Yorkshire. Charlotte glanced up at me, her eyes wide, but said nothing.

"Any word of a journal?" I asked.

She shook her head. "No."

"Not unusual," Mycroft insisted. "Unlikely the Athenaeum set would want to draw attention to the missing journal. I doubt they mentioned it to the police either. The theft came to our attention only when its contents were threatened to be exposed. Marlington and those fools at the club should have destroyed it long ago."

"Very likely they didn't," Dr. Watson put in, "for the same reason I doubt your employer will. Because no matter the danger to themselves, the journal holds information with which to control others. The journal equals power." He turned to me. "And that, my boy, is why we have this muddle, as our esteemed guest here so aptly put it."

Mrs. Hudson cleared her throat. "If you are quite done with me, I have business to attend to."

"Since your information sheds little light on the matter," Mycroft replied, "by all means, proceed with your other tasks."

She shot him a disapproving look and strode from the room. I walked to the sofa and sat in the place she had just vacated. Unlike Mycroft, I knew Mrs. Hudson had given us valuable information—information that perhaps Sherlock Holmes, trapped as he was in a difficult convalescence, wanted to convey.

I exchanged a questioning look with Charlotte. A little shake of her head indicated that we should not share this knowledge with our imposing new acquaintance. In this instance, I concurred; best to wait and see where this was going.

"How is the stolen journal connected to the murder of Sadie Gaines and the attack upon Charlotte?" I asked instead.

"I didn't say they were," Mycroft retorted.

"Why else are you here?"

He chuckled. "Why, indeed, my astute young friend?" He spread his hands before him. "Until my brother regains his senses, we are unlikely to know exactly where we stand in this matter.

"On one hand is the thief, on the other his pursuers, which unfortunately include the dilettantes at the Athenaeum Club."

He pursed his lips in irritation. "Do not misread me, Mr. Cheng, they are dangerous men, and they are made even more so by desperation. Many of them have much to lose should the contents of the journal be made public, Lord Marlington in particular."

He placed two large hands on the armrests and hoisted himself with great effort to his feet. Dr. Watson and I stood as well.

"I spoke with Marlington and convinced him of the mix-up and that you and Miss Gaines have nothing to do with the missing journal. Quidley should bother you no further.

"As for the murder of your aunt, Miss Gaines, for which I give you my condolences, it appears to be unconnected to the matter of the journal. From reading Inspector Lloyddyn's account, her death was the work of a madman."

He straightened the lapels of his waistcoat, preparing to depart. "The inspector is reported to be a capable man, and I urge you to leave the matter in his hands. These amateur investigations only muddy the waters and will put you in harm's way."

At the door, he turned to us with a stern look. "Mr. Cheng, Miss Gaines, I have my ways of knowing what you are about. Mark my words. I will brook no further interference by either you or the gentlemen of the Athenaeum Club."

"Wait," I called out before he could cross the threshold. "You speak of this crime as if it were the work of one man. Perhaps the journal's theft and the extortion are connected to a criminal syndicate."

Mycroft looked back at me with some amusement. "Certainly that could be the case. These last few years have seen an increase in organized crime throughout the country, especially here in London. However, Mr. Cheng, in my experience, there is always a leader.

Who, in this case, has wisely refused to sign his real name to the missives."

He chuckled. "Treating us instead to the rather vaguely menacing alias of the Grey Man." With that, he shut the door and was gone.

Chapter Thirty-Nine

Charlotte and I stared at each other in speechless astonishment. We, of course, had certain knowledge that the extortionist and murderer were indeed the same. And perhaps, the only reason Mycroft did not is because Charlotte had removed the killer's note from her aunt's mouth and Danny's outburst at the inquest never made it into the papers.

"What an unpleasant man," Charlotte declared, recovering quickly.

"He rarely moves and is merely irritable at having to leave his club," Dr. Watson replied. "Holmes insists his brother would be a far more brilliant detective than even he if Mycroft were not so lazy."

The good doctor regarded us through narrowed eyes. "You know something."

"What do you mean?" I asked, endeavoring to look innocent.

He sat with weary resignation. "I may not be as clever as my friend or his brother, but I observed you both closely throughout the conversation, and you clearly know more than you are saying."

Charlotte and I exchanged another look.

"There . . . there it is," he stated with satisfaction. "Spit it out."

Charlotte shrugged. "What harm could it do? Perhaps another person knowing would be a safeguard. But," she insisted, turning upon Dr. Watson a fierce glare, "you must keep what we tell you in confidence."

His reluctance to accept her stipulation was evident by the warring expressions that flashed across his face. He finally settled upon a look of unenthusiastic agreement.

"Very well," he replied.

"It's a long story," I protested, hoping he would change his mind.

He gestured to the sofa. "I have time and tea."

I sat next to Charlotte and regaled him with our adventures of the last week, my friend inserting clarification where needed. We left nothing out, not even the otherworldly intercession of Sherlock Holmes.

Doctor Watson listened in grim silence. After we were done, he strode over to the window and looked out, seemingly blind to the bird watching him from the sill.

"You have not read today's paper, I assume," was his surprising first response to our explosive discoveries.

I shook my head. "No. I have not."

"Nor I," Charlotte put in.

He turned back to us. "Then you will not know of the stabbing death last night of a jeweler, Mr. Julio Bosque Jr., set upon and killed by thieves, his workshop overturned and thoroughly stripped of its valuables."

We had reason to be grateful for Charlotte's insistence on his confidence and, indeed, Dr. Watson's own sense of honor. For it took a better part of the next hour to counter his demands we go immediately to the authorities with what we knew.

Shocked by Julio's murder, I admit to wavering, but Charlotte held firm. "Why should we? Indeed, Inspector Lloyddyn and Mr. Mycroft Holmes are the ones who should be exchanging information. If the latter were not so toplofty and actually *spoke* to the inspector, he would already know the Grey Man is alleged to be involved in an excess of criminal activity. We are not withholding information either man could not get from another source."

"My dear, you took evidence from a crime scene," he pointed out, his expression one of near disbelief that so delicate a girl pulled a crumpled piece of paper from the mouth of her murdered aunt. "The connection with young Teddy, the brothel, the poem, the locket, the very fact that you spoke with the jeweler days before his death . . ." He pinned us with a stern gaze. "Need I go on? You are withholding a great deal, all of which could prove fatal, and may have already for some."

Charlotte stared down at her clasped hands. "I am very sorry for Mr. Bosque, but as you pointed out, the workshop was overturned and everything stolen. He was a rich target in that part of town."

"Yes, my girl, or it may be that wherever you two go, disaster follows," he snapped, not giving an inch.

Charlotte jumped to her feet, eyes flashing. "I am no stranger to disaster. My family has certainly known its fair share." She balled her hands into fists. "Need I remind you, Dr. Watson, it was *my* aunt who was viciously killed, *I* and *my* friend who were brutally set upon, *I* who am the recipient of sick, taunting notes . . ." Her voice cracked, and she sat, blinking back tears.

"My dear," he began.

I shook my head to quiet him. "I understand your concerns but must agree with Charlotte. I trust Inspector Lloyddyn, but he is surrounded by graft and corruption. I remind you that Lord Marlington is magistrate and privy to all we may tell the inspector. And whatever Mr. Mycroft Holmes's assurances, I do not trust his ends or his ability to keep Marlington and his henchman at bay."

Charlotte threw me a grateful look, and I continued, "My grandfather and mother know everything, and they are comfortable with my involvement thus far." I didn't feel it necessary to tell him "everything" excluded a few minor details and that Mother was notably less comfortable than Grandfather.

Dr. Watson heaved a heavy sigh. "I gave my word, and I will keep it. I just hope I don't come to regret it."

Chapter Forty

"I'll warn Mrs. Davies and send her to stay with the vicar's mother in the countryside," Charlotte insisted in a hushed voice as we made our way to Russell Square and Margaret's house.

She pressed a hand to her mouth to stifle a sob. "Poor, poor Mr. Bosque."

In the relative privacy of the cab, I grasped her hand. "As you said, we cannot be certain his death is connected to our investigation.

"What purpose does it serve anyway?" I murmured, thinking aloud. "Why attack *after* we had gleaned what information he could offer?"

"It is as Inspector Lloyddyn surmises," Charlotte answered. "This is the work of a madman."

I drew my hand back and gazed out on the everyday bustle of London. The complexity of the city fascinated me. The different levels of society met and interwove across the pavement. They mingled together in markets, trains, and shipyards, dependent on each other in myriad ways, both mundane and important.

"The one we seek might be mad, but he is not simple," I replied, inspired by the city's diversity and contradictions. "If Mr. Grey and the Grey Man are one and the same, then we can assume our madman has membership in a criminal organization, perhaps even as its leader. We know he owns a brothel. We know he is a murderer, thief, and extortionist. He may even be Teddy's mysterious kidsman."

"But you are speaking of the work of years, building such an organization," she objected. "Why the interest in my family? Why now?"

"Because you are just come to London," I proclaimed with sudden clarity. The certainty of this settled in my bones, and I knew her presence to be key to the murderer's motivations. "This is as much about *you* as your grandmother. I think you have triggered something old, something he believed buried and forgotten."

"What a terrifying thought." She smiled through her worried frown. "Strangely, Kuo Cheng, I find your blunt honesty more comforting than evasions."

We pulled up to Margaret's house. Charlotte asked the driver to wait while I walked her to the door. We stood, the space between us filled with a warm, companionable silence.

"Aunt Sadie's inquest is the day after tomorrow," she said. "I received a summons as a witness."

"I too."

The late afternoon sun broke through thin clouds and cast a wan glow over the deserted street. Charlotte turned her face up to its tepid warmth. "I feel as if this day has lasted forever, and it is not yet teatime."

"I have to go," I told her. "I am due home, but we must regroup after the inquest."

She nodded her farewell and went in, leaving me alone on the stoop. Though the distance to my home was long, I waved the driver on his way. With a pensive frown and hands shoved into my pockets, I turned my steps towards the East End. Soon, the exertion of walking pumped much needed blood through my body and into my brain.

"Yorkshire . . . Gaines . . . a property in Yorkshire," I murmured, my gaze cast downward in concentration. Was it merely a coincidence that both Jack's estate and the monastery that housed Cecil Gaines were located near Worseton-on-Tees?

And what of Jack? Yet another coincidence he knew the name and address of our dead jeweler? Like Charlotte, I could hardly believe him complicit in anything so gruesome as Aunt Sadie's murder, or any murder for that matter. Still, it was odd.

"Yorkshire . . . Gaines," I grumbled. Some other connection teased me, some shadowy knowledge just beyond my grasp.

"Look where you're going, young man." Belying her size and age, a heavyset, well-dressed old woman nimbly danced out of my way.

I tipped my hat. "Pardon me, ma'am. My mind was elsewhere."

She threw a saucy smile over her shoulder and advised, "Watch your step, lad. London cabs stop for no man."

Buoyed by this civil, pleasant exchange, I continued on my way, mindful now of the flow of traffic. I drew in a deep breath. If I had not been so familiar with my surroundings, the pungent smell of the Thames would have been signal enough that I neared home.

I stepped into our store with five minutes to spare before teatime and found my family awaiting me in the kitchen. That it now included little Joey, apparently a permanent fixture on Grandfather's lap, drew from me a contented smile.

Later that night, in the seclusion of my room, and with Joey snoring gently on his cot, I studied my collected works of John Harold Gaines. There, I unearthed the obscure piece of information that had lodged in my brain, seemingly without notice years before, only to trouble me in the present.

A dedication in one of Gaines's earlier efforts referred to his beloved wife, Mary, and the Yorkshire farm where she grew up. Here was the link that connected John Harold Gaines to Yorkshire.

I wish I could say in reading this I had some dark foreboding of tragedy. In truth, I felt only satisfaction at having tracked down the source of my vague, niggling memory.

That night, I lay down, tired but looking forward to the next day, which would be consumed with the commonplace task of sorting and cataloging the new shipment. I would not think about the dedication again until much later when, in desperation, we sought to make sense of the terrible events to come.

Chapter Forty-One

The inquest into Sadie Gaines's murder, though public, was a more sober affair than Teddy's. Instead of a boisterous pub, the Coroner's Court took place in the very room where the murder was committed, rearranged to fit the coroner, a jury, witnesses, and what members of the public could squeeze into the parlour.

A queue of hopeful spectators stretched from the stoop to halfway down the block. I slipped past them and made my way to the kitchen entrance, where Nellie let me in.

"Miss Charlotte's waitin' for ya in the housekeeper's room," she informed me.

I thanked her and saluted Cook, busy rolling out a lump of dough on the floured tabletop. "Don't go upsetting the poor dear," she unfairly admonished me. "Jumpy as a cat, she is."

I bit my tongue on a defensive reply and nodded in agreement as I passed through the kitchen and into the hallway. The faithful old retainer sought only to protect her orphaned charge.

I entered the room, now less cold and forbidding with a cheery fire in the grate, and was put out to find Margaret seated on the sofa next to Charlotte. I had hoped to have a few moments alone to get our stories straight. A flicker of annoyance crossed my face.

"Ah, Mr. Cheng." Margaret rose in a rustle of elegant blue silk. "No need to poker up so. I'm off upstairs to check on the proceedings." She glanced down at a small timepiece pinned to her breast. "Ten minutes, no more, and you must follow me."

"Yes, of course," Charlotte agreed.

Margaret left us. I walked to the fireplace and turned my back to the flames. Charlotte sat facing me. I blinked (to my chagrin), taken aback by her appearance.

"You've changed your hair," I declared, although that was the least of it.

The curly fringe was gone, replaced by an artful pile of loose curls topped with a small, black felt hat. She stood and patted the back of her head.

"Do you like it? Margaret says a woman is always first judged by her looks, and we must present a picture of calm and proficiency when in official settings." She smoothed her skirts. "I wore black for my dear old guardian, but Margaret assures me I'm not required to go into full mourning for an aunt. Still, my dress must show a certain level of respect due a close relative."

The dark, plum-colored silk dress crossed at the top over a deep-purple velvet undershirt with large, puffed sleeves. A black, crepe belt cinched her waist, and black lace gloves encased her hands. The black parasol lying on the sofa completed her outfit.

She looked like a sleek, iridescent fairy queen. I suppressed the urge to tell her just that, saying instead, "You look very well indeed."

Charlotte smiled, and a faint blush touched her pale cheeks. That those cheeks were paler than usual had not escaped my notice. She wrung her hands, and her nervous glance darted around the room. She sat, back rigid, and patted the sofa beside her.

"Sit. We must talk. If I am to lie to the authorities, so must you," she said, releasing a dramatic sigh.

"Not direct lies," I countered, sitting. "Except the one where I am your tutor, the rest are just omissions of information."

"As Dr. Watson pointed out, that is quite a lot."

"True. But once we have all the answers, we can lay them before Inspector Lloyddyn, and perhaps he will be forgiving."

She laughed and her shoulders relaxed. "Our roles have reversed, and it is I who must quash such fanciful thinking. I have no doubt he will be quite angry with us."

I nodded, amused. "You are likely correct."

Charlotte stood again and paced to the fireplace and back. I stood to join her, and she frowned at me.

"I say, Kuo, where is that floppy hat you wore when we first met?" she asked.

Her question gave me pause. Not because I needed to search for an answer (I knew exactly where the hat was), but because she had asked it at all.

I never imagined Charlotte noticing anything about me, much less my clothing. The fact that she had brought home to me the poor companion my own respectable, though well-used suit, made to her general splendor.

Only last week, Mother had let out the hem of my trousers by two inches and my jacket sleeves by as much. But even expert laundering could not hide the worn and faded crease of the old hem. A sudden wave of shame swept over me at perceiving myself as humble and unworthy.

Margaret sailed in and pronounced in her usual imperious manner, "I said ten min—"

"Not yet," I barked, using anger as a substitute for self-pity. "I am quite capable of getting us where and when we are needed."

She drew back, her color heightened. Her lips opened on an angry retort.

I hoped she would chastise me. I longed for a target against which to throw my loathing of . . . the English, the rich, myself? I wasn't sure.

Margaret snapped her mouth shut and drew in a deep breath. "I daresay you are right, but the jury is seated, and the coroner will soon call witnesses."

"Pardon—" I began, having regained my composure.

She shushed me and led us through the doorway and out into the hall. "No need for apologies. I, too, have frayed nerves. I'm to be called as a witness, even though I saw and heard nothing beyond the neighbors yelling and banging at the door."

We went up the stairs and out onto a landing off the foyer. A bobby guarded the open door, and people milled around outside on the stoop. Margaret led us to the parlour and stopped just before the entrance.

"Everything has been rearranged to accommodate the inquest, but do prepare yourselves. The last time you were here, a woman lay dead, and you faced her murderer. So, stiff upper lip," Margaret encouraged us. "Also, beware. Ian Thorngoode, the most notorious of journalists, if one can say that of such a vicious gossip, is within."

I groaned. I had no desire for my name (or by association, our store) to appear in the pages of *The Wasp*, a shameless rag that published all sorts of sordid and lurid tales, many of them disparaging of Limehouse and the Chinese who lived there. Thorngoode's column was notable for both exemplifying the worst of sensationalized reporting and being extremely popular.

"Ian Thorngoode?" Charlotte looked her confusion.

"I'll tell you later," I answered, adding for her ears only, "Don't worry about anyone else. They have no reason to disbelieve us."

Margaret straightened her shoulders. "I will go first and draw everyone's attention. You two slip in behind me and circle around the back next to the wall. Meet me on the other side, where I have secured us seats."

With this masterful piece of planning, Margaret glided into the room. I hesitated, unsure whether even the striking Miss Scott would be enough to keep all eyes from watching the door in anticipation of Charlotte's arrival.

Margaret moved with supreme confidence. The deep blue of her dress enhanced her creamy complexion and highlighted her chestnut curls. As she had predicted, every head turned to watch her pass.

Charlotte plucked at my sleeve. "Come on, now's our chance."

We slipped in unobserved and made our way to the back of the room. The plan went amiss when Lord Brudeford caught my eye from a chair in the far corner of the parlour.

He jerked his head with a "come here" gesture. At that moment, Margaret "casually" glanced back to determine our progress.

The scene would have been comical as a staged farce, but as it was, trapped between Lord Brudeford's insistent head jerking and Margaret's impatient scowl, we hovered, uncertain and petrified. Finally, Charlotte gave my hand a reassuring squeeze.

"You go to Lord Brudeford. I will go to Margaret."

"Yes," I agreed. "It is best we are not seated together."

She cast me a tremulous smile over her shoulder, and I whispered, "Courage. You can do this."

The coroner banged his gavel to call the proceedings to order just as we took our seats. "What are you doing here?" I demanded in a whisper, irritated at his unexpected appearance.

"I come bearing an invitation."

"Couldn't you have sent it round to the store?"

"No. I had to be certain you would come, and I knew you'd be here. The invitation is for tea with my mother, and"—he grimaced—"for the sake of my sanity, you *must* attend."

"Why? What does Lady Brudeford want with me?"

"That meddling woman"—he nodded to Margaret—"told my sister about our little misadventure. Her interference led to an interrogation by my mother, who deigned to visit me at the publishing house. And now she wants a word with you and your Charlotte."

"She is *not*—" I bit back an angry retort at his sly smile. "When?" I asked through gritted teeth.

"Today, after the inquest. Says she has information on Mary Gaines."

Before I could object to such abrupt notice, the coroner called, "Dr. Ronald Payne, please step forward."

I turned my attention to the unfortunately named yet nattily dressed young doctor who took the witness chair. At some inquests, the body lays on display while the doctor is questioned. I was grateful the coroner had not deemed it necessary at Teddy's inquest and doubly so here, given the grisly manner of Aunt Sadie's death.

Even without the body, the detailed description by Dr. Payne drew gasps and groans of sympathy from the spectators. I could not see Charlotte's response, having only the back view of her head.

"What kind of knots were used?" a juror asked.

"I'm not entirely sure. Some type of sailor's knot that can slide along a rope," Dr. Payne answered, his face a mask of professional detachment. "As she struggled to relieve the pain of her limbs tied behind her, the noose about her neck tightened, cutting off her airway and killing her."

Another collective groan arose from all but a burly man with a bushy black beard who scribbled away in a small notebook. The infamous Ian Thorngoode, with his broad shoulders and crooked nose, looked more like an out-to-pasture old boxer than a newspaperman.

He had a knack for sniffing out the gruesome and tragic, and happily fed the public's appetite for scandal. He also had a knack for making his stories leap off the page.

More's the pity. I hated wasted talent.

My skin twitched with the sensation of being watched. I turned from Thorngoode to find Inspector Lloyddyn's pensive gaze upon me. I nodded in greeting and looked back at Dr. Payne.

"The only other finding of note," the doctor continued, "was a small—I almost missed it—injection site between the big and second toes of her left foot."

I sat back with a silent gasp, and my startled glance met the now hard, suspicious eyes of Inspector Lloyddyn.

Chapter Forty-Two

"Injection?" one of the jurors asked. "Of what?"

I calmed my breathing and turned my attention back to the doctor. He clasped his hands in his lap and furrowed his brow.

"I can't be sure, perhaps morphine, something to render her listless and malleable. To truss up a protesting woman is difficult. Since there was no head trauma to indicate she was made unconscious in that manner, nor were there defensive wounds, we may suppose a drug of some sort."

"Could she have injected herself?" the coroner asked.

"Doubtful. There were no other marks to indicate habitual use with a hypodermic needle."

A red-faced juror stammered, "Begging your pardon, Doctor, but . . . ah . . . an injection in the foot would mean the victim was . . . ah . . . didn't have any shoes on."

Dr. Payne cleared his throat. "That is correct. She was not wearing shoes or stockings."

"Was she properly dressed otherwise?" a braver juror asked.

"She was."

The coroner frowned. "Properly dressed but no shoes or stockings? To inject the drug, both stocking and shoe, on one foot at least, would have to be removed . . . and all this without protest or injury?"

"Yes," Dr. Payne agreed. "But perhaps she took her shoes off for comfort when at home or wore slippers. I can only surmise."

Charlotte's back stiffened, and I longed to know what revelation had come to her. The coroner thanked Dr. Payne and dismissed him.

Over the next hour, the neighbors, Cook and Nellie, Margaret, and Inspector Lloyddyn were called. The inspector, notably, gave no new information and admitted that the investigation had stalled due to lack of clues.

He did not look at me again, but his voice held the barest hint of frustration. I knew he would corner me as soon as he got the chance.

I delivered my own testimony in as matter-of-fact a manner as possible. Ian Thorngoode alternated between scrutinizing my face with an intense frown and scribbling furiously in his notebook.

The few questions directed at me centered on getting a clearer picture of the attacker. But I could only give a general description of his build and clothing, noting that he wore a toilette mask to hide his face.

The coroner called Charlotte last. Thorngoode tensed and leaned forward in his chair. A hush fell over the audience. This was what they had come for—the fragile, beautiful heir to the tragic Gaines legacy.

The prose wrote itself: *Pale and drawn, yet brave, Miss Gaines, a subdued presence in deep purple, gave a harrowing account of the brutal attack. With her voice at times a mere whisper, one of the last surviving members of that accursed family . . .*

From the stoic expression on her face, Charlotte appeared unwilling to play the role of the tremulous ingénue. She spoke in a calm and collected tone, her voice easily reaching us in the back. Though she slipped, at times, into familiar dramatic gestures and clichéd expressions, for the most part, she did not give way to theatrics.

Unlike me, she endured many questions from both the coroner and the jurors. They typically prefaced these with fawning tributes to her courage and fortitude.

"She is sure to be insufferable after this," I whispered to Lord Brudeford.

"You have only to look at her benefactress to see what it is to be truly insufferable," he returned, nodding at Margaret.

I studied her lovely profile. "I didn't like her at first, but now I think Miss Scott is a better person than many of her peers."

A contemplative "hmm" was his only response.

Despite the long-winded questioning, Charlotte kept her composure. After almost three quarters of an hour, the coroner thanked her and asked her to step down.

The inquest concluded with a ruling of deliberate murder by persons unknown. This surprised no one, and people prepared to leave.

Lord Brudeford leaned over and remarked with some amusement, "I say, the jurors swallowed whole that fiddle-faddle of you being a Gaines scholar and her tutor."

For a man of such impressive intellect, Lord Brudeford lacked a basic understanding of his race. "What do you suppose an Englishman to believe?" I stood and glared down at him. "That I'm her friend? That a girl like Charlotte would associate with me out of feelings of mutual sympathy? Such a relationship is beyond their comprehension. They believe the ludicrous, because they are incapable of seeing the obvious," I finished, my throat unusually tight.

Lord Brudeford stood and placed a hand on my shoulder. "What is the obvious, my boy?"

I suppressed my anger and turned on him my most Sphinxlike expression. "That she hired me to track down the source of an anonymous poem, of course."

"Like squeezing blood from a turnip." He laughed, shaking his head, but sobered almost at once. "Let's gather up young Miss Gaines and go. My mother can be frightening when crossed."

"I have no idea whether Charlotte is available," I protested, irritated at his insistence that we meet with Lady Brudeford.

He pretended not to hear and pulled me through the milling crowd. "We must remove her from that woman's clutches," he pronounced, heading towards Charlotte and Margaret as they also tried to leave.

"Ho, there Mr. Cheng." A hand grasped my other arm, jerking both Lord Brudeford and me to a halt. "I have some questions for you."

To my dismay, these words were accompanied by a belligerent smirk from Ian Thorngoode. "I have nothing to add," I told him, removing my arm from his grasp.

He drew back with exaggerated surprise. "Well, well, you'd think an eminent Gaines scholar like yourself might want a bit of free advertisement." His voice dripped with sarcasm, and his next words realized my greatest fear. "You and that pretty miss putting your heads together studying and all. No one watching out for her . . . makes for some interesting reading. Don't you think?"

"I'd plant you a facer myself, you blackguard, if I wasn't pressed for time." Lord Brudeford stared down his nose, his mouth pursed with distaste.

They were a study in contrasts, the tall, gaunt aristocrat, disheveled, yet somehow still elegant and imposing, and the aggressive bulldog journalist who showed him no deference. Thorngoode chuckled.

"So says the disgraced scion of a fine old family. Mayhap your name'll find its way into my article. You and your little half-breed Oriental here."

My tutor scoffed with bitter cynicism. "*Mayhap*, my friend, you will then find yourself out of a job. My fine old family, while not supportive of my way of life, will crush you like a bug."

A few people inched closer to better observe the tense scene. I seethed with frustration, not wanting to draw further attention.

"Ho, now." The journalist bared his teeth in a wolfish grin. "I'm shakin' in me boots."

"As well you should be," Lord Brudeford drawled. "Ask your old colleague, hmm, what was his name? Ah, yes, Zachariah Thrum. Ask him what happens to one who goes up against my family."

The burly, quarrelsome man paled and dropped his confident smile. "You . . . your family did *that* to old Thrum?"

"Indeed. Now, without further ado . . ." My tutor once again pulled me onward, leaving behind the crestfallen man, only for Inspector Lloyddyn to accost us next.

Lord Brudeford pursed his lips with displeasure, but unlike the chastened journalist, the inspector showed no signs of pique. He held up his hand.

"No need to put me in my place. I've spoken with Miss Gaines and am aware that she and Mr. Cheng have an appointment with Lady Brudeford."

My tutor narrowed his eyes and looked over at Charlotte and Margaret as they finally made their way out of the parlour. "That woman," he hissed. "In collusion with my mother, no doubt—" He brought himself up short, realizing his indiscretion.

An amused smile quivered on the inspector's lips. "Yes, well, I wouldn't know." Turning to me, he dropped any appearance of good humor and pinned me with a stern glare. "Miss Gaines assures me she will consult with you and determine a time in the next two days to present yourselves at my office for a discussion of the case."

"I gave my testimony, Inspector. I can't see what good—"

"Fortunately, your opinion has no bearing on my decision. If you do not appear for our interview, I'll send officers to retrieve you. Is that understood?"

I nodded, and he left with little more than a grunt as farewell. Lord Brudeford patted my back. "What did I tell you? I don't like the man, but he's not stupid. He knows you and Miss Gaines are up to something."

I shook my head. "No. There is an odd similarity between Sadie Gaines's murder and the death of my friend, Teddy. In the inspector's eyes, I am a connection, a suspicious one."

"Well," he proclaimed, propelling me out of the parlour and down the hallway. "If you make a good impression on my mother, maybe she'll intimidate the police into leaving you alone."

We reached the street to find Charlotte and Margaret hailing a cab. Charlotte spied me and called out, "Kuo."

I noted the lurking figure of Ian Thorngoode and stepped back a respectable distance to avoid Charlotte's overly familiar clutch at my arm. She took no notice and leaned her head close to mine.

"Her slippers," she whispered in a fierce undertone. "Aunt Sadie had a pair of worn woolen slippers tucked away in her embroidery basket in the parlour. Her feet pained her in shoes, and she put her slippers on whenever we were alone. Her only endearing quality, I might add." She took a deep breath. "Now they're gone. I asked Cook and Nellie. They moved all the personal belongings from the parlour for the inquest and the slippers were nowhere to be found."

Margaret joined us. She and Lord Brudeford exchanged curt nods.

"I might have known," he interjected, unable to contain himself. "Conspiring with my mother are you, Miss Scott?"

Margaret tossed a tendril of chestnut hair over her shoulder. "On the contrary, I have better things to do than involve myself in your business, but I, too, was summoned. Lady Brudeford is not one to be ignored."

"How well I know," he conceded.

A brief moment of camaraderie flared between them. I took the opportunity to whisper to Charlotte, "Beware, Ian Thorngoode stalks us. We mustn't be seen as too friendly."

Her eyes widened with understanding, and she drew back. Margaret put an arm about her shoulders.

"Come, Charlotte, our cab awaits. We will meet you at Brudeford House," she pronounced, and swept the girl away.

Chapter Forty-Three

Seated in our own cab, I ventured to ask Lord Brudeford about the exchange between him and Ian Thorngoode. "Who was Zachariah Thrum and what happened to him?"

He laughed, a real one where he threw back his head and could hardly catch his breath from the force of it. "Old Thrum," he replied when able to speak, "used to work at *The Wasp*. Probably mentored that scoundrel Thorngoode, for a nastier pen you couldn't find.

"Thrum had gathered some, um, unflattering information about my late father. In this case, it wasn't a lie or an exaggeration. Mother, being no fool, offered the man a generous sum to bury it and retire. Of course, the old wretch put out a terrifying story of being set upon and beaten, broken fingers and such, and warned never to write again. He even walked around in bandages for a full fortnight before leaving London." Lord Brudeford snorted. "Thrum lives in comfort on a nice little property outside of Manchester, where he's from, courtesy of the Brudeford estate."

"Won't your mother be upset you named the family as responsible?"

He dismissed my concern with a languid wave of his hand. "Not likely. There were always rumors it was us, because Thrum let out he was working on a story about my father. The man made plenty of enemies during his long, illustrious career, so we weren't the only candidates. Thorngoode won't cross us, and I very much doubt he would publish something that explosive based on a casual remark. If there were a decent journalist among them, they'd have sniffed out this story long ago. As is . . ." He let his words drift off, and we soon approached Hyde Park, entering Mayfield, one of the most exclusive areas of London.

I've been to Hyde Park once and have since made any excuse, no matter how inconvenient, to avoid its green expanse. I enjoy the smaller pockets of nature sprinkled throughout the city but experience confusion when surrounded by large swathes of grass and trees. Like a swimmer losing sight of the shore, anxiety grips me when I can no longer see clearly the buildings and streets that serve as my daily compass.

Brudeford House sat back on Curzon Street and lay an easy walk to Stanhope Gate and the bucolic tranquility of the park's winding trails beyond. Though not as impressive as some of the grand town homes of the nobility, the building occupied its own grounds and shone white in the dull midday sun.

My tutor sprang from the cab, and I followed him to the entryway jutting out from the center of the house. The large, carved oaken doors stood open, and a white-haired butler in livery greeted us—or rather, Lord Brudeford.

"Peaks, good to see you again," he returned with a salute.

The old man's lips produced the slightest of smiles. I deduced that Lord Brudeford was likely a favorite with the staff.

"It has been too long, my lord. Her ladyship awaits you in the green room."

"Thank you, Peaks. I know the way."

I hurried to keep up with my long-legged friend as we mounted a sweeping staircase to the first floor. I barely had time to catch my breath or survey my surroundings. He moved with such speed, as if the faster we got there, the sooner he could be gone.

He opened the door, and we stepped into a calming sea-green confection. Light filtered in through the long windows and brushed the aqua walls and thick carpet, casting a soothing glow over the room. Blown glass vases in shades of green and blue sat filled with autumn flowers on the mantle and scattered tables. Charming and unique, the whole effect served to set one at ease.

"Don't be fooled," Lord Brudeford muttered out the corner of his mouth. "Mother does this on purpose to catch you off your guard. The woman's a tactical genius."

"No whispering among yourselves, unless you wish to tell the rest of us." A musical voice floated over from a large armchair situated with its back to the windows.

From Lord Brudeford's ominous warnings, I had expected to confront some type of gorgon in mid-century dress. Instead, I faced a handsome woman as gaunt as her son and as fashionably dressed as the two younger ones seated on a sofa flanking her.

She presented her cheek to Lord Brudeford, and he dropped a light kiss upon it. "Mr. Kuo Cheng," he said, "my mother, Lady Edwina Brudeford."

I made a slight bow. "Your ladyship."

A charming smile lit up her face. She stretched out her hand, and I stood for a moment, uncertain.

Her smile widened. "You are not required to kiss it. A simple shake and we are done."

Our hands clasped briefly and dropped away. She gestured to the unoccupied sofa on the other side of her chair.

"Please, do sit."

We faced Charlotte and Margaret on the opposite sofa, with Lady Brudeford seated in the middle, as if at the head of a table, or more like, a monarch holding court—genius, indeed. A footman padded across the carpet and set a tea tray on a low table in the middle.

"Clive." Lady Brudeford turned her sparkling blue eyes on her son. "Don't blame Margaret for this situation. She had nothing to do with it. I have other means of gathering intelligence, as you well know."

Lord Brudeford swallowed a bite of coconut macaroon. "I don't believe you." He regarded Margaret through heavy, drooping lids. "Talebearer."

"Know-it-all," Margaret shot back.

"Busybody."

"Insufferable bore."

"Enough," Lady Brudeford commanded. "You sound like squabbling babies. And you, Clive, the older and a gentleman."

"I make no claim to that title, Mother."

A pained expression crossed her face, and Lord Brudeford dropped his gaze. For the first time, I saw something akin to shame animate his patrician features.

Lady Brudeford waved her beringed, fine-boned hand. "I have no need for either of you. Clive, take Margaret into the gardens. I wish to speak with these children alone."

"Mother, I—"

"Lady Brudeford, there is no—"

"Be quiet, both of you. You have served your purpose in bringing them to me. Be gone."

Lord Brudeford rose and, with a stoic expression, presented Margaret his arm. She took the crook with the very tips of her fingers, and they left walking as far apart as courtesy allowed.

I turned back to Lady Brudeford and found her gaze upon me. "It pains me to ask this of a stranger, Mr. Cheng, but is my son well?"

I studied her solemn face, laugh lines etched deep at the corners of her eyes and mouth. "No, he is not," I answered.

She looked down at her lap and ran a hand across a prayer book almost lost in the folds of her skirt. "I know something about your grandfather. I make such things my business. I am not sure I approve of either him or you. Nevertheless, he is well regarded, and you are his apprentice. It would please me to know his opinion."

I bristled at her slight, but replied with composure, "He believes your son would benefit from some introspection regarding his time in Afghanistan. Face his demons, so to speak."

She stiffened. "Are you suggesting my son is a coward?"

I hesitated. Her reaction did not bode well, but this might be the only chance I had to help my tutor. "It is not a coward who looks on slaughter and death and cannot stomach what he sees, cannot reconcile his principles with his actions on the battlefield. One could say it is cowardly to turn a blind eye, to make excuses, and accept the incongruity."

"Clive is a peer of the realm. I'd rather it not known he was unable to face the heat of battle."

"He served, and honorably so. Would you rather he was known for what he has become? That he continues to waste his abilities in an opium haze?" My resentment bubbled to the fore. "Is this a mother's love?" I bit my lip, knowing I had pushed too far.

"You dare," she snapped. Her eyes flashed a steely blue.

With some effort, I returned her gaze. "Forgive me. I spoke out of turn."

Lady Brudeford dropped her forehead into her hand and sat silent for a full minute. Charlotte and I exchanged a concerned look.

"Your ladyship?" I prompted.

She waved a languid hand in a gesture much like her son's. "Let us speak no more about it. We have gone far afield of why I asked you here.

"Charlotte," she continued. "I knew your grandmother, Mary, and wished to impart some information to you."

My friend had sat quiet during the whole of our exchange. She stood now and crossed the short distance to sit beside me. An act of solidarity that threatened my composure more than anything Lady Brudeford could say or do.

Charlotte smoothed her skirt and folded her hands on her lap. "Yes?"

A sad smile quivered on Lady Brudeford's lips. "Mary had such spirit once. Nothing has made me feel old more than the sight of you . . . ah, well." She cleared her throat. "I was not born into the aristocracy but married into it, as you see. Perhaps I am stricter in manner and custom, because I operate under the judgmental eyes of those who are."

She shrugged. "No matter the approval of my peers, I had a very happy childhood and met Mary when we were girls at school together. Oh, but she was a wit, always writing, always coming up with some new play. All of us girls adored her, and for two years, we were inseparable."

Lady Brudeford reached for a mother-of-pearl inlaid box on a side table. She set it atop the prayer book in her lap. "One day, a photographer came to the school. We were allowed to have our portraits taken in whatever grouping we wished and wearing the most outlandish costumes."

She took from the box a photograph, old by the look of it, and handed it to Charlotte. I peered over her shoulder.

Two girls stood dressed in Roman togas with laurel garlands in their hair and strappy sandals on their feet. Their arms about each other's waists, they raised wooden swords into the air.

Though stilted as many old daguerreotypes were, I could see the girls struggle to suppress laughter and to maintain fierce, warrior expressions. They were a pretty pair—the fair, willowy Lady Brudeford a contrast to the dark and curvaceous Mary Gaines.

"Mary had a beau, John, as you know. They met when she was only fifteen. He studied with her father, who was a farmer, but also a rather renowned scholar of Roman history." She pursed her lips in distaste. "I never liked him. John, that is. He proclaimed a grand passion for Mary, pursued her, even sending her poems and stories he wrote to the school. She loved him madly in return.

"Mary had dreams of writing, but John wouldn't hear of it. If they were to marry, she must devote herself to him."

Lady Brudeford stood and set the box and prayer book on the vacated chair. "Come with me. I have something to show you."

Chapter Forty-Four

We followed her down the hallway to an impressive library set with shelves of thousands upon thousands of books. Nooks with comfortable chairs for reading beckoned, and a large stained-glass window glowed above us, casting a hushed sanctity over the room. From a heavy, imposing desk she picked up a small volume bound in rich leather with the following words embossed in gold lettering: *From the Ingenious Mind of the Marvelous Mary Gaines (née Stafford).*

"I took all her plays, stories, and poems and had them printed and bound. I gave her this book as a wedding present. It came back to me with a note from Mary, thanking me but saying that John had thought the book boastful and immodest."

She handed it to Charlotte. "Have it, my dear. Someone in her family should know her brilliance."

Charlotte clasped the book to her and whispered, "Thank you."

"They married, as you know," Lady Brudeford continued. "She gave up everything to be with him—her writing, even her religion. The Stafford family was devoutly Catholic, but John was famous for his opposition to the religious order. Nevertheless, Mary was happy and supported him in his endeavors." She drew in a deep breath. "Until she changed sometime after Emma died, her youngest sister, that is."

Lady Brudeford walked to the fireplace and stared down at the banked embers. "They make much of John's sorrow over Emma's death, but Mary was inconsolable, and it wasn't only grief, but also rage."

"What did she die of?" Charlotte asked.

"Consumption, I believe. She was so weak, poor girl. She never left the house in the final months of her illness." Lady Brudeford fell silent, contemplating the long-ago demise of poor Emma.

"Is there more?" I prompted.

"Don't tell my son," she said with a smile. "But Margaret did have a hand in this. When she told me of meeting Clive, in what condition, and with whom, I was compelled to see him.

"When I visited his lodgings, he told me of your investigation and recited the poem. In that verse, Mary's fury reached out to me as if from beyond the grave." She clenched and unclenched her hands, finally clasping them before her. "John had nicknames for Mary, just as he did for the children. At first, they were affectionate and loving, but as she grew older, they became increasingly derisive. During the only holiday our families spent together in the Lakes District, he referred to her as his Glowering Goose. She hated it, feeling it cast her as old, silly, and discontented."

Lady Brudeford's eyes flashed with anger. "I believe Mary is the author of the poem, and that *she* is the Glowering Woman."

Her pronouncement rang through the stately library. Charlotte and I exchanged a meaningful glance.

"I can tell from your expressions this is not news to you," she observed, somewhat deflated that we had not met her information with audible gasps.

"Oh yes, it is, indeed," Charlotte insisted. "We knew she wrote the poem but had no idea the Glowering Woman referred to her."

I nodded. "The poem takes on greater meaning knowing the author and subject are one and the same."

"No need to placate me with undeserved credit, young man," she scolded. "Still, the words haunted me, until I was certain the Glowering Woman was Mary and the cowardly man was John."

Charlotte recited the verse aloud:

"*The lowering sky benights the day,*
and the cowardly man has his way.
The sister lost, betrays the nave,
and the glowering woman defies the grave."

"Not one of her best," Lady Brudeford admitted. "But what does it mean? If indeed she is the Glowering Woman, how did she defy the grave? She is dead. Who is the sister lost? Emma, lost to illness, or Ava, lost through betrayal?"

"Or neither," I interjected.

"At least the first part is clear," Charlotte reasoned. "The 'cowardly man,' my grandfather, has his way by committing her to an asylum, thus blighting her life."

"Twice I visited her at that dreadful place—certainly better than Bedlam, but a prison, nonetheless," Lady Brudeford told us, indignant. "But Mary refused to see me, and I never received an answer to my letters.

"Now." She shooed us towards the door and out into the hallway. "I have told you everything I know and see you are in the thick of it, as they say. I cannot force your confidence, though I'm inclined to try. I am usually quite successful with my own children."

She laughed at our closed expressions and instructed the butler to call for the carriage. "Peaks, inform Lord Brudeford and Miss Scott it is time to leave." She turned to us. "I hope that greater familiarity has engendered some understanding between those two."

I looked skeptical, and she raised her eyebrows. "You think it unlikely?"

"Not impossible, certainly," I hedged.

At that moment, Lord Brudeford and Margaret appeared from around the corner of the house walking slowly and in conversation. I glanced up at our hostess. A superior, knowing smile spread across her face as they approached.

I reassessed my impression of her as, though formidable, a rather typical representative of her class. But did her haughty charm hide a Machiavellian mind?

"I'm only a concerned mother, Mr. Cheng," she said, and I started, fearful she had somehow read my mind. "But I am also observant and unafraid to take action. Clive believes I'm grateful for his absence, but I'll do whatever necessary to bring my son home."

As the couple neared, Margaret sparkled with animation, talking, and Lord Brudeford listened, a smile hovering on his lips. They made a striking pair. I could see how it made sense to Lady Brudeford.

"Even if it means sacrificing a young woman to his demons?" I asked. "No one, Lady Brudeford, can save your son but himself."

"You are impertinent, young man," she snapped, an angry flush on her cheeks.

"Oh yes," Charlotte chimed in. "Kuo's known for that. Margaret doesn't like it either, though she pretends not to care."

This forced a reluctant laugh from her ladyship. "I can imagine. Tell me," she said. "Is Mr. Sherlock Holmes involved in this case?"

I frowned, perplexed by the sudden turn of our conversation. "No, not in any meaningful way. He has been ill and is under my grandfather's care."

"You wonder at my question," she declared. "Well, I will tell you. It was he who introduced my son to opium after his return from Afghanistan. Clive refuses to tell me the whole, but I know it involved some nefarious dealings. Would it shock you, Mr. Cheng, to know that I hope Mr. Holmes suffers?"

I noted again the steel in her steady gaze and replied, "Not in the least."

Lord Brudeford and Margaret joined us, and we waited in silence for the carriage. When it arrived, pulled by a matched pair of dappled grays and sporting the family crest, Lady Brudeford bid us goodbye. We sped away, kicking up a spray of dust and gravel.

Neither Lord Brudeford nor Margaret showed any interest in what Lady Brudeford had told us. They sat across from each other, conversed not at all, and studiously avoided meeting the others' gaze.

It was with some relief Lord Brudeford asked to be let down on Garrick Street, not far from his lodgings. Margaret, released from his binding presence, said to Charlotte, "I have a meeting and must part with you for the evening."

"You needn't worry about me," my friend replied. "First, I'm going home to get Rose-Marie and check on Cook and Nellie before dinner. I hope they weren't too inconvenienced by the inquest."

"As you will," Margaret returned. "I'll see you afterwards. Perhaps a game of whist before bedtime."

Charlotte smiled her agreement. "I would like that."

Margaret left us at Russell Square. Charlotte and I looked at each other from across the spacious carriage.

She laughed. "*What* has happened to them?"

I smiled but said in all seriousness, "A budding yet disastrous romance."

"The gardens at Brudeford House must be magical indeed to affect such a change," she replied. "But I must agree with you. Despite his title and family fortune, Lord Brudeford does not appear to me a stable prospect for marriage."

On that massive understatement, we stopped before number fourteen Gower Street. We had hardly alighted when Nellie rushed up from the kitchen. She clutched Rose-Marie under one arm and held a worn woolen slipper in the other hand.

"Oh, miss," she cried. "Some . . ." She gasped for air. "Something terrible, I'm sure."

The blood drained from Charlotte's face. She stretched her arms out for the dog. "What has happened to dear Rose-Marie?"

"No, miss, it ain't the dog," Nellie replied, handing off a robust Rose-Marie into Charlotte's arms. "It's this." She waved the slipper in front of our faces. "I let the little dog here out in the garden for a . . . a break, and he come back with this."

"He found one of Aunt Sadie's slippers."

"Look inside," Nellie urged.

With Charlotte's arms full, I took the slipper from the agitated housemaid. My heart thumped hard as I pulled from its depths an envelope addressed simply to: *Miss Charlotte Gaines.*

"You see," Nellie declared. "This letter is just like the other one, the one Miss Charlotte got on her birthday."

Charlotte pressed the dog close and rubbed her cheek against its wiry fur. "Read it, Kuo," she whispered, her voice atremble.

I took from the envelope a piece of ordinary stock paper with gold ink around the edges. I read:

Oedipus's daughter, Judas whore, I will cast your filthy carcass into the infernal fires of Hell–The Grey Man

The words had barely left my lips when Charlotte emitted a long, lingering sigh and swayed. I caught her before she hit the pavement. Nellie snatched Rose-Marie from her limp grasp, and I lifted her slight frame with little effort. We rushed down the stairs into the kitchen.

Not easily overset, Cook directed me to lay my burden on the table. She put a cool, wet towel on the girl's forehead.

I stood back, breathless and uncertain, my years of training somehow forgotten. A nugget of information gleaned from the many novels I'd read featuring delicate heroines resurfaced. "Smelling salts?"

Cook shook her head. "No need. She's already waking."

Indeed, she was. Charlotte's breast rose on a deep breath, and her eyelashes fluttered.

"Rose-Marie?" she murmured, starting up in alarm.

Cook grasped her elbow and helped her to sit. "Don't worry. That creature is just fine."

Charlotte put a hand to her forehead. "Did I faint? How mortifying."

"A completely rational response to this," I replied with feeling, waving the paper around in the air. "These messages have become increasingly deranged. The danger is too great. We must go now to Inspector Lloyddyn with what we know."

Charlotte shook her head and groaned. "Ugh, I shouldn't do that." Pulling in another breath and straightening her shoulders, she declared, "No. I want to get as much information as possible before we report to him. Tomorrow, we visit Broxburn Inn, and the day after that, we go to the inspector."

I studied my friend—not she the delicate heroine of popular novels. I admired her brave stance but feared it a foolhardy one.

"Your life is at risk," I protested. "This man is out there close by, close enough to give Rose-Marie one of your aunt's slippers with this vile note."

Cook took it from me. She scanned the paper. "Dear God, Miss Charlotte."

"No need to take on so." Charlotte gave her arm a reassuring squeeze. "I believe my aunt was made vulnerable by the presence of Mrs. Marshton. I, on the other hand, am surrounded by those I trust—*and* I am forewarned."

Charlotte pushed off the table and stood with one hand gripping the back of a chair. "Do not waste effort in trying to gainsay me. I've made up my mind." She met my eyes, questioning. "But I do not risk danger alone. I cannot ask you to put yourself in further jeopar—"

I cut her off with an impatient shake of my head. "I'm in this to the end."

Chapter Forty-Five

After a quick confab to plan our next move, Cook and Nellie bundled Charlotte off to Margaret's house. I stood alone in the kitchen.

The paper with its golden edges glared up at me from the table. I knew immediately what "Oedipus's daughter" alleged and hoped Charlotte did not.

Judas, of course, referred again to an act of betrayal, and "whore" seemed more a rambling insult from an unhinged mind than a serious accusation. But the final words left me with little doubt Charlotte's life was in grave danger, and I debated whether to take the note directly to Inspector Lloyddyn.

Knowing the killer's hand had touched the paper, I suffered an unaccustomed bout of superstition and pocketed the thing with great reluctance. The words, written in the now familiar elegant, decorative script, frightened me as little else had before in my life. Nevertheless, I honored Charlotte's request to remain silent and made my way home.

I did not tell Grandfather or Mother of the note's existence. I could not risk the possibility they would forbid my further involvement or go themselves to Inspector Lloyddyn with the information.

The next morning, I arose early and headed out to the station at Aldgate East on my way to meet Charlotte. The brisk air held the promise of winter to come and sent my blood pumping. I scanned the buildings and various perches for Felix, and hoped that he, my ancestors, or even Mr. Wei kept me in their sights.

I arrived at Baker Street Station and searched the crowded platform for Charlotte. Looking somehow taller in a narrow skirt and tailored jacket, she waved me to her side, saying in some agitation, "I was afraid you'd miss the train."

I didn't point out that we had a good five minutes to spare before departure and assured her, "You needn't have worried. I'm never late."

They stoked the engines, and smoke from the train washed over the platform. We had little opportunity to speak as we located our compartment and squeezed next to our fellow travelers on the bench seat.

The trip to Wembley passed in a blur of trees and grassy fields. Unmoored from familiar surroundings, I drew in a deep breath to settle my emotions. The next several hours would be spent beyond the outer edges of London, and I prepared myself to endure the full force of nature.

Wembley Station opened in May to coincide with the completion of the park. Over the summer months, Wembley Park had attracted thousands of visitors to its lake, gardens, sporting fields, and bandstands. The crowd shoved together in our compartment was evidence that the brisk fall air had not deterred Londoners from seeking its pleasures.

"Have you been to the park before?" I asked.

Charlotte shook her head. "Aunt Sadie found it vulgar and would never take me. Margaret suggested we should go boating on the lake someday but has been too busy to set a date."

The train slowed as we neared the station and came to a smooth stop. People stood, straightening their hats and jackets, and prepared to disembark.

We stepped onto the platform to meet a brilliant autumn morning, resplendent in fluffy white clouds and ringing with birdsong. Beads of sweat stood out on my forehead.

"Are you alright?" Charlotte frowned up into my face.

"I need a moment to get my bearings. I don't like large expanses of grass or trees. I find them hard to navigate."

Always proclaiming the beauties and superiority of the countryside, I expected Charlotte to renounce my sentiment. To my surprise, she nodded in agreement.

"I know exactly how you feel." She took my arm and steered me through the multitude. "I had the same sensation when first coming to live in town. The noise overwhelmed me, and the buildings hovered, ready to pounce." We skirted the northern border of the park on a broad walkway.

"Where are we going?" I glanced around. "We should find a custodian or local resident to ask our way."

Charlotte flashed me a triumphant smile. "No need. I know the way. I questioned Margaret last night about Broxburn Inn. It is quite notorious."

"She's comfortable with us coming here together?" I asked, doubtful.

"Um. Margaret doesn't actually know I'm here. She's occupied with her women's issues, and I, um, ah . . ." Charlotte hesitated, adding in a defiant rush, "She is not my guardian. I don't need her permission to do anything. She's only three years older than I and does whatever she likes."

I laughed. "Have you told her that?"

"Certainly not. Better to avoid any unpleasantness unless absolutely necessary."

Charlotte turned us down a one-track lane heading due north of the train station. The lane, bordered by tall hedgerows on both sides, almost like a flower-scented London alleyway, gave me a greater sense of ease, and my shoulders relaxed.

"What did Margaret say of Broxburn Inn?" I asked.

"The place is infamous among lady radicals." She imparted the information in a breathless tone. "The asylum has housed many inconvenient women, and by that, I mean wives, and mothers, and sisters, and"—Charlotte lowered her voice to a bare whisper—"mistresses who are outspoken and difficult. But also, women like my grandmother, who are no longer wanted by their husbands or other male relatives."

A quarter of a mile on, and with the sound of birds and insects as our constant accompanists, we stopped before a drive flanked by two ancient oak trees. The well-manicured lawn stretched before us and led to a large, three-story, Italianate farmhouse.

A light four-wheeled carriage and a hansom cab stood parked together on one side of the house. The two drivers lounged on their respective perches and conversed while waiting for their fares to return.

A nurse in a starched uniform and cap came out onto the porch as we approached. She held a teacup in one hand and a saucer in the other. The woman paused in the act of bringing the cup to her lips.

"Who might you be?" she asked, her tone brusque.

The plain uniform and hair pulled back in a severe bun gave the impression of age, but her smooth, youthful complexion told a different story. I guessed she had not been working long as a nurse, and certainly not long enough to have met Mary Gaines.

"I am Miss Charlotte Gaines, and this is Mr. Kuo Cheng," Charlotte introduced us. "I'm here to speak with someone who might remember my grandmother."

"And who might she be?"

"Mrs. Mary Gaines. She entered here in '78 and died the next year."

The woman came down the steps. "Mary Gaines, the wife of John Harold Gaines?"

"Yes," Charlotte confirmed.

"You're the granddaughter, my Lovely Lit—"

"Yes, indeed." My friend cut her off with a brittle smile.

The woman hesitated, silently thinking the matter over. She shrugged and sloshed tea over the rim of her cup. "Well, come on in then. We don't allow unscheduled visits as a rule, but perhaps Dr. Larkin will speak with you."

We followed her up the steps and into a broad foyer with polished wood floors. A crystal chandelier gleamed from the vaulted ceiling. A reception desk blocked the hallway and was clearly the woman's sentry post.

"Wait there," she instructed, pointing to a row of chairs lined up against the wall. "I'm not sure the doctor will see you, but I won't be a moment."

We sat. She put her teacup on the desk and strode down the hallway, disappearing near the back of the house.

An undercurrent of murmured voices and creaking floorboards settled in around us. We both startled at a loud clatter from above, followed by angry, raised voices. Another nurse emerged from a doorway off the upper landing and rushed across our line of sight, wiping hands on her crisp, white apron.

"How many women do you suppose live here?" Charlotte asked in hushed tones appropriate to the oppressive atmosphere of the house.

"I don't know. Assuming the staff lives on the premises as well, it may all depend on how they partition the rooms. If they're private—"

The hard click-clack of hurried footsteps cut off my words. We stood as the now grim-faced nurse rounded the reception desk and grabbed us each by an elbow.

"Dr. Larkin won't be seeing you. Do not return," she warned and shoved us out the door, slamming it in our faces.

Chapter Forty-Six

"How rude," Charlotte exclaimed.

We stood for a breathless moment staring at the pineapple-shaped brass door knocker.

"Rude and telling," I replied. "There's a story here."

Charlotte stretched her hands out as if beseeching the house. "They threw us out."

I looked around and spotted a path heading into a sparse forest. "Let's take a walk," I suggested. "It—"

"I know," she returned with a laugh. "Clears the mind and helps you to concentrate."

"Precisely," I replied, willing to brave the beauties of nature for a chance to think on our next move.

The path meandered through a charming, well-maintained wood turning to fall colors. A narrow brook ran along the shallow embankment. Its ambient noise added a soothing element to our surroundings.

We strolled in silence. The trail eventually turned out of the wood and into a formal garden at the back of the house. Women walked and sat among the general splendor of a sprawling English garden. Sprinkled about were the starched, watchful figures of nurses.

"The velvet glove," I whispered.

"What?"

"Or a gilded cage, whatever you want to call this." I gestured to indicate the view before us.

Charlotte nodded. "A pretense, you mean, to make everyone feel better about committing these poor women to an asylum, however pretty."

A trill of piano scales floated out over the verdant scene. The hairs rose on the back of my neck.

"A harsh judgment there, young lady, but fair enough, in some cases."

We jumped and turned in unison to find a short, sturdy old man standing not three feet from us on the path. Charlotte pressed a hand to her breast.

"Goodness, you gave me a fright. Where did you come from?"

He wore a woolen jacket over loose-fitting trousers stuffed into rubber Wellington boots. The old man carried a short shovel and pointed the blade at a newly tilled border along the edge of the wood.

"Been planting bulbs, don't ya know. Be right pretty in the spring with irises growing along there."

"You're the groundskeeper," Charlotte declared.

The old man touched the brim of his flat cap. "Alfred Johnson, miss. I've been gardener here since before it were a hospital, so to speak. Dr. Larkin, he don't like us calling it an asylum."

I perked up at the mention of his length of service. "How long has this place been a, um, hospital?"

"Goin' on thirty-five years now. Old Dr. Larkin, young Larkin's pa, he bought it off the folks who built the place, and I come with it."

"What did you mean about her judgment being harsh?" I asked.

He cupped his chin in one hand and pulled down at the sides of his mouth. "Well, from what I seen, most patients here are treated kindly and find comfort in the place. But there've been a few over the years who've suffered at the confinement."

"My grandmother was here," Charlotte confessed, embarrassed and indignant at the same time. "She died here, and Dr. Larkin won't speak with me. The nurse threw us out."

Mr. Johnson nodded. "Them's the rules, right or wrong. I figure it were that new girl brung ya in. None of them others would've even let you past the threshold."

To my surprise, Charlotte pulled a handkerchief from her handbag and dabbed at her eyes. I placed a comforting hand on her arm. She cast me a speaking, sidelong glance and sniffed.

"I never knew my grandmother. Most of my family is dead. I just hoped"—sniff—"to learn something about her final days."

The groundskeeper frowned. "Now, don't go on so. There've been quite a few through here in my time. Mayhap I remember her."

"Oh, do you think so?" Charlotte clutched the handkerchief in her little fist and released a dramatic sigh. "My name is Charlotte Gaines, and my grandmother was Mrs. Mary Gaines."

The old man opened his eyes wide. "You don't say. Well, I can tell you Dr. Larkin ain't likely to go diggin' that mess up."

"Why?" I asked.

"It were a right scandal. Not the type you'd read about in the papers, mind, but the type that brought important people here to argue on her behalf. Why, I remember some uppity Lady Somethin' or Other pitching a right fit, demanding to see Mrs. Gaines. And she weren't the only one." He pulled on the brim of his cap. "Thing is, your grandma weren't one of them patients who chafed to be gone. A sadder, more heartbroken woman I'd never seen. Only time she showed any spark 'o life was when her sister visited."

Charlotte and I exchanged a startled glance. A fluffy, white cloud obscured the sun, casting an isolated pool of shade around us. I shivered.

"Her sister?" Charlotte pressed him.

He frowned. "It were a strange thing."

"What was?" Charlotte and I asked as one, leaning in with eagerness.

Mr. Johnson stepped back and cleared his throat. "Why, I don't rightly know. They were alike, though I could tell her sister was the older. Her visits sure lifted Mrs. Gaines's spirits. Anyone could see that." He pointed towards the wood.

"Down there by the creek were the only time I had words with your grandma. Didn't know it was her at first. She'd taken to wearing them veils. You know, the type women wear to church. She stood next to the water. I feared, at first, she was trying to escape. There'd been a few over the years followed the creek into Wembley. Not her, she just stood there, silent." He shook his head with a mournful sigh. "I come up beside her, checking to see if she was alright. She clutched at a locket round her neck and held it out to me, saying, 'My husband give me this. I hope to be buried in it.'"

He blew out a long breath. "And that's all I know about your grandma."

Charlotte reached into her handbag and took out the necklace. "Is this it?"

The sun reemerged. Its rays drew from the locket a glint of gold. The old man squinted down at her open palm.

"Very like it. I remember the dragonfly. Poor lady, not even that simple request granted her."

Charlotte dropped the necklace into her bag. "Thank you, Mr. Johnson. So kind of you to share your memories with me."

A blush stole over his weathered cheeks. "Weren't nothin', miss. Now, you'd best be heading back through the wood. So's you won't be seen from the house."

We had just reached the tree line when the old man called after us. "Almost forgot. Her son visited once. Stayed with her the whole day."

"Uncle Cecil?"

"I didn't get his name. He sure unsettled the nurses though. Him being one of them religious types in robes and with the top of his head shaved."

"A tonsure," I informed him.

"If you say so." He shrugged. "As I said, he unsettled the womenfolk. Had a look about him, you know, one you see in the religious, severe-like. One 'o them grey monks from up north, I do believe."

Chapter Forty-Seven

"It can't be," Charlotte protested for the hundredth time since we left Alfred Johnson behind and took the country lane back to the park. "How could it be him? Uncle Cecil is in seclusion at the monastery."

We sat at a small table on the patio of a refreshment stand. I stared down at my teacup and nibbled on a piece of shortbread. "We don't know for cer—" I began, mostly from habit.

Charlotte held up her hand. "No. I forbid you to say it."

"A monk . . ." I mused instead and straightened in my chair with sudden enlightenment. "How stupid of me not to realize. An illuminated text . . . that's what they're like." I looked at Charlotte as if she could read my mind.

"What do you mean?" she asked.

"The notes . . . something has always bothered me about the notes. The gold edging, the beautiful, decorative script, it all reminded me of a thing I could never put my finger on." I sat back and crossed my arms, nodding with satisfaction. "An illuminated text, the notes resemble those religious books with elaborate calligraphy and colorful illustrations *and* gold leaf edging, like the gold ink used to decorate the notes." I nodded again, this time with conviction. "However improbable, the killer must be your Uncle Cecil."

The color drained from Charlotte's face, my statement having made real the fact that her uncle was most probably a deranged murderer. "The verse," she said, making a visible effort to contain her emotions. "Ada must be the sister lost. But to betray the nave . . . what does that mean? She wasn't a nun. Nobody in our family, except for Cecil, was devout."

I studied the people strolling past our table. Many were well-to-do couples, but there was also a smattering of young mothers in twice-turned dresses with their children in tow. How different their perspectives must be from each other's. How would each describe their visit to Wembley Park—as a commonplace occurrence or a special treat from the hardships of daily life?

Inspired by this observation, I suggested, "The poem is your grandmother's work. We must look at it from her point of view. Gaines puts her in an asylum. Ada chooses to stay with him but later returns to Mary, betraying the nave, meaning . . ." My voice trailed off, and I lost any thread of logical thought.

Charlotte gasped. "Yes, indeed, that's it. Ada doesn't betray God or the Church but my grandfather." She turned to me eyes, bright with discovery. "To a married woman, her husband is as good as God. She has nothing of her own, not even her children. She can do nothing without his consent. By defying my grandfather and reconciling with her sister, Ada betrays the nave."

"By Jove," I exclaimed. "I think you've solved it."

We basked for a moment in this victory before remembering the final line of the poem. Charlotte dropped her head in her hands.

"Defying the grave," she grumbled. "How?"

"Your grandmother still had two living children, as well as you," I suggested. "Perhaps it means nothing more than she will live on in her offspring."

"Hmm," was her doubtful response.

I gazed out at a distant game of cricket, and my mind turned to that of the shadowy figure who kept house for Gaines, a woman who drifted away unremarked after her sister's death. "What became of Ada?"

"Maybe they are together, Ada and Cecil," Charlotte theorized. "Maybe they are taking revenge on those who wronged my grandmother."

"In which case, why you? You were a baby when she died."

"Oedipus's daughter," she quoted, a painful blush on her cheeks. "He believes me to be the child of some unholy union, no doubt."

"I was hoping you didn't know."

"I didn't," she admitted. "Margaret, however, is a font of information, and she told me the story of the man who killed his father and married his mother."

I grasped her hand. "Who can understand a sick mind or know what insanities he weaves to justify his actions. He could have hated your father, Thomas, for being a favored son, or some such thing, and you by extension. You mustn't put any stock in such a vile message."

Charlotte returned my clasp with a brief squeeze. "You know that isn't true. Where is your detached judgment when I need it most, Kuo Cheng? We must put stock in his words, no matter how vile. It is the only way we will catch him," she declared with a militant glint in her eyes.

**

In the crowded compartment of the train, Charlotte and I sat in silence and got off at the Gower Street Station. We turned our steps towards Russell Square and Margaret's house. The shortened autumn days caught up with us, and we walked in the gloomy dusk, illuminated by the glow of streetlamps.

Since leaving Wembley Park, I had mulled over Charlotte's dramatic pronouncement and now broached the subject with some misgivings. "How do you propose to catch your uncle?" I asked.

"We must go tomorrow to Worseton-on-Tees," she replied. "You will send ahead to your friend Jack Hughes of our arrival. From there, we will pay a visit to the monks of Wickersham Abbey. Only then can we be sure Uncle Cecil is the killer."

The plan was solid, with only one snag. "The inspector," I reminded her. "He is expecting us tomorrow."

Charlotte shrugged. "So, he waits another day. What can he do to us?"

"To *you*, nothing," I retorted with some heat.

Her hand flew to her mouth. "I am sorry. You are right. We must . . . unless . . ." She clutched at my arm excitedly. "I will go to Wickersham Abbey and you to see the inspector."

We stopped, having arrived at Margaret's house. I opened my mouth to object to this harebrained scheme when a ragged urchin stepped from the shadow of the entryway.

"Kuo Cheng?" he asked.

"Yes."

He held out an envelope, smudged with dirt from his fingers. "This is for you."

I hesitated to take it. "From whom?"

The boy snorted. "Dunno. He didn't give me no name. Just told me to deliver the letter here."

"How did he know I'd be here?"

"You askin' me?" The boy's voice shook with impatience. "Here, take it." He waved the letter in my face

I took the grubby envelope, and he scampered off into the deepening London gloom. I opened it with shaking hands and pulled the familiar and terrifying gold-edged paper out.

From the dim light of a nearby streetlamp, I read the missive and sank onto the stoop with a groan. "He has Danny."

Chapter Forty-Eight

Charlotte took the note from my limp fingers and read aloud, "*I have the little tart. If you don't want me to slit her throat, come alone to the Expedition.*"

She sat beside me. "We must go."

I jumped to my feet. "*I* must go."

"Not alone. It's a trap," Charlotte insisted.

"I know. But what can I do? Danny's in this mess because of me." I pulled off my cap and ran anxious fingers through my hair. "I can't have you, too, in—" I stopped, breathless, unable to utter another word.

Charlotte stood and grasped me by my arms. She shook me as much as her small stature would allow. "You are *all* in this mess because of me."

"This isn't a game, Charlotte," I warned. "He intends to kill us."

She stepped back and placed her fists on her hips. "I'm not an idiot. I know very well this isn't a game. Which is why I have a knife in my boot and a gun in my handbag."

**

We alighted from the cab a block from the Expedition. In this busy part of SoHo, people gathered in groups along the street and out front of the ubiquitous public houses.

I led Charlotte down the street, sticking close to the buildings and avoiding light from the streetlamps. We ducked into the alleyway across from the entrance where I had first surveilled the club.

"Let's wait here," I suggested. "See who's coming and going."

It didn't take long to figure out the place was closed. A quarter of an hour passed and no one entered or left. Not even a sliver of light escaped from the curtained windows.

"The note didn't mention where in the Expedition to meet," I commented, frowning over at the ominously silent building. "Still, I'd rather not walk in the front door. There's a mews entrance." I poised to cross the street.

"Wait." Charlotte pulled from her handbag a small Remington Derringer and shoved it into her belt. "Easier to get at this way."

I shook my head in disbelief. "Where did you get a gun?"

"Aunt Beatrix, the dear, always said a woman alone cannot depend on anyone else for protection. I've had a bit of target practice, but it's really more for show."

We made our way to the narrow lane between the buildings, emerging into the mews behind the brothel. The heavy wooden door leading into the servants' quarters stood ajar.

"Bloody hell," I whispered before remembering my companion. "I say, pardon—"

"Oh, for heaven's sake . . . bloody hell, bloody hell. There, I said it. Now, what are we going to do?"

I pushed the door inward. It opened halfway and stopped with a dull thud. The unsettled feeling in the pit of my stomach moved its way up into my throat. I peeked around the doorframe. An inert form lay on the floor.

I knelt over the body of a woman. "Penny," I blurted, recognizing the dress and the painfully thin figure. She groaned.

"She's alive," Charlotte declared.

I turned her over, forcing myself not to recoil at the sight of her sliced and battered face dripping with blood. "Help me take her outside."

We each grasped an elbow. So emaciated was she it took little of our strength to move her. We set her down against the wall just outside the door. Charlotte ripped a piece of material from her petticoat and used it to staunch the blood. I checked her pulse.

"The wounds are superficial, and her heartbeat is strong. I don't believe she is in immediate danger of dying." I swallowed my misgivings at leaving her there. "We have to get Danny. We'll come back for her."

A thin, boney hand shot out and clamped my wrist in a vise-like grip. Charlotte suppressed a shriek.

"The attic," Penny croaked through swollen lips. "He's a monster. He'll kill us all."

"Where is everyone?"

"Gone." Her fingers dropped away, and she slumped forward. Charlotte gently laid her down.

My friend stood and pulled the knife from her boot. "Take it."

I took it. She drew out her gun, and we entered the club. The hallway stretched before us. Light flickered from gas lamps and cast wavering shadows on the walls.

"Where to?" Charlotte asked.

"There's a servants' stair to the upper floors."

We stole with bated breath down the hall and found the staircase near the kitchen entrance. The first step creaked as I made to go up, and I drew back.

"Walk as close to the wall as you can," Charlotte whispered. "No one ever really steps there, so it's more solid."

"How—" I began.

"You've never had to sneak out of a house full of sharp-eared women, have you?"

I admitted that I had not and led our now silent way up the

stairway. With every step that brought us closer to the attic, my muscles tightened.

Fear heightened my senses. I attuned my hearing to the empty house and strained for any minute sound. My sight sharpened and swept the space before us.

"Fear you can use, but panic will kill you," my grandfather had told me when discussing the body's response to dangerous situations.

I fought to overcome my rising panic. Our lives depended on staying clearheaded.

We reached the landing. I pushed open the attic door, fearful of meeting yet another body.

It swung inward without obstruction. Weak light wavered from the sconces on the walls.

We crossed the threshold. My lungs froze on an inward breath.

A waist-high table pushed up under a small, soot-stained window stood covered in glass beakers, tubing, and syringes with hypodermic needles. Stacked up against the back wall were tools, everything from wrenches, pliers, and screwdrivers to knives, hammers, and saws. Shelves bent under the weight of clothing, wigs, hats, tins of stage makeup, and glass jars filled with shriveled organs. Some were clearly from animals, but others I easily identified as human.

My gaze swept the room. Pieces of people's lives hung from the walls: jewelry, a lock of white-blond hair, a red velvet ribbon, and more.

"Villain," Charlotte cursed through gritted teeth. "Where are you?"

"Here." A quiet, raspy voice sent a shiver up my spine. We turned.

He had slipped in while we gaped, stupefied by the revulsion around us. Like the scene of Aunt Sadie's murder, he used shock and terror to render us immobile.

He blocked the door. With features obscured by the sickening pinkish hue of rubber, his gloved hand pressed a butcher's knife to Danny's throat.

Chapter Forty-Nine

Danny's pale, tearstained face burned the terror from my mind. Fury coursed through me.

"Let her go," I demanded, surprised at the steady force of my words.

"I will," he rasped. "Once you put down your weapons."

We hesitated. He pressed the knife into her flesh.

Danny yelped and sobbed. She shook so hard the tattered hems of her trousers flapped against her bare ankles.

"Alright, don't hurt her."

Not trusting him, but not knowing what else to do, I dropped the knife. Charlotte placed her gun on the floor.

"Let her go," I repeated.

He jerked Danny closer. I held my breath. Charlotte covered her mouth with both hands.

"She's served her purpose." He laughed and shoved the girl from him.

Danny fell to the floor. She struggled to rise, her muscles weak with fright.

"You're strong, Danny," I said, keeping my voice low and calm. "Run. You can do it. Run."

With a whimper, she lunged to her feet and out the door. Her panicked, stumbling descent echoed back up the staircase. I knew an instant of relief.

"She can't help you." His muffled laugh sent my pulse racing. "I'm glad you didn't follow my instructions. With dear Charlotte here, you'll both be dead and me long gone before anyone comes to your aid."

"Why do you hate me so, Uncle Cecil?" Charlotte asked the simplest, most essential question.

He gripped the knife and swayed. I inched closer to her, certain he would lunge. But he skittered back against the wall and into the shadows. His eyes glowed, pinpricks of insanity in the darkness.

"You are the source, the reason everyone is dead," he hissed. "The reason I'm going to hell."

He skirted the wall like a rat, wedging himself into a dark corner nearest the door. "*She* wanted it done. She wanted revenge for my brothers and sister, and your mother."

"Who wanted revenge?" Charlotte asked, her voice steady, though faint with fear. "For what? My mother died in a carriage accident with my father. It was no one's fault."

His cackle turned into a howl of pain. He clutched his hair.

We made for the door. His head snapped up.

"Stay put," he growled, brandishing the knife. "She wanted him dead, his whore too." He swayed and leaned for support against the wall. "I sneaked aboard the night before they set sail and rigged the boat to sink. With each swell, it took on water. Slowly, slowly, so they wouldn't notice until too late."

Charlotte gasped. "You murdered them too? You killed my grandfather and Nora?"

"Don't say her name," he shrieked and staggered down the wall to the middle of the room.

An eerie high-pitched keen filled the attic, made even more

unnatural by the fact that it came from behind the blank, emotionless mask. "I killed them and consigned myself to hell. But redemption is nigh. You are the filth that sullied us all."

"Aunt Sadie?" Charlotte cried, holding her hands out, placating, keeping him talking. "What had she done?"

"Sadie," he croaked. "We had an old score to settle. Betrayal, hers and others, set me on the path to damnation." His shoulders tensed, and his hand tightened on the knife.

"He's coming for ya, mate." Teddy's whispered warning brushed past me.

I dove for the knife and grasped it. A glass jar containing a human uterus flew past me as I sprang to my feet. The jar hit and shattered square on Cecil's shoulder.

He staggered back against the table. Charlotte whooped with success and scooped up her gun.

We ran.

"I'll kill you," he screamed. "I'll kill you."

Charlotte turned and squeezed off a wild shot. The bullet hit a gas sconce. Flames exploded from the wall.

"Bloody hell," I cursed.

I grabbed Charlotte's arm and pulled her out into the hallway. We sped down the stairs. Smoke and flames raced us along the ceiling.

We burst through the door and grabbed Penny at a run. The explosion knocked us off our feet as we threw ourselves behind the mews.

Chapter Fifty

"Your uncle, Cecil Gaines?" The inspector stood with his hands behind his back, his red, puffy eyes the only indication he'd been pulled from his bed in the early hours of the morning. "A deranged killer?"

We sat in the parlour of Margaret's house on Russell Square. I barely registered my surroundings, merely absorbing an overall impression of elegance and comfort.

A fire crackled in the hearth. I was grateful for its warmth and the soft, soothing candlelight that lit the room.

Though host, no doubt, to many a friendly gathering, the parlour was unusually crowded for such a late hour. Along with Inspector Lloyddyn were Constables Eaton and Farley standing at attention near the door. Grandfather sat next to me on an embroidered loveseat. Margaret paced the room, her supremely indulgent parents having long since retired. Danny, wrapped in a blanket, huddled on Cook's lap. Nellie stood unobtrusive near the window.

At the center of all this sat Charlotte, still clad in her ash-covered clothing and with Rose-Marie curled up on her lap. Though pale and drawn, she commanded our attention.

"Yes, as I have explained *twice* now, Inspector." Charlotte brushed a weary hand across her forehead. "I've told you everything."

He narrowed his eyes, both angry and skeptical. I could hardly blame him.

"You've withheld vital information for days, and you expect me to believe that?"

"The burned husk of a brothel in SoHo," Margaret snapped, stopping to direct her ire at the inspector, "should be evidence enough that these foolish children have come to the end of their detective games."

I didn't know who she was angrier with, the inspector or us. I couldn't blame her either.

I avoided looking at Grandfather for fear of seeing not anger but disappointment. Other than assuring himself I was uninjured, he had said nothing. He attentively followed the conversation, having given up all pretense of not knowing English.

"So, you believe this Grey Man, otherwise known as Mr. Grey, and possibly your uncle, Cecil Gaines," Inspector Lloyddyn continued, ignoring Margaret's outburst, "not only targeted you as some unholy fiend who destroyed his family, but has also established a criminal syndicate in London."

"Yes, Inspector," she replied.

"I don't know about a syndicate, exactly," I added. "But certainly some type of organized crime that, well, trades in defenseless people, at the very least."

"Your friend, Teddy Tooley?" he asked, no doubt recalling the similarity in his and Sadie Gaines's murder.

"Yes."

"Very well," he reasoned. "If Cecil Gaines is the Grey Man, how is it that Miss Gaines here received a letter from the monks at, ah . . ."

"Wickersham Abbey," I put in.

"Yes."

"Besides him admitting to being my uncle—" Charlotte began.

"Not exactly," I interjected, reluctant to gainsay her but wanting to be precise. "He never identified himself as such."

"And he wore a mask," Inspector Lloyddyn pointed out. "You cannot be sure who he was."

"Really, Inspector," Margaret protested. "What *other* murderous lunatic would claim to drown her grandfather and seek to kill her?"

He rubbed his eyes. "A fair question, Miss Scott, one on which I will not think further tonight. Suffice it to say you three and that young woman, Penny, were lucky to get out alive. I don't believe anyone stuck up in the attic could survive the fire. By all odds, we can bury the Grey Man and Cecil Gaines with him, if you believe they are one and the same."

"Well, I'm not sure I like your odds." Charlotte stood and held Rose-Marie close. "And I have no intention of waiting to find out. I leave tomorrow for Yorkshire. I'll see for myself whether Uncle Cecil is spending his days in solitude and prayer at the Wickersham hermitage."

A moment of stunned silence met this pronouncement, followed by a babble of objections from Inspector Lloyddyn, Margaret, and even Cook.

"I cannot agree with such a fool—"

"How can you contemplate—?"

"Oh, Miss Charlotte, do you think that's wise—"

She held up her hand. "My mind is made up, and no one can stop me."

"Well, if you're adamant," Margaret replied. "I'll come with you."

Inspector Lloyddyn puffed out his cheeks and released them with an exasperated sigh. "I had hoped to get some rest tomorrow, but I'd be derelict in my duty if I let you two go on your own."

Charlotte shrugged. "As you wish." She turned to my grandfather. "The only one I'd like to come with me is Kuo. But I can understand, Mr. Cheng, if you'd rather he not." She turned away with a muffled "Goodnight" and rushed from the room.

I suppressed a tremendous urge to go after her and was grateful Nellie followed. Charlotte needed a friend.

We all stood to leave. A grubby hand tugged at my arm.

"That Constable Farley is taking me home," Danny informed me. "Cook is coming too. She's to deliver a letter from Miss Scott explaining what happened. Hoping it'll help smooth things over with my mother." She shook her head. "Looks like my days of freedom are over."

She was taking the loss of her alias better than I could have hoped. I imagine being kidnapped and held at knifepoint by a raving lunatic put things into perspective.

"I'm sorry, Danny."

She sniffed and dabbed her eyes with the end of one grimy sleeve. "I'm better off than that poor woman, her face all cut up. She tried to stop him dragging me upstairs. And he . . ."

I dropped a comforting hand on her shoulder. "She'll survive. I'm taking Joey to visit her at hospital in a few days if you want to come."

She nodded and added with false bravado, "With the constable and Cook as audience, Mother'll cry and clutch me to her breast. It shouldn't be too bad."

"Come on with you, Miss Danny, we're ready to go," Cook said, shooing her out the door.

**

Grandfather and I rode home in silence. At this hour, thick fog muffled sound, and the city was as quiet as it ever got.

Not far from home, he spoke. "I believe you should go with your friend to Yorkshire."

His words surprised me into looking at him straight on. I dropped my gaze almost at once, my cheeks flushed with shame. "I am sorry for being dishonest, Grandfather."

He sighed. "Your mother as well . . . when I discovered she had applied to Mr. Wei for help."

I drew back in surprise. "How did you find out?"

"It was he who came to the store to report the fire."

"Mr. Wei followed me?"

Grandfather nodded. "Yes, as your mother had instructed him. He followed you to the brothel, unaware of the actual danger, and watched from without. When you did not reappear, Mr. Wei sought entry." He shook his head with a mirthless laugh. "The explosion threw him back from the entrance, but he wasn't harmed. He stayed long enough to see you were unhurt and came to tell us."

"I thought the police had summoned you," I replied, remembering my relief when his calm, strong figure materialized from the ash and smoke to embrace me on the street. In the chaos of the police, the fire brigade, the neighbors, and gawkers, I knew a moment of peace and security.

"Grandfather." I leaned over and grasped his arm. "In that room . . ." My voice shook, and I swallowed threatening tears. "There were items, personal items, and jars with human body parts."

He covered my hand with his own.

"There was a lock of white-blond hair tacked to the wall," I continued, tears spilling over onto my cheeks. "Teddy warned me, Grandfather. He was with me in that room, and he saved my life."

Chapter Fifty-One

Margaret delayed our departure the next morning, insisting on posting a letter to the Hughes estate. "If you must stop first to greet your friend, we have to give him and his sister some warning, however brief. Worseton has a perfectly fine inn, but I fear Miss Hughes will feel obliged to host us."

"It is more than a greeting," I replied with some annoyance at her high-handed commandeering of our trip. "As a prominent local landowner, Jack will know something about the abbey and how best to proceed. It's important to get some understanding of the situation before we find ourselves in the middle of it."

"Says the young man who walked into a brothel at the behest of a killer."

"With a knife to my friend's throat, I would do it again," I snapped.

"Please," Charlotte pleaded. "No bickering. I don't think I could take hours of this."

At the train station, Inspector Lloyddyn strolled in only moments before departure, incurring Margaret's censure. He and I exchanged a look of fellow feeling.

"Probably still laboring under some shock from last night, poor lady," he said in an aside to me, with greater sympathy than I felt.

The journey north sped by, primarily because we slept most of the way. By the time we arrived at our stop, Margaret was in a better mood, and Charlotte, though still uncharacteristically quiet, looked less pale.

The reservoirs of courage that had sustained us on our rescue mission last night were now severely depleted. I understood her withdrawal as if it were my own and drew comfort from our silent camaraderie.

We hired a carriage to take us the final eleven miles to Worseton-on-Tees and Jack's estate just beyond. I sat next to the window and tried to overcome my unease with nature, anchoring my sight on whatever landmarks appeared, whether natural or manmade.

This far north, the sun brushed the horizon and cast a red glow over the fields and woodlands. A glimmer of stars appeared in the dark blue sky of dusk.

Ignoring my protests, Margaret demanded we stop to admire the river Tees. Standing on the bank, Charlotte came close beside me and whispered, "Do you think that monster is dead?"

I shook my head. "Almost certainly not."

She nodded. "I, too, feel he is alive. I think he is close, and we will find him here."

The river flowed by in a dark green rush, brushing the reeds and the low-hanging branches of the willow trees. I closed my eyes and listened to the muted roar of volumes of water on the move.

"This is lovely. I'm glad we stopped."

Margaret smiled with pleasure at my praise. We piled back into the carriage and soon passed through the village and out the other end on our way to the Hughes estate.

Just outside of Worseton, a sign stood next to the road, almost hidden behind an overgrowth of hedgerow, with the words "Incitatus Farm" written in faded white letters and barely discernible in the fading light. An arrow pointed down a narrow track through dense woodland.

I stiffened and cleared a sudden lump of fear from my throat. I knew now with certainty our answers lay hidden in this pastoral landscape.

The carriage turned off the road onto a long drive through well-manicured parkland. Margaret sat forward and stuck her head out the window. "I see it."

We swept up to the estate via the circular drive, and a large Jacobethan-style manor house came into view. The house possessed an impressive portico and three stories with an attic floor above.

We alighted from the carriage. The heavy doors burst open, and a young woman strode out, her arms outstretched in greeting.

"So good to see you again, Miss Scott, and your friends with you."

Lucy Hughes exhibited many of the same characteristics as her brother, being both tall and handsome. She looked very like him, though instead of blue, a pair of large, warm brown eyes enlivened her face.

Unlike Jack, she had an ease of conversation and manner that made us at home in an instant. She introduced herself and directed the footman to retrieve our luggage.

"Please, no objections," she begged. "It has been long since we were jolly with guests. Jack is out—an obligation he could not rearrange—but will be back directly."

She ushered us into an entrance hall with a vaulted ceiling and a central grand staircase branching off in two opposing directions at the top. A chandelier hung from above, and various tapestries, coats of arms, and paintings adorned the walls. Though decorated to assume the trappings of age and permanence, I judged the house to be no more than a couple of decades old.

"We've laid out tea in the parlour," Lucy told us, leading the way down a wide corridor to an imposing room that ran half the length of the house. "You must be famished after so long a journey."

She arranged us with graceful self-confidence around the massive hearth, placing the inspector in a large chair on one side of her and Margaret on the other. Charlotte and I sat on the settee beside Margaret. The footmen poured tea and passed around plates of cakes, scones, and sliced fruit.

"I would have preferred to have tea in the atrium since the autumn colors are so vibrant this year, but Mrs. Clayton, our housekeeper, is particularly conscious of the 'family dignity' since our parents died." She laughed. "Now that I have satisfied her demands, the rest of your stay will be mercifully lacking in formality."

Margaret, the only other one in the room to have any long-term experience with servants, replied, an arch smile on her lips, "Yes, we, too, have an old retainer who is quite exacting about our behavior."

"Aunt Beatrix and I never had any servants," Charlotte put in. "Just a village lady who came in to cook and clean during the week. When I arrived in London, I was grateful for Cook and Nellie. They have been good friends to me in this trying time."

To my amusement, the two ladies squirmed as their condescension turned to discomfort. Lucy was the first to rally.

"How right you are, Miss Gaines, to remind us a faithful servant is to be appreciated and treasured." She flashed Charlotte a warm smile.

I admired her quick mind and open manners. Clearly, she had received the lion's share of intellect in the Hughes family.

"Where has your brother got off to, if I may ask?" Margaret deftly changed the subject.

Lucy's cheeks lit with an attractive, rosy color. "Of course. He has gone to speak with my betrothed about a matter upon which they are both being very closemouthed. I fear they are meant to surprise me, and I can only hold my breath as to what it is."

Margaret smiled. "I read of the engagement. You are to be congratulated."

We added our congratulations to Margaret's. Lucy's blush deepened.

"It has been the strangest affair. I can tell you. To wake up one morning and find the boy with whom you ran wild through the woods and fields is now your devoted admirer, and even stranger, that you are his. Well, I think it has startled us both.

"But enough of my engagement," she declared. "I'm all eagerness to hear of this mysterious errand that has brought you to our doorstep, and with a police inspector, no less—"

"Hello," Jack called as he entered the parlour and strode across the expanse of carpet, trying hard not to look only at Margaret. He glowed with health and manly vigor, still attired in his riding dress.

We stood to greet him, and Margaret returned a tight smile. I felt a twinge of sympathy at her discomfort. Applying for help to a man who was clearly in love with her but for whom she had no amorous feelings was no easy task.

"My apologies for not being here to welcome you," he said, winking at his sister and throwing an arm about her shoulders, deftly placing himself next to Margaret. "I had some important business to attend to."

Lucy laughed and blushed again. "Jack, everyone you know except Inspector Jonas Lloyddyn, here."

Jack beamed. "Another Welshman," he declared. "An uncommon name, Lloyddyn. My Welsh is rusty, but that would roughly translate into Wise Man, or more literally, Grey Man. That's it, is it not, Inspector?"

Chapter Fifty-Two

Charlotte, Margaret, and I stood immobilized by horror and disbelief. My sight telescoped.

Jack and Lucy grew distant. They stood, unknowing and unprotected, trapped with a monster on one side of a chasm.

In that fraction of a second, the Grey Man knew no hesitation. Wielding terror and shock as effectively as any weapon, he drew a knife from his jacket and plunged it into Lucy's heart.

No scream escaped her lips. No blood gushed from a wound sealed tight with the hilt of a knife. She sighed and dropped, falling into her brother's arms.

Jack stared, incredulous at the limp figure of his sister. His mouth worked in silent incomprehension, unable even to sob.

"Oh God, no," Margaret forced the words from between frozen lips and broke the spell.

Sound burst back into the world. Jack wailed his sister's name, cradling her on the floor.

"What . . . what has happened?" he cried.

Margaret fell to her knees beside them. "Charlotte, alert the house," she barked. "Call for a doctor."

Charlotte ran from the room, yelling frantically for anyone within earshot. I tore my eyes from the pitiful sight. With everyone's attention riveted on Lucy, the Gray Man had disappeared. I knew where he was headed.

I raced from the room, down the hallway, and out through the entrance onto the circular drive. My heart galloped in my chest, so full of emotion it nearly burst.

Gravel crunched and sprayed up from beneath my pounding feet. I ran the length of the drive and skidded to a stop on the lane.

"Kuo," Charlotte called, breathless from behind me. "Wait."

I turned and she threw herself into my arms. I closed my eyes, gritting my teeth against a sob. "That dear lady . . . fool, I'm a fool."

Charlotte's arms tightened around me. Her tears soaked through my collar. Time suspended, and my heart slowed to a sedate canter.

She sighed and loosened her grip. We released each other and stepped back.

Charlotte wiped her face, blotchy from crying. Did I look as drained and haggard?

"Do you blame yourself for not knowing Welsh?" she asked. Tears ran unheeded down her cheeks. "Imagine me. Can it be possible that Uncle Cecil is both the Grey Man and the inspector? My own uncle, a murderer responsible for . . ."

She pressed a fist to her lips. I gripped her shoulders.

"Do you have your gun?" I asked.

She nodded.

"Good. I know where he's gone."

Charlotte drew in a deep breath. "I figured as much," she replied with a hint of her old quarrelsome tone. "What have you discovered?"

"It is only in these last hours," I explained, letting her know I'd held nothing back, "that the threads of this mystery have unknotted and come together into something like a pattern."

I turned us towards the village and set a brisk pace down the narrow country road. The dark sky spread out above, resplendent with stars. They cast a surprising amount of light and revealed the path before us.

"How far?" Charlotte asked.

I pointed up the road. "We passed a sign for a farm on our way here."

"Why would he go there?"

"You remember Lady Brudeford telling us that Mary's father was a scholar of Roman history?" I explained. "According to Gaines's biography, her father taught at a boys' school in Edinburgh until he inherited a farm. Of course, no one really pays attention to these little details only meant to flesh out the life of a great man. I certainly didn't at the time."

"What farm?"

A sign materialized out of the darkness, and we stopped. "This one."

Charlotte squinted in the dim starlight. "Incitatus Farm? How could you possibly know this is it?"

"A connection between your family and Yorkshire vexed me," I explained. "Until I went through my books and found a dedication in one of Gaines's early works. He acknowledges the influence of the Yorkshire farm where Mary grew up. Gaines gives no specific location, but Incitatus was the name of Caligula's favorite horse."

She gasped. "And the abbey."

"Yes. Wickersham Abbey being so close, and the family devout Catholics, as well as your Uncle Cecil . . . when I saw the sign, it all came together here."

We stared down the dark path, overhung with the thick branches of massive oak trees. "To think we once suspected Jack," she remarked with a sad laugh.

"Indeed." I shook my head, grief for that good man threatening to overcome me. "A deadly coincidence."

"Do you believe any of this a coincidence?" she asked. "I do not. The fates have led us here, and I'm grateful you're with me, Kuo Cheng."

With the dramatic flair of old, Charlotte pulled the gun from her pocket. She grasped my hand, and we made our silent, watchful way down the path together.

Chapter Fifty-Three

The neat, two-story farmhouse, surrounded by an overgrown English garden, stood back behind a picket fence. Windows glared at us, malevolent and dark as empty eye sockets. Only a wavering light shone from between the curtains of a window on the ground floor.

Alert for any hostile presence, we pushed open the door and entered a small foyer. The low ceiling and heavy wood paneling pressed in on us. Our pounding hearts and quickened breath reverberated in the confined space.

Charlotte, her gun at the ready, led us down a narrow hallway to the candlelit room. A woman sat on a worn sofa beside the dying fire. Cecil Gaines lay stretched out, his head resting on her lap, and his face even paler than usual.

"Aunt Ada," my friend announced. "It is I, Charlotte, your niece."

The woman smiled. Creases around her mouth and eyes deepened. The faded, parchment-like skin enhanced the mad, piercing intelligence of her blue eyes.

"You are, indeed, my niece, but I am not Ada."

I knew a moment of blinding realization, the threads finally woven together into a clear and terrible design.

"*And the glowering woman defies the grave,*" I pronounced,

stepping out from the shadow of the doorway. "Mary Gaines, you defied the grave by switching places with your sister Ada."

"Hmm." The old woman looked me up and down. "You're the Chinese boy my poor Cecil raged about." She gazed at her son's face and brushed back a stray lock of hair from his forehead.

"Is he dead?" I asked.

"Oh yes. It was time," Mary answered with a sad shake of her head. "I administered quite a heavy dose, so his death was quick and painless," she assured us and nodded at Charlotte. "You can put down the gun, my dear. There's no one here to hurt you."

Charlotte frowned. "I don't understand."

Mary turned to me with a sickly-sweet smile. "Ah, but young Mr. Cheng here does."

"What does she mean?" Charlotte pleaded. Her voice cracked with stress. "How is she my grandmother, and yet I am still her niece?"

I gripped her shoulders. "Your mother was not Frances Gaines but Emma Stafford. I'm guessing her illness was the final months of pregnancy, and that she died giving birth to you."

She frowned. "Then who is my father?"

Mary laughed. "Oh, you are an innocent, my dear."

Charlotte began to shake. I tightened my grip on her shoulders.

"Don't listen to her. Look at me." She met my eyes with a wide, panicked stare.

"Your father was John Harold Gaines. That's why Cecil referred to you as the daughter of Oedipus. When a husband has, um, relations with his wife's sister, it is considered incest. Even if the wife were to die, they cannot marry. It's illegal."

The gun dropped with a clatter from her limp fingers. I picked it up, grateful the thing hadn't fired, and put it in my pocket.

"Sit." I led her to a chair as far away from the horror on the sofa as possible.

"I would offer you a cup of tea." Mary gestured to the pot resting on a low table. "But I fear it would do you more harm than good."

"Poison?" I asked.

She ignored my question. "We should get on with the story. I don't have much time."

"You changed places with Ada," I stated matter-of-factly. "It's the reason she refused to see your friend Lady Brudeford at Broxburn Inn."

"Excellent. Right again." Mary flashed a mad grin. "Ada came to me contrite, and, as it was, dying. Though she was the older, we were enough alike to pass for the other, and I had moped around for weeks, covered in shawls and veils. No one noticed the difference. Old women are as overlooked and interchangeable as bed linen. We did have to pay off the old doctor and his son. Took me selling all of my jewelry."

"Your locket?" Charlotte asked, her voice steadier.

"Buried with Ada." Mary placed a hand to her breast and swayed. "Ah, I'm feeling it now." She swallowed hard and continued, "The locket Cecil had the very poor judgment to send you was Emma's, given to her by John. Months after she died, I discovered it among her things. Emma never let on who fathered her baby, but that locket told me everything I needed to know."

"Your husband placed Charlotte with your son and his wife," I prompted.

"Yes, quite the elaborate scheme. We all came together supposedly to save poor dead Emma's reputation. Of course, I didn't know about the locket then. Thomas and Francis left for the continent, meeting up with a nurse we'd hired to take Charlotte. They stayed long enough to make the story seem plausible."

Her head drooped. She forced it back up on an indrawn breath. "I told no one but Cecil of John's betrayal, and later, Ada. I was, at first, content to stay hidden away at Broxburn, but then Thomas died in a carriage accident, the result of a wager."

Spittle slid down from the corner of her mouth. "Do excuse me. I am not at my best," she quipped, wiping it away. "John craved attention, sought the public's adulation. He had all sorts of clever ideas that were meant to make him interesting, to keep him in the news. They usually involved parading about in society, attending salons and readings. In a bid to impress the noble and wealthy members of that idiotic club he belonged to, he bet Thomas could break the speed record from London to Bristol." She shook her head. "My poor Thomas, always game, always striving to win John's favor, and Frances with him.

"Their deaths were the final blow," she seethed, showing anger for the first time. "I'd given everything, lost everything to John. Eliza died in a fire at a school in Scotland *he* insisted she attend. Little Archie caught scarlet fever at an orphanage John toured, my precious baby a mere prop in his arms."

Her eyes glowed with grief and lunacy. "I played by the rules. I put my husband first, relegated my own ambitions to the dustbin. I bore children, just to watch them die one by one from the hubris of a vain man. I did what he asked of me and still he cast me aside. My crime? Growing old and tiresome." She wagged a finger at Charlotte. "Let that be a lesson to you, my girl. The game is rigged, and not in our favor."

"And Cecil," I demanded. "On whose head is his death, and those he murdered, those who have suffered at his hands?"

"Just like a man. Blame the woman." Mary shrugged and sank further into the sofa. "Cecil sought revenge as ruthlessly as I did," she insisted. "After we killed John and that sniveling little nobody, Nora, I retired here, and he returned to the abbey."

She stroked Cecil's head. "Over the years, my boy left for London more and more often, until he rarely came home. Father McCleary covered for his absences at my request, and, of course, contributions." Tears ran down her ravaged cheeks, now drained of all living color. "Until I discovered John's journal and Cecil's own diary filled with rantings of one horror after another, I had no idea of the level of depravity to which he had sunk, of his imposture and the criminal organization he'd built, or of the terrible things he did to try and cleanse his soul. When you, my dear niece, arrived in London, to his mind, killing you was his only true path to redemption.

"If anything, Mr. Cheng, you can blame the church for filling his head with the nonsense of eternal damnation. And that's on men." She sobbed, her chin now resting on her chest. "I burned his diary, but knew one day I would have to stop him."

Gathering her strength for the last time, Mary struggled to look up at Charlotte. "You're the only one left, dear child. Cecil's crimes have made you richer than you can imagine."

Charlotte stared back at her, eyes filled with revulsion. "I want none of it, stained with the blood and suffering of others. None of it, I tell you."

"Ah, my Lovely Little Lottie Love, you have no idea."

Mary slumped back against the armrest. Her dead eyes stared down at the floor.

Chapter Fifty-Four

An early freeze coated the churchyard in a wintry rime. It weighed down the grass and touched the headstones with a sparkling frost. We stood, our breath hanging in the air, next to a newly dug grave still awaiting a granite marker. The mounded turf lay strewn with wreaths and bouquets of pine needles, colorful leaves, berries, and autumn flowers.

After a fortnight of police and interviews, shocked neighbors and curious townspeople, a grieving Jack and inconsolable Edward Martin, we prepared to take our leave. Charlotte, Margaret, and I bowed our heads in sad farewell to a woman we had known barely an hour, but felt the enormity of her loss, nonetheless.

"How will Jack get on without her?" Charlotte asked.

"As he must," Margaret replied. "As we all must when tragedy strikes."

The impatient jingle of the horses' harness drew us back to the carriage. We climbed in and arranged ourselves for the short trip to the train station.

"I'll be glad to get home," Charlotte declared, settling herself back against the cushions. "Never thought I'd say that about London, but Cook and Nellie have set everything to rights, and your things have arrived as well, Margaret."

"Oh, good," her friend replied with an absentminded nod. Her gaze lingered on the dwindling churchyard until it disappeared round a bend in the road.

She sat back and smiled. "Did I tell you? I received a letter from Mrs. Fawcett. She's found just the right person for a respectable companion."

"I suppose Mrs. Fawcett is to be trusted to know," Charlotte replied, a doubtful frown upon her brow. "But I do so hope she's not some fussy old woman always ready to poke a stick in our plans."

I stared out the window. My sight grew vague and their voices distant. I relived again those frantic moments after Mary Gaines had breathed her last, when Charlotte sat stunned, and I searched the room for the only thing that could save my friend from ruin.

I discovered John Harold Gaines's journal, as I believed Mary meant us to, on a small writing desk, the deed to the farm pressed within its pages. I shook Charlotte from her stupor. We rushed back to the Hughes estate to find the house in an uproar and Margaret in a state of extreme agitation.

"Where've you been?" She practically breathed fire. "The police are here. The doctor, too . . . though it will do no—" She pressed a hand to her lips.

I drew them into a quiet corner. "Say nothing about Cecil Gaines. Say nothing about Mary, the abbey, none of it," I instructed them.

"Mary? Mary Gaines? What have you discovered?" Margaret demanded.

I shook my head. "I'll tell you all when we have time. Right now, you must trust me and say only that we came here at the behest of Inspector Lloyddyn to track down a clue to Sadie Gaines's murder. Do you understand?"

They nodded.

"We're shocked—which just so happens to be true—to find the inspector himself the deranged killer. Rage as much as you like,

Margaret, at the incompetence of the London police for not knowing a lunatic lurked in their midst. Do whatever it takes to divert them from the truth, at least for the time being."

I found the constable and told him I'd followed the fleeing killer to Incitatus Farm.

"The old Stafford place?" I only knew he spoke by the words emanating out from behind his enormous walrus mustache.

"Yes, sir," I replied. "He was within, and an old woman. Both dead."

"Good God, you can't be serious?" he expostulated. "Old Ada Stafford? No one has seen her in years. A recluse, they say. Why would he go there?"

I shrugged. "Can't say."

"A girl," the constable added. "That Miss Scott said there was a girl missing."

"Not missing," I assured him with some trepidation, knowing my next words would surely anger Charlotte if she found out. "Poor thing panicked and hid in the garden. She's back now."

The constable drew in a deep breath. "Well, can't say as I blame her. This is a right calamity." He had clapped me on the back. "Well done, lad. I'll get some men over there on the double."

"Perhaps I shall never marry." Margaret's voice drew me back to the present. "To give one's life over to a man to rule at his whim . . ." She shook her head.

"Not all men are John Harold Gaines," I protested.

"No?" she countered. "How are we women to know? To the world, Gaines was beloved, renowned, a defender of women, but to his wife, who gave him everything, an oppressive abuser."

"Well—" I began, ready to do battle for my sex, however undeserving.

"We're at the station," Charlotte announced, looking at me with amusement, though the trauma of that night still lingered in her eyes. "You two can debate this matter when I'm out of earshot."

"Right you are," I replied, returning her smile, grateful that she would come to no more harm.

I jumped from the carriage and helped bring down the luggage, handing it to the porter. I patted my trousers, pretending to have lost something.

"I'll be right along. Some change must have slipped from my pockets. I need to check the cushions."

They entered the station, and I told the coachman to drive on. The carriage swept away, revealing a stand of silver birch next to the station house. I recognized the man by a single sprig of holly pinned to his lapel with a black ribbon.

"Mr. Kuo Cheng?" he asked upon my approach.

"Yes."

"Do you have it?"

"Yes," I repeated.

"Ah, well, Mr. Mycroft Holmes sends his compliments and hopes you are pleased with the outcome."

Since the murderer was dead, the magistrate had determined an inquest to be unnecessary. No mention was ever made of Ada Gaines. Other than a few sensationalist articles decrying the killer policeman, no inquisitive journalist dug too deeply into the motivations of a madman. In fact, none, other than Ian Thorngoode, had taken the bait laid out by Mycroft and his associates. Only Thorngoode spent his time sniffing around the dark corners of London for a shadowy syndicate, finding just enough clues to keep him far from the banks of the Tees River and a sad, deserted farmhouse.

He might even discover some useful information. Anything was possible.

I nodded, satisfied that the Gaines family and, more importantly,

Charlotte would be free from scandal. I pulled from my breast pocket a small journal.

"Mr. Holmes may find a gap or two in the entries," I said, handing it off to him.

The man startled in the process of slipping the book into his jacket. "What? That wasn't the deal. He'll be most unhappy to discover pages missing."

"If he has any complaints, he knows where to find me," I threw over my shoulder, turning to leave.

I drew in a deep breath of the fresh morning air, strangely sterile after a lifetime of the potent London broth. The engine stoked as I stepped onto the platform. Charlotte waved to me through the smoke and steam billowing up from the tracks.

I hastened to join her. I, too, would be glad to get home.

Afterword

Holmes stood at the window looking out onto the street below. Since his recovery, we had learned nothing more of what transpired before a massive dose of opium almost killed him. Though he maintained his usual impassive demeanor, I knew the memory loss rankled. He would not rest until those stolen days were restored to him.

"Look, Watson." Holmes summoned me to the window. "They are arguing."

I joined him. "*She* is arguing. Young Kuo is, like you, stoic in the face of opposition."

"Stoic?" Holmes narrowed his gaze. "No. The boy is merely calm and controlled."

I shrugged. Kuo came regularly to visit me, and though Holmes joined in our conversations when it suited him, he more often than not made himself scarce. Still, I conceded to him the point, knowing his powers of observation to be superior to my own.

"What do you think of the girl?" I asked, for this was the first time Charlotte had joined Kuo on one of his visits.

An almost imperceptible smile touched his lips. "She is adept at getting what she wants."

I glanced down once again at the couple, Kuo now handing

Charlotte into a cab. Before he could step back, the girl touched his cheek with a gentle, fleeting caress.

I shook my head. "I'm afraid, Holmes, that is one thing she cannot have, and Kuo knows it."

He turned away from the window. "There are exceptions to society's rules, and regardless, Miss Gaines is in a position to flout them. Nevertheless, my dear Watson, you may be correct. The boy's pride and sense of honor are the sticking points, and we have already seen to what lengths he will go to protect her, even if from herself."

He sat in his chair and picked up the newspaper. I wandered over to the fireplace.

"I assume Mycroft has employed you to track down the missing entries," I prompted, referring to the pages Kuo had taken from the journal.

He snorted. "My esteemed brother exerted himself to raise his voice. The boy left just enough to give him a good idea to whom the pages referred. Mycroft may be lazy, but neither he nor his employer are to be trifled with. Your young friend plays a dangerous game."

"He does so for Miss Gaines." I jumped to Kuo's defense. "The boy is well aware of the fickle nature of politics. Who knows what may happen in the future? What person Mycroft's employer may wish to harm with damaging information? How readily they might renege on their promises if it suits them. No, Holmes, he was wise to make assurances."

He did not reply, and I asked, "Do you have any clue what Kuo has done with the pages?"

"After reading that"—Holmes nodded at a manuscript tucked up under some heavy tomes on the desk. "I've a good idea."

I stiffened, angry that I'd given him the means by which to foil the boy. It was I who had convinced Kuo to write the details of his adventure down on paper.

He shook his head, amused. "You needn't blame yourself, Watson. I would've cracked the case without it. Still, I told Mycroft to let his employer know the task was beyond my capabilities. As with young Kuo, I also detest bullies."

I raised my eyebrows. "To let anyone, much less the Crown, believe you incapable of solving a mystery . . . admit it, Holmes, you like the boy."

"He is exceptionally intelligent and observant, as well as unusually sensitive to his environment. How else to explain the phenomenon he refers to as supernatural intercession?"

Unlike his missing days, Holmes was much less dispassionate about his role as a passive intermediary for Kuo's ancestors. He rejected the thought of being a powerless vessel to any creature, whether natural or supernatural.

Holmes believed he must have absorbed some understanding of the Chinese language through his wanderings, as well as knowledge of the investigation by overhearing our discussions in his sleeping presence. Almost exactly what Charlotte had suggested, as I pointed out to him (much to his displeasure).

"Contrary to the elder Mr. Cheng's determination of my character," Holmes had argued, "I'm not at all averse to believing the unconscious mind capable of seeing what the conscious mind ignores."

I smiled at the memory but did not probe further, knowing how it annoyed my friend. "One thing puzzles me," I said, changing the subject. "Why would Cecil Gaines seek to kill you after you had been successfully removed from the investigation?"

"Perhaps he feared I would recover and remember all," my friend replied. "Though I am not entirely convinced it was he." Holmes tapped two fingers against his head. "I believe the answer is in here, and until I can recall that hidden memory, we may never know." He unfolded the paper and snapped it open, burying his head within its pages.

I walked to the desk and pulled the manuscript from beneath the books. Unlocking the bottom drawer, I placed it atop a pile of similar papers, locked it again, and tucked the key into my breast pocket. Like the many of our adventures Holmes deemed too sensitive to publish, I hoped the story of Kuo and Charlotte's courage in the face of such terrible hatred would one day be told.

Dr. John Watson
London, England 1895

About the Author

Diana Lee lives and writes (mostly) in California.

www.ingramcontent.com/pod-product-compliance
Lightning Source LLC
Chambersburg PA
CBHW030416180626
46812CB00005B/2034